STAR OF
EMPIRE

Books by Leonard Sanders

THE HAMLET WARNING

THE HAMLET ULTIMATUM

SONOMA

FORT WORTH

TEXAS NOON

STAR OF EMPIRE

STAR

O F

EMPIRE

A Novel of Old San Antonio

—

Leonard Sanders

Delacorte Press

Published by
Delacorte Press
Bantam Doubleday Dell Publishing Group, Inc.
666 Fifth Avenue
New York, New York 10103

Library of Congress Cataloging in Publication Data
Sanders, Leonard.
    Star of empire : a novel of old San Antonio / by Leonard Sanders.
        p.   cm.
    ISBN 0-385-29916-8
    1. San Antonio (Tex.)—History—Fiction.   I. Title.
PS3569.A5127S7   1992
813′.54—dc20   91-45852
                                                             CIP

Designed by Ann Gold
Manufactured in the United States of America
Published simultaneously in Canada

September 1992

10 9 8 7 6 5 4 3 2 1
RRH

For Florene

AUTHOR'S NOTE

Sources consulted for this novel include journals, diaries, and writings of William Fairfax Gray, his wife Millie Gray, Adolphus Sterne, Ann Raney Coleman, Mary A. Maverick, John Holland Jenkins, Noah Smithwick, Thomas J. Green, William Bollaert, John L. Linn, Thomas W. Bell, George Wilkins Kendall, Dr. J. H. Barnard, Mary Austin Holley, William Preston Stapp, Sam Houston, John James Audubon, and the mysterious Ohio gentleman who toured Texas in 1837, who wrote of what he saw, and whose identity has continued to elude generations of scholars.

The day-to-day drama these writers witnessed set in motion events that almost doubled the size of our nation in one brief decade. Although Cornelia and Tad Logan and most of the other characters in this novel are fictitious, their experiences and dreams are fact, as recorded by these early Texans. Historical figures—such as Sam Houston, Mirabeau B. Lamar, Robert Potter, Thomas Jefferson Rusk, and "Old Paint" Caldwell—are presented espousing their known views and causes in the proper times and places.

Leonard Sanders
Fort Worth, 1992

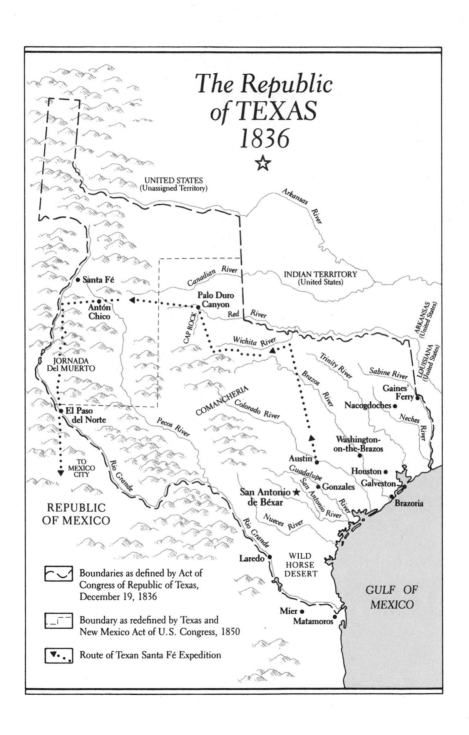

The Republic
of TEXAS
1836
☆

UNITED STATES
(Unassigned Territory)

Arkansas River

Santa Fé

Canadian River

Palo Duro
Canyon

INDIAN TERRITORY
(United States)

Antón
Chico

Red River

CAP ROCK

ARKANSAS
(United States)

Wichita River

LOUISIANA
(United States)

JORNADA
Del MUERTO

COMANCHERIA

Colorado River

Trinity River

Sabine River

Gaines'
Ferry

Brazos River

Nacogdoches

El Paso
del Norte

Pecos River

Neches River

Washington-
on-the-Brazos

TO
MEXICO
CITY

Rio Grande

Austin

Guadalupe River

San Antonio River

Houston
Galveston

REPUBLIC
OF MEXICO

San Antonio ★
de Béxar

Gonzales

Nueces River

Rio Grande

Brazoria

Laredo

WILD
HORSE
DESERT

GULF OF
MEXICO

Mier
Matamoros

Boundaries as defined by Act of
Congress of Republic of Texas,
December 19, 1836

Boundary as redefined by Texas and
New Mexico Act of U.S. Congress, 1850

Route of Texan Santa Fé Expedition

"Westward the star of empire takes its way."
—John Quincy Adams
Oration at Plymouth, 1802

PART ONE

The Republic

Have you ever been in San Antonio, the beautiful San Antonio de Béxar? [This] is almost the first question which is asked by the early settler of Texas who wishes to inspire the recent immigrant with a high idea of the beauty and richness of his adopted country. I had learned so much of Béxar from young and old that I determined, as soon as an opportunity was presented, to make a pilgrimage to the place which fame represented as the Eden of Texas.

Anonymous 1837 traveler in
the Republic of Texas

--- 1 ---

Late in the afternoon Corrie tired of lawn games. The April sun was warm. Not a breath of air stirred. She knew she should preserve her strength for the cotillion ball. If past Threadgill parties were any indication, she would be dancing till dawn. Surrendering her croquet mallet, along with her place in the tournament, she walked away from the wickets and searched for an unoccupied stretch of cool green shade. The grass was crowded with Charleston society, for an all-day Threadgill party was not to be missed. As Corrie made her way toward the distant trees, she caught sight of Grandmother Threadgill seated alone on a cast iron bench under a spreading live oak. Tiny and birdlike, Mrs. Threadgill was at least a year older than God. Corrie went to pay her respects, as was only proper. Mrs. Threadgill and Corrie's great-grandmother O'Brien had been girlhood friends. Sometimes Mrs. Threadgill told stories of the early days, and Corrie loved to listen to them.

Mrs. Threadgill smiled as Corrie approached. "I've been watching you. You're good at that game. I fear I never was."

"I can't imagine you not excelling at anything," Corrie said. "I remember my grandmother O'Brien telling how you used to take the high jumps."

Mrs. Threadgill's blue eyes crinkled in delight. "Oh, my, but that was long ago. I'm surprised anyone remembers. Come sit with me, child. We'll send for a cool lemonade and talk."

Corrie sank to the bench. The soft down pillows felt comfortable. Liveried servants circulated about the lawn, dispensing drinks to guests. Corrie raised a gloved hand and caught the eye of one. Corrie suspected he had special orders to keep watch on the

Threadgill matriarch, for the lemonade appeared within minutes after the order was given.

Mrs. Threadgill placed a bony hand on Corrie's cheek. "How nice it must be to know you're the envy of all your friends," she said. "Don't you dare risk turning your back on a single one of them today!"

It was Corrie's turn to laugh. Her betrothal to Ramsey had been announced only last week. In a case or two Mrs. Threadgill's warning might be apt.

"You're too kind," Corrie said. "But I'll admit, at the moment I couldn't possibly be happier."

"You've chosen a good man," Mrs. Threadgill said. "I've known his family through five generations."

Corrie felt any response to that would be immoderate. She and Mrs. Threadgill sat for a time in comfortable silence. Behind them, beyond the box elders, rose the Threadgill home, a three-story brick structure that dated back to before the Revolution. Its wide verandas and marble columns commanded a vast stretch of the lawn where the party was in progress. In the middle of the lawn, a score of single adults were still playing croquet. Exclamations and applause followed each shot. Beyond, over by the pink-flowering dogwood, the younger matrons were seated, talking of babies and gowns and their difficulties with servants. The older women sat to the left, near the crape myrtle bushes. There the subjects would be the aches and pains of age, interspersed with tidbits of community gossip. On the other side of the lawn, the older men stood discussing the price of cotton and rice, the prospects for recent plantings, and, inevitably, politics. The young married men also stood apart, talking of horses, hunting, and liquor. Boys and girls too young for serious courtship, but too old for the playground behind the house, kept to their own groups. Corrie did not know why lawn parties divided in this way. But it had always been so, as long as she could remember.

The Threadgill house was large, yet inadequate to sleep all the guests. A small tent-city stood down by the river, where soon most everyone would nap before dressing for tonight's ball.

"When's the wedding?" Mrs. Threadgill asked.

"We haven't yet set the date," Corrie said. Mrs. Threadgill's eyebrows rose, prompting Corrie to explain. "With Mother's illness, we thought it best to wait."

Mrs. Threadgill shook a forefinger in the air. "Child, never put off a wedding! Not ever! Life goes on. Affections wander. There can be tragedy! I've seen it happen!"

Somewhat taken aback, Corrie wondered if Mrs. Threadgill was more senile than everyone assumed. "Oh, don't worry, Mrs. Threadgill," Corrie said. "Ramsey and I have known each other all our lives. Besides, Mother's urging us to go ahead. We probably will."

Mrs. Threadgill seemed reluctant to leave the subject. "You and Ramsey have waited too long already. I'm telling you, child. If you wait longer, you're asking for trouble."

Corrie caught sight of Ramsey circling the croquet players. "You can judge for yourself, Mrs. Threadgill. Here he comes."

As Ramsey approached Corrie felt a burst of love and pride. She had always thought him handsome. But since his return from the university a year ago, she had found him irresistible. Today he wore perfectly tailored dark broadcloth. His black cravat formed a dramatic contrast to his frilled white shirt. His pencil-line mustache and close-cropped beard were immaculately trimmed. At twenty-two he was only four years older than Corrie, but his dignified bearing gave him added maturity. As he drew near he swept off his broad Panama, releasing the wealth of dark brown curls fringing his ears. "Mrs. Threadgill," he said, bowing. "You're looking especially lovely today. And what a marvelous shawl. Is it new?"

Corrie repressed a smile. Mrs. Threadgill's shawl, worn to every social affair, summer and winter, had become a Charleston institution. Of black lace, appliquéd with gold thread, it was truly a work of art. But it had seen better days. Only Ramsey would have the grace to pay it yet another compliment.

Mrs. Threadgill's face brightened. "Thank you. This shawl was given to me by Mr. Threadgill more than thirty years ago. It came from the West Indies. You have good taste, young man."

Ramsey again bowed, then seated himself on the other side of Mrs. Threadgill. Although he gave his attention to Mrs. Threadgill, his gentle eyes kept coming back to Corrie.

"Mr. Threadgill was in shipping," Mrs. Threadgill went on. "That was before rice and cotton. Most of the planters here then grew indigo."

Corrie listened avidly, hoping Ramsey could get her talking about the early days, when Corrie's great-grandparents had come to these shores. Those had been lively times, filled with pirate attacks, Indian raids, and romantic wars. Corrie often wished she had lived in those years.

"In four more years I'll turn a hundred," Mrs. Threadgill went on. "I've seen many things."

"I'm sure you have," Ramsey said.

"People come and go, but quality stays. It has always been that way in Charleston. You two make a lovely couple. I trust you intend to stay and manage Osborne."

"Of course," Ramsey said, smiling at Corrie.

"I remember when your great-grandfather started that plantation. It was considered only swampland. He turned it into the best place on the coast. He was truly a remarkable man."

"So I've heard," Ramsey said.

Mrs. Threadgill seemed primed for one of her stories. But Corrie was distracted by a curious silence at the croquet court. Play had stopped and the players stood looking toward the drive.

Two horsemen were approaching under the towering live oaks and Spanish moss. At first Corrie's attention was drawn to one of the horses. It was a black stallion at least a hand taller than ordinary. His shoulders were flecked with foam, evidence of recent hard use. Yet he tossed his head with restless energy. As the daughter of a horse breeder, Corrie recognized superb horseflesh. And horsemanship. The rider held a firm rein.

Corrie studied the man in the saddle. He was long of limb, broad of shoulder, and wore a dark frock coat. Brass buttons gleamed. His high-topped boots were polished to a smooth sheen. He wore a huge hat, with a brim of much greater span than the Panamas currently in fashion. His face was square, with wide-set eyes and a massive jaw.

The other rider was almost as resplendently attired. Initially

Corrie assumed he also was a gentleman. But as they drew rein she saw that the second rider was a light-skinned Negro.

Mallets in hand, the croquet players hurried across the lawn and crowded around as the tall man dismounted. There was much excited chatter, but Corrie could not hear the words.

Ramsey and Mrs. Threadgill became aware of the new arrivals.

"Who is that?" Corrie asked.

"He's a stranger to me," Ramsey said.

"That's Thaddeus Logan, up from Savannah to take his cousin Anne to the ball," Mrs. Threadgill said.

Ramsey's eyes narrowed, as they always did when he was making connections. "Of the Donegal Logans? I wasn't aware you were related."

"His grandfather was my first cousin," Mrs. Threadgill said.

Corrie did not bother to pursue the exact relationship. She had little patience with extended genealogy, a prevailing preoccupation for most Charlestonians.

"I've sold Negroes to Frank Logan at Donegal," Ramsey said.

"Frank's a brother," Mrs. Threadgill explained. "Frank's older. He runs the plantation. Thaddeus is a lawyer. He's just back from Texas. He was a hero in the fighting out there."

Corrie was intrigued. During the Texas Revolution three years ago she had read every account she could find. Then fifteen, she had thought the battles deliciously romantic. She had wept over the heroic death of the men in the Alamo.

"Is that a Donegal Negro?" Ramsey asked, eyeing Logan's servant.

"Yes, that's Jack, Tad's body servant. Tad's grandfather—my cousin—gave Jack to Tad at birth. They were born on the same day. They're inseparable. Tad even took Jack to Texas with him."

Corrie was familiar with the custom of such a special birthday gift when a slave baby and a white were born on the same day.

Trailing admirers, Logan left the drive and came across the lawn. Corrie realized he was coming to pay his respects to Mrs. Threadgill and suddenly wished she were elsewhere. She did not want to become a part of the giggling gaggle swarming about the man. But there was no escape.

Corrie felt Logan's gaze linger overlong on her, and from that moment she began to bridle. His sky-blue eyes were far too bold. His voice was deep, and a trifle loud, as if unaccustomed to polite use. "Aunt Mary," he said, bending to take her hand. "You're growing younger every time I see you."

His gaze kept returning to Corrie, as if to include her in his flowery tribute to his grandaunt. His admirers stood back respectfully, taking in the scene. Corrie thought of slipping off her left glove so Logan could see her engagement ring, and thus be warned. But she decided that would be too obvious.

Mrs. Threadgill made introductions. Irritated, Corrie met Logan's gaze with her own as he bent to kiss her hand.

"Are you related to John McNair of Moultrie Hill?" he asked.

His eyes were still locked with her own, for she refused to be intimidated. And he still had not relinquished her hand. "He's my father," Corrie said.

He smiled down at her. "Then perhaps I'll be seeing you again. I'm hoping to buy some of your father's famous mares."

Even under the circumstances Corrie felt she should make an overture. With the depressed market for cotton and rice, Moultrie Hill had not turned a profit in the last two years. "I'm sure Father will be happy to see you," she said. "I happen to know he does have some stock for sale."

Again Logan bowed. "I'll be looking forward to my visit."

Corrie pulled her hand free. Ramsey was aware of the byplay. On his introduction, he quietly but firmly assumed control of the conversation. "Mrs. Threadgill tells us you've been in Texas. Is that country as promising as claimed?"

Logan took Ramsey's measure before answering. "To my mind, there could be no exaggeration about Texas. The land is vast, and offers untold riches."

"Are the Texans concerned about further incursions from the Mexicans?"

"Not especially. If they come, we'll whip them again."

Logan's admirers laughed. Ramsey gave him the trace of a smile. "Then I take it you plan to return."

"As soon as I can get outfitted."

"To practice law?"

"That's my profession. But I expect to devote myself at least partially to land speculation."

"I'm trained in law as well," Ramsey said. "We have that in common. I regret you don't plan to start a law practice here. We might explore our mutual interests professionally."

"Perhaps we shall some day," Logan shot back.

Logan's circle of admirers was following the exchange avidly. Ramsey and Logan reminded Corrie of two bulls circling each other warily, sizing each other up. Corrie thought Ramsey was holding his own. His calm, gentlemanly poise was unshakable. But there was a power, a presence, about Logan that could not be denied.

Again his eyes came to rest on Corrie. Mrs. Threadgill, still sharp to nuances, interrupted the game. "Mr. Cothburn and Miss McNair are betrothed," she announced rather pointedly.

Logan did not appear surprised. Again he offered Ramsey his hand. "My congratulations, sir."

Ramsey made gracious acknowledgment. But Corrie sensed that Logan's aggressive manner was beginning to wear on him. She spoke to free him from the situation. "It's growing late. If everyone will excuse me, I'll go take my nap."

Ramsey picked up his cue. "I'll walk you to your pavilion." He glanced at Logan. "No doubt we'll see you tonight."

Glancing toward Corrie, Logan said, "You can count on it."

They strolled down the grassy slope toward the pavilion. "What did you think of the Threadgill cousin?" Ramsey asked.

Corrie needed time to sort out her reactions. "He seemed interesting," she replied noncommittally.

"I was impressed. He's clearly not an ordinary fellow."

Corrie did not want to appear to be yet another victim of the man's charms. "I thought him more than a trifle overbearing. I didn't feel comfortable with him."

Ramsey frowned. "There must be something odd about him. I've come to know his brother Frank rather well and in all the time

I've dealt with him he never mentioned a brother in the Texas fighting."

"Maybe the occasion never arose."

"But it did. I remember we talked at length about the Texas Revolution. Frank had firm opinions. But he never once hinted he had a brother involved."

"Maybe there's bad blood between them."

"That's what I'm thinking. The Logans were friendly enough, and good hosts. But there's a coldness about them I can't define. The old man is still alive, a fierce old Irishman. Yet Frank is very much in charge. Donegal's a fairly large place, with more than two thousand acres under cultivation. You'd think Frank would need help with the management."

"Maybe Thaddeus has been disowned."

"That's possible. There was a younger brother, a tall, lanky boy, so removed from the family circle I first assumed him to be mentally afflicted. But I later found him intelligent enough, just shy and uncertain. Frank's married, and has sons. Yet in all the time I was there, I saw no women, save the servants. In all, I found the Logans a very peculiar family."

They arrived at the pavilion. Ramsey pulled out his watch. "Quarter to five. Shall I pick you up about eight?"

Corrie hesitated. A two-hour nap, and an hour to dress. "Eight will be fine."

Ramsey gave her a quick kiss and walked away. Corrie stood and watched him go, savoring his firm, manly stride. They had fallen into an easy, comfortable relationship, and Corrie anticipated a good marriage. She was not eager to assume the role of a plantation mistress. But one could not stay young and carefree forever. As the owner of the most successful plantation in South Carolina, Ramsey had been considered the catch of her generation. Soon she would have him all to herself.

She entered the tent. Her servant girl, Hattie, was perched on a low stool, polishing Corrie's dancing slippers. The tent was warm, but Hattie had opened vents. A cool cross-breeze made the interior tolerable. Corrie's dresses and gowns, and those of her fourteen-year-old sister, Pruella, lined the walls of the tent. Corrie moved toward them. "Is my gown ready?"

"Will be when you're ready for it," Hattie said. "Miss Corrie, where's Miss Pruella? Your momma expects me to take care of the both of you. How can I do it when I'm working here? I haven't seen that child since noon."

"She's all right, Hattie," Corrie assured her. "I saw her a few minutes ago. She'll be along shortly."

"We shouldn't have come, with your momma sick and all," Hattie fumed. "You've got your man. You don't need any more of this foolishness. It's too hard on everybody."

Corrie tended to agree. A twenty-four-hour party required at least five complete outfits for herself, and five more for Prue. They each needed traveling dresses for the twenty-mile carriage ride, a morning dress to wear through the noon dinner, an afternoon dress for the lawn games, and a gown for the evening supper and ball. The clothing alone took a month of planning and work. Two field hands were needed to load and unload the tent, cots, chairs, dressing mirrors, and trunks. With Hattie and the carriage driver, Ben, the party demanded the use of four servants who could be better employed at home. But when Corrie had suggested sending regrets to the Threadgills, her mother had refused to listen. "Of course you're going," she had said. "McNairs, O'Briens, and Pendletons have been attending Threadgill parties for a century. You'll be expected."

"We can't always do what we wish," Corrie told Hattie. "We must keep up appearances."

"Keeping up appearances is what's going to put us in the grave. We ought to be home taking care of your momma," Hattie retorted.

Corrie did not argue. In a way Hattie was just as much Sarah McNair's daughter as herself or Prue. Years ago Sarah McNair had seen that Hattie was too small ever to succeed as a field hand. She moved her into the house and trained her to be a body servant. In the years since, Hattie had worked for Sarah with dedication and devotion. Only fifteen when Corrie was born, Hattie had cared for both Corrie and Prue as babies.

She was as black as the inside of a coal bin and her eyes were large. She long ago had earned her place in the McNair family, and knew it. "Miss Corrie, you better take your nap," she warned.

"In a minute," Corrie said, going down the line of dresses and gowns. Every costume required accessories, and something always seemed to disappear at the last moment. Corrie was checking each item when her sister came into the tent.

Prue was breathless from running and seemed animated even beyond her usual high spirits. "Well!" she announced. "My sister has really set tongues to wagging!"

Prue plainly was relishing whatever was on her mind. "How?" Corrie asked.

"By flirting with the Threadgills' Savannah cousin, right in front of Ramsey and Anne Threadgill!"

Corrie was irritated. She had merely stared the man down. Surely no one could have taken that as flirting.

"They say he couldn't take his eyes off you," Prue continued. "They say Anne Threadgill's fit to be tied. They're teasing her about losing her cousin to you before his horse was unsaddled."

Corrie could not judge how much of Prue's report was true and how much stemmed from Prue's tendency to overdramatize. "I've never heard anything so ridiculous," she said.

"I saw the whole thing! That man sure stirred up the fillies. It was like when Father turns the stallion in among the mares."

Hattie looked up. "Miss Pruella! Your momma hear you talking like that, she'll take a whip to you, sick or not."

"Oh, phoo."

Corrie was amused. Prue was at the stage when one never knew what she might come out with. "How do you know about such things?" she asked.

"I hid in the hayloft and watched."

Corrie had done the same thing, years ago. To this day she remained confused as to exactly what she had witnessed.

"Anyway, the man has sure turned some heads," Prue said.

"Well, mine is not among them," Corrie told her.

Lately Prue had become a perfectionist where her appearance was concerned. She examined her gown and found that the balloon sleeves did not flare the way she thought they should. She and

Hattie argued over whether the loose fabric should be pleated. Prue wanted the sleeves full to hide her bony arms. Hattie insisted the sleeves looked nicer hanging straight. Corrie listened to the debate, taking no part. Prue won her way.

"Miss Corrie, if you don't take your nap, you're going to look like death warmed over tonight, right when Master Ramsey want you to look your prettiest."

Corrie silently agreed by turning so Hattie could unhook the back of her afternoon dress. She slipped out of it and lay full length on her cot.

But sleep would not come. The incident with Thaddeus Logan had disturbed her in ways she did not understand.

After thinking at length, she concluded that there might be some truth in the talk among Prue's friends. Perhaps she had handled the situation badly. There had been no point in challenging the man.

Tonight, at the ball, she would be polite, but pointedly ignore Thaddeus Logan.

Tad took his evening clothes out of the carpetbag and tossed them to Jack. "I'm going to sleep about an hour," he said. "When I wake up, this coat and trousers better not have a wrinkle in them."

"Does anything ever, after I've worked it over?" Jack asked. "And I'll press out that red cravat. That'll set you off fine tonight."

"The black one," Tad said. He sat on a Threadgill chair and stretched out a leg for Jack to pull off the boot.

"The red one, Marsh Tad," Jack said, tugging the boot free. "A gentleman should wear something red when he's trying to catch the eye of a lady. Red puts them in the proper mood."

Tad laughed. "What makes you think I'm trying to attract any lady's eye?"

Jack pulled off the other boot. "I saw the way you looked at that red-haired lady this afternoon. I'm not so dumb."

"You'll do until someone dumb comes along. As it happens, the lady is spoken for."

"If I know you, Marsh Tad, you won't let a little thing like that stand in your way. And it seems to me you're already fooling with the lady. I heard you telling her you might buy some horses off her papa. What you going to use for money?"

"You let me worry about that."

"That I will. One thing I don't have to worry about is money. If I had any, I'd ride into Charleston tonight and toss myself a little spree. Give those Charleston women a treat."

Tad considered Jack's oblique request. He would not need Jack for the rest of the evening. Jack deserved a night out. "There's a couple of dollars in my trousers. I'll write you a pass through the patrollers. But I want you back here by dawn, sober and ready to ride."

"I'll probably be in better shape than you, Marsh Tad. We going back to Savannah tomorrow?"

Tad hesitated. "I haven't thought it out yet."

Jack looked at him strangely but asked no further questions. He gathered Tad's evening clothes and went out to borrow an iron from some compliant household maid.

From throughout the house came the sounds of preparations for supper. Tad lay back on the bed, lit a cigar, propped his feet against the footboard, and began to sort out the diverse thoughts that had flooded through his mind since his arrival.

For years a drastic plan had been nibbling at the edges of his consciousness. This afternoon, while he was talking with Cornelia McNair, the entire plan had fallen abruptly into place.

Jack was right. He was completely captivated by her. But his interest went far beyond her beauty. He was more intrigued with what he sensed in her.

For a time he allowed himself the luxury of remembering her abundant auburn hair, the green glint to her eyes as she boldly met his gaze, the sensuous curve of her lips as she smiled. This was no submissive Southern belle, like scores he had courted during the last year. She was like Perrault's Sleeping Beauty, waiting to be awakened.

Tad snuffed out his cigar, rested his head on a pillow, and closed his eyes.

To hell with Cornelia McNair's engagement. She was made for a far more challenging life than Ramsey Cothburn offered.

Through the next few weeks, he would awaken this sleeping beauty to that fact.

The next quadrille had been called. Everyone milled about the dance floor in search for his or her home partner. Cautiously Corrie moved through the crowd, hunting for Ramsey while making every effort to avoid Thaddeus Logan and his red cravat. The man had been eyeing her all evening.

"There you are. I thought I'd lost you." Ramsey was behind her, pulling his dance card from a pocket. He held it up to the light. "Let's see, our station for this quadrille is at the north wall."

Relieved, Corrie went with him toward their place. She leaned close to his ear. "I saved the next waltz for you as I promised."

"Corrie, I'm sorry," he said. "I forgot. My card is filled." He looked at his card. "I'm committed to Anne Threadgill. Shall I tell her I'm in error?"

Corrie opened her mouth to say yes, but reconsidered. She should not put Ramsey to such an inconvenience. Surely she could find someone still uncommitted.

They reached their station. She glanced across to the opposite couple. There stood Anne Threadgill and Thaddeus Logan.

Corrie's thoughts flew ahead to the coming quadrille. When the time came to change partners, she would be dancing with him. There was no way to avoid it.

The string orchestra opened the quadrille, setting a lively pace. Corrie concentrated on the steps, advancing with Ramsey to meet Anne Threadgill and Thaddeus Logan, offering a two-beat low curtsy, retreating backward three steps, turning twice with Ramsey, and moving forward to the center as the four couples in her set formed a star. Then she was on Logan's arm, promenading the length of the room. He moved smoothly, confidently, with flourishes that proved him to be a superb dancer. He bent close to her ear. "You look absolutely ravishing tonight."

Ravishing was not a word Corrie was accustomed to hearing.

She was not even sure it was proper. "Thank you," she said with a tone she attempted to place between coolness and politeness.

"And such a lovely dress. I don't think I've ever seen one cut quite that way. Refreshingly different. Is it new?"

Corrie was brought up short. Men usually offered compliments in generalities. The cut of the fabric against the bias had been her idea. Sarah and Hattie had been opposed. Not until the dress was completed was the success evident. Corrie could not prevent a note of appreciation from creeping into her voice. "Yes, it's new."

"Lovely," he said again. "I tried to speak with you earlier. I've saved a few dances, hoping you still have one free."

In a moment Corrie would be swinging away with another partner. "Oh, I'm sorry," she said. "But my card is filled."

The lie came easily. Surely she would be able to find someone in the crowd before the dance arrived.

She was spun away by her next partner. She felt momentary relief. But on reflection, she could see a complication developing.

If Tad Logan saw her idle during the waltz, or fleeing from the dance floor, he would know she had lied.

She did not want to give him that satisfaction.

When the quadrille ended, she asked Ramsey to excuse her.

In the hall she encountered Prue. "I told you these sleeves wouldn't hang right," Prue complained. "Just look at them!"

Even in the face of her own troubles Corrie felt a wave of sympathy. Prue was striving so hard for adulthood. Yet at fourteen she still retained the thin body of a tomboy. Corrie glanced into an adjoining bedroom. A lamp was lit, but the room was deserted. "Come in here," she said. "We can pin some tucks."

They found pins in a Threadgill dresser. Corrie went to work. She tried to make her question sound casual. "Is your dance card full?"

"Of course."

"Who is your partner for the next waltz?"

Prue searched through her card. "Owen Threadgill."

Fifteen years old. He would have to do. "Can I have him?" Corrie asked. "Just for that dance? You can make some kind of excuse, can't you?"

Prue took a step backward and looked at her. "For the Lord's sake! Why?"

Corrie tried to explain. "It was a mixup. I saved that waltz for Ramsey. He didn't know, and made another commitment. Now I'm left with it open. Thaddeus Logan has been so forward, I'm attempting to avoid him. I don't want to insult him, because he's coming to buy horses from Father."

Prue frowned. "Good Lord, Corrie. It's only a dance. Everyone knows you're engaged to Ramsey. What could Logan do to you on the dance floor, surrounded by people?"

"You don't understand. His boldness has grown awkward."

Prue studied her pointedly. "I hear what you're saying. But I'm also hearing something else. I'm hearing you may not be as immune to him as you claim."

"Just yes or no. Will you make excuses to Owen Threadgill or not?" Corrie snapped, reflecting that recently Prue had become far too outspoken on matters beyond her grasp.

Prue shook her head. "What am I to tell him? That I've suddenly broken a leg? Turned my ankle? Think how it'd look! I bow out and push you at him. What will he think? What will everyone else think?"

"Then you won't help me out of this awkward situation?"

"Corrie, dancing with Owen Threadgill would be even more awkward."

Even in her agitation Corrie could see the humor. She laughed. Owen was short and fat. Maneuvering him into dancing with her would be too obvious. She would have to think of a different tack.

The sleeves were done. Gathered into folds, they billowed nicely. Prue examined them in the mirror. "That's much better."

"We should be getting back," Corrie said. "It's about time for the next set."

They returned to the dance floor. Corrie caught sight of Logan searching for his next partner.

Prue's accusation still stung. It occurred to Corrie that similar thoughts might have gone through Logan's mind.

She wanted no misapprehensions. On impulse, she intercepted him. "Mr. Logan, I regret I gave you wrong information a while ago.

Through mixed signals with my fiancé, I do have an open dance, if you're still of a mind."

He smiled down at her. Was it her imagination, or was there mockery in his eyes? "How fortunate for me. Which dance?"

Corrie held out her dance card. Logan matched it against his own, and penciled in his name. He bowed. "I'll be looking forward to that waltz," he said.

He hurried on to his partner for the next set. Ramsey came to Corrie. He had seen the exchange, and was regarding Logan with an odd expression.

"Now my card is complete," Corrie said lightly. "Mr. Logan is honoring me with a waltz."

Ramsey did not respond. The orchestra began the next number, and he swirled her away.

Now that she had dispensed with the lie, she felt much better. For a time she lost herself in the music. But as the waltz approached, a shapeless dread slowly settled over her.

The next quadrille concluded. Logan and Anne Threadgill came across the floor to Corrie and Ramsey. Corrie concentrated on the proper amenities. The two men exchanged partners. Ramsey and Anne walked away. Corrie was left alone with Thaddeus Logan.

At close range his broad face and wide shoulders made him seem larger than life. His blue eyes, darker in the soft lamplight, gazed down at her with a disturbing intensity. His mere presence was overpowering. Even though he had not yet touched her, Corrie felt as if he had her enveloped in a strong bear hug, squeezing the breath from her lungs.

She sought refuge in polite conversation. "When are you returning to Texas?"

His deep voice transcended the clamor around them. "My plans are uncertain. I have a few legal matters to clear up, horses, slaves, and equipment to buy. Probably next fall."

Corrie wanted to ask if he would be spending time in Charleston. But that would be prying, and she did not want to suggest that she was even remotely interested. She sought another subject. "I've doted on Texas for years. I'd love to see it someday."

He did not answer immediately. His eyes narrowed as if in

thought. "I hope you have the opportunity. Texas is beautiful beyond description. But the Republic offers much more. There's a spirit, an *élan vital*, about Texas that is beyond compare."

Corrie's finishing school had provided her with two years of French. But never before had a male used a French phrase in her presence without condescension. "In what way?" she asked.

Again the hesitation, the narrowing of his eyes, as he sought the proper words. "The Texas colonialists are men and women who were not content to accept the structured, limited life made for them in the East. They seek more. Consequently, in Texas you have around you men and women with a more vigorous attitude toward life. It's difficult to explain."

"I think you're doing rather well," Corrie said.

"Don't misunderstand me," he said, again locking his gaze with her own. "I love the South. But our ancestors built it. Now there's nothing left for us to do except preserve it against its slow decline. Out there is a new land, waiting to be created. Texans enjoy a warm camaraderie of shared purpose in the building of a new nation."

"That sounds thrilling!"

Logan smiled down at her. "I find it so."

Earlier, Corrie had been impatient for the music to begin. Now she hoped it would not. She had dozens of questions to ask. "I read every account I could find during the Texas Revolution. Yet you've given me an entirely different picture."

Logan laughed. Corrie noticed the way his eyes crinkled at the corners, the sensuous curve of his mouth. "Most accounts did us a great disservice. We weren't a ragtag bunch of malcontents, as portrayed, no more so than our ancestors at Lexington, Concord, or Yorktown. The American Revolution has been reborn in Texas."

Corrie's response sounded lame, even to herself. "I'll be wishing you every success."

The waltz started. It was one of Corrie's favorites, "Old Smokey." Logan guided her onto the floor with a firm, controlled grace. The lyrics of the old song came to Corrie's mind:

> *I can love little*
> *And I can love long.*

I can love an old sweetheart
Till a new one comes along.

Corrie had always been proud that Ramsey was such a superb
dancer. Thaddeus Logan, however, was better. He led her so
smoothly, she felt she was floating.

The waltz ended all too soon. She returned to Ramsey with a
warm afterglow. While she danced to other tunes, the beat, rhythm,
and lyrics of "Old Smokey" lingered. She finished the night in a
daze.

Ramsey walked her back to her pavilion. He seemed unusually
thoughtful and subdued. The first hint of dawn was showing in the
east. They were tired, and talked little. At the tent he kissed her
good-night and walked away.

Prue and Hattie were asleep on their cots. Corrie found herself
too restless to lie down. Within three hours the trunks would be
packed, the tent loaded, and she would be returning to Moultrie
Hill.

She left the tent and walked alone by the river, under fading
stars and the growing light of dawn. Thaddeus Logan's face, voice,
and words kept a firm hold on her mind.

She did not understand what was happening to her, and was a
bit frightened. All evening she had acted like a flighty schoolgirl,
first avoiding Logan, then totally yielding to him.

Old Mrs. Threadgill's warning came to her: "Never put off a
wedding. Not ever. Life goes on. Affections wander. There can be
tragedy!"

Everyone in Charleston had known for years that someday she
and Ramsey would be married. She herself had never doubted. Her
parents, his family, expected it. Her trousseau was prepared. Only
Sarah's illness had delayed the wedding.

For weeks Sarah had been urging Corrie to ignore her illness,
and to set the date. Ramsey was gently pressing.

Why had she been resisting?

Corrie decided she had been foolish. She would not wait longer,
and risk any external threat to her happiness.

She returned to the tent. After two hours of fitful sleep, she summoned Old Ben and had him drive her up to the Threadgill paddocks, where the men were saddling and harnessing horses for the return to their homes.

Ben fetched Ramsey. He leaned into the carriage with a faintly puzzled expression.

"Mother has been after me again to go ahead and set our wedding date," she told him. "I've thought it over. Would June eleventh be satisfactory?"

Ramsey could hardly contain his elation. He opened the carriage door, stepped in, and kissed her. "You've just made me the happiest man in the world."

--- 2 ---

Jack pulled open the heavy drapes, allowing the early-morning sun to flood the room. "Marsh Tad, when we going back to Charleston?"

Tad rolled into a sitting position in the bed. After almost twenty-four hours in the saddle, he and Jack had arrived at Donegal two hours before dawn. Yet Jack was up, dressed, and already thinking of going back to Charleston.

"It'll be a few days," Tad told him. "Hand me my boots."

"What we going to do today, Marsh Tad?"

"I'm going into Savannah. You're going to stay here and see to having the horses shod. If I'm not back by dark, you can come on into town. I'll be at the Manigault House. Lord knows I could use some sleep." Tad slipped into his trousers. "Who's up?"

"Marsh Frank and his boys done finished breakfast and gone. Marsh Larkin and Marsh Whit are still at the table."

Tad felt relief. He was not in the mood to tangle with Frank. Not before he put his plan into effect. "You can go along now, Jack," he said. "I'll be leaving for town in an hour or so. Have the bay mare ready."

Jack left the room. Tad shaved and walked downstairs to the dining room.

His brother Whit and father, Larkin, were seated at the long dining table. The cook, Brita, was clearing the table in the wake of Frank and his boys. Frank's wife, Lizette, seldom came down to breakfast, but had it brought up to her room.

Brita poured Tad a cup of coffee. He buttered a piece of toast and nibbled as he awaited his breakfast.

"What time you get in last night?" Larkin Logan asked.

"About three," Tad said.

Larkin snorted derisively. "Somebody's going to shoot you, prowling around the country that time of night. What business you have in Charleston, anyway?"

Tad was accustomed to the verbal abuse. It no longer bothered him. "I escorted your niece Anne Threadgill to a ball."

Again Larkin snorted. His wild mane of thick gray hair was uncombed, and his pale blue eyes were as sharp as rapiers. "Dancing? I thought you was a cripple."

Tad did not bother to answer. The old man's fierceness no longer frightened him. His concern was for his brother Whit, who sat ramrod straight in his chair, cowed like a scared rabbit, awaiting permission to leave the table. Tad wondered how many times the old man's ham-sized fists had lashed out over the years, knocking the boy to the floor. It had happened to Tad too many times to count. He still remembered the stunning swiftness of the old man's Irish temper, the pain, the brilliance of the lights shooting through his head.

Tad had taken the abuse and endured.

And today he intended to call in the chips.

"When Frank was wounded at Horseshoe Bend, they brought him back on a pine board," Larkin said. "He was up and around in a matter of weeks."

"I suppose Frank's just tougher than me," Tad said, winking at Whit. "Took me more than a year to get over a little ol' Mexican musket ball through the kneecap."

Whit grinned uncertainly. Larkin Logan missed the byplay, but he sensed it. He glowered at Whit. "Boy, go on out and help Frank's boys with the horses. Make yourself useful."

"Yes, sir," Whit said, rising.

Even after all his months at home, Tad was still amazed at how much Whit had grown. His fifteen-year-old brother was a six-foot-two beanpole.

A beanpole with the heart of a scared rabbit.

It pained Tad to look at him.

Whit shuffled out, leaving Larkin and Tad alone.

"What you going to do with yourself?" Larkin asked. "You decided on anything yet?"

Tad's breakfast arrived. "I've been intending to talk to you about that."

"Then talk."

"Later," Tad said. "I don't want the servants in on it."

Larkin glared at him for a long moment, then stood up abruptly. "I'm not one to dawdle at the table. If you want to talk, like as not I'll be on the gallery."

He ambled from the room. Tad ate his breakfast leisurely, thinking back over his childhood, allowing his anger to build, for today he would make use of it.

He had lived in the shadow of his brother Frank from the day he was born. No matter how he tried to please his parents, he found that in their eyes his every accomplishment had been done earlier, and better, by Frank, seventeen years older.

He had endured the old man's blows, hoping adulthood would bring improvement. But his future was made plain on his return from college. Already Frank was firmly in charge of Donegal. Frank's three sons were growing up, the heirs apparent. Larkin Logan was so blinded by his love for his grandson, he failed to see that he had not left a place at Donegal for Tad.

And even in the depths of his rage, Tad understood that Whit's plight was worse.

Whit had been born in his mother's forty-second year. His difficult birth caused her death. For months Larkin Logan would not enter the room where the baby lay. For the most part the boy had been reared by servants. Innocent, uncomprehending, he had faced the cold hatred of Larkin Logan every day of his life.

Whit had sought attention, approval, affection, so long that it now had become a habit. The very sight of him touched Tad's heart and angered him in the same breath.

In Whit, Tad saw repetition of his own childhood. But where Tad's anger had reshaped him into an independent, self-sustaining adult, Whit was of too gentle a nature for his own good. The most he could muster toward anger was an occasional low-keyed, puzzled resentment that soon vanished.

Unable to improve Whit's condition, or his own, Tad had gone to Texas. He had returned a hero to everyone except Larkin and

Frank Logan. At Donegal, Tad's Texas experiences only revived talk of Horseshoe Bend, where Frank had served as a boy hero beside Andrew Jackson in the same year Tad was born.

If the situation at Donegal had changed, it was for the worse. Larkin had grown even more self-righteous and set in his ways. Logic could not budge him. He was convinced that he had created his own dynasty, coming to full flower in his grandsons.

Tad finished his breakfast. Brita came and cleared the table. Tad lingered over coffee, reluctant to rekindle all those old raw emotions.

But it had to be done. In no other way could he turn dreams into reality. He thought ahead to the prize within reach.

Out in Texas, along the San Antonio River near San Antonio de Béxar, lay rich, virgin land as far as the eye could see, well situated for irrigation, with water in abundance from hundreds of limestone springs. Beyond the river, green pastures swept away to vistas of stunning immensity. In that country grew enough grass to supply horses and beef for all the armies of the world.

An empire was there for the making. As a Texas citizen, he was entitled to a league and a labor of land—more than forty-six hundred acres. He was due more land as a hero of San Jacinto. And the land was cheap. With a little money, he could buy thousands more acres.

Over the weekend, Cornelia McNair had become a part of this dream. With a wife such as Cornelia, he would found his own dynasty in that new nation. And in time his Texas empire would dwarf the piddling two thousand acres Frank Logan had schemed and plotted all his life to steal.

Tad remembered the way Cornelia McNair had looked in the lamplight, the expression on her face when he told her about Texas. He had planted the seed. Betrothed or not, Cornelia McNair was there for the taking. He intended to devote himself completely to the task.

But first he must contend with Larkin and Frank Logan.

He returned to his room and packed a bag. When he walked out of the house, Larkin was seated in his rocking chair on the front gallery. Frank's sons and Whit were training colts in the paddock below the house. Larkin was laughing, enjoying their sport. In the distance, Donegal Negroes were plowing with four-horse teams, preparing the ground for spring planting. Tad dropped his bag on the porch and perched on the gallery rail, facing his father.

"You asked what I plan to do," he said. "I've decided. I'm going back to Texas. So I want my inheritance now."

Larkin looked up at him, not understanding. "You what?"

"I want my inheritance. My part of Donegal."

Larkin's teeth gnashed. He dropped his voice to a whisper. "You always were a cold-blooded bastard. But I'd have thought you'd have the common decency to wait until I die."

"Frank hasn't waited," Tad pointed out. "He has taken everything. And you've let him."

Larkin gestured to the paddock. "Frank has sons. He stayed, worked the land. You've never turned a hand to do anything."

Tad did not want to argue. But there was much that needed to be said, and the opportunity might never come again. "I'll have sons too. You were giving Frank whatever he wanted before I was out of short pants. There was never a place here for me."

"You only had to take hold. To speak up."

"I did. Time after time. You were always so wrapped up in Frank, you never noticed what I was doing, or listened to me. That used to hurt. It doesn't anymore. I just want out."

Larkin stared into the distance, refusing to look at Tad. "Then get out. I won't have an ungrateful son under my roof."

"If you had built Donegal, it might be different," Tad said. "But Grandfather built this place. You haven't added to it. I know Grandfather would want me to have a part. He recognized my situation. I think that's why he gave me Jack."

Again Larkin gnashed his teeth. "You can damned well wait till I die. I've made provisions. That's all you'll get."

Tad was surprised at how calm he felt. "I can't wait. I need the money. Let's look at it legally. I'm your son, and I'm being done out of my prospects by you, in collusion with my brother. That'll be easy to establish in any court of law."

Larkin jerked as if stabbed. He glared up at Tad. "Are you

threatening me? Then by God you can damned well sue. See what it gets you. I'll cut you off! You'll never inherit a penny!"

"I wouldn't be so sure, if I were you. I sat through law school gathering precedents. I've compiled a goodly list."

Larkin snorted. "You're not half as smart as you think you are. I know something about the law. I'm alive. I can do anything I god-damned well please with my property."

Tad leaned close and lowered his voice. "Not if you're found incompetent. Not if you've been dethroned of your reason by a calculating older son."

Larkin jumped to his feet, fists waving. "By God, I'll show you how incompetent I am. Get out of my house! Get off my property! Don't you ever come back!"

Tad moved from the porch rail and took a step back. He held up his hands, palms outward. "I'll go. And I'll leave you with this thought. You haven't managed your own affairs for twenty years. Frank has signed every paper, made every trade, written every check. Given that evidence, what would any jury decide about your competency?"

Tad turned and walked away. Larkin's shouting had reached the ears of his grandsons. They looked at Tad curiously as he walked into the stall where Jack had left the saddled bay mare.

He rode into Savannah and to the Manigault House. There he took a suite and went to bed. Two hours after dark Jack awakened him, fumbling about the room and lighting a lamp.

"Marsh Tad, what did you say to your daddy? He's been having a fit ever since you left. He came down to the smith and told me to take your horses and git. He said none of your horses would ever wear a Donegal shoe again."

Tad sat up and lit a cigar from the lamp. "I said some things I should have said a long time ago."

"What we going to do now, Marsh Tad? Did he run you off?"

"We'll stay here a day or two. Then we'll see."

The next morning Tad went to a lawyer and spent the day drawing up papers. He was reviewing them the following day in his suite when a boy knocked on the door. He handed Tad a note:

Tad, I'm downstairs with my lawyer. I want to talk with you.

Tad turned the note over and wrote a brief reply:

No lawyer. I try my cases in court. If you want to talk, come
on up.

Frank arrived a few minutes later. He refused a chair. He seemed to
have aged in the two days since Tad last saw him. The Old Man's
temper tantrum must have been monumental. Deep worry lines
creased Frank's face and his shoulders sagged. He jabbed the air
with a finger. "First, I want to say that what you've done to your
father is despicable. If you were anyone else, you'd be talking to my
seconds. I'm trying my best to be reasonable about this."

"That makes two of us," Tad said.

"You can't possibly do what you've threatened."

"I can, and I will. The suit is prepared. It'll be filed within the
week if no action is forthcoming from you."

Frank waved his hands. "It's ridiculous on the face of it. Even
assuming you have legal grounds, which you don't, you can't divide
a plantation."

"Maybe I can't. But a court can."

Frank ran a hand through his hair. "Tad, I don't understand you
at all. What is it you want?"

"My share, Frank. You're running Donegal as if it were your
private fiefdom. But part of it is mine. Part of it is Whit's. I'm sure
your lawyer has advised you that I have a good case."

Frank sank into a chair. "Tad, I'm here only because I don't
want to put Father through this. Is there any chance you and I can
come to an understanding?"

"That depends. I only want to be fair. I know you've worked
hard, built up the value. I'm not out to hold you up."

"How much?"

"A third. We can bring in appraisers, settle on the average of
sealed evaluations of land, slaves, and livestock. I'm not after the
profits you've made and banked through the years. I acknowledge
you've worked for what you've earned. I recognize the profits helped

send me to college. But one third of the actual value of the property is mine. One third is Whit's. You can buy us out. I'll sign a quit-claim."

"I can't do that. Not two thirds. I don't have that much cash. I've been hit hard by the Panic."

Tad had anticipated that difficulty. He offered a solution. "Whit won't reach his majority for another six years. You could settle with me now, and agree to buy Whit's portion on his twenty-first birth-day, at current prices. Then you'd be rid of both of us. You and your sons would own Donegal free and clear."

Frank's eyes betrayed him. "We might be able to work something out. How soon would we start the process?"

"We've started. All that's left is to confer with your lawyer. When we've drawn up an agreement, I'll table my suit."

Frank prepared to leave. He paused in the doorway. "Father's very angry. I don't think you should come home for a while."

"I don't intend to," Tad said. "Not ever."

Tad spent the following day with Frank's lawyers, drawing up the agreement. When he returned to his suite late in the afternoon Whit was waiting.

A deep cut and dark bruise covered Whit's right cheek. The eye was swollen almost shut. "What happened to you?" Tad asked, knowing.

"He knocked me down with a board," Whit said. "I've run away."

Tad sent Jack down to the kitchen for a plate of food. Whit looked up at Tad in his most pleading manner. "Tad, if you're going back to Texas, I want to go with you. I'll work. I'm big for my age. I'm strong. I can be a lot of help to you."

Tad shunted the subject aside for the moment. "We'll see. What set the Old Man off? Why'd he hit you?"

"Uzziah left the granary door open. Some of the horses got in and bloated. Two died. Uzziah lied, told him I did it."

Uzziah was the stableboy. But he could not be blamed. Larkin

Logan once beat a Negro named Buford to the point of death with a log chain. "Have you put anything on that cut?"

Whit shook his head. "Didn't have a chance. That's not the worst of it. He took a poker to me."

He raised his trouser legs. Cuts, bruises, and dried blood covered both shins. The marks were a signature Tad recognized: Larkin tended to go for the shins.

Tad felt his temper rising. He bore the scars of similar beatings.

"I'm not going back," Whit said. "If you won't take me with you, I'll run away."

"I won't make you go back," Tad assured him. "You can stay here for the present. Frank will be in tomorrow to sign the papers. I'll talk to him, see what we can work out."

Whit persisted. "Will you take me to Texas with you?"

Tad hesitated. "Whit, I'll try. I don't know if it'd be possible. Frank and the Old Man could accuse me of aiding and abetting your runaway. I might win Frank over to helping us. He wants Donegal. Maybe I can make that part of the deal."

Jack returned with the food. As Whit moved to a table to eat, Tad noticed that his trousers were too short, his coat too small. The sleeves lacked a hand's width of reaching the wrists. The coat was too snug to button. "Those the only clothes you brought with you?" Tad asked.

Whit nodded.

"You've grown out of that coat," Tad told him. "While I'm with Frank tomorrow, go with Jack and buy yourself some decent clothes."

Whit looked at his short sleeves. "I'll be beholden."

"It's not charity. I'll keep a running account and take it out of your share of Donegal, six years from now. Jack, you'll be spending Master Whit's money. Don't be stingy. As soon as the papers are signed, we'll go up to Charleston and buy some horses and maybe a few Negroes."

Jack laughed.

Whit looked up at him. "What's so funny?"

"Marsh Whit, we may buy us some horses and darkies. But it won't be horses and darkies Marsh Tad'll be looking at."

*   *   *

Sarah stood in the doorway, looking at her daughter. "Corrie, this isn't like you. I can't imagine you not being gracious. There's something you're not saying. What is it?"

Corrie had not wanted to bother her mother with the difficulties Thaddeus Logan had posed. Now she saw she could not avoid the subject. He was coming to supper and she was expected to be there. "It's only that Mr. Logan was unseemingly forward with me. Everyone noticed. Even old Mrs. Threadgill felt it necessary to tell him, rather pointedly, that Ramsey and I are betrothed. But that didn't stop him. He continued to act as if I were unattached."

"There must have been some misunderstanding. Your father was most impressed with him."

Corrie saw that Thaddeus Logan was precisely the type of man her father would admire. Articulate. A superb horseman. A military hero. Logan would be able to write his own ticket at Moultrie Hill. "He's a charmer," she admitted.

"Apparently he's also a Freemason, and you know the store your father places in that."

Corrie nodded. John McNair often pointed out that the aristocracy in England, including the kings, were Freemasons, as were American presidents and most members of Congress. He said the secret signs, passwords, and handshakes of the order provided instant recognition among outstanding individuals, who otherwise would be strangers. "I didn't know he was a Mason," Corrie said. "No wonder Father was so impressed."

"Your father has invited Mr. Logan to be our guest through the weekend. Tomorrow the men will look over the horses. On Sunday Mr. Logan will go to church with us, and to dinner-on-the-grounds afterward."

Corrie was appalled. She could not begin to imagine living under the same roof with Thaddeus Logan for three days. "I hope I won't be expected to entertain him at that length. I have too much to do."

Sarah looked at her for a long moment. "I've been intending to speak to you. Corrie, I think you're devoting yourself too much to superficialities." She gestured to the work in front of Corrie. "Those wedding invitations needn't be so elaborate. You should be spending your time with Ramsey instead."

Corrie did not understand. "I spend time with him."

"Not alone. Corrie, while it's true you've known Ramsey all your life, I have the feeling you two have never been close in the way you should be. I see none of the intimacy that should exist in a couple on the verge of matrimony. I don't think this distance is on his part. You tend to hold him at arm's length. I've seen you. And I've seen the puzzlement on his face in unguarded moments."

Corrie was shaken and confused. "What would you have me do?"

"Talk more with Ramsey. Not about parties and socials and such. But about the two of you. I believe you each expect certain things of each other, and you may be disappointed. It would help if you'd learn what's in each other's mind."

Corrie did not respond. What else was there to know about Ramsey? About their future together?

The duties of a plantation wife had not changed in three generations. Corrie had grown up observing that life. She would have no difficulty in falling into the routine of managing the Osborne household, entertaining Ramsey's friends, and maintaining an active social life. What else was there to know?

"Mr. Logan is to arrive about an hour before sunset," Sarah said. "His brother may be with him. No doubt they'll be tired from the road. I think it would be nice if we received them on the front gallery for a cool drink before supper."

Corrie nodded assent. She supposed she could not avoid the ordeal.

She summoned Hattie and asked her to prepare the green taffeta with the yoke neckline. While Hattie worked, Corrie hurried her toilette. She decided to wear her hair loose and flowing, and limited her jewelry to a small heirloom locket. She allowed herself only a bare hint of perfume.

When Corrie descended to the front gallery, Prue was seated on the glider. She looked up in amusement. "That's quite an outfit. I thought you didn't like the man."

"You just hush!" Corrie said. "I'll not take any smart talk out of you tonight!"

"Perish the thought. . . . You think he's really coming to trade horses? Or is he coming to see you?"

Corrie had not mentioned that possibility to anyone. But she had wondered. "He'd better be coming to trade horses," she said. "That's all the man will get at Moultrie Hill."

A few minutes later John and Sarah McNair came out onto the gallery. Corrie and Prue moved to make room for Sarah on the glider. Corrie thought her mother appeared pale. She put a hand on her arm. "Mother, do you feel all right? Are you up to this?"

"I'm only tired," Sarah said. "I'll feel better with a cool drink."

The wait was brief. Three riders appeared on the road from Charleston, turned into the Moultrie Hill lane, and came up the gravel drive at a fast trot.

As the three riders drew rein, the Moultrie Hill groom, Nedabiah, stepped forward. Logan swept off his huge hat. "Good day to you all. Please allow me to introduce my brother Whitfield."

The brother was a younger, thinner version of Thaddeus—the same wide face, blue eyes, and full jaw. But there was a vulnerable quality about him that Thaddeus Logan lacked. He reminded Corrie of a lost pup, constantly searching for a friendly face. As he removed his Panama, Corrie first thought he had a black smudge across his left cheek. But then she saw it was an ugly cut, surrounded by a deep bruise.

"Welcome to Moultrie Hill," Corrie's father said from the gallery. "If you'll surrender your horses to Nedabiah, and join us on the gallery, we'll have a cool drink before supper."

The Logans dismounted and came up the steps. Corrie's father made introductions. Corrie and Prue curtsied.

"I had the pleasure of meeting Miss Cornelia at the Threadgill ball and sharing a waltz with her," Logan said. "Since I've now met you, Mrs. McNair, I see from whom your daughters derived their beauty."

It was blarney, pure and simple. Corrie was rather chagrined to see her mother reveling in it. A rosy glow came to her cheeks. "You're too kind, Mr. Logan." She seemed to feel the need to acknowledge Whitfield. "That's a painful-looking cut, Master Logan. What in the world happened to you?"

The boy seemed stricken, unable to answer. Corrie assumed he was unaccustomed to being the center of attention.

"He got caught between an unruly horse and a paddock gate," Logan said. "The horse won. But no harm done. I think the paddock gate can be repaired."

In the laughter following Logan's joke, Corrie happened to be watching the boy's face. She sensed that the paddock gate story was as new to him as to the other listeners. She wondered if he had been injured in some brawl.

Corrie's father led the way to the seats on the gallery, and lime drinks were served.

For a time Thaddeus Logan was full of compliments for the house, the plantation, the crops he had seen from the road.

While Thaddeus talked, his younger brother sat so quietly that Corrie could understand how Ramsey first thought him mentally deficient. But he followed the conversation avidly, and smiled occasionally at his brother's clever phrases.

At dusk Corrie's father escorted them into the house. While the men washed on the back porch, Corrie and her mother made last-minute preparations.

Although lamps were lit in the parlor, supper was served in the dining room by candlelight. As was the custom at Moultrie Hill, they ate leisurely, allowing ample time for relaxed conversation.

"Mr. McNair tells me you're going back west," Sarah said, fending off talk of horses. "We've met few Texians, and you're an eloquent man, Mr. Logan. Could you describe Texas for us?"

Logan gave her his wide smile. "To do it justice, Mrs. McNair, I would have to be a poet. I fear I fall far short. But I'll try. The first salient fact about Texas is its vastness. Less than half of the Republic has been explored. In the parts I've seen, you can ride for days through an ocean of grass, broken only by small mottes of trees. Birds and wildlife abound. Sometimes you pass through prairies of wildflowers stretching as far as the eye can see."

Logan turned his smile on Corrie, making her aware that she

was listening with open mouth, scarcely breathing. She could not imagine a land so lovely.

"There are streams that traverse those prairies with greenery, for all the world like an emerald necklace," Logan continued. "On farther west, the land grows more harsh, with cactus and thorned plants. But even those desert regions possess a certain beauty."

Corrie found herself longing to see what Logan described. In her eighteen years she had hardly been out of the tidewater.

"Tell them about the buffalo and deer," Whitfield burst out, overly loud. Even in the candlelight his face showed red from his embarrassment over suddenly asserting himself.

Logan seemed not to notice. "Deer, buffalo, antelope, and elk are unbelievably abundant. I once spent three days riding through one immense herd of buffalo. It's seldom you lack fresh food for your supper."

"What about the Indians?" Corrie's father asked. "Have they proved troublesome?"

"At times. But I don't believe them to be the savages portrayed in most accounts. A friend of mine, David Burnet, once fell from his horse in the wilderness on the upper Colorado, and was gravely injured. He was found by the Comanches, who restored him to health, though it took two years. I've gathered evidence of similar acts of compassion. I'm encouraged to think we may be able to make peace with them."

"I've seen the maps," Corrie's father said. "Where are most Texians situated?"

"At present, in the older communities near the Louisiana border, and on the original colonial grants along the lower portions of the rivers in the interior. When I left the Republic, the newest activity was on the coast, at Galveston Island, and in a town called Houston, named for the general."

"Is that where you plan to settle?"

Logan slowly shook his head. Although he addressed her father, Corrie had the uncanny impression he was speaking for her benefit alone. "No, Mr. McNair. I plan to go on farther west, to San Antonio de Béxar. It's the fairest site in all of Texas. The San Antonio River rises from limestone springs just to the north and winds its way southward through the settlement, feeding expanses of large trees along its course. The Spanish fathers built missions there along the river. The ruins still stand. The fathers also directed the digging of a network of canals. You are never far from water, and with irrigation crops grow abundantly with a minimum of effort. To my mind, the biblical Garden of Eden must have been something like San Antonio de Béxar."

Again Logan turned his smile on Corrie, jarring her from the spell of his words.

"What about the surrounding country?" Corrie's father asked.

"To the east lie the central grasslands I've described. To the north and west rise low mountains, the rugged country that provides the source of ample water. To the south stretches flat land. It's called desert, but that may be a misnomer, for the region supports great herds of wild mustangs. I believe that land someday will prove ideal for cattle."

Corrie's father then asked Logan about the mustangs. Corrie was disappointed, for now there would be talk of little else but horses.

"Good mounts are at a premium in Texas," Logan said. "I hope to drive a small foundation herd west with me, and raise and train good saddle horses. It should be a profitable enterprise."

"Well, I hope we can be of service," Corrie's father said.

"I'm sure you will be. I've heard repeatedly that you have the best horses available. If you don't mind, tomorrow I'd like to see a demonstration of their abilities."

"That can be arranged," Corrie's father replied. "We happen to have at this table the two best equestrians in South Carolina."

Corrie felt her face grow hot. "Father!" she said. But there was no stopping him.

"Our carriage driver, Ben, probably knows horses as well as anyone around Charleston. As a boy, he rode as a jockey for Grandfather McNair. He taught my daughters to ride from the first day they could sit a horse. Taught them all he knows."

Corrie felt driven to speak. "My father badly overstates the case, Mr. Logan."

"I doubt that, Miss Cornelia. I do hope we can prevail on you. I would love to see the horses at work."

Under the circumstances, Corrie could not refuse. "It would be my pleasure," she said.

"Miss Pruella?"

"Of course, Mr. Logan."

After supper the men withdrew to the parlor for cigars, brandy, and, no doubt, talk of horses and politics. Corrie felt she had made her contributions to the evening. She asked to be excused and returned to her room.

Again she set to work on the invitations. But she could not concentrate. Her mind kept wandering to Thaddeus Logan and his descriptions of Texas.

Faraway places and exotic lands had always held enormous appeal for her. She often envied her great-grandparents, who had come from England to Charleston by way of the West Indies early in the last century. At Charles Town they had helped to build a crown province celebrated for its wealth and high level of culture. All of her life she had thrilled to the family stories of Indian attacks, marauding pirates, and romantic wars. The lives her grandparents had lived made her own hopelessly prosaic by comparison. She always wished she had lived in those days, when adventure and great accomplishment were routine.

Irritated with herself for dawdling, she forced herself to concentrate and labored over the invitations long after the house had stilled. Consequently she was late to bed, and sound asleep the following morning when Hattie brought her breakfast.

She awoke vaguely disturbed. Thaddeus Logan had figured prominently in her dreams. She tried to recall details but failed, for Hattie's chatter chased away every lingering image.

Prue came into the room. Years ago they had developed the habit of braiding each other's hair for riding.

Corrie set to work. As usual, Prue talked. "Do you suppose Thaddeus Logan's man is a bright Negro?" she asked.

Corrie was mildly shocked at the thought. The term was commonly applied to Negroes who were kin to the family who owned them. "Prue, you shouldn't say such things. It doesn't become you."

Prue sniffed her exasperation. "Well, did you believe that story about Whitfield and the paddock gate?"

Corrie did not want to speculate. "It sounded plausible."

"I think he was in a fight. He's strange. He looks like God started out to make another Thaddeus, and the effort didn't turn out quite right."

Corrie suppressed a laugh. "Whitfield's young. Someday he may be as handsome as Thaddeus."

Prue glanced up. "Then you *do* think Thaddeus handsome!"

"There's no denying that," Corrie conceded.

"More so than Ramsey?"

Corrie hesitated. The two men were so different.

Prue burst out laughing and again turned to look at Corrie. "See? You're having to think about it! Thaddeus Logan has truly caught your eye!"

Corrie yanked a braid to turn Prue's head straight. "I hesitated only because I was thinking how different they are."

"Well, I prefer Ramsey," Prue said. "I always know what he's thinking. Thaddeus Logan makes me uncomfortable."

"In what way?" Corrie asked, gratified that the effect was not limited to herself.

"For all his big words, and what father calls his eloquence, I feel he's not telling everything he's thinking."

Corrie laughed. "Few people do. And that's a habit you could well acquire."

She tied a bow and tugged a braid to let Prue know she was done. They exchanged places.

"He talks about Texas like it's a religion," Prue said as she divided Corrie's hair. "And I guess we're in for another dose of it tomorrow. Father said he plans to ask Mr. Logan to speak on Texas at dinner-on-the-grounds."

Again Corrie did not respond.

She was swiftly getting her fill of Mr. Logan.

Corrie stepped from the mounting block onto Titan. She squeezed her right leg firmly into the sidesaddle, arranged her skirt, and tugged her riding cap down tightly. Prue was already up on Ladyship.

"What does Father want us to do?" Prue asked.

"I don't know," Corrie said. "Let's go ask."

She led the way, riding down the track to where the men sat on their horses. Thaddeus Logan was up on the big black stallion, and Whitfield on a dun gelding. Corrie's father was riding Old Solicitor, his longtime favorite horse.

As Corrie approached, the Logans swept off their hats and bowed from the saddle. Corrie acknowledged their presence with a nod. Her father was explaining his theory of selection with an eye to strength in the legs and loins.

"Titan, the horse Cornelia is riding, is the grandsire of most of the horses I have for sale," he concluded. "He has taken best-in-show everywhere he has competed for the last six years. I've striven to preserve his attributes. Pruella is on Ladyship, now the grand dam of my line of horses. Few of the two- and three-year-olds you've seen today are fully trained. But by observing Titan and Ladyship you can gain perspective on the potential of their progeny. Corrie, would you and Pruella please give Mr. Logan a demonstration of their gaits."

Corrie turned the stallion and rode away at a fast trot. Prue fell in behind her. Around the turn, as she rode back in front of the men, she put Titan into a walk, a trot, a canter, and a gallop. Riding close behind, Prue followed her lead.

From the far end of the track Corrie returned with Titan maintaining a high-stepping pace. The gait was not Corrie's favorite, for it was unnatural. Yet it was always a crowd pleaser. On the next return she kept Titan in a rack, a gait she liked even less.

She made her last return at a fast canter and waited until they were even with the men. "Now!" she said to Prue.

Titan and Ladyship changed leads in unison. It was their best trick. The simultaneous flying change of leads always brought down the house. Corrie had never heard of it being done by any other horses in or around Charleston.

"Now!" she said, and the horses changed back. Corrie broke stride to a trot and rode across to where the men waited.

Logan again swept off his hat. "Absolutely stunning horseman-ship. I've never seen anything like it."

Corrie could not hide her pleasure. "Ben trained them to do that. He deserves the credit."

Logan turned to Corrie's father. "Much of Texas is rough coun-try. My buyers will be wanting strong animals. Are they good jumpers?"

Corrie's father turned and raised a hand. "Ben! Nedabiah! Put up the jumps."

The bars were set just above midpoint. When all was ready, Corrie and Prue aligned their horses and rode down the course, taking the jumps together.

All went smoothly. Corrie did not hear a single hoof strike wood. Neither horse bobbled in stride. She drew rein and walked Titan back to the men.

"Very impressive," she heard Logan saying to her father. "But are they strong jumpers? Could they clear a high fence, if they had a man's hand to guide them?"

Corrie did not await her father's reply. She turned and loped Titan over to where Ben stood. "Top peg, Ben," she ordered. "The whole course."

Ben shook his head. "Miss Cornelia, you can't—"

"Top peg," she said again.

She wheeled Titan and rode to the end of the course. She knew she was being foolish. A good horseman should take a horse to the higher jumps gradually, building the animal's confidence. But Lo-gan had plainly implied he was seeing only timid horsemanship.

She would show him what a McNair horse could do.

Prue rode up beside her. "Corrie, I've never jumped a full course on top peg. Ladyship is getting long in the tooth. I don't know if she could do it. And I'm not about to break my neck for any man, including Thaddeus Logan."

"Then get out of my way," Corrie said.

The bars were up. Corrie heard her father calling to her. She ignored him. She reined Titan into a small circle, then started him down the course.

She gave him his head, allowing him to time his jumps, and

concentrated on helping him by keeping her weight well forward. They sailed over the first bar with inches to spare. Corrie took care not to settle back into the seat until two full strides after the landing.

They fell into a routine, taking each jump, preparing for the next. Only twice did a hoof graze wood. Neither time did the bar fall.

Corrie trotted Titan back to where the men waited.

"Corrie, don't you ever do anything like that again!" her father said. "Think how we would have felt if Titan had taken a header, and you had been injured."

"I knew he could do it," she lied.

Logan was giving her that smile she was beginning to find infuriating. "That horse probably could clear any fence in Texas."

Titan was excited from the exertion. He kept tossing his head, tamping his feet. "He needs to work off some of his energy," Corrie said to Logan.

She took Titan twice around the track at a full-out run. She slowed to a trot to allow him to catch his breath. But he was still tossing his head, snorting. Thaddeus Logan rode up beside her.

"He's fast," Logan said. "Could he do even better, if he had some competition?"

Corrie glanced meaningfully at Logan's stallion. "He could," she said. "If he had some competition."

Logan gave her a deep, vigorous laugh. It was a good sound, and Corrie was struck by the fact that this was the first time she had seen him lose his serious demeanor. He seemed like a different person. "Four times around the track?" he suggested.

Corrie nodded agreement.

"Loser loses his hat?"

Laughing, Corrie again nodded agreement.

"Let's trot once around to get warmed up. When we come back here, we'll go."

They trotted down the track together. Logan's stallion also tossed his head, eager to run. "What's his name?" Corrie asked.

"Midnight. When he was born, Jack took one look and said 'black as midnight,' and he's been Midnight ever since."

"You raised him from a colt?"

"From the day he was born. He's quite a traveler. He has sweethearts all over Texas."

Corrie laughed, enjoying Logan's lighter mood. "What about yourself?" she asked. "Do you have sweethearts all over Texas?"

He answered with mock seriousness. "No. Single women are as rare as hens' teeth in Texas. I had to come back to Georgia."

"And did you find any there?"

"A few. But by then I had changed my ideas as to what I desired in a woman."

The conversation again had turned serious. But Corrie felt driven. "And what might that be?"

Logan gave her an analytical glance. "An outlook on life compatible with my own."

"Could you define that?"

Again Logan paused while he studied her. Corrie fully understood she had overstepped. But she was spurred by curiosity.

"It's an outlook beyond definition," Logan said. "Beyond words. But I recognize it when I see it."

Corrie was irritated, and disappointed. Logan had drawn her out until she placed herself at risk, then answered her with a nonanswer. She reined Titan away from Midnight and tightened her grip on the sidesaddle. "We're about to the mark," she said. "Get ready."

They set off neck to neck, pounding toward the far turn. Midnight held the advantage of a longer stride. But Titan knew the track. Corrie held him back going into the turn and released him at the proper moment. Midnight swung too wide. Titan emerged from the turn ahead by a neck.

Midnight closed the gap on the straightaway, but again swung too wide at the next turn. Titan regained the lead.

The pattern was repeated each lap. As they rounded the final turn Titan again led by a neck. Midnight closed steadily. They crossed the finish line nose to nose.

Corrie and Logan drew rein, laughing in exhilaration. They turned back up the track with both horses blowing heavily.

"I'd call that a dead heat," Logan said. "I don't believe anyone lost his hat."

*   *   *

Ramsey and Corrie sat together near the lectern. As he had done every Sunday for the last year, Ramsey had escorted Corrie to church. On the way and during the dinner following the sermon, Corrie had remembered her mother's admonition and had attempted to talk more with him. She asked about Osborne, the prospect for spring crops. But Ramsey had seemed preoccupied. Corrie had filled the silences by telling him of her work on the invitations, and how she and Titan had matched Logan and his big black horse. Now they sat quietly. Thaddeus Logan was about to speak and Corrie was curious, even eager, to hear what he would say.

Brother Lane introduced Logan as a McNair houseguest who happened to be a hero of the Texas Revolution. He said Mr. Logan had been prevailed upon to say a few words about the new republic bordering the United States on the west.

Logan received polite applause as he made his way to the lectern. He acknowledged the courtesy with a nod.

He began his talk with his description of the beauty of Texas, and of the Republic's commercial possibilities. Then, just as Corrie was beginning to think she had heard it all before, he abruptly changed his tack.

"I find that by and large the significance of what happened out in Texas has not yet been fully appreciated in the United States," he said. "Especially in Washington."

He paused. Corrie wished she had not chosen a seat so near the lectern. Logan's physical presence was overwhelming at short distance, his deep voice spellbinding.

"As we look back over history, we find man's course has been ever upward," he said. "The ancient Greeks gave us a love of learning. The ancient Romans left us the concept of the citizen state. In England the Magna Charta proclaimed that man must be accorded certain inherent dignities. Our American Revolution established the belief that no decree should be levied without the consent of the governed. And now, out in Texas, a new chapter has been written, proving that tyranny cannot prevail against a determined populace, no matter what the odds."

Again Logan paused, gazing out over his audience. The silence around Corrie told her Logan had everyone enthralled.

"Thermopylae had a messenger of defeat," he said. "The Alamo had none. Every man there knew the odds. Fewer than two hundred men against an army of six thousand. They could have fled. They could have retreated. But they held out for thirteen glorious days. Have you ever wondered what prompted such courage?"

Logan gave his audience a moment to ponder the question before resuming.

"I think we can find the answer in the letter that came from the Alamo eleven days before its fall."

Logan quoted the letter word for word without notes, his voice thundering out over the audience. He spoke slowly, giving each word full impact.

" 'To the People of Texas and all Americans in the world. Fellow citizens and compatriots: I am besieged, by a thousand or more of the Mexicans under Santa Anna. I have sustained continual bombardment and cannonade for twenty-four hours and have not lost a man. The enemy has demanded a surrender at discretion, otherwise the garrison are to be put to the sword if the fort is taken. I have answered the demand with a cannon shot and our flag still waves proudly from the walls. I shall never surrender or retreat. Then, I call on you in the name of Liberty, of patriotism, and everything dear to the American character, to come to our aid, with all dispatch. The enemy is receiving reinforcements daily and will no doubt increase to three or four thousand in four or five days. If this call is neglected, I am determined to sustain myself as long as possible and die like a soldier who never forgets what is due to his own honor and that of his country. Victory or Death.' "

Logan paused dramatically. "The letter is signed Lieutenant Colonel William Barret Travis."

Corrie could not stop her tears. She had wept for those men three years ago, when the news first came, and she wept for them now.

Logan lowered his voice, as if in deference to the dead. "It was this legacy that enabled a few hundred of us to destroy a Mexican army twice the size of our own at San Jacinto."

Lowering his gaze, he seemed to speak directly to Corrie, jarring her out of a trance.

"Today this appeal from Colonel Travis remains valid. We won independence for Texas on the battlefield of San Jacinto, but the story doesn't end there. We now must gather the fruits of victory. At this very moment the northern provinces of Mexico are in revolt. They should be encouraged to cast their lot with Texas. California is another plum ready to fall from the tree. She should be enticed to rally around the Lone Star flag. The Oregon country also may soon look to Texas for strength and guidance. I believe the borders of Texas are destined to reach from Louisiana to the Pacific, from the Arkansas River to the mountains of Coahuila. In time Texas will be a sister republic to the United States, and rival her in size."

A murmur of surprise swept through the crowd. Corrie assumed the grand idea was as new to the other listeners as to herself.

"Our task is immense," Logan went on. He looked out over the crowd. "The French came to Texas and hardly left a trace of themselves. The Spanish came with their armies and missions, and lingered for almost three centuries. But they could not hold her. The Mexicans came, and also failed. But I believe we Americans are equal to the task. Not only will we hold Texas. We will build Texas into an empire beyond compare."

Again a murmur swept through the crowd. Corrie felt goose bumps. She had never dreamed that what her grandparents accomplished might be repeated in her own lifetime.

Logan seemed to pick up her thoughts. Again his gaze dropped to her. "When our grandfathers and grandmothers landed on these shores, they brought culture, refinement, and the Word of God to the wilderness. When they opposed injustices, and won independence, they inspired the imagination of freedom-loving people everywhere. Men and women of compatible minds came to America, to take up the American way of life."

Corrie recognized the phrase *compatible minds*, and knew that Logan was indeed speaking to her. He was conveying a private message in a public speech.

He was telling her they were of compatible minds, that she was what he desired in a woman.

"The American Revolution continues in Texas, in a government modeled on the one in Washington," Logan went on. "And just as freedom-loving people everywhere came to the assistance of our grandparents, so we need them in Texas today, to complete the building of an empire that is there for the making. Thank you."

The abrupt ending was followed by a moment of silence, then thunderous applause. Men stood and shouted approval. The applause went on and on.

Corrie sat shaken to the core. In a few brief minutes she had wept, thrilled to new concepts, felt joy, sadness, and undeniable challenge.

Ramsey was on his feet, applauding. He looked down at her, concerned. "Are you all right?"

Corrie seized the opportunity to hide her turmoil. "I feel giddy. I think it's the crowd. Could we please leave?"

Ramsey helped her to his carriage and summoned his driver. Within minutes they were driving away from the crowd, on the way back to Moultrie Hill.

They did not discuss the speech. Ramsey's avoidance of it was pointed. Clearly its effect on her was all too apparent.

Corrie went to bed and slept through supper. When she awoke she felt better. Moultrie Hill appeared normal. The sky had not fallen. Chances seemed good that in time she would recover her equilibrium.

Corrie remembered that earlier Ben had reported that Titan was favoring his right foreleg. Concerned that she might have injured him, she walked down to the sheds near the paddock, and to the stall where he was being kept overnight.

The sun was setting. She led Titan around the stall in semidarkness. Although she could see he was limping, the shed was too dark for her to explore the injury.

"Do you have a lantern?" Logan asked behind her.

Startled, Corrie pointed. "Over there."

Logan reached for the lantern, struck a lucifer, and lit and adjusted the wick. "I hope we didn't hurt him with our fun."

"I don't think it's serious," Corrie said, examining Titan's leg. "A mild sprain, at worst."

Logan stroked Titan's neck. "I was concerned. Now that I own his offspring, I feel I have a vested interest in him."

As a member of his host family, Corrie felt she should acknowledge Logan's entertainment at the church. "I enjoyed your speech. I was very moved by what you said."

He lowered the wick and hung the lantern back on its peg. The reduced flame cast a soft, warm glow over the interior of the shed. He spoke in a low voice. "What do you think would happen if Titan were kept in this stall for the rest of his life?"

Corrie failed to see the point of the question, but she had no doubt as to the answer. "He would waste away and die."

Logan nodded solemnly. "Corrie, to my mind you are like Titan. You don't belong cooped up here." He gestured toward Moultrie Hill, the community. "You should be free to live your full potential."

Corrie was shocked. He was telling her she should not marry Ramsey. He had done so without mentioning Ramsey's name.

"Mr. Logan, perhaps you've misunderstood my situation. I'm to marry Ramsey Cothburn in June."

"Ramsey Cothburn is a fine man," Logan said. "I've had that report from all quarters. But, Corrie, he's not the right man."

For a moment Corrie was flooded with conflicting emotions. She felt anger, indignation, intrigue, alarm, and curiosity in the same breath. "What gives you the right to sit in judgment?"

"The right of a devotee. Corrie, I've loved you since the time I first saw you, sitting on the Threadgill lawn. I knew then that you were the one I wanted. In our brief acquaintance, you've proved to be all I anticipated in that moment."

He had not placed a hand on her. But Corrie stepped back defensively. "Mr. Logan, this conversation has become improper."

"Yes, it has. But it's an improper situation. Think to the years ahead, Corrie. What will you do? Meet with the quilting society? Crochet? Attend afternoon socials and teas? Sit around and exchange family pedigrees with women who have never done one practical thing in their lives? Corrie, you're capable of far beyond that."

Corrie was left speechless.

"Come with me to Texas, Corrie," he continued. "We'll live a life of adventure, accomplishment. That's what you were born to do."

"I hardly know you!" Corrie said. She opened her mouth, searching for words. He quickly stepped forward and placed his fingers across her lips.

"Wait! If you answer now, you'll only say what you think you should say, not what's in your heart. Please think very seriously about what kind of life you want. I've bared my heart to you and I think I know what's in yours."

He removed his hand. Uncertain of what to say, Corrie remained silent.

"My affairs will keep me occupied the next three weeks. Then I'll come back and play the role of a proper suitor. I only ask that you think seriously of me, and what I've said."

Before she could answer, he kissed her hand and vanished into the night.

Corrie stood for a time in the dimly lit shed, unable to stop trembling. Clearly Logan had seen her leave the house and followed, with the intention of catching her alone.

She endured a restless night, trying to decide what to do. Toward dawn she concluded she would not tolerate Logan's attentions any longer. In the morning she would confront him, thank him politely for his interest, and tell him that to return as a suitor would be pointless.

Relieved with the decision, she slept.

When she awoke, the Logans were gone.

--- 3 ---

Larkin Logan was squatting in the middle of the field, examining the tender shoots of early cotton. He looked up as Tad approached on Midnight, cupped a hand, and shouted. "I thought I told you never to come back to Donegal."

Tad rode closer but did not dismount. "I'm not here by choice," he said. "I've come to tell you I'm keeping Whit. I'm taking him west with me."

Rising, Larkin faced Tad with legs widespread. "I'll be damned if you will. He's underage. I'll get the law after you."

"I wouldn't mind going to court with it," Tad warned. "I'd only have to show the marks you put on him. No judge or jury would send him back here for more beatings."

"A judge would understand the need for discipline."

Tad laughed. "Is that what you call it? Knocking him down with a board? Taking a poker to his shins?"

"He sassed me."

"He refused to tell you who left the granary door open because he knew you'd beat the guilty party half to death. And you would." Tad slowly turned Midnight, taking care not to trample the rows of seedling cotton. "I'm not going to argue further. I just came to tell you."

Larkin took a step forward. "Why are you doing this to me?"

Tad halted Midnight and turned in the saddle to look back at his father. "I'm not thinking of you. I'm thinking of Whit."

"I'll see you in hell before I'll let you take him off. File your goddamned lawsuit. You buffaloed Frank and his lawyers. But you don't scare me."

Tad sat on one hip in the saddle and met his father's gaze over

Midnight's rump. "You want it all to come out?" he asked quietly. "The beating you gave poor old Buford with a log chain? Whippings and beatings you've given other Donegal Negroes? The way you used to beat me? And now Whit?"

"I never whipped you," Larkin said.

Tad could hardly believe his ears. "I have marks on me that prove otherwise. You once took a poker to me. Don't you remember? Jack and I were playing and left the north gate open. Some of the horses got out."

"Hell, yes, I remember," Larkin shot back. "Brian Nelson's scrub stud got to two of my mares. I gave you the whipping you deserved. I wouldn't call it a beating."

"A jury would, if I showed the scars," Tad said. "I can assemble witnesses to your beatings, strip you of the shred of reputation you have left. Is that what you want?"

"Go ahead with your lies and half truths," Larkin said, his voice breaking. "I won't let the boy go with you. I didn't raise him to be killed by wild Indians."

Tad was not surprised to see tears running down his father's cheeks. Larkin Logan's life was ruled by abrupt and irrational swings of mood. He could beat a victim one moment, and weep for him in the next. Tad understood, for he had inherited the trait.

"I'll look after Whit," he promised. "But I mean what I say. You'd better think it through before you try to stop me."

He put the spurs to Midnight and trotted away.

Larkin shouted behind him. "Why you doing this?"

Tad did not stop to answer, not trusting himself to speak. He regretted what he was doing. In time he probably would relent. But not until he had Whit well away from Donegal.

That evening he took Whit to one side and broke the news. "I've talked to Father. I think he's going to agree for you to go west with me."

Whit laughed and performed a little dance. "What'd he say?"

"He's opposed. But I threatened to take him to court for beating you. I don't think he'll give us trouble."

The revelation tempered Whit's joy. He sat for a time in silence. "When will we leave?"

"Not for a while," Tad told him. "I have to buy wagons and equipment. We'll go back to Charleston and buy some Negroes. Right now, with the Panic, it's a buyer's market up there."

Tad hesitated, reflecting that perhaps Whit should have a full explanation, to circumvent any awkwardness that might occur from his not knowing. "And I plan to ask Cornelia McNair to marry me," he added.

Whit blinked in bewilderment. "I thought she was going to marry someone else."

"She may," Tad said. "We'll see."

Within a week of Thaddeus Logan's departure, Corrie became convinced she was losing her mind. His face and voice were with her every waking moment. She kept reliving the way he had looked by lantern light in Titan's stall, solemnly declaring his love for her. At night she tossed and turned, besieged by vivid dreams.

The worst of it was that she knew Logan's estimate of her future with Ramsey was true.

With Thaddeus Logan the most exciting part of her life would still lie ahead. And she could not deny that he fascinated her more than any other man ever had on such short acquaintance. But she recognized that her intense feelings might only be an acute case of infatuation. And even if it proved to be love, how could she pledge herself to a virtual stranger? How could she possibly abandon her engagement to Ramsey? How could she justify herself to her parents, to the community?

The dilemma would not go away. She lost her appetite, skipped meals, and spent more and more time in bed, thinking, yet getting nowhere.

One evening Sarah came and stood over her. "Corrie, I want to know what's wrong with you. Are you ill?"

"Not really," Corrie said. "I'm just not feeling well."

"I'm sending for Doctor Powers. This isn't like you." She started for the door.

"Please, Mother," Corrie said.

Something in Corrie's voice stopped Sarah. She turned and looked back. "Corrie, what is it?"

Once Corrie started talking the whole story tumbled out unbidden. She told of her helpless fascination with Thaddeus Logan, his persistent attention, and her resulting confusion. She told of his declaration of love, of his impending proposal, and of her uncertainty.

Sarah sank to the edge of the bed and folded her hands in her lap. "Oh, my," she said. "Does Ramsey know?"

Corrie fought back tears. "It hasn't been mentioned. But I think he suspects."

Sarah took Corrie's hand. "Do you love Mr. Logan?"

Corrie hesitated. "I don't know. I've never felt like this about anyone before. When I'm near him I can hardly breathe. But I've only known him a few weeks. I must be crazy to take his attentions seriously."

"Don't blame yourself," Sarah said. "We can't help the way we feel."

"But what'll I do?" Corrie asked. "I've thought of nothing else since he left."

Sarah did not answer immediately. But a moment later she spoke firmly. "This will be difficult. You should tell Ramsey of your doubts."

Corrie shook her head. "I can't."

"You must. Corrie, you're entertaining the affections of two honorable men. You must be honest with them. The first step is to tell Ramsey the truth."

"I can't," Corrie said again. "I couldn't do that to him."

"You have no choice. Three lives are at stake in this. You can't marry Ramsey deceitful with him about your true feelings."

Corrie could not argue with that logic. "All right. I'll tell Ramsey. But what shall I do about Thaddeus Logan?"

"The answer to that must come from your own heart," Sarah said. "No one else can help you."

*   *   *

That Sunday, Corrie went to church with Ramsey. On the way back she waited until the carriage crossed a small freshwater creek flowing through a green meadow. "Let's stop and walk for a bit," she suggested. From his solemn demeanor Corrie suspected he knew exactly what was on her mind.

They strolled through lush spring grass to the fallen sycamore where they had whiled away so many hours in the past. Corrie took a seat on the trunk and watched the gently flowing water. Ramsey stood over her, patiently waiting.

Corrie's carefully prepared speech suddenly went right out of her head. She began, uncertain precisely what she would say. "Ramsey, I want you to know I love you as much as ever. But I must tell you that in the last few weeks I've become confused. I'm concerned because it wouldn't be fair for me to continue our engagement in my present state of mind."

Ramsey did not move. "What has happened?" he asked quietly.

Corrie had been determined to keep her composure, but now could not hold back tears. "I've developed an emotional attachment to Thaddeus Logan. I know it's irrational. But I'm no longer certain of myself. Do you understand?"

Ramsey seated himself on the far edge of the tree trunk. He nodded, looking down at his boots. "I'm not blind. I've seen this coming. I haven't known what to do about it."

"This isn't a flight of fancy," Corrie said. "Ramsey, I'm not a fickle person."

"I know you're not."

"I've agonized more than you can imagine. I hate myself for doing this." She paused, hesitating. "But under the circumstances, I think I should return your ring."

She slipped it off and held it out to him. For a long moment she thought he would refuse to take it. Then he relented, and allowed her to drop it into his palm. His lower lip trembled, and she thought he, too, would weep.

Eventually, he looked up and met her gaze.

"Is there any hope you'll reconsider?"

Corrie attempted to dry her eyes. "I don't know. I need time to think. Maybe I'll regain my sanity. But I can't promise anything."

Ramsey moved over beside her. "Corrie, I love you so much. Your happiness is the most important thing in the world to me."

He paused. Corrie waited.

"I believe the trouble is that we've been locked in this stage of our relationship too long. I've recognized this, and worried about it. We've allowed routine to intervene, and our relationship hasn't progressed as it should. I'm confident that as we go on into the next stage, as man and wife, we'll experience a deepening of our love, and it'll be all it was meant to be."

"I would like to think so," Corrie said.

"I've felt this lack between us," Ramsey went on. "I'm sure that is the cause. Our love for each other isn't at fault. It's our failure to nurture that love as we should."

Ramsey's argument seemed logical. Corrie's confusion was renewed. "Perhaps you're right," she said. "Please give me time to think about it."

"We've meant too much to each other for too many years for me to give you up so easily," Ramsey said. "I've always loved you. I always will."

Again Corrie gave way to tears. He put one arm gently around her. She felt dangerously close to losing her resolve. "Please, Ramsey," she managed to say. "This is only prolonging the agony. I want to go home."

He helped her back to the carriage. They drove on to Moultrie Hill in silence.

Ramsey left her at the front door. "I'll be waiting, Corrie," he said softly.

That evening Corrie told Prue that she had ended her engagement to Ramsey.

Prue seemed strangely angry. "What? Why? God never made a better man than Ramsey Cothburn."

"I can't help the way I feel," Corrie told her. "I know it's hard for you to understand. And, God knows, I may be acting foolishly. I'm not even certain at this point if Mr. Logan will be coming back."

"He paid Father for the horses, then left them," Prue said. "So he'll be back for the horses, if nothing else."

Corrie's ordeal continued through the next two weeks. But when Thaddeus Logan at last returned to Moultrie Hill, she soon wondered why she had ever doubted. Within a week she felt completely at ease with him. And within two more weeks she was certain of her heart.

He was gentle and attentive. He took her for long rides in a landau carriage he had purchased. Sometimes they saddled Titan and Midnight to explore coves along the tidewater.

On an evening in early June, more than a month after his return to Charleston, Tad drove her to a tidewater cove they now frequented. They walked away from the carriage and sat for a while on grass, watching the sunset.

Tad took her hands in his own. "Corrie, I hope you've given thought to what I said in the paddock that evening. I told you I'd wait until we were better acquainted. I now feel it's time to speak. Corrie, will you marry me?"

She looked him straight in the eye and said, "Yes, of course I will."

He put his arms around her and gently drew her to him. "I've known from the first time I saw you that we belong together. Nothing in the world has ever been more right."

He kissed her. How long they lay enveloped in each other's arms Corrie never knew. She was hardly aware as he guided her back to the carriage.

The McNair family was delighted with the news. John and Sarah had developed a great liking for Tad and had come to believe that he was the man for Corrie. Even Prue seemed to have become accustomed to the idea.

So the wedding was set for the last Sunday in September. Tad and Corrie made plans to leave a month later, so they would arrive in San Antonio de Béxar in ample time for spring planting.

*   *   *

Corrie sat dividing her books into those she would take and those she would leave behind. Never in her life had she been so happy. The only disturbing element in her life through the summer was a nagging remorse over the way she had treated Ramsey. She kept remembering the old ballad of Barbara Allen, of the cruel way Barbara had treated Sweet William, and of her later fatal remorse. The memory of her Sweet Ramsey, and what she had done to him, remained with her constantly, like a small dark cloud on an otherwise perfect day.

Prue helped Corrie, wrapping in newspaper the volumes selected. As they worked they talked about the books, remembering the stories, the times in their lives when they first read them.

Sarah came and stood in the doorway for a time listening. Corrie noticed that her face was pale and drawn, and when she spoke she sounded upset. "Corrie, if you have a minute, could you go with me to the peach orchard? Prue, Hattie is taking the Pendleton china down from the high shelf. I'm afraid she'll fall. Why don't you go down to the pantry and help?"

Aware she was being excluded from whatever Sarah had on her mind, Prue grimaced at Corrie. But she went without complaint.

Corrie put on a bonnet and followed her mother out of the house and to the orchard. There Sarah began picking ripe fruit, showing her the variations among the peaches, suggesting she take along pits from each.

Corrie began picking fruit from each variety. After a few minutes work she felt her mother's hand on her arm. "Corrie, I've brought you here to tell you something. You must be brave. I don't want Prue or anyone in the house to know."

Corrie felt a wave of premonition.

"Only your father knows this. Doctor Powers says I have only a few months to live."

Corrie felt as if all air had been torn from her lungs. For a moment she thought she would faint.

Sarah gripped her by the elbows. "Corrie, I'm depending on you! Let's not draw attention. You must help me keep this a secret."

Corrie's mind was reeling. The day was warm. She felt overheated. She found she could not speak.

"Doctor Powers says I have cancer. That's what has been wrong with me all through the last year."

"How long have you known?" Corrie managed to ask.

"Since Lent. I told your father. I saw no reason to tell anyone else."

Corrie thought back over the months. All through her own tumult over Ramsey and Tad, her mother had been living with this terrible secret. She remembered the times her father's hand had gone to cover Sarah's at odd moments, the way they now sometimes paused and touched each other.

Corrie had assumed her own impending marriage had rekindled a sense of romance in them.

How vain and unobserving could a person be?

"Mother, I'll tell Tad to go on west without me. I'll join him later. I can't leave you like this!"

"You must. That's why I'm telling you now. I want you to take Pruella with you. Your father's a wonderful man. But he isn't in good health. And even if he was, he wouldn't be capable of rearing an adolescent daughter alone."

It was too much to assimilate. Corrie put her hands to her face and leaned against a peach tree.

"Your father and I have discussed this thoroughly," Sarah went on. "Times are not good. That has been a burden on him. Surely you've seen how he has aged in the last two years. We want you to take Pruella and Hattie, and possibly Old Ben."

Corrie was too stunned to think clearly, but she managed to say, "If that's what you want, I'll do what I can."

"You also might as well take the good furniture, silverware, and china. Pruella isn't interested in it now, but she will be later. We can decide her portion now."

Corrie's shock gave way to tears and, for a time, she and her mother stood embraced, weeping.

At last Sarah pushed away. "Enough, Corrie. We can't have Pruella suspect anything beyond the sadness of your leaving."

"How can we possibly handle Prue?" Corrie asked. "She's quick to pick up on things."

Sarah smiled. "Let's play a little trick on her. You might mention the remote possibility of her going. Then your father and I can let her talk us into allowing her to go. You can be persuaded first. She'll be so busy convincing us that she'll never suspect."

Corrie thought the plan could work. On the following day she told Tad. He quickly agreed to the plan.

That afternoon she set the trap. She and Prue were packing some of the silverware for the trip west. "I wish you were going with me," Corrie said in an offhand way. "You could help me get settled into my new home."

"Oh, I'd give anything to go," Prue said. "If I could arrange it, would Tad take me along?"

"As a matter of fact, it was Tad who mentioned it," Corrie lied. "He said we could bring you home by sea a year or so from now, when we return for a visit. I told him I wished we could take you, but that I doubted Father and Mother would allow it."

"They probably wouldn't," Prue agreed.

But Prue remained preoccupied through the remainder of the day. The idea had taken hold and the campaign began.

During the next few days Prue went back and forth between her mother and father, constantly introducing new arguments. Corrie supposedly spoke with each in Prue's behalf, proclaiming her need of a travel companion, an extra set of hands in establishing her new home. Later, as the plot progressed, Tad purportedly talked with Prue's father, assuring him that Prue would be escorted safely home. Gradually, after two weeks of resistance, Sarah and John McNair yielded, and told Prue she could go.

Prue was so elated with the victory that she never once suspected. She was the envy of all her friends, and thought of nothing else but the trip.

Corrie and her father went down to the paddock to give Old Ben his choice of whether to go or stay.

He did not have to ponder. He said he would go west, if needed. "I'se had a good life here, Mastah John," he said. "But I guess it don't make no difference where I leave these old bones. I'd like to serve my little misses, long as I'm able."

When the question was put to Hattie, she wept, and predicted that if she went to Texas she would be killed by Indians. But eventually she reconciled herself to the trip.

"Miss Corrie, you can't do without me and you know it," she said. "If Miss Pruella was staying here, I might need to stay and look after her. With you both going, there's nothing left for me to do but go."

Corrie began to feel the burden of the lives placed in her care. She worried most about Prue, and what would happen to her over the next few years. She felt that in time Prue might forgive her mother. But as preparations for the wedding and trip entered the sweltering months of late summer, Corrie began to wonder if Prue ever would forgive her sister.

The wedding day had been planned in such minute detail that for Corrie it was like seeing an oft-told story come to life.

Her father gave her away. Resplendent in soft yellow linen, Prue served as maid of honor. Whit was best man, so solemn and intense Corrie wanted to laugh every time she looked at him. Brother Lane recited the ceremony without a bobble. Tad, attired in a new dark coat, ruled over all with his silent, imposing presence. Corrie could not have wished for a more perfect wedding.

Of all those invited, only a few sent regrets out of loyalty to Ramsey Cothburn. Apparently most felt greater loyalty to Corrie, and to Sarah and John McNair.

After the reception at Moultrie Hill, Corrie and Tad drove into Charleston, and for seven glorious days and nights Corrie had Tad completely to herself. They remained in their rooms for the most part, ordering meals sent up. Only twice did they venture out in the evening. On each occasion they encountered acquaintances, and Corrie found herself eager to return to their rooms, where she was not required to share Tad with anyone.

She had fully anticipated the richness of the spiritual side of marriage. But the physical took her by surprise. At first her uncontrollable passions frightened her. Only gradually did she learn to yield to them, to allow herself to be swept away in the throes of ecstasy.

As they spent more time in intimacy, Corrie began to see a different facet of Tad. It surfaced at odd moments. Occasionally she would arouse from slumber to find him fully awake, lost in thought. At times he appeared to surrender himself to darker moods, sitting silent for long intervals, lost in a trance. Corrie soon learned to leave him alone during these infrequent spells. Twice she saw his anger flare: once when other guests at the inn became too noisy, and once when supper arrived cold. Each time his rage was brief. But she sensed that there existed fury in him that he barely controlled. Slowly she came to understand that her husband was a far more complex man than he permitted the world to see.

All too soon their honeymoon ended, and they returned to Moultrie Hill to complete preparations for the road.

As the day of departure approached, the wagons were loaded. Grain, tents, clothing, and other goods that would be needed on the road were placed near the endgates for easy access. The furniture, china, and other items were put in the middle. Corrie made a complete list of every wagon's cargo. She was kept so busy, she had little time to grieve over the impending departure.

At last the day arrived. Corrie awoke to the lowing of oxen being led to the wagons. Dawn was just breaking, but already the men had breakfasted and were getting ready for the road.

Corrie dressed hurriedly. Not until she was descending the stairs was she struck by the enormity of the moment. She had lived all of her life at Moultrie Hill, and now she was leaving, perhaps never to return.

At the foot of the stairs she stopped, leaned against the banister, and sought to compose herself. Prue came down behind her, carrying blankets they would need in the landau.

"Oh, phoo," Prue said. "Not you too! Mother is crying her eyes out. How can I be so happy to be leaving, with everyone carrying on so?"

Corrie put an arm around Prue and looked into the parlor one last time. "It just hit me all of a sudden how much I'll miss this place," she said.

"One thing you can be sure of," Prue said. "This place will never change. It hasn't one iota in the almost fifteen years I've known it."

Their mother came from the back of the house, weeping. Prue went out with the blankets. Corrie and her mother followed. "Your father has sent for the carriage," Sarah said between sobs. "We'll go a little way with you."

Corrie shrank from the prospect of a protracted farewell. She knew it would be agonizing.

The McNairs rode together in the landau—Corrie, Prue, Hattie, and Sarah and John. Corrie and Sarah remained embraced, unable to control their tears. Hattie huddled against them, sobbing. John McNair sat leaning forward, his head lowered, a hand on Sarah's arm. Up on the driver's seat Old Ben also was weeping, his shoulders shaking. Prue sat alone in the corner of the carriage, looking out at familiar scenes, disdainful of the rampant sentimentality, yet sensitive enough to withhold comment. Corrie was concerned that she might yet perceive that the emotions around her were excessive for a simple departure, but she could not control her tears.

The oxen plodded down the road at the pace of a drunken man's stagger. Accustomed to horses, carriages, and speed, Corrie wondered if she could endure the tedium of day-to-day travel with an ox train.

The farewell ride seemed interminable. But six miles from Moultrie Hill Sarah collapsed, sinking to a deeper level of sorrow.

Corrie's father gripped her arm. "Sarah, I think it's time to head back," he said.

Corrie and her father helped Sarah to the McNair carriage. Corrie and Prue hugged and kissed their parents one last time while Hattie cried. Then the McNair carriage headed back down the road toward Moultrie Hill. Corrie stood and watched it go, certain this would be the last time she would see her mother, and probably her father.

--- 4 ---

In the golden hour of sunset the landau trundled safely off the tiny ferry. Corrie felt transformed. From the moment the wheels touched earth and purred softly along in sand, the pine forest rose higher around her. The sky fused into a deeper shade of blue. Along the riverbank, wildflowers bloomed in greater profusion. The birds sang with more vigor.

Common sense told her all this was only her imagination. But the illusion did not surprise her. For months along the road she had heard of little else but the wonders she would see in Texas. Now, with the crossing of the river, she at last was leaving the United States and entering the infant Republic of Texas. The change in citizenship was a bit frightening. But in a way she felt she was coming home. Her husband had helped to win independence for this new nation. Now she was to be a part of it.

Prue sat up straight and looked ahead with interest. "Texas! I was beginning to think I'd never live to see it."

The carriage was moving away from the ferry, weaving through trees, progressing up a long slope. In the distance, silhouetted against the setting sun, a clearing came into view, and with it a small settlement. Already a modest cluster of humanity had emerged from the low, chinked-log structures and stood staring down at the new arrivals.

Tad came splashing out of the river astride Midnight. He was leaning forward in the saddle, holding the reins taut with one hand, calming the horse with the other. Even after four months of marriage Corrie's heart quickened at the mere sight of him. He came trotting to her side of the carriage, reached in, and took one of her hands in his own. She searched his face for a hint of his mood. He was unsmiling, but his voice held a jesting tone. "See? Didn't I tell you? Back on dry land. Safe and sound. Tonight you ladies will sleep in proper beds, in the sovereign Republic of Texas."

He kept Midnight trotting alongside the carriage, squeezing Corrie's hand with gentle reassurance. Oblivious to the byplay, Prue looked back at the muddy river bottom and sniffed. "Texas doesn't look any better than Louisiana to me."

Tad released Corrie's hand. He winked at her but spoke to Prue. He and Prue had been waging a lighthearted duel of wits all the way from South Carolina westward. "Careful what you say, Miss Pruella. There's a customs house here. It imposes a heavy tax on tongues critical of Texas."

"Then I'll just have to stay in Louisiana," Prue shot back. "I'm known for speaking my mind."

"Well! Now we know! That accounts for the long silences."

Hattie giggled. "That's telling her, Mistah Tad."

Prue refused to accept defeat. "Look at that river. Don't tell me you call it beautiful."

Tad gave an extravagant sigh. "Prue, the Sabine has served as a border for a long, long time. First between France and Spain. Then between the United States and Mexico. Now between the United States and Texas. It's just worn out."

"That makes two of us," Prue said. "I feel like I've been traveling forever."

"You can take heart. We've only four hundred and fifty miles to go. We're almost there."

Prue groaned.

Corrie hardly listened. Studying the scene ahead, she tended to agree with Prue. After a day spent in the natural splendor of the forest, the village, no more than a double row of dull and drab log cabins, seemed a travesty on its surroundings.

On the road rooms were always at a premium. She presumed she again would be forced to share a bed with Prue, as she had so often on the journey, and lose the chance for another night in Tad's arms. "Tad, couldn't we go on?" she asked. "I wouldn't mind sleeping in the wagon. Really I wouldn't."

Tad frowned. Lifting his big hat, he squinted at the sunlight slanting down through the trees. "We'll have to stop and clear through customs. Besides, this is a crossroads. I'm hoping to get some decent news. We'll get an early start in the morning."

Corrie did not protest. She knew Tad was troubled over the contradictory rumors they had heard on the road concerning conditions in Texas.

A chorus of yells sounded from the river as Whit, Jack, and two Negro drovers brought the horse herd out of the water. On the knoll where the crowd stood, heads swiveled in unison as the villagers turned to monitor the sudden burst of activity.

With a gesture to Ben, Tad halted the carriage. He rode back toward the river, waved his hat, and shouted. "Whit!"

Whit raised a hand in acknowledgment and guided his gelding toward Tad, using his firm control to make the horse pace.

"The big show-off," Prue said.

Tad raised his voice. "Whit, swim back across and see to the wagons. Make sure they're tied down before the ferry leaves the bank. Tell the drivers to keep their teams snubbed. Tell Jack to corral the horses in that clearing yonder. We'll hold them there tonight."

Whit gave Tad a quick, military-style salute, wheeled his horse, and dashed back to the horse herd.

No longer the primary object of curiosity, Corrie was free to study the village and its citizens from beneath the rim of her parasol.

The town contained fewer than a dozen dwellings, all of chinked-log construction. Most were of the double-room and dog-trot plan Corrie had seen so often west of the Mississippi. A few were larger, but only one rose two stories high. Corrie assumed it to be the tavern. At its front was a marvel: the first glass windows she had seen since Vicksburg.

At least two dozen men stood beside the road at the top of the hill, devoting their attention to the horse herd. Each might have been outfitted for a role in a stage play. A few wore faded home-spun, others fringed buckskin. Ponchos and tight-legged leather trousers were common. A few preferred coonskin caps, but most were topped by various versions of the wide-brimmed hat Tad preferred. The costumes were colorful and varied, but there was a unity: every trouser leg was tucked into high boots for protection from the mud. Corrie made a mental note to remember to write her father of the attention his horses received on their arrival in Texas.

Beyond the crowd four men of a different sort stepped out of the tavern and strolled toward the road. They wore store-bought clothing of a more fashionable cut. Tad stood in his stirrups and waved his hat. The men waved back.

"Now maybe we'll get some news," Tad said. "Ben, drive on up to that two-story building."

Ben acknowledged the order. Tad put spurs to Midnight and pounded up the hill. He reined to a stop in front of the tavern, leapt from the saddle, and hugged each of the four men.

Never before had Corrie seen grown men embrace in public. In her part of the South it was not done, except perhaps among brothers, and even then on the rarest of occasions.

The men in front of the log house continued to laugh and pound each other on the back like schoolboys. Corrie was surprised by another strange display. Jack came riding up to the men, bold as a prince, and dismounted to shake hands. He held hat in hand, but Corrie could discern no other deference.

She could not imagine a polished gentleman such as Tad standing by and condoning such conduct from one of his Negroes. She wondered if he had lost all perspective in his close relationship with Jack, leading him to tolerate unacceptable liberties.

Ben clucked the team into a trot. As he drew to a stop in front of the house, Tad led the group of men out to the carriage, laughing in sheer exuberance.

"Gentlemen, allow me to present my lovely bride, the newest citizen of our fair Republic, Cornelia McNair Logan. Corrie, please meet my most honored friends, General Thomas Jefferson Rusk, General David Rusk, the Honorable Robert Potter, and Major James Gaines. Major Gaines will be our host tonight."

Corrie offered her hand. Each of the gentlemen stepped forward and bowed to kiss her glove. Corrie was impressed by their courtly bearing and manners. For the instant, she easily could have imagined herself on a velvety lawn in Charleston, instead of mired in mud before a log cabin in Texas.

The two Rusks bore strong resemblance. Corrie assumed they were brothers. Potter was short and solid, thick of neck, with a strong Napoleonic cast to his features. His brown eyes rested on her so intently, she felt color rising to her cheeks. Major Gaines was portly and middle aged. He offered her a warm smile.

Tad stepped forward. "Gentlemen, I'm also proud to present my sister-in-law, Miss Pruella McNair. Miss McNair has come west on a visit to our new Republic."

Prue offered her hand. The ceremony was repeated. Prue blushed prettily.

Major Gaines assumed his role as host. "Gentlemen, if you will go on into the house, my servants will see to your needs. Colonel Logan, with your permission, I'll attend to the ladies' baggage, and see them to their rooms. I'll join you shortly."

Corrie caught the plural, "rooms." Tad gave her a slight nod, signaling confirmation.

With a lingering glance back at her, he accompanied his friends into the house where, Corrie assumed, a jug of liquor awaited. There he no doubt would learn some of the news he had been seeking. She was puzzled over his being addressed as "colonel." He had never once mentioned holding military rank.

Major Gaines helped Corrie and Prue from the carriage. He looked back toward the house. "Mrs. Gaines said she'd be right out. I don't know what's keeping her."

As if in answer a tall, graying woman stepped from the cabin, accompanied by three half-grown Negro boys. Although her dress was plain, she carried herself well, and Corrie sensed background and breeding. Gaines made the introductions.

Mrs. Gaines smiled at Corrie. "I apologize for not being here to greet you. Our cook wandered off, when he knew we had guests tonight."

"I hope we're not too great an imposition," Corrie said.

"No imposition at all," Major Gaines answered. "My wife and I have been here taking care of travelers since Spanish days. We've endured two revolutions—the Mexicans against the Spanish, the

Texians against the Mexicans. We've seen some lively times. But we've survived." He examined the boot of the landau. "Mrs. Logan, if you'll point out what needs to be carried in, I'll see to having it done."

"Those two trunks," Corrie said. "But most of what I'll need is in one of the wagons still across the river."

"In that case, perhaps Mrs. Gaines can escort your sister up to her room, while you and I wait for that wagon."

Prue and Hattie went on into the house with Mrs. Gaines. The three boys followed, struggling under the weight of the trunks. Across the river, Whit was dashing about, shouting, bossing the drivers. During the last several weeks Tad had been giving him increased responsibilities, and sometimes he was overly conscientious in carrying them out. His voice rose as he scolded one of the drivers.

Corrie assumed she would be dining with the men she had just met. Although they obviously were Tad's close friends, she knew nothing about them. "Major Gaines, with all the worries of the road, Thaddeus and I haven't had the opportunity to talk much about his Texian friends. Who are the Rusk brothers?"

Gaines was unable to hide his surprise. "Why, Mrs. Logan, Tom Rusk is probably the most popular man in Texas. He'd be president of the Republic today, if he hadn't withdrawn his nomination. People tend to blow hot and cold on the subject of Sam Houston. Or Mirabeau Lamar. But no one in the whole Republic has a bad word to say about Tom Rusk."

Embarrassed at her ignorance, Corrie felt explanation was necessary "I've been so busy the last few months—the wedding, the trip west. I don't know much about Texas, or my husband's friends. I have much to learn."

Gaines gave her a knowing smile. "Well, I think I can easily bring you up to date on your fellow guests. When we delegates met at Washington-on-the-Brazos to declare Texas independent three years ago, we named Tom Rusk as our secretary of war. We chose Robert Potter, the former United States congressman you just met, as our secretary of the navy." He paused, watching as a wagon was driven off the ferry. "Those were perilous times, Mrs. Logan. We were fortunate to have men such as your husband to lead us."

Corrie found the surprises coming too rapidly to absorb. First was the revelation that she had just met—and was talking with—some of the Founding Fathers of this new nation. Second, and most surprising, this apparent signer of the Texas Declaration of Independence had termed Tad one of their leaders.

Now she wanted to know more about Tad and his past. "My husband has mentioned that he was at San Jacinto. But as you probably know, he's a modest man. I'm somewhat chagrined that he has such close friends and experiences that I know so little about."

Gaines nodded. Again he paused, as if deciding how much he should tell. When he resumed, his voice was softer, huskier. "To understand what happened at San Jacinto, you have to think in terms of those terrible times. Santa Anna, the Mexican general, had declared no quarter. And he had kept his word at the Alamo, slaughtering the defenders to the last man. Fannin's three hundred and forty-two men were put to the sword at Goliad. The whole populace of Texas was fleeing eastward, ahead of the Mexican army. So when your husband and about six hundred of us met the enemy at the mouth of the San Jacinto River, we knew that if we lost the battle, we'd be dead, one way or another. We were depending on each other. It's been my experience that friendship forged in such heat tends to be made of sterner stuff. All over Texas there are select men who share this rare friendship. Your husband is one of them."

Corrie was grateful for the insight. But the exchange had grown too personal. She sought a lighter vein, and changed the subject. "I expected to find rustic conditions in Texas. Somehow, I assumed the people would be a match. But thus far I've been pleasantly surprised by the obvious quality and attainments of the Texians I've met."

Gaines smiled. "Mrs. Logan, I've watched emigrants cross this river into Texas two decades. Those who came as colonials before the Revolution, such as your husband, are generally of a higher sort. Most were accomplished men before their emigration. Most were energetic, adventurous, educated men. But in the last three years—since Independence—I've seen a different sort. We've been overrun by rapscallions who now seek to profit from the bravery and deeds of others. Shysters. Speculators. They don't bode well for Texas."

Gaines seemed to be thinking aloud. Corrie felt comfortable with his ruminating monologue. Her father had the same habit.

With sunset, rosy hues were forming beyond the darkening greenery of the trees. A stillness had fallen over the river bottom. "I'm amazed to find Texas so wooded," Corrie said. "I've always thought of Texas as wide-open spaces."

Gaines laughed. "You are now on the edge of the Piney Woods of East Texas. This heavy timber extends roughly a hundred miles into the interior. From there on, at least for the next six or seven hundred miles, you'll find all the open country you could wish." Again he paused. "Where does the colonel plan to settle?"

Corrie hesitated, unsure how to answer. In talking with strangers on the road Tad had been secretive. She assumed he must have good reasons. "I don't think he has fully decided."

Gaines raised his eyebrows in surprise. "Well, I'm sure he'll choose the proper place. With all that Texas has to offer, he can hardly go wrong."

Once in the house, Corrie found herself wondering what further surprises her husband and this new Republic of Texas held in store for her.

Corrie turned the lamp low in Prue's attic room, softening the harshness of the raw log walls. "Did you see Whit's big performance at supper?" Prue asked. "Smoking that big cigar? Drinking with the men? Acting like he was one of them? And Tad didn't say a word!"

Corrie did not answer. It would not help to point out that Whit was within three months of his sixteenth birthday and, under Tad's supportive tutelage, was proving to be unusually mature for his age.

At the start of the journey Corrie had been concerned that Prue and Whit, thrust together on the road, might become too close. But the opposite had occurred. Everything Whit did seemed to annoy Prue. For his own part, Whit blithely went his own way, acting as if Prue did not exist.

Prue slid under the comforter and pulled it up under her chin. "You ever notice the way he walks? Putting each foot way out, trying to ape Tad? But he's too skinny. He looks like a big, long-legged bird. From behind, it's funny."

Again Corrie did not answer. She hid a smile.

Prue sighed and fell silent. On the road every moment of rest was precious. Already Hattie was asleep on a pallet in the corner. Major Gaines and his wife had suggested that a cot behind the kitchen might be more appropriate, but Corrie had held her ground.

As Corrie prepared to leave the room, she stood for a long moment looking down at Prue, once again feeling the burden of the secret she was keeping from her.

By now, their mother might be dead. She had no way of knowing. The last she had heard was a single letter at Vicksburg. Sarah had written, enigmatically, that her health was "some worse," which could mean anything.

Corrie's exasperation with the one brief letter was heightened by the fact that in the same mail Prue received four long, chatty letters from friends, filled with inanities.

In replying to her parents, Corrie had asked that her next mail be sent to Nacogdoches, Republic of Texas, now two days away.

Corrie picked up the lamp, backed out of the room, and quietly closed the door. She descended the narrow steps to the upstairs hall and crossed to her own room.

Tad was down on the gallery, drinking and talking with the men. Corrie changed into her nightgown and crossed to the window, freed the latch, and pushed open the hinged window panel. She sank to the floor, rested her head on the window, and savored the cool night air, the mingled fragrances of pine and cedar. From below came the voices of the men, smoking and talking on the downstairs gallery. In the still night air Corrie could hear every word.

For a time the men talked of the unusually mild winter, the prospects for spring crops, a court session in the nearby town of San Augustine, and the favorite male preoccupation, politics. Uninterested in the subjects, Corrie only half listened, enjoying instead the flavor of the conversation. Seldom did she have the opportunity to hear men in unaffected talk. At supper the Rusks, Congressman Potter, and Major Gaines had been on their best behavior, sticking to gentlemanly topics.

Now the men were in high spirits, joking and swapping anecdotes. At the mention of Sam Houston, the president of Texas, Corrie raised her head to hear.

"You'll find him a changed man, Colonel," said Major Gaines. "What would be your reaction if I told you your friend Sam has taken the pledge, joined the Sons of Temperance, and preaches almost every Sunday against the evils of Demon Rum?"

Tad laughed. "I'd say you could tell me that the sun, the moon, and all the stars have changed their course in the heavens, and I'd believe you. But what you've just told me exceeds all credence."

"I'll drink to that!" someone shouted.

Corrie laughed along with the men. With the mention of Sam Houston, talk again turned to politics, the appointments in the new administration. Not knowing the names, Corrie lost interest.

The night air was growing colder. She shivered, and was about to turn away from the window when she heard General Tom Rusk speaking to Thaddeus. "Colonel, where do you expect to establish your home?"

Corrie stopped breathing, hanging on Tad's answer, hoping he would not contradict her reply to Major Gaines on the question.

"It depends," Tad said. "On my last visit, I was most taken with the country in and around Béxar."

Corrie could not determine if the murmured reaction was favorable or unfavorable. It seemed mixed.

"Colonel, not many Texians have gone back to Béxar to stay since the war," Major Gaines said. "Not much there now but Mexicans. When you come right down to it, we have to remember that the war with Mexico isn't over. We have no peace treaty. If hostilities resume—and that could happen—Béxar will be the first to know. Settling there now could be risky."

Corrie's heart sank. Surely this news wrecked all of Tad's carefully made plans.

"What about the army?" Tad asked. "I expected it would return to Béxar, use the Alamo as headquarters."

"The plain truth is that Texas has no army," Gaines said. "This hasn't been bandied around, but President Houston furloughed the army, without pay. He had to. There was no money in the treasury to pay them."

"The Republic's in sad shape, Colonel," Rusk agreed. "The line of settlement has retreated all along the frontier. The government can offer no protection. Besides the Mexican threat, there's the Indians to consider. The Comanches pretty well rule the roost from the Colorado westward."

"Then I take it San Antonio de Béxar is beyond the line of settlement," Tad said.

"A full two hundred miles beyond," Rusk replied. "Travelers going there usually wait up at San Felipe until enough of a force is assembled to risk it."

"What about the Old Presidio Road?"

Again Corrie held her breath so she would not miss the reply. She had seen Tad's map. The Old Presidio Road was the route Tad intended to follow.

"Out of the question," Rusk said. "The Comanches know the route as well as any white man. I wouldn't chance it, Colonel. If I had it in mind to go to Béxar, I'd try the southern route, through San Felipe."

"Why don't you consider settling around San Augustine or Nacogdoches?" Gaines suggested. "Or maybe down around Liberty? You could serve your turn in Congress, help us establish our court system. It'd be much safer for your family."

"I'll certainly consider it, Major," Tad said. "But I grew fond of that country around Béxar. Surely the Republic's difficulty is temporary. What about the foreign loans?"

Talk turned to the prospects of Texas borrowing money from England, or perhaps France. Corrie was growing chilled. Quietly she closed the window and slipped into bed.

For a time she lay awake, aching with disappointment as much for Tad as for herself. Plainly his dream of settling in San Antonio de Béxar was beyond reach, at least for the present.

There had been forewarnings. Last night in Louisiana she and Tad had been entertained by army officers and their wives at Fort Jessup, the last military outpost on the United States frontier.

Throughout the evening Corrie had been disturbed by implications, especially from the women, that Fort Jessup was the jumping-off place for civilization, that nothing but barbarism lay to the west. Several times Corrie caught the women regarding her with poorly disguised curiosity, as if wondering why she would subject herself to Texas.

When she mentioned her impression to Tad, he laughed and said conditions in Texas could not possibly be that bad.

Now all the reports they had heard on the road had just been confirmed, and by his friends.

Corrie tried to remain awake, but weary from the long day, she fell asleep.

A short time later Tad kissed her from deep sleep. Stirred by the long evening of anticipation, Corrie was quickly aroused. For a time she yielded to mindless pleasure, oblivious to anything else.

But afterward, with Tad drowsily holding her in his arms, she recalled the talk on the gallery.

"Tad, I overheard what Major Gaines and General Rusk said about San Antonio de Béxar," she whispered.

He stirred sleepily. "Heard? How?"

"The window," she said. "I opened it and listened."

He playfully thumped her with his palm. "You scamp!"

He said no more. Corrie pushed further. "Did they change your mind about going there?"

He held her closer. "Not really. I've always known there'd be risk."

"But no army. No protection! Shouldn't we reconsider?"

Tad was almost asleep. "We'll see," he said.

Gradually Tad's breathing lengthened into sleep. Still held in his arms, Corrie thought back over what had been said on the gallery, and Tad's response to it.

Slowly she understood that Tad was going to take her and everything he owned to San Antonio de Béxar, two hundred miles beyond the line of safe settlement, precisely because the risks were greater, as, no doubt, were the potential rewards. And she began to realize that Tad's drive and ambition were even greater than she had imagined.

*   *   *

Tad was worried. Clearing through customs had taken longer than anticipated. He had not been able to get the wagons back onto the road until well after sunup. Now he doubted he would be able to reach San Augustine before dark, and this stretch of the Piney Woods had a long history of banditry. Years ago the United States and Spain, unable to agree on a boundary, had established a neutral ground. Later the Mexicans enlarged on the strip by prohibiting settlement within twenty leagues of the Sabine. The no-man's-land became infested with fugitives from both countries. Tad dreaded traveling through the section.

Thirty yards ahead, the horse herd grazed along the edges of the road, driven gently along by Whit, Jack, and two Negro drovers. The two colts were romping, nipping playfully at each other, kicking up their heels, frisky in the cold morning air.

The road had deteriorated considerably since Tad last traveled it, six months after San Jacinto. Trees still formed its boundaries, but saplings as tall as horse and rider grew in profusion in the road. Vines, heavy underbrush, and fog lent the surrounding forest a dark, forbidding aspect. Tad worried about the dangers of a breakdown in this region. Rough roads through Louisiana had taken their toll on the wagons. Several were badly in need of repair.

Whit left the horse herd and came to ride beside Tad in a stillness broken only by the occasional snap of a bullwhip, the murmur of wheels on soft ground.

"I hadn't expected roads in Texas to be this good," Whit said. His voice was growing deeper every day.

"Most aren't," Tad told him. "This is the main pike. Wait till you see some farther on."

"Lot of work, cutting all those trees."

"The Spanish always made sure they had plenty of help. Peons. Convicts. Indian captives."

"Which way we heading out of Nacogdoches?"

Tad had not yet made a decision. But from what he had learned at the Gaines House, the answer appeared inevitable.

"The southern route, I suppose. Down to Houston, across to San Felipe."

Whit made no effort to hide his disappointment. "Hell, Tad, all that talk back there didn't scare me. We could take care of the Indians."

Tad glanced at his younger brother. Usually Whit talked and acted like a man. At other times he still showed immaturity. "Don't be foolish. You and I wouldn't have a prayer against twenty or thirty Comanches."

Whit did not answer immediately. Again they rode for a time side by side in silence.

"We could arm the Negroes."

Tad had considered it. He had brought along extra rifles, just in case. Arming slaves was illegal in the Southern states. No doubt by now the Republic of Texas also had such a law. Tad believed a valid argument could be made that Negroes had a right to defend themselves. But he was hesitant about putting theory into practice.

"Jack is good enough with pistol or rifle," he said. "And John McNair said Old Ben is handy with a shotgun. But I don't know enough about the rest to put a gun in their hands."

"The two of us would be worth several men."

It was not an idle boast. The new five-shot repeating pistols were accurate and dependable. He and Whit each carried one at the waist, and another in their saddlebags. With an extra cylinder for each pistol, they could each fire twenty rounds without reloading.

But such firepower would be inadequate against even a handful of Comanches. "Whit, we have four hundred miles to go. Believe me, the fewer Indians we see, the better."

The talk on the Gaines House gallery had left Tad deeply disturbed. Apparently the worst of the rumors he had heard were true. In the first three years of the Republic, nothing had been accomplished. The Republic was floundering.

It was a sobering prospect. All his worldly possessions were here on this road, including twenty-six thousand dollars in gold, the last from his settlement with Frank.

Whit also was thinking of the previous evening. "Tad, didn't it bother you last night the way other men keep looking at Corrie?"

Tad hesitated, not certain what prompted the question. "Not especially. When you marry a beautiful woman, you soon learn to live with the attention."

Whit rode for a time in silence. "Maybe they couldn't help staring. She was like a picture, there in the candlelight."

Tad understood. The attention had bothered Whit, who was developing a strong attachment to Corrie. Tad felt no jealousy, for he knew it was calf love. But he recognized that the infatuation could become unhealthy, and should be discouraged. He glanced back at the carriage. It was out of earshot. "Pruella's also growing into a beautiful woman," he said. "Or haven't you noticed?"

Whit snorted. "Prue? She's too skinny."

"Someday I'll remind you that you said that."

This time it was Whit who glanced back at the carriage. "Well, she'll never be anywhere near as pretty as Corrie." He hesitated. "Why did General Rusk and those other men keep taking you aside last night? What did they want?"

"They all need a professional associate in San Antonio de Béxar. They were asking if I'd be interested."

"Are you?"

Tad laughed. "Of course. It gives me the start on a law practice."

"What kind of lawyering will you be doing?"

"All kinds, I imagine. These gentlemen need land titles cleared in Béxar for their clients. Last night they promised me enough work to keep me busy for quite a while."

The fog continued to lift. Patches of blue sky were breaking through. Ahead, the road curved. The horse herd was almost out of sight around the bend. Tad felt a wave of apprehension. "Whit, go tell the men to keep the horses within sight of the wagons. They're letting them get too far ahead."

Whit spurred his sorrel and rode off at a gallop. Horse and rider were one, easily leaping a pile of fallen timber, dodging to avoid a patch of underbrush. Tad was consumed for a moment with a rush of love for his younger brother, mingled with pride for his precocious manliness.

A breeze stirred the tops of the trees. The sun was growing

warmer. The fog was vanishing. Tad wheeled Midnight and rode back toward the wagons. The top of the landau was still up, but the curtains were open. As he passed, Tad raised a hand to Corrie, exchanged a smile with her, and rode on.

He held Midnight to a slow walk and studied every wagon and team closely. The oxen were gaunt. He had brought along plenty of grain, for little was to be had in Texas. But the oxen needed rest, the one thing he could not grant them. Even when they reached San Antonio de Béxar, they immediately would be put to work turning ground for spring planting.

Pausing beside each six-ox team, Tad searched for signs of any sores that might be developing under the yokes. He monitored hooves for splits or undue wear. He examined each wagon wheel. Several tire rims were thin. If the metal broke, the wheels would fall apart. He listened for the squeaks of a dry hub. He talked briefly with each driver, making sure all was in order.

The inspection trip took him the length of the train, to where his overseer, Newt, brought up the rear.

Of all his purchases Tad was most pleased with Newt. Trained as a blacksmith, he was a hard worker, and conscientious. The other Negroes were afraid of him, so Tad had made him overseer.

"There's a wheel wobble on number four," Tad told him.

Newt had a self-possessed, calm manner of speaking. "Needs a shim, suh. Ah'll fix it, next we stop."

"We'll make San Augustine about dark. You can do it there."

"They got a forge?"

They had not seen a good forge since Vicksburg.

"San Augustine's a small place," Tad said. "I doubt they'll have one. But there'll be one in Nacogdoches, a day farther on."

Newt shook his head. "Suh, we got three rims almost gone."

Tad nodded. It was a worry he could do nothing about. He left Newt and rode forward on the other side of the train, studying the wagons and oxen from the different perspective.

Still worrying about the wheels, Tad returned to his customary place in front of the landau, where he could keep an eye on the horse herd ahead, and the wagon train behind.

The road now ran straight and narrow, between walls of pine

trees. The ground was of the rusty hue that led Texians to call this the Redlands. On each side underbrush grew in profusion.

On seeing Tad, Jack left the horse herd and came trotting back down the road. He turned his mare to ride beside Tad. "That buckskin mare's about to foal. Marsh Whit said to tell you."

Tad groaned. Another problem. "How soon?"

"Tonight. Maybe tomorrow early."

The horse and foal were too valuable to lose. He might have to stay over a day in San Augustine.

Jack's brow was wrinkled in a way that revealed he was troubled. Tad knew his every mood.

"What's eating on you?" Tad asked.

Jack was reluctant to answer. "Fella back there said he knows a Nigra in Texas that owns other Nigras. Could that be?"

The question tugged at a vague memory. Tad patiently tracked it to the source. "There's a freedman in Nacogdoches who owns a Negro family. He rents them out as servants and field hands. That may be the fellow your fellow was talking about."

Jack slowly shook his head in disbelief. "A Nigra owning other Nigras? That just don't seem right."

"Jack, you think too much. I should never have taught you to read."

Jack laughed. "Why, Marsh Tad, I was thinking before I was reading." He watched the horse herd for a time in silence. "How'd this fella get to be a freedman?"

Tad gave him an appraising glance. Not since they were children had they discussed the institution of slavery. In college Tad endured many hours of debate on the subject. He never took part. As far as he was concerned, slavery was a fact of life. Approval or disapproval was a futile pursuit.

He considered Jack's question, the reasons behind it. "From what I remember, he's a blacksmith. He may have earned his freedom working at odd jobs with his owner's permission."

More likely the Negro was freed under the probate of a last will and testament. Tad did not mention that possibility.

"You think maybe someday I could be a freedman out here in Texas, if I work hard enough?"

Tad hesitated. He would not have tolerated such talk from any other Negro. But this was Jack.

"It's not that simple. A freedman still must have a white sponsor, to satisfy legal requirements."

That was not exactly true, but it was close enough. A freedman invariably needed white protection of some sort to survive. Generally, he was not accepted by the whites, or the blacks. If he traveled far from home, he might be seized by some unscrupulous white and sold back into slavery.

For a moment Tad was nagged by a twinge of conscience. On the eve of San Jacinto he had left Jack at Harrisburg with the baggage train. He had also left a letter with the commander there, certifying that if he was killed, Jack was to be given his freedom.

After the victory, wounded and needing Jack's care, Tad retrieved and destroyed the letter. Jack had never known of it.

Never before had Tad suspected that Jack might want to be free. Jack had grown up amid advantages unknown to most Negroes. This revelation of his thinking felt almost like a betrayal.

Before Tad or Jack could say anything more, three mares wheeled away from the herd and came running back down the road. The two Negro drovers raced in pursuit, trying to turn them. Tad tensed, waiting for the right moment to spur Midnight to block the mares, prevent them from going past him.

"Look there, Marsh Tad!" Jack shouted, pointing to blurred motion in the brush beyond the horse herd.

Abruptly five mounted men burst from the forest, firing pistols and rifles.

In an instant all was confusion. The horses bolted into the trees on the left, fleeing the gunfire. Tad drew his pistol. But Whit rode into his line of vision, placing himself between the attackers and the horse herd. Tad held his fire.

Erect in the saddle, hat brim flattened in the wind, Whit charged the five riders. His gun sounded three times, leaving three balloons of black smoke in his wake.

Under Whit's onslaught the riders swerved back into the woods to Tad's right. Whit emptied his pistol. Tad fired twice at uncertain targets moving past him through the underbrush. Midnight, not yet

completely broken to gunfire, reared and bucked, keeping Tad preoccupied. He was aware that Whit was plunging into the woods, either
not knowing, or not caring, that his pistol was empty.

Tad brought Midnight under control. He cupped a hand to his
mouth and yelled. "Whit! They're gone. Come back!"

Whit reined in his sorrel so abruptly that it sat back on its
haunches. Tad holstered his pistol and calmed his stallion.

The horses had disappeared. Tad heard them crashing through
underbrush in the distance. He winced inwardly, thinking of thorns
and briars ripping tender horseflesh.

He rode over to Whit, who was still clutching his empty pistol.
His face was pale. "Tad, I killed one of them. He's over yonder." He
pointed.

A nondescript bundle lay at the edge of the woods.

Tad glanced back at the wagon train and motioned to Newt,
who came forward at a gallop.

Tad fished in his pocket for keys. "Jack, go tell Miss Corrie I said
everything's all right. Then go back to the third wagon and open the
arms chest. I want you and Newt to give powder, shot, and a rifle to
everyone who knows how to shoot. Use your judgment. Bring Ben
his shotgun. Tell him to stay with Miss Corrie. Whit, reload. Give
Jack your extra pistol. We've got to go into the timber after those
horses."

"Won't those men have them by now?"

"I doubt it. I think you ran the bastards off."

Tad rode over to the body and dismounted. He rolled it face up
with the toe of his boot. The dead man was white and appeared to
be in his late thirties. He wore a stubble of black beard, tattered
homespun clothing, and homemade boots. An old flintlock rifle lay
beside him. A single-shot percussion pistol lay a few feet beyond.
Whit's ball had entered the center of the man's chest. He had died
so quickly that the wound had lost less than a cup of blood.

Tad remounted. "Let's look over there. I may have hit one."

He rode into the woods. Whit followed. Tad trailed the tracks
through sodden dead leaves. At the place where he had aimed, several leaves glinted crimson. A few yards farther he found more
blood.

"We could go after them," Whit said.

"I'm more concerned with the horses," Tad said.

They returned to the road. Tad went over to the carriage. Corrie pulled back a curtain. "Tad, what is it?"

Both Corrie and Prue appeared calm. Tad took this as further proof that the McNair sisters were of rare quality.

"Horse thieves," he said. "They're gone now."

"Is anyone hurt?" Corrie asked.

"Not on our side. Whit drove them off. He charged right at them. It was something to see."

"Is Whit all right?" Prue asked. She moved her head, trying to peer beyond Tad. "What's he doing?"

Tad could not think of a way to soften facts. "Whit killed one. He and Jack are taking care of the body."

Prue and Hattie gasped.

"Will we have to camp here?" Corrie asked.

"No. I still hope to reach San Augustine tonight. But the horses scattered. We're going into the woods after them. I'm posting a guard. You'll be safe. Ben has his shotgun."

Tad reached into the carriage, squeezed her hand, and for a moment she took his hand between her own.

Whit and Jack rolled the body into an old ground cloth. Tad dismounted and helped them load it into the back of a wagon.

He then led Whit, Jack, and the two drovers into the pine forest, following the trail of the horses.

The search was difficult. The ground was covered with vines, underbrush, leaves, and dead branches. The horses were neighing to one another, trying to get back together. Tad, Jack, and Whit followed the sounds and assembled the horses, one by one, turning them over to the two drovers to hold.

It was slow work. But at the end of two hours only three were missing—two mares and a colt.

Tad did not want to give up.

Again they spread out and searched. A few minutes later Whit found the colt in a ravine, lying in a pile of dead timber, whimpering, eyes wide in fright. Both front legs were broken. Tad took one of the rifles and dispatched it with a single shot.

Whit stood looking down at the dead colt. When he spoke, his voice was so choked that Tad had difficulty understanding him. "Now I don't feel so bad about killing that bastard."

Tad put an arm around Whit's shoulders. "Whit, I'm so proud of you I could bust. I couldn't have done better on my best day."

Whit wiped his nose with the back of his hand. "It happened so fast! I can't even remember drawing my pistol."

Tad thought back to Concepción, San Jacinto, other battles. "That's always the way it is," he said.

Whit's face remained pale. But he was regaining his composure. "What'll happen now?"

"We'll take the body in and turn it over to the sheriff."

"Will I be charged?"

Tad felt he should not minimize matters. "It's possible."

"What'll happen?"

"That depends. The Rusk brothers said court's still in session at San Augustine. If you're charged, we might get it cleared up quickly."

"They were thieves!" Whit said.

"That might be difficult to prove, since they didn't succeed," Tad pointed out. "But we have a good case for self-defense. There were five men riding toward you, shooting. I saw it. Jack saw it. So did the drovers."

"Then we shouldn't have any trouble, should we?"

Tad wanted Whit prepared for the worst, in case it came. "Nothing's ever certain in law," he warned. "The man's friends could show up with a completely different story."

Not until the horses were returned to the road was the full extent of damage visible. Tad was sickened. Hardly a single animal remained unmarked. Most had long, bleeding cuts. Tad was not certain the mare near foaling would make it as far as San Augustine before dropping the colt.

Jack brought creosote and patented salve from the utility wagon. For the better part of an hour they doctored the horses. While they worked, lowering gray clouds moved in from the north, accompanied by drizzling rain and a cold, strong wind. Within minutes the temperature dropped to near freezing.

At last Tad called a halt. "We've done all we can for now. We must get on if we're to make San Augustine before midnight."

They roped the horses into strings and pushed on. Tad rode down the line of wagons in the icy wind, making sure each of the drivers had a warm coat. He urged them to use their whips on the oxen to step up the pace.

He wanted to stop to see to the comfort of Corrie and Prue, but the flaps of the carriage were buttoned against the wind. He could not stick his head in without exposing them to the cold.

With the heavy overcast, darkness came early. Lacking even the light of stars, Tad ordered lanterns lit and hung from the rear of each wagon. They traveled mile after mile with the swaying lights sending shadows dancing in the gloom, making an eerie, weaving tunnel through the trees.

For a time the road seemed endless. But at last the rain slackened into a ghostly mist, and amber pinpoints of light came into view in the distance. Tad rode on ahead with a hooded lantern, hoping to get into San Augustine before all of its residents retired for the night.

Most of the log houses on the outskirts were dark, but light gleamed through the shuttered windows at the Whittlesey Tavern. Tad rode to it, tied Midnight to the hitching rail, snuffed his lantern, and entered.

A group of men were gathered around a log fire. Tad recognized several fellow lawyers. In years past he had spent many such evenings in posttrial conviviality, rehashing cases, swapping views on public affairs and politics. All looked up in surprise that a traveler would be wandering in so late on such a cold, wet night.

His friends rose to greet him, and to welcome him back to Texas. Several minutes passed before he could make his wants known. When it was learned a wagon train was on the way, the town came alive. Two of Tad's friends surrendered their rooms. A barn was made available for Tad's Negroes. The livery stables and attendant corrals were opened for the care of the animals. By the time the wagons arrived in town, preparations were completed.

When Corrie and Prue arrived they went straight up to their rooms. Tad asked that warm food be sent up from the kitchen.

Then, with his most immediate concerns met, he returned to the fire and described the trouble on the road.

His friend Adolphus Sterne of Nacogdoches was first to recognize the urgency. "Thaddeus, court has adjourned. Judge Love is spending the night here with friends. But he plans to leave for Jefferson first thing in the morning."

"And I want to get on to Nacogdoches," Tad said. "I was hoping to take care of any legalities tonight."

A servant was sent to rouse Sheriff Kimbro and Judge Love. Within minutes they arrived at the tavern. The body was carried from the wagon and unwrapped on the floor.

Sheriff Kimbro held a lamp high. "Hell, it's Cletus Fowler. He was in town day before yesterday. Him and two brothers."

"Who was he?" Tad asked.

"Squatter up in the Strip," Sterne said. "There's a big family. Up toward Pecan Point. Been there twenty years."

Tad understood. Living on prohibited land, the family was unable to obtain a clear title.

"He ever in trouble before?"

"Nothing serious," Kimbro said. "Moonshining, fighting, drunkenness, is about the extent of it."

Tad noted with concern that thievery was not mentioned.

Judge Love spoke to the sheriff. "Bill, I can understand Colonel Logan's desire for action on this tonight. I'm not inclined to leave it unresolved until my next circuit. Why don't we go ahead and conduct a preliminary hearing? I can either make a preliminary ruling on the findings, or bind the case over for trial. Anyone have any objections to that?"

"Seems to me we'd only be presented with one version," said one of the lawyers Tad did not know.

Judge Love frowned, apparently giving the observation some thought. He spoke to Tad. "This incident happened about noon?"

"A little earlier. A good two hours before the norther hit."

"And you then spent two hours hunting your horses? And an hour doctoring them before you came on with an ox train? It seems to me that if we are to hear from the other parties, we would've done so by now. I believe we can get on with it."

Tad sent for Whit, who was seeing to the feeding of oxen and horses. A few minutes later he entered the tavern wet and shivering. He was given space close to the fire.

Tad made introductions. A small table was brought for Judge Love, and the public room of the tavern was turned into an impromptu court, with Exhibit A lying on the bare plank floor.

Judge Love opened by identifying everyone present, and defining the nature of the hearing. He then spoke direct to Tad. "Colonel Logan, will you please describe for the court exactly what occurred on the San Augustine–Sabine Road, at approximately eleven-thirty in the morning on this date."

Relying heavily on his legal experience, Tad gave his testimony in unadorned fashion, adhering to the facts, offering no opinions. He told of the five men charging from the woods, and Whit's countercharge. As he talked, all eyes shifted to Whit, who sat with head lowered.

"And your brother is not yet sixteen?" Judge Love asked.

"He will be sixteen in May, Your Honor," Tad said.

Judge Love looked at Whit. "Mr. Logan, when those men broke from the woods, shooting, was it your impression they were shooting at you?"

Whit looked up, hesitating. Tad wished he had taken the time to tutor Whit on how best to offer his testimony. But his worries were unfounded. Whit spoke strongly. "Yes, sir."

"They were not shooting up in the air, merely to scare the horses into stampeding?"

"No, sir. The muzzles were aimed at me. I heard the balls buzz by my ears."

"And yet you spurred toward them? Why?"

"I knew they were after the horses, sir."

The judge gave Whit the trace of a smile. "How many shots would you estimate were fired at you?"

Again Whit hesitated. "I'm not sure, sir. Eight, maybe."

"They had both pistols and rifles?"

"Yes, sir."

"How many shots did you fire?"

"Five, sir."

The judge paused, doubt crossing his face. Tad intervened.

"With the court's permission. My brother and I both were armed with these five-shooters."

He passed his loaded gun to the judge. Instantly the new Colt's revolving pistol became the focus of attention. The judge examined it critically. Spectators crowded around him. Tad was asked several questions about the gun and his experiences with it. He told them it was a dependable weapon, even though he would have preferred a larger caliber bore.

The judge returned to questioning Whit. "Mr. Logan, do you know which of your five shots took effect?"

"The second, sir."

"You missed with the first?"

Again Whit hesitated. "Yes, sir. I was surprised, not thinking straight. The pistol went off before I was ready."

"Your brother says you've been practicing with the pistols. Why did you miss with the other three shots?"

Whit cast Tad a pleading glance. Tad could not help him.

"Well, sir, when the man fell from his horse, the others turned. They were going away. I just shot to run them off."

"I see. You shot the first man while he was riding toward you, firing. But when the others turned, you emptied your pistol without intending for the balls to take effect?"

Whit was on the verge of losing his composure. He put a wrist to his mouth. The room was deathly still while the court awaited his answer. "I never shot anyone before, sir. Right then, I just didn't want to shoot anyone else."

The judge turned to Tad. "Colonel Logan, I believe you said you fired twice as these men passed you, and possibly wounded one. What was your reasoning at that moment, your justification for shooting?"

Tad took his time, going back over the action, the confusion. "The horses had bolted into the woods. I didn't know if Whit, or any of my Negroes, had been hit. The thieves were riding parallel to the road, toward the wagons. I didn't know what they yet planned to do. My wife and sister-in-law were but a few yards away. I had their safety uppermost in mind."

Judge Love paused. For a time he appeared lost in thought.

"Colonel Logan, can the court depend on you to keep the court informed as to your whereabouts, and the whereabouts of your brother?"

"Of course, Your Honor. I can tell you now. We'll be in San Antonio de Béxar, where I'm establishing a law practice."

A murmur of surprise swept through the room. Judge Love laughed. "Colonel, not many of your colleagues are willing to risk their scalps in Béxar. I gather you'll have plenty of offers for professional association before the evening is out."

"That's good to know, Your Honor," Tad said.

Judge Love glanced at his clerk, and spoke slowly so his next words could be duly recorded. "It is the finding of this court that the deceased, identified as Cletus Fowler by those who knew him, died in the commission of a felony, to wit horse thievery, and that his death at the hands of Whit Logan was an act of justifiable homicide. It is further the finding of this court that Whit Logan, not yet in his majority, conducted himself commendably in the defense of his family and the property in his charge."

Again Judge Love paused, allowing the clerk to catch up.

"This finding of facts does not constitute a ruling, but shall serve as such, until such time as further facts come to light that conceivably could tend to alter this action."

"Thank you, Your Honor," Tad said.

Judge Love smiled. "Colonel Logan, unless the companions of the deceased come in before morning with a reasonable explanation of why they shot at you and ran off your horses, this frees you to go on to Nacogdoches in the morning, and myself to leave for Jefferson. I'm confident this puts the matter to rest, legally."

As the judge had predicted, Tad was preoccupied for a time discussing legal work he might do in Béxar in association with the attorneys present.

Afterward, although exhausted, he pulled on his heavy coat and went back out into the icy wind. He made certain his slaves had been fed and were bedded down and comfortable. He then spent almost two hours with Jack, Ben, and one of the drovers, tending the foaling mare. Eventually a healthy male colt was born into the world.

By the time he returned to the tavern, everyone had retired except his friend Adolphus Sterne. "I prevailed upon our host for a bottle of his best brandy," Sterne said. "It's middling passable liquor. I thought you might wish a nightcap."

Tad was numb from the cold. He took off his coat and rubbed his hands. "Old friend, I appreciate your thoughtfulness more than you'll ever know."

Whit was bedded down on a cot in the corner, beside other male guests of the tavern. Tad walked over to check on him. He appeared to be sleeping peacefully, untroubled by dreams from having killed a man during the day.

Tad and Sterne moved to chairs by the fire. The pine log that had blazed so well earlier was now only glowing embers. Sterne took a poker from its rack, punched the coals into flame, and placed another log on top. He then sat down with Tad and poured two glasses of brandy.

For a time they sat in silence, enjoying the brandy and quiet companionship. Lamps had been lowered in deference to the sleeping men. Light from the burning logs cast moving shadows on the walls. There was no sound, save soft snores from the corner and an occasional snap of pine knots in the fireplace.

Sterne, usually a talkative man, seemed to be in a contemplative mood.

Tad first had met him while en route home from San Jacinto. On the road Tad's wound had reopened and festered. Jack had built a lean-to shelter for him beside the road. Sterne had come along, returning from a wedding on the Bayou Attoyac. He had stopped, assessed the situation, and helped Jack carry Tad back to Nacogdoches. There he took Tad into his home, sent for a doctor, and supervised Tad's slow return to health over the next three weeks.

During that time Tad and Sterne became friends. Gradually Tad learned much about him, and found him an interesting man. He had been born in France. But at sixteen, facing military conscription for the Napoleonic wars, he fled to America. He landed penniless in New Orleans. There he clerked in a store and studied law. Later, trading goods upriver, he drifted into the Mexican province of Texas. During the first Texas effort toward freedom he smuggled guns for the insurrectionists. He was caught and sentenced to hang. After a year in chains he was released on his vow never to take up arms again against Mexico. He had kept his word. During the Revolution he organized and financed volunteers from the States, known as the New Orleans Greys. Most of them died fighting. Sterne spoke six languages and was a dedicated reader. Few men had done as much for Texas. And few knew it better. Tad was eager to learn Sterne's views of conditions in Texas.

"I'm told Houston's presidency has been a disaster," Tad said. "What's your opinion of it?"

Sterne gave a deep sigh. "Colonel, times have never been so hard in Texas as they are now. I'm thoroughly convinced the Republic is in a state of collapse."

Tad was swept by foreboding. His dreams of empire were implicitly linked to the future of the Republic. "What about President Lamar? Will his administration be successful?"

"Lamar and Houston are so deep into land speculation they can't think of anything else—Houston in the town they named for him, Lamar in his new site for the Capitol up on the Colorado. I'm disgusted with both of them. I had some hope for Lamar. In his inaugural speech he said we'd march to the south until we got more fight than we could handle, and there we'd place our southern border. Plainly, with no army, it was nothing but empty air. Besides, he was so distraught over Sam's speech, he had to ask someone else to read his own. His inaugural was a disgrace. And he'll get no help. Congress is made up of demagogues. We've been attempting to make great men out of trash!"

"Do you think the war with Mexico will be resumed?"

Sterne spoke slowly, gazing into the fire. "If the centralists return Santa Anna to power, we're in for it. I happen to know that a plan of attack exists. Gunboats will land troops at Sabine Pass and at Galveston, while a land army invades through Matamoros. Texas has nothing under arms to stop them."

Tad remained silent. If the Mexican army moved north from Matamoros, it would pass through San Antonio de Béxar.

"If we could make peace with Mexico, we might have a chance." Sterne went on. "Or effect a treaty of annexation to the United States. But I foresee neither happening anytime soon. We're hopelessly adrift."

"Have you heard from Sam lately?"

"Nothing of any warmth. I sponsored a rally in Nacogdoches for Lamar. My friendship with Sam Houston has cooled."

That was a surprise. Tad was disturbed over the repeated reports that his old friend Sam Houston had changed.

"What'll Sam do, now that he's out of office?" Tad asked.

"He's gone into legal partnership with old John Birdsall in Houston. That won't last, though. He'll be back in politics before the birds fly north again. San Augustine has put him on the ballot for Congress, and my guess is he'll accept."

Then Sterne pulled a large silver watch from his vest pocket. "It's getting toward morning. Perhaps we should get some rest. Naturally I'm expecting you and your family to make my home your headquarters while you're in Nacogdoches."

Tad hesitated. He was deeply obligated to the Sternes for their kindness during his long convalescence. He was reluctant to impose on them further. But Sterne, his wife, and their home would provide Corrie with a wonderful introduction to Texas. "I accept," he said. "But on the condition that you ride in the landau today and keep my wife and sister-in-law entertained. I fear they have found this a long and tedious journey."

Sterne chuckled. "Clearly I'm gaining the best of the bargain." He finished his brandy, rose, and paused. "Perhaps I should mention, Colonel, that you may not yet be done with this Fowler case. They're a clannish lot. I can imagine the other brothers taking up what they perceive as family honor."

Tad thanked him for the warning. They said good-night, and Sterne moved off into the semidarkness. After several minutes a cot creaked under his weight. Again silence fell.

Tad sat finishing his brandy, reluctant to leave the fire.

He felt deeply depressed. He had heard nothing the slightest bit encouraging since his arrival back in Texas. It was growing plain that after the euphoria of independence, Texas had fallen into a fatal paralysis.

Everywhere he looked he saw difficulties. He needed land. But the Republic's land office was not yet functioning. War with Mexico was likely. Yet Texas had no army, no navy. Two thirds of the Republic was populated by hostile Indians, including the region where he planned to make his home. The Republic was flat broke, and in debt. Texas currency was worth only forty cents on the U.S. dollar.

Yet the riches were there.

He thought once again of the abundant waters of the San Antonio River, the vast stretches of virgin land sweeping away to distant horizons, and all that awaited him there.

As the fire burned low, he concluded that the detour to the south to avoid Indians might be a blessing in disguise. On his swing by the Gulf, he would visit the Capitol of the Republic in the new town of Houston.

There he would talk with Sam Houston, the departing president, and Mirabeau B. Lamar, the incoming president, and other friends and fellow veterans of San Jacinto, now senators, congressmen, and appointed officials of the Republic.

He would not ask for action.

He would demand it.

--- 5 ---

Tad bowed low before Corrie. "Mrs. Logan, may I have the honor of this dance?"

He spun her through a lively version of "Springfield Mountain." By the time the music ended, Corrie was breathless. She tugged at Tad's arm. "Please, I'm exhausted," she said.

They strolled to a row of chairs as the music started for the next dance. Across the room, Whit led one of the Raguet daughters onto the floor. The young lady was tall and slim, and they made a good-looking couple. Whit was a good dancer, except that he tended to take too long a step. Sterne was dancing with Prue, turning her in elaborate curlicues that made her bell skirt flare prettily. Sterne truly loved to dance. He had not been off the floor a minute while music was playing.

"The wagons are almost ready," Tad said close to Corrie's ear. "We'll be able to leave sometime tomorrow morning."

Corrie felt a pang of regret. They had been in Nacogdoches two days and she had developed an affection for the town and its people. She had found unexpected worldliness and romance in their lives. On the road from San Augustine, Sterne had kept Corrie and Prue laughing with anecdotes of his boyhood flight from Europe and his survival in New Orleans. Later Corrie learned Mrs. Sterne had come from Germany as a child, was orphaned when her parents died of yellow fever, and had been reared by a French family in Louisiana, the Bossiers.

Corrie also had become privy to the local social intrigue. Out on the dance floor was Anna Raguet and a suitor, Dr. Robert Irons. Anna had been expected to marry Sam Houston as soon as he received his divorce from a long-ago marriage in Tennessee. But now

92

Nacogdoches was abuzz, for Anna had jilted Houston. The town was sharply divided. Anna was twenty, and some said that Houston, at forty-six, was far too old for her. But others thought Anna was missing her chance for greatness. They argued in complete sincerity that if Texas was annexed to the United States, as some hoped, Sam Houston surely would rise to the White House, and need Anna as his first lady.

As Corrie watched the dancers she found herself yearning to be a part of all this. She had overheard the Sternes, and other prominent people, urging Tad to stay, to open a law practice, to represent them in Congress. Why was Tad not content to settle here, where they might raise a family in comparative safety?

She had not yet quite recovered from an incident during the afternoon. Mrs. Durst, the outspoken wife of a local planter, had not been able to contain herself when she learned Tad was taking Corrie to San Antonio de Béxar. "Oh, honey! That's way out in the wild country!" she said. "Don't go! If the Mexicans don't kill you, the Indians will!"

Mrs. Sterne had smoothed over the remark, but Mrs. Durst's bluntness put into words hints everyone had been dropping since Corrie's arrival in Texas. She had gathered a unified impression that everyone considered her foolish for blindly following her husband to San Antonio de Béxar.

She glanced at the clock on the opposite wall. It was well after midnight. Sterne had said these dances often lasted until morning. Tad was preoccupied with repair of the wagons, and in getting back on the road. If she did not take the initiative now, she might not have a private moment with him for days. She badly wanted to talk with him about her growing doubts.

"Tad, couldn't we go back to the house now?" she asked.

He looked at her with concern. "Are you ill?"

"No. Just tired. I don't want to make a fuss. Couldn't we merely slip away?"

"We're the guests of honor."

"Which means we should be the first to leave."

Tad hesitated. "If you want. We'll say good-night to the Sternes."

They walked back to the Sterne house in the crisp February night. In the guest bedroom, Tad removed his coat and vest and kindled a fire. He then sat on a straight chair to remove his boots. Corrie stepped behind the folding screen to remove her ball gown. The house was silent except for the rustle of silk as she removed her clothing. Prue and Whit were still at the ball. Hattie had retired for the night. On the small dressing table behind her lay three letters that had awaited their arrival in Nacogdoches. She had read all three until she knew them by heart.

Two were from her mother. In one Sarah said, "I am some worse." In the other she said, "I am about the same." Both letters were totally devoid of factual information.

Somehow this evasiveness brought home to her, as nothing else before, a recognition that Sarah was truly dying.

Looking ahead into her own future, Corrie now could see that she no doubt had left home forever. If her father died soon afterward, as she expected, nothing would be left for her in South Carolina save a few aunts and cousins.

The third letter was from one of Prue's friends. "Ramsey Cothburn has turned into an absolute drunkard since Corrie threw him over!" the friend said. The word *drunkard* was underlined three times. At first Corrie had dismissed the label as adolescent drama. But on further reflection she wondered if there was some truth in it.

Thwarted, Sweet Ramsey might drown his disappointments.

And she was responsible.

Had she made a mistake after all? Should she have married Sweet Ramsey?

Was she as foolish as people thought? If the dangers were so widely believed, could they not exist? Was Tad's obsession so complete that he was ignoring common sense?

She badly needed reassurance.

Pulling a robe over her nightgown, she stepped from behind the screen, crossed to a chair facing Tad, and asked the first question that came to mind. "Tad, is the war with Mexico likely to be resumed?"

He studied her face in the soft lamplight. In her part of the South—and she supposed in Texas as well—women were expected to concern themselves with household and social affairs. Men took care of politics, commerce, warfare. Still she met his gaze and did not retreat.

For a long moment she thought he might not answer. But when he spoke, his tone was solemn. "That depends on events in Mexico. If Santa Anna regains power, it's a possibility. Why do you ask?"

Corrie took a deep breath. "Tad, I've heard considerable talk. It has left me very disturbed. Most people here think the Mexicans may again invade. They say Béxar also is exposed to Indian attack, its defenses inadequate. I'm wondering if we're being unwise in going that far west so soon."

He continued to look at her without expression. For a long moment she thought he might be angry. But he spoke softly. "There's some risk. But I won't subject you to any danger that can be avoided."

"Tad, if there's no army, no protection, how can we possibly be safe? Why don't we stay in Nacogdoches? I've heard the men begging you to establish here. In two days I've learned to love this place. Couldn't we at least consider it?"

He smiled. "I'm glad you'll be seeing all the settled parts of Texas on our way to Béxar, so you can make your own comparisons. From here we'll travel a hundred and fifty miles almost due south to Houston. On the way you'll see fine plantations. From Houston we'll go west, through the country where Stephen Austin's original Three Hundred families are settled. Then, when we arrive in Béxar, you'll see it's like nowhere else in Texas, or on earth. Corrie, I'm so confident you'll be happy there that I'll make you a promise. If you don't fall in love with San Antonio at first sight, we'll return anywhere you say."

"Why are our prospects so much better there than here?"

"The best land is taken, over the settled parts of Texas. What's left is mediocre. Surely we don't want that."

"But I've been told there are plans to drive the Cherokees off their land here. Won't that make more land available?"

Tad shook his head. "The Indians were given that land under treaty with Spain, Mexico, and now Texas. If the Republic goes back on its word, it'll be a sad mistake. I wouldn't want land under those circumstances."

Tad leaned forward and took her by the shoulders. "Corrie, out there along the San Antonio River are hundreds of *thousands* of acres waiting to be acquired. There we can build our own empire. I've seen that land. It can be ours!"

Corrie had never seen him so exhilarated. She hesitated to dash cold water on his enthusiasm. Yet she felt reality should be faced. "Is it worth risking our lives?"

He shook her gently. "Corrie, you must understand. This danger you're talking about is temporary. Eventually there'll be peace with Mexico. We'll make peace with the Indians, or failing that, they'll be driven back to the north. Texas will win diplomatic recognition from all the countries in Europe, and there'll be monetary stability. We'll be the principal landholders in San Antonio de Béxar, where it all began. As Texas grows and prospers, so will we. Corrie, you've said you admired your great-grandparents, what they accomplished. I promise you, we'll do much, much more!"

"Tad, all I want is a home."

"And you'll have one that'll outdo any in the South."

"But it all sounds so impossible!"

Tad raised his chin. "I don't recognize the word."

Corrie thought he was joking. Then she saw he was deadly serious.

Tad gave her a long look. "Corrie, you don't question destiny," he continued. "All this is there to be done. And we'll do it."

Abruptly he rose and blew out the lamp.

Shaken, Corrie continued to sit in the glow of the fireplace while he removed his clothing and slipped into his nightshirt. He eased between the covers and turned his back, signaling that the conversation was over.

Corrie rose, peeled out of her robe, and slipped into bed. Tad did not reach for her, and she knew for certain that he was angry. But she could not let the matter rest.

"Tad, I must think of Prue, as well as myself," she said. "If Béxar is as dangerous as I've been told, I won't go."

His voice came from the darkness at the far side of the bed. "What will you do?"

"I'll wait for you here, or some other safe place, until conditions change."

Silence reigned in the darkened room for a full minute.

"Let's go on to Houston," Tad said. "If you're still of a like mind, I'll send you back here, or you can stay in Houston."

Tad lingered across the street from the Capitol, watching as members of the Third Congress emerged. The ten-day trip from Nacogdoches to Houston had been unexpectedly difficult, and he was tired. From the tent city he had seen here three years ago, Houston had grown into a bustling, crowded town. He had found a room in a private home for Corrie and Prue. But tonight he would have to sleep alone in a wagon.

The hour was late. He was tempted to abandon his search and wait until morning. But he had heard that Sam Houston would be leaving soon on a visit back to the United States, and he did not want to miss him.

Lamps burned on the lower floor of the Capitol. Inside, men moved to and fro, their shadows flickering on the window panes. The building, of plank construction, rose two and a half stories. It was saved from a boxlike appearance only by six dormers, four chimneys, and long galleries on each floor. It remained unpainted and unweathered, the raw lumber attesting to the newness of the Republic it served.

Tad crossed the muddy street and entered the large front doors. Groups of men stood talking the length of a long, wide hall. General Sam Houston was far down the hall, addressing a sizable group. Tad strolled within earshot. He quickly gathered that Houston was lobbying the congressmen, trying to keep the Capitol in his namesake city.

"If not here, where we have adequate facilities, why not then at Washington-on-the-Brazos?" Houston asked. "There we at least would have the benefit of the hallowed setting where our glorious independence was declared, our constitution written. Lamar's proposed site offers nothing, save the appended name of Stephen F. Austin who, unless I'm woefully in error, was fortunate enough never to have gazed upon the place."

The group laughed. The wall lamps in the hall were spaced at a sufficient interval to cast portions in semidarkness. Tad remained in the shadows to wait until the general was free.

"We've built this edifice at a considerable cost to the Republic," Houston went on. "President Lamar's proposed site has nothing to compare. Think of its distance from your wives and families! The Congress will have to travel there and back in a body for protection. Anyone knows indiscriminate mixing of congressmen is dangerous!"

Again the group laughed.

"I'll tell you what is to come, gentlemen," Houston continued. "If President Lamar's Indian policies prevail, and the Comanches get wind of them, they'll come calling on Lamar's new Capitol. Congress will find itself in adjournment *sine mora, sine die.*"

This time the laughter spilled down the hall, attracting the attention of other groups. Tad's Latin was equal to the joke: without delay and without a day set to reconvene.

"So I ask you, gentlemen, to consider this proposed relocation most carefully. You owe it to yourselves, your constituents, and to your Republic."

Sam Houston moved through the congressmen, shaking hands, extracting commitments and promises, ingratiating himself with each individual in his accomplished manner. Tad studied his skill in projecting effusive friendliness, clothed in implicit aloofness. It was rare art. Slowly Houston worked his way toward Tad. Not until he was a few feet away did recognition come. "Colonel Logan!"

Houston stepped forward and seized Tad in a warm abrazo. Tad returned the embrace.

"I'm glad to see you back in Texas," Houston said. "Where are you located?"

"Nowhere yet, General." Tad forced himself to speak. He was shocked by how much Houston had aged in three years. "My goods are still aboard wagons outside of town. My wife, brother, and a sister-in-law are with me. I'm bound for Béxar. I'd like to talk with you for a few minutes, if I may."

"Very well, let's walk. It's a fine evening. Almost spring."

They strolled out of the Capitol. The streets now were slightly less crowded. A constant uproar came from taverns and gambling halls. Only three years old, Houston had gained a reputation as a town that never slept.

General Houston donned his fur sombrero with its long eagle plume. He walked with long strides, using his gold-headed cane. Tad noticed a pronounced limp. He wore a conventional frock coat, but strikingly prominent was his vivid panther-skin vest. Clearly the general had not yet completely abandoned his Indian ways.

At forty-six, Sam Houston could be taken for sixty. Yet he remained a vigorous man, tall and ramrod straight.

Tad was fully aware he was walking with a living legend. Houston had become a boy hero at nineteen, fighting under Andrew Jackson. He studied for the law and served Tennessee in the U.S. Congress, and as governor. But a few days after his marriage he had resigned and left Tennessee to live with the Cherokees in the Arkansas Territory. There he was called "The Big Drunk." Later—no one knew exactly when or for what purpose—he rode into Texas, accepted command of the army, became the hero of San Jacinto, and was elected president.

Speculation was wide in both Texas and the United States that during the Texas Revolution Houston had acted in secret collusion with President Jackson. Now Houston was going back for a visit with Jackson in Nashville. Tad wondered what the two ex-presidents might find to talk about. Rumors were plentiful that the two old warriors were plotting to bring Texas into the United States by annexation. Others said Houston was opposed to annexation. One wit claimed Houston tended to favor annexation when sober, but opposed it when drunk. No one knew. Houston had never committed himself on the subject.

"General, I've returned to Texas to acquire land along the San Antonio River, to raise horses and cattle," Tad said. "Now I hear Béxar is endangered by both Comanches and Mexicans. I must know. If I settle there, how soon can I expect relief?"

Houston walked several strides before answering. "As you no doubt know, that's now out of my hands."

"But you've been dealing with it. Surely you have some idea of what may happen."

Again Houston did not respond immediately. "Colonel, all the Republic's troubles dwindle down to money. Congress won't pass funding bills. That's the long and short of it."

"What about England? France? Can we expect help from them?"

"That depends on Lamar. England and France are wary of granting us diplomatic recognition, for fear of harming their trade with Mexico. But they also are chary we may be annexed to the United States. They foresee that a border with Mexico would give the United States the edge in trade. The United States, on the other hand, has granted us quick recognition, fearing that any treaties we make with France and England will give them an entrée into the Western Hemisphere. It's a delicate poker game. I doubt Lamar is equal to the task."

"Is there hope our troubles with Mexico can be put to rest?"

Again Houston hesitated. "If we could secure mutual protection treaties with England and France, we most certainly could make peace with Mexico."

Obviously such treaties would anger the United States. "Then you're opposed to annexation?" Tad asked bluntly.

Houston stopped and faced Tad under the light of a lantern. He casually glanced up and down the street to make sure they were not overheard. Yet he answered in his usual oblique manner.

"Colonel, it could well be that annexation is inevitable. We've all fed too long at the same trough. Our citizens still call themselves Americans and think of themselves as such. They celebrate the Fourth of July with as much enthusiasm as San Jacinto Day."

Tad persisted. "The last I heard, you had withdrawn the petition for annexation."

"I have. You see, we've been rebuffed like a foolish, overanxious young lady seeking a quick marriage. It's time to back off, entertain other suitors, and renew the game."

"Then you believe the possibility of annexation is alive?"

"Definitely. It may be our eventual salvation. But the moment is not propitious. Calhoun and the other old mossbacks in the U.S.

Congress have retarded the western movement of the United States for two decades. They can't endure forever. Who knows? Perhaps it's God's plan, a United States stretching from the Atlantic to the Pacific. That's what France and England fear the most, a world power in the Western Hemisphere. And it may come to pass."

Tad felt the discussion had gone too far afield. He narrowed it to his specific situation.

"If we fail to obtain mutual protection treaties with France or England, is Mexico apt to renew the war?"

"Who knows? The Centralists have enough troubles of their own. As long as Mexico isn't provoked, I don't look for renewal. I fear the impetuosity of our citizens far more than I do the Mexicans. If we had an army, most members of Congress would insist that it march on Mexico tomorrow morning. It's a delicate situation, Colonel. Any incident along the border or at sea could renew hostilities, when neither we nor the Mexicans desire a war, or are in any shape to fight it."

"What about the Indians? Do you anticipate successful treaties with the Comanches?"

"The Indians have different ways, but they're men. They desire peace, the same as we. If they're abused, they'll fight, the same as we. If Lamar is allowed his war of eradication against the Cherokees, the Comanches will take their cue. Settlement along our frontier will be set back thirty years."

As a boy Houston ran away from home and lived among the Cherokees in East Tennessee. He never allowed anyone to forget his strong Indian sympathies. Tad felt he should voice a warning to his old friend. "General, I've sampled the waters in San Augustine and Nacogdoches. The people there seem to be heavily in favor of the Cherokee removal plan."

Houston grimaced. "Tom Rusk, Adolphus Sterne, others up there, have spent too much time listening to Lamar. I've no doubt as to what our course should be. I've warned them. If we go back on our Cherokee treaties, we'll never be trusted again. Our children will be fighting Indian battles well into the 1870s."

"The safety of my family is a prime consideration," Tad said. "Should I be concerned about the Indian threat in Béxar?"

Houston frowned. "The volunteer Rangers there offer adequate protection for the town itself. It's true that a hundred or more lives have been lost to Indians around Béxar in the last two years, mostly through carelessness. But with prudence, I believe your risk will be minimal."

Tad was taken aback. A hundred deaths from Indians in two years? In a town of less than a thousand souls? "I hadn't realized it was that bad."

"The Comanches don't favor pitched battles. They lie in wait for the lone herdsman, a surveying party poorly armed. With sensible precautions, I doubt you'll have difficulty."

"General, I must have more guarantee than that. I'm deeply troubled. What has happened to Texas? I remember our state of mind after San Jacinto. We'd won independence, and we had a nation to build. Now I find regression everywhere."

Again Houston turned to face him. "I'll tell you what happened, Thaddeus. Too many Texians have shirked their plain duty. San Jacinto should have been the start of our endeavors, not an end. If you want to make Texas all it should be, go on out to Béxar and build your home. Start your family. Come serve with me in Congress. With God's help, maybe, just maybe, we can save the Republic from three years of Lamar's administration. If the Republic is still afloat after three years, perhaps I'll regain that crown of thorns. It'll be a long road. And I'll need your help every step of the way."

"I haven't given serious consideration to serving in Congress," Tad admitted.

Houston slapped him on the back. "If you'll toss your hat, I'll speak in your behalf. We'll be a good team."

They resumed walking, on past the collection of stores called the Long Row.

"How long will you be in town?" Houston asked.

"Two or three days."

"I'll be here through Friday. We've yet to build a church, but we offer two fine theaters. I hope you and your family will be my guests tomorrow evening. Corri's New Theater is presenting Sheridan's *Rivals*."

"We would be most honored," Tad said.

At the next corner Tad and Houston shook hands and parted. Houston turned up Main Street toward his lodgings. Watching the solitary figure fade into the night, it occurred to Tad that despite all of Sam Houston's fame and esteem, he was in many ways a lonely man. His long-ago first marriage had hardly lasted until the ink was dry on the license. Whether intolerable heartache followed, no one ever knew. Houston never allowed the subject to be mentioned in his presence. Rumors persisted of an Indian wife back on the Arkansas and, some insisted, a papoose or two. Houston ignored the rumors, never dignifying them with a denial. And now Anna Raguet, the object of Houston's attention the last four years, had thrown him over. He had many acquaintances, and many enemies, but no close friends. He confided in no one.

Turning his back on the clamor of the town's taverns and gambling halls, Tad walked through the night toward the wagons, marveling over the scope of Houston's mind. From this small hamlet on Buffalo Bayou, the general managed to keep abreast of political situations in Mexico, France, England, the United States, and all sections of the Republic. Only a few weeks out of office, he already was preparing to serve in the Texas Congress, to do what he could to save his beloved Republic from the disasters he was sure to come under the new administration.

A few minutes later Tad arrived at the wagons. Everyone was asleep except Jack, who was puttering around a campfire, fixing himself a midnight meal. Tad laughed when he saw that Jack was drunk. Tad called to him, "If you can manage without spilling it, fix me some coffee."

He went to his wagon and removed his coat and gun belt. By the time he returned to the fire, Jack was seated on a log, eating. The coffee was boiling. Tad removed it from the fire.

"Fella tonight tried to get me to run away with him to Mexico," Jack announced. "He say we could work our way there on a ship. Then we'd be free."

"Free to what?" Tad asked. "Starve?"

"He didn't say. I don't know exactly what he had in mind."

"I doubt he thought that far ahead. His plan wouldn't work.

First place, no ship would take you. Second, you'd be worse off than the lowest Mexican, and that's pretty low."

"He set me to thinking, though. What'd you do if I did that, Marsh Tad?"

Rustling up a cup, Tad poured coffee. He knew Jack was testing him. "I'd go down there, find you, bring you back, and flay your black hide."

Jack threw back his head. "Whooee! You'd do that? To me?"

Jack had allowed the coffee to boil too long. It was bitter. "Of course I would. I couldn't let it be said I let a man run off and did nothing about it."

Jack laughed. "We sure couldn't have that, now, could we, Marsh Tad?"

"Jack, you seem to be hung up on freedom lately. I didn't invent the way the world is. But we both have to live in it. There are many ways of being free. Remember when we were boys, and I had to go in to my books? You could go fishing, do any damned thing you wanted. I had to study."

"I guess we free—and not free—in different ways, Marsh Tad," Jack replied. Then, grinning, he said, "I done thought up something that'll make us both rich."

"Then maybe I'd better hear it," Tad said.

"I'll run a school for gentlemen. Most gentlemen here don't know how to be gentlemen. They buy a good suit and then wear it with a bandana sticking out. Pants leg stuck in their boots. I'd teach them no lady likes for a gentleman to chew tobacco and spit. I don't know about Galveston, but in Houston it's spit, spit, spit everywhere. I'd teach these gentlemen how to be gentlemen."

Tad laughed. He could envision Jack lecturing aspiring gentlemen on the art of dressing and conducting themselves properly.

Jack could do it.

"I've seen nothing out here like Charleston or Savannah, Marsh Tad."

"You won't, Jack. Not for some time to come. The men here are devoting themselves to building, creating. What you're talking about comes later."

"Then maybe we should have stayed in Savannah. What's going to become of us out here, Marsh Tad?"

"We'll get rich. Build a fine home. You'll be a part of it."

He finished his coffee, went to his wagon, and prepared for bed. He heard Jack clattering around awhile, then came silence.

Tad found himself missing Corrie. He sat for a time on the wagon tongue, savoring the stars, the night air. He was too restless to sleep.

Slowly his anger began to build. From what Sam Houston had told him, the whole country had fallen into mediocrity. His entire plan was in jeopardy. And he was partially to blame.

From Houston's criticism of others, Tad now could see the fallacy in his own thinking. When he received a musket ball in the knee at San Jacinto, he felt he had done his share. Now he was returning to Texas to claim his reward in land, protection, and riches. But as Houston pointed out, San Jacinto logically was the *start* of the Republic.

More work, and perhaps much fighting, remained to be done.

The dangers were real, and could not be ignored. He no longer could pretend to himself, and to Corrie, that the hazards would be eliminated overnight. Corrie could not be blamed for refusing to establish a home in a small village where fifty of its citizens were murdered every year.

If he had to go it alone, leaving Corrie behind, his plans would be delayed for years. He needed her with him, to help build a home, a family, to share in all he was trying to do.

Now that he had won her, he could not live without her.

But he recognized that if he urged her to go on to Béxar with him, he would be asking more from her than he had any right to expect.

He sat on the wagon tongue and brooded over the dilemma until the stars paled and the roosters of Houston announced the approach of dawn.

Only then did he lie down for an hour of troubled sleep.

* * *

"Where were you?" Whit asked Tad.

"Over there, under those trees," Tad said, pointing. "That's where we formed up and waited. Burleson's regiment was on our right. The regulars were in the center. Sherman's regiment was on the left."

"Where were the Mexicans?"

Again Tad pointed. "Just beyond those mottes of timber. On past that little hill."

Ever since their arrival in Houston Whit had been eager to see the San Jacinto battlefield. Tad at last had given way to his pleas, and invited Corrie and Prue along. But now Corrie regretted she had come on the outing. Plainly Tad was deeply affected. She had never seen him so solemn.

"The twin sisters were over there," Tad said to Whit, gesturing to the left. "They opened the attack, raked the enemy position. It was about three-thirty in the afternoon. Santa Anna and his men were taking their siesta."

Corrie knew about the Twin Sisters, two cannon given to the Texas revolutionaries by the city of Cincinnati.

"My men and I first fired about here," Tad said to Whit. "The enemy answered with a volley. Three of my men were hit."

Whit studied the ground, as if searching for blood. Corrie shivered. She could not imagine why Tad was subjecting himself to this. He rode on ahead, as if searching. Whit rode with him. Corrie and Prue followed at a more leisurely pace. Subdued, Prue was devoid of her usual witty observations.

The aura of mortality caused Corrie to renew her worry that by now her mother also might be dead. Since their trip south to Houston was unplanned, their next mail would be received in San Antonio de Béxar, still weeks away.

Ahead, Tad reined in Midnight. "Along about here the enemy had put up a barricade of saddles, supplies, boxes," he told Whit. "When we reached it, we used it for our own purpose. The hottest of the fighting was done right here."

Tad and Whit rode in circles, searching for evidence of the barricade. Corrie and Prue sat on their horses and waited.

"How gruesome!" Prue whispered to Corrie. "This place gives me cold chills. I'm sure it's haunted."

Corrie did not respond, but she tended to agree. The bright morning sun failed to lighten the grim atmosphere.

Tad and Whit returned. "Here the battle became a rout," Tad said. "The Mexicans broke and ran into that little stand of timber over there. Most left their muskets behind."

They rode on to the narrow band of trees. At the far edge they came to a small brook, only a few feet wide and no more than six inches deep. Tad stopped. Corrie reined in beside him. Before them lay a low marsh. Beyond was San Jacinto Bay, and Corrie became oriented to the drawings she had seen of the battlefield. To their left was Buffalo Bayou. On farther north was the place where the San Jacinto River emptied into the bay.

"It had been raining off and on for six weeks," Tad said. "That marsh was knee deep in mud. There's where the enemy went, and there's where we finished them off. Four or five hundred. Maybe more. There in the mud."

Whit glanced back at the trees. "Where were you firing from?"

"Little shooting was done beyond this point." Tad paused. "It was work for swords and rifle butts."

"Oh, my God!" Prue whispered.

If Corrie had not been watching Tad's face, she might have missed a rare moment. His lower lip trembled, and for a fleeting instant he almost lost his composure.

She started to reach out to touch him but hesitated. The quarrel between them was not yet resolved, and on the road there had been no opportunity for private, serious discussion. She did not want him misinterpreting the gesture as appeasement.

Whit remained oblivious to Tad's mood. "Where were you hit?"

Tad looked, rather than pointed, into the marsh. "About thirty yards out there. Three of my men brought me over here, propped me against that tree there. After a while they carried me to the surgeon. I didn't think it was serious. It didn't fester until later."

"Where were the Mexicans buried?" Whit asked.

"They weren't. Least not right off. They were left where they fell. I don't know what happened to the bodies."

Again Corrie shivered. She easily could imagine skeletons lying in the marsh a few yards away. Prue rolled her eyes skyward and Corrie knew they were sharing the same thought.

Tad turned Midnight. "So much for the battlefield. If you've seen enough, we'd best be getting back into Houston."

They rode back through the trees and into the wide green expanse beyond. Prue and Whit moved on ahead, talking and laughing, the horrors of the battlefield already forgotten. On the previous evening, to the amusement of General Houston, Prue had been totally convulsed by the antics of Mrs. Malaprop in the play. Now Prue and Whit were making up their own malapropisms, attempting to outdo each other.

Corrie glanced at Tad. He remained unusually solemn. She was sure at least a part of his melancholy stemmed from the issue between them. She wanted him to understand that it was just that—an irreconcilable issue—and nothing more. She put an intimate, friendly tone to her voice.

"Tad, why did you subject yourself to this? It must be painful for you."

He took his time answering. "I told myself Whit should see it. But I suppose I mostly wanted to make myself remember." He met her gaze. "Corrie, I feel I must never forget what the Republic cost us."

Ahead, Prue sat tall in her sidesaddle, statuesque. Whit, lanky and awkward, rode next to her.

"They make a handsome couple," Corrie said.

Tad chuckled. "Oil and water."

Corrie was surprised. "Why do you say that?"

"They're so different. Whit open, trusting, innocent. Prue sharp, cutting. She rides circles around him in the smarts department."

"I'm not so sure of that. Whit has a lot to offer."

She was saved from further argument as a small sternwheel steamboat came into view on the bayou. It was loaded with people headed downstream toward the bay and, Corrie assumed, Galveston Island. The engineer blew his diminutive whistle. The sound was almost lost in the vastness of the terrain.

Prue and Whit waved their hats. The people on deck waved back. Then the steamboat moved into trees lining the narrow bayou and was lost to sight.

Corrie and Tad rode for a time in silence. When Tad again spoke, he seemed troubled.

"Corrie, during the last two days I've talked with a number of people who've just come back from Béxar. I have to confess. The situation is worse than I thought."

Corrie was glad he had raised the subject. She wanted it out in the open. "In what way?" she asked.

"Indians. Lack of protection. What's worse, I've also talked with many old friends who are now senators, congressmen, cabinet officials. They're dubious of relief anytime soon."

Corrie remained silent, allowing him to talk about it freely. Tad rode on several minutes before continuing.

"So the danger exists. I understand your concern. I'll do whatever you wish. If you want to go back to Nacogdoches, or stay here in Houston, I'll establish a comfortable home for you until it's safe to go on to Béxar. I could go on west alone and make preparations. When the situation eases, I'll come get you."

Corrie felt her heart sinking. "How long would that be?"

Tad shook his head. "I don't know."

Corrie could guess. Months. Maybe years.

"It isn't what I planned," Tad said. "It isn't what I want. But I'll take you anywhere you choose."

Aside from Nacogdoches, Corrie had seen no place in Texas where she would want to live. Despite Tad's promises, on the long trip south from Nacogdoches she had seen nothing she would call a grand plantation. True, they had passed huge fields under cultivation. But the owners lived in dogtrot log houses, hardly a step up from the rows of cabins that served as slave quarters. Only belatedly had she understood that for Tad, and perhaps all Texas men, a "grand plantation" was one with plenty of good land amply stocked with slaves. She mistakenly tended to think of a "grand plantation" as a sumptuous, multistoried home staffed with well-trained house servants.

She rode on in silence for a time, attempting to hide her disappointment. "How serious is the danger?" she asked.

"I'm told that once we reach San Antonio itself, we're safe. Thus far the Indians haven't ventured into town. They lie in wait on the outskirts and ambush the lone traveler, or at most a small body of people."

"What about the situation with Mexico?"

Tad sighed. "Sam Houston is convinced the Mexicans don't want a renewal. But he fears Lamar may aggravate them into some kind of an adventure. I don't know. I'm to talk with Lamar tonight. Maybe I can gain a better evaluation from him."

The town of Houston came into view. Corrie knew she would not care to remain here. The entire settlement was too raw, unfinished. All was in constant motion, the streets crowded with carts, wagons, horses, men. Every person in view seemed to have scores of tasks to accomplish and not enough time to do them. Buildings were going up everywhere. From dawn to well after dark the town was noisy with the sounds of saws, hammers, and shouted orders. She could not imagine herself living alone in Houston—or anywhere, for that matter.

"What do you think you'd like to do?" Tad asked.

Corrie rebelled against making the decision. She needed more time.

"I don't know," she said. "Please allow me at least a few hours to think about it."

"I'm pleased you've returned to Texas, Colonel," Lamar said. "I think if I were in your position—starting a family, looking to the future—I'd also be heading for Béxar."

Tad did not respond. He remembered that Lamar was a widower who had first come to Texas as a desperate diversion from his grief.

"As for your questions, Colonel, I believe I can put your mind at ease," Lamar went on. "I'm preparing to put into effect improvements that will give the frontier considerable relief."

Lamar leaned back in his chair and lit a big Mexican cigar called a "puro." He was a moderately small man, of delicate build, with dark, almost feminine eyes and mouth. The wall behind him was graced with four paintings by his own hand. Lamar not only was an artist, but also a poet, an expert fencer, and a hopeless romantic. Tad had never been able to decide whether he liked the man. Yet even in his indecision, Tad could understand how Lamar had been able to win the support of such men as Adolphus Sterne and Tom Rusk, along with a majority of Texian voters.

He was personable and charming, and his courage was beyond question. Surely few men had risen to high office so quickly. On first word of the siege of the Alamo, Lamar had left his home in Georgia and ridden pell-mell for Texas. He had enlisted as a private just before San Jacinto. On the eve of battle Tom Rusk and his men had found themselves surrounded by the enemy. Lamar, shedding all caution, charged the Mexican ranks full tilt, creating enough of a diversion for Rusk to escape. No one who saw Lamar's charge that day would ever forget it. He was promoted on the spot to colonel in command of cavalry. Ten days after the battle, with Sam Houston wounded and Rusk in command of the army, Lamar was named secretary of war. Five months later, he was elected vice president of the new republic.

Lamar blew a ring of blue smoke over the shaded lamp on his desk. "I'm aware, Colonel, that you're a great admirer of Sam Houston. Please understand I'm not being critical of him personally when I say that he never understood the role of the navy in our victory at San Jacinto. As hard as we fought, if our navy hadn't prevented Santa Anna from receiving supplies, we wouldn't have had our victory."

Tad was not inclined to argue. It was a moot point.

"I'm rebuilding the Texas navy," Lamar went on. "You see, once we regain control of the seas, Mexico won't dare invade, for she'll be unable to supply an army on Texas soil. I'm also remobilizing the army, and allocating funds for more Ranger companies. I plan to establish new military posts on our frontier. We'll take the war to the Comanches, and remove the Cherokees from East Texas. That should end our Indian troubles."

"How will all of this be financed?" Tad asked.

Again Lamar smiled. "Desperate times require extraordinary means. I'm attacking that problem on all fronts. I'll prevail on France, England, Belgium, for loans. I'm proposing a levy on the

Santa Fé trade. And we've hardly begun to exploit our most valuable asset, land. We'll issue more land script."

Tad was not encouraged. From all he had heard, Texas already was awash in land script, so deflated in value it had become a joke. It was true that considerable trade was moving along a route from Missouri through Santa Fé to Chihuahua, crossing land claimed by Texas. But a levy on that trade would be difficult to enforce, because of the remoteness, and no doubt would anger the United States. Sam Houston had been seeking loans from France and England for three years, and the money seemed no closer now than it had at the start.

"I take it you're against annexation," Tad asked.

"Emphatically!" Lamar answered, thumping his desk with his fist. "As long as we remain independent, our opportunities remain unlimited. With our navy we'll be able to affect policies among other nations. We can form an alliance with the revolutionists in the Yucatán and put pressure on Mexico. With our remobilized army we can control our border with Mexico. We can form alliances with the Oregon country, the Anglos in California. Colonel, I believe the final borders of Texas are not yet drawn on any map."

The words could have been Tad's own. Yet, coming from Lamar, they sounded hopelessly grandiose.

"I'm also disturbed over the failure of the Land Office to function properly thus far," Tad said. "Can I also expect relief in that quarter?"

"Most assuredly," Lamar went on. "You see, one of the benefits of relocating the Capitol to the upper Colorado will be greater responsiveness to the people. In time, Austin will be much more centrally located to the Republic's population."

Tad persisted. "Then if I go ahead and locate land, I can be reasonably certain my application will be acted upon?"

"Colonel, if you have any trouble at all, just let me know. I'll see to whatever needs to be done."

Tad felt he could not expect a firmer commitment. He rose and offered his hand. "I promised I wouldn't take much of your time. I've enjoyed our talk."

Lamar rose and shook hands. "I hope I've put your mind at ease,

Colonel. I'd beg you to stay, but I've a cabinet meeting convening shortly. Please feel free to drop me a line, anytime."

Tad thanked Lamar and left the room. In the hall he paused to shake hands with John Watrous, the Republic's attorney general, and James Webb, secretary of state. But he did not linger. Apparently the cabinet meeting was about to open.

He went out into the night and walked the streets of Houston, seeking the source of his dissatisfaction with Lamar's elaborate promises. After walking several blocks deep in contemplation, he came to a conclusion.

While he and Lamar shared the same goals, and were both dreamers, he sensed that Lamar was too impractical, totally incapable of facing hard realities.

Tad felt that he himself entertained no illusions. He was convinced that if peace could not be obtained, the hostile Indians must be subdued. This would take time, money, lives. He felt that Mexico would remain a threat until soundly whipped by force of arms. He could see that diplomatic recognition and foreign loans would require skillful maneuvering. He felt Lamar lacked the necessary expertise and patience.

He found himself in a paradox. While he disagreed with Sam Houston on many policies, and distrusted him on the question of annexation, he recognized that the Old Warrior was a past master in handling the affairs of the nation.

There was method in Houston's equivocation. No one ever knew exactly where Sam Houston stood on any issue. He kept both friends and enemies guessing, and his options open.

Lamar was too outspoken, too naive.

Reluctant to return to his room, and to press Corrie for her answer, Tad walked the streets of Houston, contemplating the bleak outlook for the future he had planned.

Corrie's thoughts kept going in the same circle. Clearly Prue, Hattie, and Ben were her responsibility. She should not take them into a situation where their lives were in jeopardy. Moreover, she was Prue's guardian. She herself must survive to fulfill her obligations.

But this conviction inevitably led to the alternatives. The thought of begging Tad to abandon his dreams was becoming ever more repugnant to her. His dreams in large part were what had attracted her to him in the beginning. If she asked him to settle in some safe place, he would become ordinary, and they would lead ordinary lives.

Yet she could not see herself living alone—a virtual widow—during the years Tad spent accomplishing his dreams. She had married him to share those dreams.

This conclusion led her back to where she had started: She did not bring Prue west to put her in mortal danger.

Still uncertain what she would say, she waited for Tad's arrival, hoping his interview with President Lamar would produce some solution.

Earlier Tad had managed a separate room for Prue and Hattie. Tonight Corrie would have Tad all to herself. But the rare prize held little joy. The gulf between them was growing, and threatened to create an irreparable schism.

He returned late. Corrie could not fathom his mood. Without speaking he removed his cravat and coat, and pulled off his boots.

"How did it go?" Corrie asked.

Tad looked at her, sighed, and she could see his exhaustion. "He promises everything. But I don't know if he can deliver."

Corrie was swept by renewed hope. "What kind of promises?"

"An army to hold off the Mexicans. A line of forts and companies of Rangers to keep the Indians in check. The question is how he'll pay for all this."

Corrie found cause for some encouragement. "Still, it seems he's at least trying," she pointed out.

Tad shook his head slowly. "I must tell you. I believe he's inadequate to the task. He's like a child who makes up stories and thinks the telling will make it so. He's a poet, a romantic. He doesn't have his feet on the ground."

Once more Corrie had come full circle. Tad's skepticism dashed the hope she was attempting to build on Lamar's leadership. She was reluctant to leave the subject. "Does President Lamar think the war with Mexico will be renewed?"

"He holds the theory we won at San Jacinto because the Texas navy prevented Santa Anna from being supplied by sea. He plans to rebuild our navy, make alliances with pirates and freebooters. He says Mexico won't invade if she loses control of the seas, for she can't supply an army in Texas by land."

"Is that true?"

"I'm not so sure. A Mexican soldier can march all day on a handful of beans. Santa Anna brought a good-sized supply train with him last time. A sea route might not be much of a factor in his thinking."

Again Corrie's search for reassurance was thwarted. But the mention of pirates triggered the memory of a family story. Years ago her great-grandfather and great-grandmother McNair, on their way from Jamaica to Charles Town, were chased by a pirate. By day the larger schooner they were on would gain ground, but by night the pirate's lighter sloop would close the gap, until one dawn the pirate was only a cable length away. As boarding appeared imminent, muskets and pistols were issued to the passengers. Corrie's great-grandmother McNair was told to leave the main deck so the pirate would not see her. But according to the family story she refused to budge. "I want him to see I'm armed and ready," she explained.

As Corrie contemplated her own plight, the family anecdote took on added meaning. In those days pirates and privateers abounded in the Caribbean. Surely her great-grandmother knew the danger before the ship set sail from Jamaica. And if she and others like her had refused to go, Charles Town would never have become Charleston.

"Have you decided what you'll do?" Tad asked.

Corrie's decision was newly hatched, but she did not need to ponder over it. She knew it was right.

"I feel my responsibility to Prue immensely," she told him. "I shouldn't endanger her life, or mine. But I didn't come all the way to Texas to sit around and twiddle my thumbs. I have my own dreams to fulfill. I'll go on to Béxar with you."

Tad's face lit up with a smile. He hugged and kissed her. "I've been praying you'd say that. I couldn't imagine going on without you."

--- 6 ---

A low line of trees slowly assumed form on the western horizon. Corrie hardly dared hope they were not an illusion. But soon Whit rode back to the carriage and pointed ahead. "That's the Brazos. Tad says we should be into San Felipe before noon."

San Felipe de Austin, the old headquarters of the Austin Colony. From here they would run the gauntlet of Comanches across the final hundred and fifty miles into San Antonio.

Prue cocked her head at Whit from beneath her parasol. "San Felipe. Is this where we leave our last will and testament?"

Whit grinned down at her. "No. You keep it with you, so it'll be found with your bleached bones."

Hattie gasped.

"Stop it, both of you!" Corrie said, her thoughts flying once again to her mother.

Whit laughed and rode toward the horse herd. Prue's gaze followed him. "Shoot, Corrie. We might as well have fun about it."

Corrie did not respond. The landscape around them was so peaceful, she found it inconceivable they were approaching land held by hostile Indians. Since leaving the bayous of Houston a week ago they had traveled mostly through vast treeless prairies. Immense flocks of geese and ducks flew overhead. Often herds of deer sprang up from the tall grass and bounded away. Every night the wagon train dined on fowl and venison.

For two days they had passed among the surviving members of Stephen F. Austin's original colonists. Their homes were far apart, and invariably crude imitations of log cabins. But the people were friendly and helpful.

Yet, even with the ease of travel, Tad had grown ever more

116

troubled. Corrie was worried about him. He never seemed to rest. He started the wagons earlier, and often did not call a stop until well after sunset. At night, when he finally lay down to sleep, he tossed ceaselessly.

Each night they camped where the wagons rolled to a stop, and when morning came, they went on, ever alert for Indians. The Negroes were scared, and their fear was infectious.

Three mornings ago Tad handed out rifles to the Negroes and drilled them in loading and firing. Now they carried the rifles everywhere they went.

Tad and Jack rode ahead to scout the river. A few minutes later they returned and reported they had found a suitable crossing. But when Corrie reached the river, she could not hide her unease. The banks were steep and the current was swift.

"There've been hard rains far upriver," Tad said. "Probably somewhere a white man has never seen."

The horse herd was driven across first. In midstream the water rose to their haunches. The animals emerged on the opposite bank wet and dripping.

Gingerly, the first wagon was eased into the water. Tad rode beside it, giving instructions to the driver. All went well until midstream. There the oxen lost their footing, began swimming, and were swept downstream. The wagon, tugged sideways, overturned, spilling its contents into the river.

Whit and Jack plunged into the water to help Tad rescue the driver. Corrie left the carriage, ran to the riverbank, and stood helpless. She recognized Grandmother McNair's chiffonier floating away, and realized that the wagon had contained her most valuable heirlooms. The driver was fished from the water. Whit raced downstream in pursuit of the chiffonier. He jumped off his horse, held the chiffonier for a moment, lost his footing, disappeared underwater, and came up battling the current. Jack rushed to help. Corrie held her breath while the two wrestled the chest to safety on the opposite shore.

Shouting, Tad directed efforts as chairs, tables, and boxes were rescued. Afterward, the men crisscrossed their horses through the current, searching for more. The damaged wagon was pulled from the water.

Before the next wagon entered the river, ropes were attached to the wagon and the lead oxen. Whit, Jack, and the two drovers rode across upstream, holding the ropes taut, preventing the oxen from drifting with the current. The wagon crossed safely.

With such painstaking care the other wagons were driven safely across the Brazos.

Ropes were attached to the landau. Slowly Ben drove it down the bank and into the water. Corrie felt her heart racing as the river lapped against the underside, threatening to turn the carriage into a runaway boat. Hattie's eyes were shut tight. Prue leaned forward, enjoying the thrill.

As they reached the deepest part of the river, the carriage indeed floated. But the lines held fast. The wheels again found bottom. Ben drove the carriage onto the bank.

A few minutes later they reached the top of the bluff, and entered San Felipe de Austin.

Corrie's heart sank. San Felipe was a wretched, decaying, half-burned cluster of five stores, two disreputable-looking taverns, and perhaps two dozen unpainted, pitiful houses.

She had expected far more from one of the most famous towns in Texas, the headquarters of Austin's first colonists, the seat of the first provisional government of the new Republic.

Was this a foretaste of what she would see in San Antonio?

Tad came over to the carriage and leaned from his horse. "I'll go see about finding accommodations for you."

She stopped him. "Tad, I'd prefer to stay in the wagon."

He did not object. "I've put four Negroes to unloading the furniture. You can tell them how best to dry it. I'll go see if there's anyone forming a group to cross to Béxar."

Corrie looked at the depressing town. "I hope we won't have to stay here long."

Tad followed her gaze. "General Houston burned San Felipe to prevent it falling into enemy hands. It hasn't been built back like I expected."

He rode toward one of the taverns, taking Whit and Jack with him.

By late afternoon Corrie, Prue, and Hattie completed the work at the damaged wagon. Corrie suddenly felt giddy. She walked to her wagon and the burlap-wrapped jug of cool water kept there. A wave of blackness swept over her. She reached for a wagon wheel, but could not find it.

The next she knew, she lay in her own bed in the wagon. Hattie was bathing her face. Prue held her hand. Corrie felt her stomach churn. She tried to rise. "I'm going to be sick!"

Hattie reached for a wooden bucket used to ladle out grain to the horses. She got it in place just in time. For several minutes Corrie was racked by nausea.

Gradually the worst moments passed. She lay back on the quilts. The wagon canopy above her seemed to be swirling and she could not focus her eyes. Again Hattie bathed her face.

Corrie could not imagine what had made her so sick. She thought back to their hurried noon meal, to breakfast, to supper the evening before. "It must have been the venison," she said. "We kept it too long. It didn't taste right."

Hattie stopped wiping her forehead. "Miss Corrie, I think I know what's wrong with you, and it ain't venison."

Corrie did not understand.

"Miss Corrie, when you last catch your time?"

Corrie remembered being late—where? In Alabama, maybe Mississippi. She had blamed worry, lack of sleep, too much activity. It had happened before. But in a rush of intuition, she knew Hattie was right.

"Corrie, if only you could see your face!" Prue said, giggling.

Hattie laughed too. "Miss Corrie, looks like you got a secret to tell Mistah Tad."

"Not yet. I want to be certain."

"You going to be a lot more than certain before long. You better lie back and rest for a while and get used to the idea."

Corrie obeyed. When she awoke she heard Hattie telling Tad she was not feeling well, and was lying down. He came to the wagon, frowning with concern. "Are you ill?"

She wanted to tell him the news, but this was neither the time nor place. Besides, she was not yet sure. "I overexerted myself," she told him. "I'll be fine after a bit of rest."

He glanced back toward town. "You may have time for a long rest. There's no one waiting to go on west. Three men were here ten days. They've now gone downstream to Richmond in hope of finding others crossing there. I hired a man to go after them."

"Will three men be enough?" Corrie asked.

"Depends on the men," Tad said.

He went away to supervise the never-ending repair of wagons and the feeding of livestock. Feeling better, Corrie sat up and gazed out at the sunset over the miserable little town.

Gradually, she absorbed the probability of her pregnancy and the realization that she now had much more than a marriage invested in this western adventure.

Her own change of citizenship had been a bit frightening. Legally a Texian, she still thought of herself as American, and she had the comfort of knowing that, if necessary, she could go back at any time.

But for her son—and somehow she knew it would be a son—the view of the world would be different. He would be a native-born Texian, with no claim to U.S. citizenship.

Corrie found this reality even more disturbing than that she was now with child, preparing to set off across a one-hundred-fifty-mile strip ruled by Comanches.

"I'm not keen on setting out with an ox train," said the red-haired man. "We'd be twice as long on the road. The risk would be double."

Tad did not respond. He had no intention of begging. The three men were gathered around the campfire. Whit stood back at the edge of the light, listening. After having waited two days for the return of the three, Tad was in no mood to pamper them.

"How many effective guns do you have?" the man asked.

He had introduced himself as Andrew Bates from South Carolina. He said he had arrived in Texas two months ago, purchased three soldiers' land bounties in Houston, and was on his way to Béxar to clear the titles. He claimed to have been an Indian fighter back east, against the Seminoles and Creeks.

Tad considered his answer carefully. "My brother and I each have a brace of five-shot revolvers, with extra cylinders. I have two single-shot percussion pistols, a ten-gauge shotgun, and twelve percussion rifles, fifty-caliber bore."

"And there are only the two of you?"

"My man Jack is a good marksman. All of my Negroes have some acquaintance with guns. I've been training them."

The three exchanged glances. Clearly they did not favor arming slaves. The tall one had been introduced as Christopher Sowers of Georgia. The third, a towering Alabaman, was named James Shippen. All three were land speculators.

"So you total six pistols, twelve rifles, and a shotgun," Bates said. "We each have two pistols and a rifle. That's twenty-eight barrels. How's your skill with weapons, sir?"

Tad held his temper. "I've always found it adequate. How's your own, sir?"

For a moment Tad thought Bates would take offense. His eyes narrowed, and even in the firelight Tad could see the red hues of his face darken. He hesitated. "I can hold up my end."

Tad looked at the other two. "And you gentlemen?"

"I've never had any complaints," said Shippen.

Tad liked that. The other man, Sower, merely nodded.

"My brother's young, but he has proved himself in a tight situation," Tad said. The three men glanced at Whit. Tad went on. "I wish we were greater in number, but I'm not inclined to wait longer. I'm prepared to chance it if you are. I'll be most happy to have you along. You're welcome to share our table."

"I don't know," Bates said. "Your oxen won't be able to make more'n ten or fifteen miles a day. The Comanches will be onto that horse herd like ants on sugar. I'd like some guarantee that if we get in a bind, we'd abandon the wagons and make a dash for Béxar. We're well mounted. We could outrun them."

"No," Tad said. "Under certain circumstances, I might give up the horse herd. But not the wagons."

A brief silence fell.

"I'm in," said Shippen. He glanced down at Bates. "Andrew, I'm tired of waiting. I think this is our best bet."

"I'll go along," Sowers said.

Bates looked up at the two who had just deserted him. "I don't know," he said again. "You say you know the road?"

"I've been there," Tad said.

"After the Revolution?"

"Before, during, and after."

Bates shrugged. "All right. I'll go."

The three rose, shook hands with Tad, and walked back to their camp. Whit came forward and knelt by the fire. "Bates struck me as a blowhard. What'd you think of the other two?"

Tad was pleased that Whit was learning to read character. "Shippen seems all right. Sower could go either way. But you're right about Bates. I don't think I'd trust him in a pinch."

"Tad, what are our chances of getting through?"

Whit did not appear to be asking out of undue concern. Tad gave him an honest assessment. "I doubt we'll see trouble between here and the Colorado. But for the last hundred and thirty miles, across the Navidad and the Guadalupe to Béxar, we'll be lucky to get by without a scrape."

"Should we chance it? I mean, with Corrie and Prue along?"

Tad spoke with a confidence he did not feel. "I lied to Bates. If necessary, we'll abandon the wagons. We're well-mounted, and Corrie and Prue can ride as well as you or I."

West from the Colorado the landscape gradually yielded to grand vistas of stunning beauty, and Corrie began to understand Tad's obsession for this country. Far away, in diminutive detail, ranged herds of deer, antelope, and wild mustangs. Clumps of post oak formed islands in an ocean of grass. Great quantities of wildflowers gave the prairie the appearance of a cultivated garden.

The carriage now traveled closer to the center of the wagon train. Tad insisted the new position was safer. The horse herd no longer ranged ahead, but was held close to the wagon train. The three travelers rode with Tad, Whit, and Jack out ahead of the wagons, with rifles across the pommels of their saddles.

On the third morning beyond the Colorado, Tad called a halt at the top of a high hill. The men all rode forward and sat on their horses, staring into the distance.

"What do they see?" Prue asked, shading her eyes.

Corrie searched the horizon but saw nothing.

Prue pointed. "What is that to the left of those trees?"

Corrie saw movement. "It looks like a herd of wild horses."

"No," Prue said. "I think I see riders on them."

A few minutes later Tad came down the length of the wagon train, stopping to talk to each driver. He reined in beside the carriage. His face was grim.

"It's Indians. Fifteen or so. We'll keep moving, give them a look at our guns. Maybe they'll leave us alone." He nudged Midnight closer and spoke to Corrie. "If it comes to a fight, we'll put the carriage in the center. You, Prue, and Hattie get under it. Ben will be there with his shotgun."

Tad hurried on past to speak with the other drivers. Corrie tried to calm her thumping heart. Hattie was rigid with fear.

Prue's face was pale. "Well, I came to Texas for adventure," she said. "I guess this is it."

Corrie reached into her reticule and grasped the pepperbox pistol Tad had given her. The cold metal gave her no comfort.

The horse herd was brought in close, roped into strings, and tied to the back of the wagons. Tad returned to the front, gave the signal, and again the wagons rolled forward.

The Indians came toward the wagon train at a steady trot. A few hundred yards away they stopped. Tad raised an arm, bringing the wagons to a halt.

Corrie recognized that these Indians were different from those she had seen in the South, or encountered drunk in the streets of Nacogdoches. These sat erect on their horses and their gaze was proud. For weapons they carried bows and arrows, shields, lances and, here and there, muskets. They wore their hair long, free to the wind.

Abruptly one Indian rode out from the rest, making elaborate signs with his hands and arms.

Tad rode forward to meet him, also making signs. Corrie held her breath as the two stopped within a few feet of each other and continued to talk in signs.

The conversation seemed to go on forever, with much pointing and gesturing. But at last Tad turned and rode back to where Whit, Jack, and the three men waited. They talked for a moment. Then Tad came to the carriage.

"They're Tonkawas," he said. "Friendly Indians. They'll be riding with us for a way."

Corrie was aghast. "Traveling *with* us?"

Tad nodded. "They claim they fought yesterday with some Comanches. The way I understand it, the Tonks were winning until a bigger bunch of Comanches showed up. The Tonks ran. They've come to us for protection."

Corrie had a sudden image of the Indians talking their way into camp, then murdering them all. "Does that story sound true?"

Tad nodded. "Other tribes claim the Tonks are cannibals. They make war on them constantly. Several of these Tonks have been wounded. They say they're hungry, and haven't had time to hunt. Their horses are used up. So I think they're telling the truth. But we'll stay on our guard."

Ahead, Whit and Jack drove a spare ox out onto the prairie. Corrie recognized it as the one with a split hoof, unable to work. Whit and Jack had been doctoring it.

Whit and Jack left the ox and rode back toward the wagons. The animal stood, uncertain what to do. Its indecision was brief. Two Indians sent arrows completely through the animal. It dropped to its knees, then fell over, legs twitching.

Indians swarmed over the dying ox. In hardly more than the blink of an eye the carcass was opened, the hide thrown back, and the flesh sliced into long strips. The Tonkawas sat on the ground and began eating the raw meat, wiping their hands carelessly on thigh and stomach.

Even in her revulsion Corrie was struck by the primitive grandeur of the Indians. Tad, Whit, and Jack sat unobtrusively on their horses a short distance away. Corrie found comfort in Old Ben's shotgun, lying across his lap.

"No one at home will ever believe this," Prue whispered. "They'll say I made it up. Corrie, I want you to write a note for me, saying it's true."

Corrie did not answer. Two of the Indians were wrestling over a slice of liver, apparently a choice morsel. She felt her gorge rising and tried to shift her mind to pleasant thoughts.

The ox did not last long. Soon only skin, bones, and offal remained, and the Indians remounted. The carriage caught the eye of one. He approached to investigate. Others followed.

"Oh, my God!" Prue whispered. "What'll we *do?*"

Corrie clung to the handle of the pepperbox pistol, still hidden in her reticule. Hattie was so petrified she was beyond making a sound. She sat trembling. Prue shrank into the far corner of the carriage.

"Smile, try to act friendly," Corrie said. "The men are here to protect us. Ben, don't shoot!"

Old Ben's voice remained deep and untroubled. "I'll be careful, Miss Corrie. But I got us two barrels of buckshot here if we need it."

The curious Indian rode close to the landau and peered inside. From his manner Corrie assumed he was a chief. *"¡Hola, mujeres!"* he shouted.

Corrie had read that after two centuries of association, many Indian tribes used Spanish as a lingua franca. A powerful odor of blood, sweat, and rancid animal grease filled the carriage. Corrie smiled. "Hello," she said.

The Indian put a hand on the frame of the carriage. When he felt it give under his weight, the purpose of the leaf springs apparently dawned on him. He pushed again, harder, rocking the carriage. He laughed and said something to his companions in their language. Other Indians, mouths still wet with blood from their meal, leaned from their mounts to test the springs. The landau rocked violently.

The chief smiled at Corrie. *"Como una niña,"* he said, cradling his arms as if holding an infant.

For a moment Corrie thought that in his closeness to nature, the Indian had divined that she was with child. But then she understood what he was saying: She was being rocked in the carriage like a baby. She smiled. "Yes, like a child."

The Indian's gaze came to rest on Hattie. He rode closer to peer in, and said something to the others. They also came close to look at Hattie.

Rigid with fear, Hattie could do nothing but stare back. After a long moment, Tad's voice came in a phrase of Spanish. The Indians turned away.

Tad came to the carriage and looked in. "Are you all right?"

"They gave us a scare," Corrie said. "That's all."

"They meant no harm. They're just curious."

He returned to the front of the wagons, gave the signal, and again they were on the move, with the band of Tonkawas riding a short distance to their left.

The Indians remained close to the wagon train. Occasionally one or two rode off to a high ridge and gazed for a time into the distance. The Indian who seemed to be chief rode forward to confer with Tad. A short while later Tad came to ride briefly beside the carriage.

"The Tonks claim we're being trailed by Comanches," he said. "I haven't seen any sign of them."

"You think they'll attack?" Prue asked.

"As long as the Tonks are with us, I doubt it. But we'll take no chances."

In late afternoon they passed over a rise and descended into a wide valley covered with buffalo. Whit and Jack spurred their horses, raced into the herd, and quickly brought down four animals. The Indians shouted their approval. The buffalo stampeded, and for a time the ground trembled with the thunder of their passage. The herd disappeared to the north, leaving the oxen strangely disturbed. Usually docile and plodding by nature, they were suddenly difficult to control. It was as if the buffalo had fanned some forgotten spark within them. For a time the wagons moved at a faster pace.

That evening the Tonkawas camped a few yards away and accepted choice cuts of buffalo meat.

"Don't bother to cook mine," Prue quipped. "When I travel, I prefer to follow the customs of whatever country I happen to find myself in."

Whit laughed, and Corrie began to suspect that Prue had found an admirer.

Tad could not seem to relax. "I believe it'd be best if you, Prue, and Hattie slept in our wagon," he told Corrie. "I'll be up through the night. The Comanches may try to slip in and steal the horses. And I don't fully trust the Tonks."

Later, when Corrie went to the wagon, she was surprised to find Old Ben seated on the ground beneath it, a blanket around his shoulders, his shotgun across his lap. "I'll sleep right here, Miss Corrie," he said. "Don't you worry none."

"I'll get you an extra blanket," she said.

Perhaps because of the precautions the night passed peaceably. Before dawn Corrie awoke to the sounds of the drivers raising the wagons and greasing the wheels. By first light the wagons again were rolling.

The Tonkawas remained with them through the morning and into late afternoon. At last a narrow line of timber came into view. Tad said it marked the course of the Guadalupe. The Tonkawas were jubilant. Apparently the river was a goal in their flight. They thanked Tad repeatedly for his protection, then rode away toward the north. The wagons continued on.

In the hour before sundown they reached the battered old town of Gonzáles. Not much of it was left—only a half dozen cabins and piles of charred debris.

Corrie knew the town's story, for it was a part of the Texas legend. Three years ago the thirty-two men of this town rode away to the defense of the Alamo. They never returned. Their widows fled eastward, ahead of the advancing Mexican army. In retreat, Houston burned the town to discourage the invaders.

Now only a few people had returned. A general store, a tavern, a blacksmith shop, were the only evidence of occupation.

Tad positioned the wagons on the river below town. Corrie, Prue, and Hattie spread blankets on bushes as a screen and bathed in the cool water.

On returning to the wagons in the last rays of the setting sun,

Corrie saw Tad standing alone on the riverbank, gazing off to the west. It was the time of day when usually he would be supervising the feeding of the animals, seeing to the upkeep of the wagons. His abrupt withdrawal was so unsettling that Corrie forgot herself and asked of Jack a question she otherwise would never have uttered. "What in the world is Tad doing?"

Jack gave her his slow, sad smile. "Marsh Tad's in one big blue funk, Miss Corrie. You see, this was the place where we got word about the Alamo. Marsh Tad was on his way there. But that lady come up that road there with her little baby and said everybody in the Alamo was dead."

Corrie had not known that Tad was on his way to the Alamo when it fell. He had never mentioned it.

But she knew the identity of the lady Jack had mentioned. Newspapers all over the world that spring carried heart-rending stories about "The Messenger from the Alamo," Suzanna Dickinson, and "The Babe of the Alamo," the infant Angelina.

Mrs. Dickinson's husband was among the dead. The victorious Santa Anna spared her life, and gave her escort to Gonzáles, where she informed General Houston and all of Texas that the Alamo had fallen.

Tad had been here! He had witnessed that heartrending scene! Why had he never mentioned it?

It logically followed that if he was here when word came from the Alamo, then he had participated in the long retreat of the Texas army from this place, in rain, all the way to the battlefield at San Jacinto.

Suddenly this portion of the Texas story became intensely personal for Corrie. The many miles she had traveled from the battlefield at San Jacinto, and considered a hardship, Tad and his companions had trudged in the opposite direction under terrible circumstances.

No wonder he was in a big blue funk.

She walked up the riverbank to where he sat. Twilight had deepened. She could not see the expression on his face. He glanced up but did not speak. She sat down beside him.

"Jack told me you were here when word came from the Alamo," she said. "I didn't know that."

When he spoke, his voice was low, and hoarse. "Albert Martin was my best friend. He led the men from here into the Alamo. If word had reached me in time, I would have been with him."

Corrie did not press. They sat for a time in the darkness without speaking.

"We had chased the Mexicans out of Béxar once," Tad said after a time. "We thought the job was done. So I went back to East Texas."

Corrie understood. A few months earlier the Texians had routed the Mexicans from the Alamo, from San Antonio, and sent them packing back to Mexico. Tad had been there, for he had fought in the Battle of Concepción. But Santa Anna had returned the following spring with an army of six thousand.

Tad sighed in the darkness. "I knew many of the men in the Alamo," he said. "Bowie. Travis. Martin. All the men from here. I should have been there."

"I'm glad you weren't," Corrie said.

"I was off in the bayous, locating land. If I'd been in Nacogdoches, Liberty, any of the towns, I would've heard. I keep wondering why the news came too late for me."

Corrie felt that the time had come. "Perhaps there's a providence," she said. "Perhaps you were spared for San Jacinto. For me. For what you're now doing. For the son you'll have before long."

She felt his eyes trying to pierce the darkness. "Son?"

"I'm certain it'll be a son," she said.

His voice was so heavy with emotion that the word came almost as a sob. "Corrie!"

He pulled her to him and held her tight, her cheek against the soft buckskin of his shirt. He said nothing more.

--- 7 ---

Bates turned his horse to face Tad. "Mr. Logan, we've talked it over. We've elected to go on. I figure we're safe now."

Tad was not surprised. The day before he had seen Bates, Shippen, and Sowers with their heads together. He had guessed the subject under discussion.

They now were at the Cíbolo, a day's ride from San Antonio aboard a good horse, but two full days of travel for the oxen.

"Mr. Bates, if you ride on, you're endangering us all," Tad said. "I'm told the Comanches hang around Béxar and wait in ambush for small parties of travelers."

"The Tonks wouldn't have left us if they thought there was any danger," Bates insisted. "There's a company of Rangers in Béxar. I figure we're inside the safe zone."

Tad gave Bates a long, hard stare. "Mr. Bates, you agreed to accompany this wagon train to Béxar. We're not yet there. You're going back on your agreement."

"We're past all danger."

"And I say we're not. Mr. Shippen, are you also backing out on your commitment?"

Shippen glanced uneasily at Bates before replying. "We're eager to get on, Mr. Logan. I understand there's quite a scramble for land. We don't want to lose out. Way I see it, we'd just be scouting on ahead for you. I promise. If we see Indians, we'll come back to help protect the wagons."

"Mr. Sowers?"

Sowers spat into the dirt. "I think we're close enough to Béxar to call our agreement completed. One day could mean considerable difference in locating land."

130

Tad thought of Corrie, Prue, his unborn child. For once he could not control his anger. "Then ride on, you cheap sons of bitches. Never expect any favors from me."

Bates turned red of face. His hand moved toward his pistol, then stopped. "You take that back right now, Mr. Logan! Apologize! You've got no call to talk to us that way!"

"By abandoning women in a situation like this, you've given me reason to call you any damned thing I can think of."

"Let's go, Andrew," Shippen said. "We don't want trouble."

Bates sat rigid, as if he might yet fight. Tad wheeled Midnight and rode toward the wagons. Whit and Jack had finished with the last-minute details. They came to meet him.

"Where they going?" Whit asked, staring after the three.

"Béxar," Tad said.

"They're leaving us?"

"You called the shot on Bates. We're best off without him."

They started the wagons westward. As a precaution, Tad guided them off the main road. He spent much of the morning ranging ahead, scouting post oak and mesquite mottes, making sure no Comanche war party lay in wait.

It was a tension-filled day. Repeatedly he was startled as a jackrabbit, a covey of quail, or a deer burst from cover.

Late in the afternoon he rode into the valley of the Salado. The wind shifted direction. With the fresh breeze came the faint sound of gunfire. Tad listened for several minutes, ascertaining the location. He then turned and raced back to the wagons. Whit saw him coming and rode out to meet him.

"Gunfire ahead," Tad said. "Slightly to the south. Let's take the wagons to the north. We'll camp along the river."

Whit cupped an ear. "I hear it. What do you think it is?"

"Could be Bates, Shippen, and Sowers," Tad said. "That'd be the route they took."

"They should be in Béxar by now."

"Not if their trip was interrupted."

Whit listened for a moment. "Shouldn't we go help?"

"They made their decision," Tad said. "They'll have to live or die with it. I'll not sacrifice the women to their ignorance. Let's get moving."

Corrie, Prue, and Hattie lay under the wagon, listening to night sounds. The stars were out, but no moon. Corrie could make out only vague shapes of bushes near the wagon.

Before sundown Tad had selected a place to camp in a grove of post oaks beside a small stream. Now the men were keeping watch in the post oaks all around camp.

"This is just like a Halloween party," Prue whispered. "Except it's real."

"Those weren't ghosts, Miss Prue," Hattie whispered back. "I heard them shooting. Plain as anything."

Prue nudged Corrie with an elbow. "Well, if anybody was killed, they'd be ghosts now, wouldn't they?"

"Prue, hush!" Corrie said.

Prue grew quiet. But Corrie could not sleep. No doubt Indians were out there somewhere. At any moment they might try to slip in to steal the horses, or split skulls with their axes. Even now some of the Negroes might be dead, murdered on watch.

From a few yards away came a resounding thump. Corrie, Prue, and Hattie jumped in unison, even though in the same instant they recognized that the sound came from a horse stomping, dislodging a heel fly.

Prue laughed nervously. "Wouldn't it be awful if we were killed *now*? Only a day away from Béxar? After coming all this way? Of course it'd be awful anytime. But think of the miles!"

"Prue, we're not in any danger. The men will protect us," Corrie replied with little conviction. Most of the men had never fired a gun until three weeks ago.

"I wish I'd worn my bell skirt," Prue whispered. "If I'm to be killed anyway, I'd like to be looking my best."

Corrie understood then that Prue was prattling only because she was scared. Corrie reached for her in the darkness and placed a palm on her cheek. Prue hugged Corrie's hand to her.

"Mistah Tad won't let us get hurt, Miss Prue," Hattie whispered. "I just don't think he will."

Corrie put an arm around Hattie. "He won't," she said.

They lay quietly for a time, listening to the night—the sigh of the night breeze in the post oak, the movement of the horses and oxen, the occasional call of a distant coyote. There came other, faint sounds Corrie could not identify—perhaps the flick of a night bird, perhaps the momentary scurrying of small animal. She remained awake, listening.

"Corrie, what will you name the baby?" Prue asked.

Corrie ignored her own admonitions for silence. She also felt like talking. "I haven't had time to think about it," she whispered. "If it's a boy, I may let Tad decide."

"I don't know if I'll ever want children."

Corrie thought back to when she was Prue's age. Ever since adolescence she had wanted the warmth of a good marriage, a family. She had never entertained any other goal.

They lay silent for a long interval. Then from somewhere deeper into the post-oak grove came the tentative hoot of an owl.

"Did that sound like a real owl to you?" Prue whispered.

Corrie reconstructed the sound in her mind and found an element that seemed almost human. But she knew the tricks one's senses could play. "I think you're imagining things," she said.

Again came the hoot of an owl, lower in tone.

"There!" Prue whispered. "You hear?"

Corrie did not answer. The hoot indeed seemed devoid of owl qualities. Scarcely breathing, Corrie strained to hear the next hoot over the beating of her heart.

Prue snuggled closer. Hattie buried her face under Corrie's arm. For a time they held each other, listening.

When the next hoot came, it sounded much closer.

They listened hard, but heard no more except the occasional movements of a horse or an ox. Corrie thought of the men on watch, the terrors they must be enduring alone out in the brush, hearing the same sounds, nurturing their imaginations.

She lay for an interminable time embraced with Prue and Hattie, alert for the soft tread of a moccasin, a stir among the horses, any sign that their screen of protection had been penetrated. The hoot of the owl was not repeated.

At last Corrie dozed from sheer exhaustion. When she awoke, the eastern sky was gray and Tad was kneeling beside the wagon.

"Dawn's coming," he said. "Jack and I are going out to look around. Whit and Ben will be here. I'll be back soon."

Corrie did not want him to go. But she recognized the necessity. They certainly should not drive the wagons out of the grove into a band of Indians. "Please be careful," she said.

After the terrors of the night, Corrie found immense relief in the morning routine. A cold breakfast was served. Whit directed the feeding and harnessing of the oxen. By sunup they were ready to move. But Tad and Jack failed to return.

Corrie's concern increased with each passing minute. The delay was unlike Tad.

Whit also was worried. He kept glancing up at the sun. "If they don't show up soon, I'm going out to look for them."

"Let's wait," Corrie said. "If they were in trouble, we would have heard their guns."

The sun was well above the horizon when Tad and Jack returned. Tad's face was drawn with fatigue. "We struck fresh tracks about two miles west of here," he said. "Looked to be about thirty Comanches. We trailed them, but they seemed to be circling. So we broke off and hurried back."

Corrie peeked out at the prairie, half expecting to see Indians. "What'll we do?" she asked. "Stay hidden?"

Tad shook his head. "No, we cut plain tracks coming in here. We'll get back on the road and make the best time possible until we hit Béxar."

The buzzards were low on the horizon, west of the Cíbolo. "Keep the wagons moving," Tad told Whit. "I'll go see what those birds are after."

He rode ahead at a slow trot, saving Midnight's strength. Frequently he stopped to listen for sounds, to watch for movement in the immense landscape.

Three bodies were lying in a buffalo wallow a hundred yards from the road. Waving his hat, Tad drove away the buzzards.

All three had been scalped, mutilated, and riddled with arrows. Tad steeled himself against the stench and rode close. Enough features remained for him to identify Bates, Shippen, and Sowers. He had nothing with him to cover the bodies, so he left the buzzards to their work. Carefully he rode in ever-widening arcs, piecing together what had happened.

He returned to the wagons and summoned Jack and Whit. "Jack, load pick, shovels, and a couple of men into the utility wagon," he said. "Bring it on ahead. Whit, you come on with the wagons. Keep to the road. I don't want the women seeing this. I'll go back and keep the buzzards off those poor bastards till you get there."

He returned to the buffalo wallow and again drove off the buzzards. Taking a small bottle of whiskey from his saddlebags, he splashed a liberal dose on his handkerchief, tied it over his nose, and searched the bodies. Bates had been carrying three land certificates. Shippen and Sowers had each carried two.

At some point during the battle Shippen had started writing a letter. It remained unfinished. Sowers had written a short last will and testament, leaving all his goods to his wife. Tad gathered all the papers and put them in his saddlebags.

Jack arrived with the wagon and two Negroes. Tad put them to work with pick and shovel. By the time they had scooped out a shallow, wide grave, the wagons arrived on the road. Whit rode close and dismounted to look at the bodies. Tad was inclined to warn him away, but refrained, reasoning that this was a necessary part of his education.

Whit went from one corpse to the next, his face contorted. "Why'd they put so many arrows into them?"

"Counting coup," Tad told him. "Everyone who puts an arrow into the victim participates in the killing."

"Why'd they cut them up so?"

"I'm told it has to do with their concept of the hereafter," Tad told him. "With his guts cut out, a man can't eat in the next world. With his thigh muscle cut, he can't walk."

"Marsh Whit, you going to be sick?" Jack asked. "This here ain't nothing to play around with."

"I'm all right," Whit said. "Why'd they attack these three, for what little they had, instead of the wagon train?"

"We ran a better bluff," Tad said. "From what I can gather from signs, the great Indian fighter Bates rode right into the middle of them. They were in that motte of post oak over there, waiting. I think Bates and Sowers were hit before they ever saw the Indians. They made it to this wallow. The Indians took their time, picked them off from cover."

Whit leaned over one of the bodies. "They must have forgot to take water from their saddles. Their lips are all cracked."

Tad felt a wave of affection for his brother. He was learning fast.

They dragged the corpses into the grave. The Negroes covered them. Jack made crosses out of old barrel staves and hammered each into the ground with the flat side of a pick.

Jack and the Negroes returned to the wagon. Tad remounted. Whit held back. "Shouldn't we say something over them?"

"We buried them," Tad said. "I'll notify their families. That's more than they had a right to expect. Come on. I want to get into Béxar before dark."

San Antonio de Béxar rose out of the earth like a mirage. In one moment there was only desert shrubbery and the usual boundless landscape. In the next Corrie was amazed to see soaring bell towers and arched stone ramparts beckoning on the horizon. The abrupt change was magical.

Tad watched her from beside the carriage, savoring her reaction. "I've approached Béxar from most every direction," he said. "It always takes you by surprise."

They entered the valley of the San Antonio River and moved toward town through the lush greenery of cottonwood, pecan, and live oaks. They passed deserted, crumbling old missions strung along the river like jewels.

From the town ahead came the soft peal of church bells, summoning the faithful to vespers. Sheep, cattle, and horses grazed in the surrounding fields. Children splashed in the river beneath the trees.

There was a softness to the air, a delicate gentleness to the quality of light. Corrie was swept by a profound sense of peace. San Antonio conveyed an unmistakable aura of permanence. Unlike the other settled parts of Texas, San Antonio seemed to have existed forever.

Tad halted the wagons, pointed, and to the right lay the fallen ruins of the Alamo. Corrie recognized it from the many drawings she had seen in newspapers. Tad took off his hat and rode close. Whit also removed his hat, sat on his horse, and waited.

"I expected it to be a shrine or something by now," Prue whispered. "I didn't know it was just an old fallen building."

Tad returned, gave the signal, and led the wagons across a shallow ford toward the setting sun. He halted the wagons before a large house, where a small delegation seemed to be waiting. Tad dismounted and shook hands with a distinguished-looking Mexican. The two embraced in what Tad had explained to her was an abrazo, a form of greeting between close male friends.

Tad was smiling. "Corrie, this is my good friend, Señor Francisco Ibarra Yturria. We won't be camping out like Gypsies the next few weeks after all. Señor Ibarra has offered us the use of his town house while we prepare our own home."

Ibarra swept off his hat and came forward to kiss Corrie's hand. When he spoke, his English was only slightly accented. "Mrs. Logan, I am deeply honored to make your acquaintance. There is a saying in Spanish, My house is your house. I hope you'll find the accommodations suitable."

For once in her life Corrie was left almost speechless. "Your generosity is most welcome, and appreciated," she managed to say. "I'm very grateful."

Ibarra was an imposing man, from his glistening, jet-black hair to his highly polished boots. When he smiled, the whiteness of his teeth contrasted well with his bronze skin.

"I could do no less for my best friend," Ibarra said.

Tad introduced Prue, who all too plainly thought Ibarra romantic beyond measure.

"If you ladies will allow me to help you from your carriage, I'll show you your new home," Ibarra said.

In the early twilight Corrie walked with Ibarra up a flagstone walk. Tad, Prue, Whit, and Hattie followed. They passed through a tiled entry hall, into a long, narrow room. The furniture was heavy, dark, and immaculate. Candelabra hung from the ceiling, lighting the interior.

Three servant girls came forward. Ibarra introduced them. "I apologize that they do not understand English," he said. "But I'm sure you can make your wants known."

Corrie was overwhelmed by the largess. Not only was she being given a house, but servants as well. "I'm sure we'll manage," she said.

Ibarra invited them to be seated and issued orders in Spanish. Wine was brought and served. Ibarra stood and raised his glass. "I offer a toast to your happiness in San Antonio de Béxar. May you find it beyond all your expectations."

"I already have," Corrie told him.

With the ceremony completed, Ibarra bowed. "I know you've had a long journey. I'll leave you to your rest. Thaddeus tells me he'll be occupied tomorrow, finding a new home, setting up his legal practice. I hope you ladies will allow me and my vaqueros to acquaint you with San Antonio de Béxar."

"His vaqueros will be armed," Tad said. "You'll be safe."

"I will be most honored," Corrie said.

Again Ibarra bowed. "Until tomorrow, then."

Tad walked Ibarra back to the street. When he returned, Corrie could not repress a mild recrimination. "Tad, I'm totally enchanted! Why didn't you tell me it would be like this?"

Tad smiled. "There's no way to explain San Antonio de Béxar. It must be experienced."

When Señor Ibarra called the next morning, Corrie received him in the long room alone, for Tad had left earlier, taking Whit and Jack with him, and Prue had dawdled late in bed.

Corrie apologized that they were not ready. Ibarra showed his white teeth in a smile. "There's a phrase in Spanish you will hear often. *No hay de nada.* It is of nothing. We have the rest of our lives to enjoy. A little delay is of no importance."

Corrie agreed with the philosophy. But it heightened her irritation with Tad. She felt he could have put off whatever he was doing and spent this one day in delightful diversion.

A few minutes later Prue emerged sleepy eyed, but dressed. Ibarra escorted them out to where ten vaqueros waited, and assisted them onto their horses. "First we will explore the river," he said. "It is the life blood of San Antonio de Béxar."

Corrie was intrigued by the vaqueros, who clearly considered today's outing a lark. Not one appeared more than eighteen. Each wore what seemed to be a permanent smile. Their dark glances kept bouncing off Prue, who was by no means oblivious. Each vaquero wore leather trousers with big brass buttons running from ankle to knee. Their white cotton shirts were bound at the waist with a red sash, and each sash held a brace of pistols. But most colorful were their wide-brimmed, high-crowned hats, often seemingly of more weight than the wearer. Corrie saw immediately that all were superb horsemen.

Ibarra led the way across the Main Plaza, passing in front of the church. He identified it as San Fernando Cathedral.

"It seems so old," Corrie commented.

"I'm not sure of its age," Ibarra said. "But it is not very old. Less than a century."

Corrie laughed. "I've just come from Houston, where no building is more than three years old. By comparison San Antonio seems so permanent. It's as if it has been here forever."

"In human terms, perhaps it has," Ibarra conceded. "The earliest Spanish explorers found Indians living here. We now will go visit the springs that make Béxar what it is."

They rode along the river under tall trees. Here and there weeping willows trailed leaves in the pale green water. The day was warm, with only a faint breeze. Billowing white clouds floated across the deep blue sky. Fields of grass and flowers bordered the river. Corrie could not readily adjust to all the lush greenness. "I've never seen a river more lovely," she said.

Again Ibarra smiled. "Several times in my life I've tried to live elsewhere. I keep coming back here."

As they rode upstream toward the springs, Corrie learned more about him. He owned a rancho downstream, where he lived with his wife and three children, two boys and a girl.

"Isn't it dangerous, because of the Indians?" Corrie asked.

"I have in my employ more than fifty vaqueros. As long as we live and travel in strength, the Indians do not bother us."

He said he had fought on the side of the Texians during the Revolution. "Thaddeus and I were together at Concepción, and at San Jacinto," he said. "We are like brothers."

"Perhaps you can prevail on him to enjoy himself more," Corrie said. "I wish he were with us today."

Ibarra laughed. "Señora, Thaddeus is *muy ambicioso*. Very ambitious. I cannot change him. He has talked long of what he wants to do. A law practice. A big rancho. A *plantación*. Now he is setting out to realize his dreams. I wish him every success."

They reached the springs. Cascades of water gushed from layers of rock. The rivulets flowed together and became a river.

"We now will go to San Pedro Springs, the start of San Pedro Creek," Ibarra said. "It is even more beautiful."

As they leisurely rode along, Ibarra explained that both the San Antonio River and San Pedro Creek were used for bathing and washing. By common agreement the acequia, dug long ago by church fathers, was used only for drinking water.

Behind Corrie and Ibarra, Prue was talking and joking with the vaqueros, and learning Spanish words and phrases.

Corrie found San Pedro Springs more appealing because of the quietness and solitude. Flowing from subterranean depths, the waters entered a pool that overflowed to start the creek on its way through town. Above the springs soared giant trees. Lush grass grew right to the water's edge.

After a few minutes at the springs, they rode on downstream. They came to a swimming hole filled with Mexican children, most as naked as the day they were born. Like the biblical Adam and Eve, the children seemed unaware that they were naked. Corrie felt warmth rushing to her cheeks, but neither Ibarra nor the vaqueros seemed to see anything amiss.

They passed huts made of mesquite posts driven into the ground and held together by mud, rawhide, and straw. From what Corrie could see of the interiors, the floors were earthen. Women came to the doorways and waved greetings. Ibarra explained that the huts were called jacales, and that most Mexicans in San Antonio lived in this way.

Ibarra's account of the town's history was so detailed, so filled with Indian raids, insurrections, and hurricanes, that Corrie retained only the most essential points. She gathered that the Spanish first had come to stay a century and a half before, and that shortly thereafter two priests had returned and founded the mission of San Antonio de Valero, later known to the world as the Alamo. Ibarra said a military fort was established nearby, and the first colonists were brought in—fifty-six Canary Islanders.

"Many here today can trace their lineage to those sixteen families who arrived in 1731," Ibarra said. "In a way, that was the start of San Antonio de Béxar. The military came and went. Even the priests failed. But the Canary Islanders stayed."

Ibarra led them south down the river to gaze upon the ruins of the old missions as he named them, one by one: San Francisco de la Espada. San Juan Capistrano. San José y San Miguel de Aguayo. Nuestra Señora de la Purisima Concepción. Corrie gathered that their stories were the same: early success, hundreds of Indian converts, irrigated fields, and prosperity, then disease, death, and, eventually, abandonment.

The ruins were sad, yet strangely comforting.

She found it difficult to believe that only a few miles away, and only a few hours ago, three men had been murdered, and that she herself had narrowly escaped death.

The return route led them to the Alamo. Once again Corrie found herself deeply affected as she gazed on the sad ruins.

"The first site for San Antonio de Valero was on the other side of the river," Ibarra said. "That building was destroyed by a hurricane. Another was started, and collapsed while it was being built. The third—this one, the Alamo—was never finished. The Indians died of disease. The chapel was used by troops. Most everyone forgot it was ever a mission."

They forded the river and returned to Ibarra's town house. Corrie thanked him profusely for the guided tour.

Prue added her own thanks. "It was marvelously grand. I want to ride out there again soon with my sketchbook."

For the first time Ibarra appeared temporarily at a loss for words. He looked at Prue. "Señorita, I myself would not go alone where we went today. I'm sure Comanches were watching us. They didn't bother us only because of my vaqueros."

Corrie was surprised. "The Indians would attack so close to town?"

Solemnly Ibarra nodded. "Last fall a party of nineteen men rode out on a sightseeing tour, like the one we took today. They were insufficiently armed. All but one were killed. Señora, I could tell you terrible stories. Please! When you wish to venture out, tell either Thaddeus or me, so we can ensure your safety."

Prue seemed sobered by the warning. After Ibarra and the vaqueros departed, she said to Corrie, "Has it occurred to you that we're prisoners in this town? We made it in. Now we can't get out. Not without an army."

"I believe this will do," Tad said.

Whit studied the house doubtfully. "Isn't it too small?"

Tad could see possibilities. "We'll knock out the wall between the two rooms on the right, and extend the whole house another twenty feet or so at the back. That'll add another four rooms." He pointed. "We can put a row of cabins along that back fence, and a barn over there. The property's deep enough for a pasture between here and the river. We can bring in the horses at night to keep them safe."

Jack whistled. "Marsh Tad, you talking a lot of work."

"We have sixteen men without a thing to do. We'll put eight to planting. The rest can do the carpentry on the house and cabins. I'll hire Mexicans to lay the adobe."

Tad walked to the back of the house. "We can put the kitchen

there, the patio here. We can haul limestone from the river. Later
we'll put a gallery along the east side of the house."

Whit looked toward the river. "Will that be enough pasture for
the horses?"

"During the day we'll graze them on our land upriver. Soon we'll
move them to the ranch. This will be our town house. We'll build a
bigger one at the ranch."

Again Jack whistled. "You sure talk big, Marsh Tad, for a fella
who don't own nothing yet."

Tad laughed. "Jack, you do have a way with words."

They returned to the horses and rode upstream. Tad was pleased
with the day's progress thus far. He had found a suitable location for
his law office, four rooms on the second floor of a building facing
the Main Plaza. The space would be sufficient for his private office,
his law library, an assistant, and, perhaps later, an associate. Now he
had found a home. The house was owned by a merchant who had
fled San Antonio during the Revolution and had not returned.

Now he needed to find a small tract suited to irrigation.

At the edge of town they passed patches of corn, beans, and
melons. The corn was less than knee high, the melon vines not yet
budded, and the beans just sprouted.

"The Mexicans plant just enough to live on," Tad explained to
Whit. "Each family raises a few goats, sheep, a cow or two, and
tends a little plot. Never more work than necessary."

Upstream Tad kept well away from the timber. "Listen to me,
both of you," he said. "Anytime you're out like this, even no more
than a pistol shot from town, be careful. Watch the woods. Never
ride up to a ditch or riverbank without circling around, checking it
out. Just assume a few Comanches are out there watching for you to
make a mistake."

"How'll we work these fields you're about to buy, Marsh Tad?"
Jack asked. "Don't the Indians kill Nigras too?"

"We'll keep one man on watch at all times," Tad explained.
"The others will keep guns handy."

A short distance below the springs Tad found the site he remembered. While Whit and Jack kept watch, he rode across the
tract, gaining a better idea of its dimensions.

"Who owns this land now?" Whit asked.

"Everybody and nobody. It's complicated. The king of Spain gave away titles to land all around here. When the Mexicans won independence, they gave away more. Now Texas. The grants overlap, and are poorly surveyed. A lot of people can lay claim, but no one owns it outright."

"So how can you buy it?"

"By purchasing the *derechos*," Tad explained. "The rights. Most of the families who were given land are now into the third and fourth generation. Dozens of heirs. I'll research the old surveys, birth records, find those who hold the *derechos*, deal with them. That's what I'll be doing during the next few years. Clearing titles. For us, and for lawyers back in East Texas."

"How can we work it, when we don't own it?" Whit asked.

"I'm entitled to a league, about forty-four hundred acres, and a labor, about a hundred and seventy-seven acres. I'll file on this as my labor."

"If you're entitled to it, why bother with the *derechos*?"

"Since I'm filing here, on land already claimed, I won't have a clear title. It'd always be subject to litigation. The heirs could get together and move me off of it."

"That sounds like a lot of unnecessary work," Whit said.

Again Tad laughed. "That's why we have lawyers."

Whit studied the future irrigated field. "How do you know where the property lines run?"

"I don't. Not for sure. I found an old survey. But later plats may overlap. Jack Hays, who commands the volunteer Ranger company here, is also the official surveyor. When his men aren't chasing Indians, they're out on surveys. I'll get him to make a new, accurate plat, and go from there."

As they returned toward town, Tad's mind was leaping ahead to all that needed to be done in the next few days.

"Tomorrow we'll put eight men to work on the house. Whit, I want you to bring oxen, wagon, equipment, and the rest of the men up here and start the plowing. Lay out the rows at a right angle to the river. Jack, I'll be needing you to run errands out of the office. Stick close. Don't wander off."

"Long as you're doing all this fancy planning, Marsh Tad, can you work in something for me to eat today? Unless I disremember, we ain't had a bite since breakfast."

Tad glanced at the sun. It was well into the Mexican siesta. "We'll go by the Ibarra house," he said. "The cooks will be gone, but Hattie should be able to find us something."

Tad rode for a few minutes in silence. "I'm going to need all the help you two can give me through the next few months," he told Whit and Jack. "It'd take an army to do all that must be done. But we three may be able to put a dent in it."

Life in the Ibarra house settled into a placid routine. Every day Tad was gone before daylight, taking Jack and Whit with him. After Corrie awoke, she and Prue ate a leisurely breakfast on the patio, served by the Ibarra household. By midmorning, they were receiving callers. First came the few Anglo women of San Antonio de Béxar. Mrs. Thomas Higginbotham. Mrs. Sam Maverick. Mrs. William Jacques. Mrs. William Elliott. Then through the next few weeks the señoras of the Mexican hidalgos came to call—Señoras García, Navarro, Soto, Garza, Zambrano, Seguín, Veramendi, and Yturri. Few of the Mexican women spoke English. Their social calls were awkward, but carried out with much ceremony.

Corrie became accustomed to the town's rhythm. In the cool mornings San Antonio stirred early. The bells of San Fernando summoned the faithful to matins, and herdsmen drove their animals out to pasture. The delicious smells of coffee, tortillas, and frying eggs filled the air. Most work was done in the relatively cool mornings. Women went to the river to wash. Children played in the streets or along the river. Men took their implements into the fields to plant and cultivate. Around eleven, as heat began to build, the town went to sleep. Men lay down in whatever shade they could find. The women retired to their homes, loosened their clothing, and reclined on rawhide hammocks. Children came home to sleep on pallets. A hush fell and remained unbroken through the heat of the day.

Not until five in the afternoon did the town again stir. Children returned to play in the streets. The herdsmen went into the fields to bring in their animals. Church bells sounded the call to vespers. Families walked to the river to bathe. Cooking fires were lit, and soon the air carried the delicious aromas of simmering beans, cooking meat, chiles, and spices.

At sundown San Antonio blossomed anew. With twilight came the first tentative notes of a guitar, a fiddle, sometimes a horn. Voices rose in plaintive love ballads. By ten o'clock the fandangos began, and the night was filled with music.

Every evening Corrie went onto the patio and listened. Moonlight, the whisper of trees along the river, the lingering smells, and the music conspired to kindle a bittersweet, pervasive, haunting ache in the heart. As Tad had predicted, she fell in love with San Antonio. She yearned to know more about its people. But there was an impassible barrier.

One evening she told Tad she wanted to attend a fandango.

He would not hear of it. "Corrie, you'd be embarrassed. Those dances are not for decent women to see."

Tad was friendly with the hidalgos. But he showed little interest in the lower-class Mexicans of the jacales. "For a hundred years they've been occupying the best land in Texas, with plenty of water," he told her. "And what have they done with it? Nothing! The mission fathers dug the acequias for irrigation. Now the Mexicans have let most go to ruin. They sleep half the day and drink and dance all night. The Mexicans won't last. When enough Americans settle here, they'll be pushed back across the Rio Grande."

Tad's attitude seemed prevalent among the fifty-odd Americans living in Béxar. To Corrie's regret, the Americans and the Mexicans tended to live apart, to go their separate ways. The American women claimed to be shocked and incensed that Mexican children were allowed to run through the streets naked. They refused to allow their children to play with them.

Only rarely did the two cultures overlap. At first Corrie was appalled by the hot, spicy dishes prepared by the Ibarra servants: eggs swimming in mouth-numbing hot sauces, beans cooked with eye-watering jalapeños, meats basted tender with chiles. But within weeks Corrie found herself acclimated, and her once-favorite Southern dishes soon seemed bland and tasteless.

Yet even her love for San Antonio could not lift her out of the melancholy that seized her at times. Prue blamed her dark moods on her pregnancy. Corrie knew it was more.

She wanted to share her new life, to blend San Antonio and her pregnancy into her marriage.

But Tad was forever elsewhere. During the days he was constantly on the move, meeting with clients, supervising work on the new house, going upriver to make sure Whit was carrying out his orders properly. In the evenings he labored over the old documents in his office until midnight and after. Often he was gone overnight with the surveyors, clearing land titles for himself, or for his lawyer friends in East Texas.

During the days and nights when he was out on a survey Corrie worried so that she found it impossible to sleep. The Mexicans said sixty people had been killed by Indians within the last year, and that twenty-six of them were surveyors.

Tad's work seemed to have no end. Mail from the east was infrequent, dependent as it was on the courage and luck of the mail rider. So far no letter had arrived from home. But each packet that reached Béxar brought more work for Tad.

As the weeks went by, a conviction grew in Corrie that somehow she must stop this deterioration in her marriage.

When Tad entered the house well after midnight, Corrie was still awake. He came down the hall and fell into bed fully clothed, totally exhausted. Corrie rose, lit a lamp, and stood over him. "Tad, you're killing yourself. Why? What is it you want that you must turn yourself into a corpse? Certainly nothing we need."

He looked at her blankly, as if she were speaking in a language unknown to him. "Let's not go into it tonight."

"I don't know of a better time. Look at you! So tired, you can hardly talk. Why? I want to know! What is worth this?"

He shook his head slowly from side to side. "Corrie, during the last three days I've located some of the best land in this country. Maybe on this continent. It won't be available forever. More land speculators are arriving every day. Soon the choice parcels will be gone. Don't you see? I must act on it *now*."

"Is it worth ruining your health? Losing your life? Tad, I die a thousand deaths every time you go out with Captain Hays. I know how many of his surveyors have been killed. What good will the land be if I'm widowed? Don't you have any consideration for me? For your child?"

Corrie burst into tears.

Tad rose from the bed and held her in his arms. "Corrie, listen. This is something I must do. Don't you see? Conditions will change soon. We'll have a home. We'll be growing crops. We'll have a rancho. The demands of my law practice will ease. We'll have time to enjoy what we've earned."

"But time is passing now," Corrie managed to say. "A new life is growing within me. That's something we should share."

"And we do," Tad said. He tipped her face upward and kissed away her tears. "Soon we'll have more time together. I promise."

His exhaustion was so plain, Corrie did not have the heart to argue further. He lay back on the bed. Within a minute he had sunk into sound sleep.

Corrie sat on the bed and held his hand.

She knew Tad truly believed the promise he had just made.

PART TWO

San Antonio de Béxar

I shall not mention the thousand and one incidents which happened in connection with the Comanches in and about San Antonio from 1838 until 1842, when we became refugees.
Mary A. Maverick
Memoirs

8

Corrie backed to the far wall and examined the bedroom critically. Although they now had been in their new home three months, she was not yet finished with the interior. She had saved this back bedroom until last.

She was spreading the drapes experimentally when Prue came rushing into the room, giggling in anticipation. "Corrie! Do I have news for you! You'll never believe it!"

Prue waved a letter. "Ramsey Cothburn has sold Osborne! He's moving to Texas!"

Corrie looked up, irritated. She was certain Prue was playing a prank. "Don't clown. I must get these drapes up."

Prue giggled. "But it's true! I swear. Read it!"

Corrie sank awkwardly into a chair. Three months to go, and already she was having trouble with balance.

The first few lines of the letter were convincing. The wealth of detail was beyond the capacity of Prue's friend to invent. Old Man Wetherill had bought Osborne. Anthony Wharton had purchased the slaves. The names were listed. Corrie remembered some, especially the house servants, who had almost become her own.

How could Ramsey bear to part with them? Corrie read back over the letter and found an item that had escaped her notice: Ramsey planned to leave the following Monday on a packet from Charleston, bound for Texas by way of New Orleans. Corrie checked the date of the letter: it was five weeks old!

If the information was valid, Ramsey was now in Texas!

Corrie read back over the letter once more. Prue could not stop giggling. Corrie returned the letter. "Prue, stop it! This is not something to be joked about. Someday you'll understand. Ramsey is a good friend. But chances are we'll never see him again. Texas is—"

"A big place," Prue finished. "How well I know. But aren't you intrigued?"

Corrie did not answer. What *was* Ramsey doing in Texas, so far out of his element?

She was tempted to sober Prue with the long letter she had received recently from their mother. Corrie had demanded more specific information. She had almost memorized the reply:

> Day to day, I see no change, but the truth is that I am steadily going downhill. The doctor has said it is only a matter of time. Now I am usually bedridden. Only occasionally do I feel well enough to sit in my chair for a while. Your father is beside himself with worry, but there is nothing I can do to ease his pain.

Once again Corrie stopped on the verge of telling her, knowing Prue would weep and wail for days, begging to go home. Under the circumstances that was out of the question.

"Prue, go fetch Hattie," she ordered. "Have her bring nails and a hammer. Unless the world stops turning, we'll at least get these drapes hung today."

Prue did not protest, but headed toward the long room, where Hattie was cleaning and polishing furniture.

Corrie arranged a wooden box by the window and climbed upon it. She experimented with the hooks and was ready when Prue and Hattie returned with the hammer and nails.

Corrie nailed the hooks to the window frame. Prue helped her thread the drapery onto the rod. As Corrie lifted all into place, the bells of San Fernando a block away began to sound.

Corrie was puzzled. It did not seem time for vespers.

"They ringing early, Miss Corrie," Hattie said.

"They're sounding some kind of an alarm," Corrie said. "Prue, go see what's happening."

While Prue was gone Corrie changed into shoes more suitable for the street. She grabbed a shawl and hurried into the front yard.

Prue came running back breathless. "Comanches!" she said. "Just outside town! They've stolen the Rivas horses and taken the little Rivas boy captive. The one they call Pablito."

Corrie was aghast. The boy was the nephew of her cook, Consuelo. Corrie had talked with him often, teased him. He was only five years old and she shuddered to think of him in the hands of the Comanches.

Behind her, Hattie began to moan.

"Hattie, hush!" Corrie said. "We're safe here. Mister Tad will be in from the fields in a minute. Go out to the kitchen and pack cornbread, whatever you can find for him. Hurry now!"

As a member of the Volunteer Rangers, Tad kept a good horse stabled close to the house day and night. His saddlebags were always packed with jerky and provisions for ten days. But surely cornbread and whatever fresh food Hattie could find would be welcome.

The Rangers were assembling in the Main Plaza, less than a block away. Corrie recognized Jack Hays, Ben McCulloch, Mat "Old Paint" Caldwell, and Sam Maverick.

Corrie heard Tad coming before he rode into view. He emerged from the trees below the house. Jack led Midnight out of the barn already saddled. The bells ceased to ring.

Corrie ran out and caught the reins of his bay. "Tad, they've taken the little Rivas boy."

Jack led Midnight to the front of the house at a trot and tossed Tad a bundle of clothing. Tad hung his sombrero and pistol belt over the saddle horn and wrestled into his big, floppy serape. "How did it happen?"

Corrie looked at Prue.

"Pablito and Manuel went out to bring in the horses," Prue said. "The Indians scooped up Pablito and ran off with the horses. Manuel jumped into brush along the river and escaped."

"How many Indians?" Tad asked.

"Manuel said about twenty."

Tad pulled on his leggings, adjusted them, and put on his sombrero. He took out his guns and checked the loads. "Jack, this may be a trick to lure the Rangers out of town. Take the bay. Go tell

Whit to bring everybody in and keep them close to the house. Won't hurt if they miss a few days' work."

"Marsh Tad, let me go with you," Jack said. "I can go tell Marsh Whit that, then catch you."

"No, Jack."

"Damn it, why not, Marsh Tad?"

"Because I don't want you going out and getting killed."

"What I had in mind, Marsh Tad, was seeing *you* don't get killed. Let me go along. That bay's got bottom. I can keep up."

"Jack, I'm not going to argue about it. It's my place to go. It's your place to stay here and look after Miss Corrie, Miss Prue, and Master Whit. Now, do as I tell you!"

Tears came to Jack's eyes. Corrie stood marveling over the exchange. Sometimes they acted like brothers.

Tad checked his saddle wallet for ammunition, supplies. Hattie brought food wrapped in a cloth. Tad thanked her, rolled the bundle into his blanket, and tied it behind his saddle. Shouts came from the plaza, telling him to hurry.

He swung into the saddle and looked down at Corrie. With his huge sombrero, belted serape, leather leggings, and large-roweled spurs, he looked like a Mexican bandit. A chill swept up Corrie's spine with the thought that within hours he might be fighting for his life.

"I don't know how long we'll be gone," he said. "With Whit, Jack, and the men close to the house, you'll be safe. I'll get back as soon as I can."

Corrie gave him a smile she did not feel. "Just bring back little Pablito," she said.

He wheeled Midnight and loped toward the plaza. Within a minute the Ranger troop was in motion, heading northward out of town. Soon the sound of hooves faded in the distance.

Jack still had tears rolling down his cheeks.

Corrie felt sudden empathy. "Don't worry, Jack," she said. "Master Tad can take care of himself."

Jack shook his head. "I *know* him, Miss Corrie. He's so bad to lose his temper. When he gets to fighting he's got no quitting sense. I ought to be there to look after him."

Corrie also was worried about Whit and the Negroes. "Jack, maybe you'd better go on and bring in Master Whit."

He nodded, mounted the bay, and rode off to the north. Corrie led Prue and Hattie back into the house.

"Hattie, lay out that dark muslin dress," Corrie said. "The one with the embroidery. I'll go call on the Rivas family."

Hattie looked at her wide eyed. "Miss Corrie, none of the white people go calling down there."

"Maybe it's time someone did," Corrie said.

"**I** wish he'd let me go with him," Whit said. "I can shoot as well as any of them. It isn't fair."

Corrie turned up the lamp. Tad had been gone ten days and her evenings, with Tad away, had fallen into a routine. After supper, Whit brought his books into the long room to study, while she drilled herself on Spanish grammar.

"Someone must keep the work going forward," she said. "Tad trusts you with that."

Whit shook his head. "Newt is better at getting work out of the Negroes. They're scared of him. Jack knows more about the crops. I've never paid much attention to them. Frank always took care of Donegal."

In the last few evenings, Corrie and Whit had developed a deeper level of intimacy. They both tended to be night owls. Hattie usually retired early. Prue wrote letters until she became sleepy, then went to bed.

"Tad tries to keep me in a box," Whit went on. "He won't let me do a thing on my own."

"He wants you to learn. He's been giving you more and more responsibility, experience you can use throughout your life."

Whit winced. "Corrie, I don't want to be a planter. I didn't want to be one in Georgia. I don't want to be one here."

"What do you want to do? Whatever you choose, I'm sure Tad will support you."

"I don't know," Whit said. The room was still, but from the open windows came the faint music of a fandango. Whit shrugged.

"I just want to get out, look around, and *find* what I want to do. I can't. When I said I wanted to go out with Captain Hays and learn surveying, Tad wouldn't even think about it."

"That's because the work is so dangerous. Tad wants to keep you safe, until you're older."

"I'll be seventeen next May. John Coffee Hays began work as a chain man in Mississippi at fifteen. He learned in the field." Whit pointed to his books. "These were written for surveying an English countryside, not Texas leagues and labors. With Hays, I could learn more in a week."

"Whit, Tad loves you. He doesn't want you killed."

Whit laughed without humor. "Learning how to take care of myself is a part of it."

Corrie did not answer. Whit had a valid point. On this barbaric frontier, surely every man should be schooled early.

"I threatened to run away from home back in Georgia," Whit said. "Now it looks like I'll have to run away from Tad."

Corrie touched his arm. "No, Whit. You'll never have to leave your home here. When you have differences with Tad, maybe I can help. I don't want there ever to be trouble between you and Tad."

Whit looked at her for a long moment, but said no more.

Not until later did Corrie wonder if she had made a promise she could not fulfill.

Corrie was working on a piece of embroidery in the long room when Jack came in the back door. "They're back, Miss Corrie," he called. "They're riding in now."

Most women in her condition would not have gone out in public. But Corrie did not care. She grabbed a shawl and hurried with Jack to the Main Plaza.

Most of the town had gathered. All of the Volunteers had dismounted except Tad, who still sat in the saddle, leaning forward, talking to Consuelo. From Consuelo's tears, Corrie concluded that the Volunteers had not recovered her nephew.

Corrie's relief on seeing Tad was so great she felt dizzy. Not until one of the horses moved did she see that his right leg was caked with dried blood from hip to knee.

"He's hurt, Miss Corrie," Jack said. He pushed their way through the horses until they reached Tad's side.

Tad looked down at her, his expression solemn. "We didn't get the boy, Corrie. But we taught them a lesson."

Close to tears, Corrie reached for and held Tad's wrist. "We've all been so worried." She looked at his leg. "Jack, go fetch Dr. Weideman."

Tad's eyes were sunken and from his face alone she could see he had lost more weight. "No," he said. "Don't get the doctor. Just help me get to bed. That's all I need. A few hours sleep. I haven't had any to speak of since we left."

At the house, Whit helped Jack ease Tad from the saddle. With an arm around each, Tad used his good leg to make his way into the house and into the back bedroom.

"What did that, Marsh Tad?" Jack asked. "An arrer?"

"A squaw with a knife," Tad said. "It's a clean wound. Didn't hit bone."

Corrie left the three in the room so Whit and Jack could strip Tad, although she was uncertain whose modesty was being preserved. She and Hattie assembled clean towels, whiskey, alum, rhubarb, and a slippery-elm poultice. When she returned to the bedroom, Jack had turned back the blanket, exposing the wound. The vicious cut was surrounded by a dark bruise.

"That looks bad, Marsh Tad," Jack said.

He bathed the wound in whiskey and carefully cleaned it with a cloth. Tad stirred and reached for the bottle. "Jack, damn your worthless hide. You're wasting good whiskey. That'll do more good internally." He turned up the bottle and drank.

Jack and Whit laughed. "You're not hurt too bad," Jack said.

"How many Comanches y'all get?" Whit asked.

Tad grimaced from the raw whiskey. "Twelve, maybe sixteen. We disagreed on the number."

Corrie wanted to ask about the squaw who had stabbed him. But she was afraid of the answer.

"How come you were out so long?" Whit asked.

Tad's eyes were again closed. He spoke sleepily. "Trails kept splitting on us. Finally we lost them altogether. Most of the men wanted to go on north, see what we could stir up, so we did. We hit a camp, mostly women, children, old warriors. We burned it, figuring the smoke would bring the braves in. It did. They kept us pinned down four days. It was no picnic."

Corrie did not want to disturb him further, but she felt driven to ask, "Did you see the little Rivas boy at all?"

Tad shook his head without opening his eyes. "We saw four captives from a distance. He wasn't among them."

Jack applied the slippery-elm poultice and bandaged the leg. As he worked, Tad's breathing became deep and regular. Jack motioned to Whit. They quietly slipped from the room.

Corrie followed. But she found she could not bear to leave Tad untended. She returned to the bedroom, sat in a chair, and watched him sleep, yielding to a warm sense of closeness.

As the night deepened, she changed into her nightgown and eased onto the bed beside him.

Unexpectedly she felt life stir within her. She badly wanted to share the moment with Tad, yet she did not want to awaken him. The movements came again, stronger, then ceased. Corrie lay quietly while her husband and baby slept.

She thought of the terrors the Rivas boy must be enduring, and sent up a heartfelt prayer for him.

She could not subdue a nagging fear. She was bringing a child into the world in a place where no family was safe.

Would her own child suffer the Rivas boy's fate in five years time?

Was he destined to grow up following in his father's footsteps, risking his life against the Indians time after time?

After a long trip to San Patricio on the Nueces, clearing up one of many *derechos*, Tad arrived back in Béxar. On a whim he rode by the Alamo.

The ruins lay pale white under a full moon. The chapel that had served two armies as a fort stood shorn of its roof and frontispiece, yet somehow retained a certain dignity in its rough stones and ornately carved doorway. Tad dismounted, feeling a twinge of pain from his thigh. He sat on low stones and contemplated the ruins.

The sight never failed to fill him with a profound sadness. Here so many of his friends had died. Jim Bowie. Albert Martin. Jim Bonham. George Kimbell. William Travis. Tom Miller. Bill and John King. The list was long. Some he had known well. He had fought beside them, sharing blankets, drinks, women. Some he had met as friendly foes in court.

Faces came unbidden from memory. He felt shackled to them forever. But for an unshod horse, swollen streams, and vast distances, his ashes would now have been lying somewhere near where he sat.

Here in the silence of the Alamo, Tad could not escape the impression that he had been spared for a purpose. He felt a tremendous responsibility to carry on for his dead friends.

Fighting Comanches and Mexicans as a single man was jeopardy enough. Now, with a wife, and a child on the way, the hazard was becoming intolerable.

He remounted and forded the river. He was tired, but he always went to check on his mail before going home to bed.

As he had expected, a fresh stack of correspondence lay on his desk. He shuffled through it, then opened the fattest, a long letter from his friend Adolphus Sterne in Nacogdoches.

In hurried phrases, Sterne told how he and others in East Texas had become convinced that the Cherokees were plotting with Vicente Córdova and other Mexican spies to overthrow the Republic.

He said he, Tom Rusk, and five hundred other East Texans had marched on the Cherokees, and in a series of battles driven them out of Texas. Sterne described the battles and pursuit. He said that he himself had commanded a company of cavalry, and that more than a hundred Cherokees had been killed.

Tad stopped reading, deeply troubled. Those lands had been granted to the Cherokees by the Spanish and Mexican governments, and later by the Texas Republic. As a lawyer, Tad could not condone the ouster of the Indians, much less their deaths.

He remembered Sam Houston's dire warning: If the Texas Cherokees were removed, other tribes would be forewarned, and Indian battles would prevail for the next thirty years.

Sterne concluded the letter with some gossip. Sam Houston's enemies said he had fallen off the wagon, and had hardly drawn a sober breath in Tennessee. Other intelligence cast doubt on this report, Sterne wrote. Sam Houston had won the heart of an Alabama beauty half his age and soon would marry.

Greatly disturbed, Tad tossed the letter aside. The Republic was in a crisis. All his accomplishments were being undermined, right at the point when he was well on his way to achieving his dreams.

His small plantation above town was nearing harvest. Soon he would have sufficient grains to feed his livestock through the coming year. His cotton had bloomed, and was making bolls. He must now find a way to gin the harvest and transport the bales to Brazoria for shipment.

The town house was completed. Downstream, between the Atascosa and San Antonio rivers, he held certificates on ten leagues of land—more than forty thousand acres. He was moving forward on clearing the titles. He must yet brand the thousands of wild cattle on the land before they strayed elsewhere.

His law practice had mushroomed all out of proportion to his expectations. Just the legal work on his desk at the moment would keep him busy through the coming year.

Yet, if the looming troubles of the Republic continued, he could lose all. He simply must find a solution.

In recent months Sam Houston, Mirabeau Lamar, Tom Rusk, and others had written, renewing their pleas for him to run for Congress. They pointed out that he had trained in United States and English law, and practiced in Mexican courts. They said his help was needed to put together a workable judicial system for the Republic. He had considered the requests seriously, but felt he could not possibly go off to Congress at the expense of his crops, land, and family.

But now he was forced to reconsider.

President Lamar's term in office would continue another two and a half years. If his present Indian policies continued, Tad would be spending much of his time chasing Indians.

He could not erase from his mind the face of the squaw who had stabbed him on that last foray. In the Rangers' charge on the village, she emerged from a clump of bushes with knife upheld. As she plunged the blade into him, he shot her in the face. In that instant, her features were burned into his brain forever.

She had been a handsome woman. Her attack had been fierce, like that of any mother protecting her young. Even in his pain Tad had felt empathy with her.

He believed there must be a better way of dealing with the Indians. He did not want his sons battling them twenty years in the future. Perhaps the solution lay in Congress.

Turning up his desk lamp, he gathered his writing material.

The first letter he addressed to Sam Houston. He conveyed his sincere congratulations on Houston's impending marriage. He then offered his assessment that public opinion in Béxar was evenly mixed on Lamar's Indian removal policy. He added his own personal view that the recent war against the Cherokees in East Texas would inflame the Comanches to commit further depredations.

He described the many private reports he had received indicating a buildup of Mexican troops south of the Rio Grande.

Choosing his words carefully, he revealed his decision to stand for Congress, in hopes of helping to establish peace with the Indians, a better judicial system, and a workable relationship with Mexico. He asked for Houston's assistance in securing the congressional seat.

The second letter he addressed to President Lamar at the new Capitol in Austin. He began with a description of the perilous situation the Comanches posed in Béxar. He listed the thirty-six individuals killed or taken captive during the last five months. Again choosing his words with care, he proposed that a well-defined Indian *peace* policy, firmly enforced, might best serve the Republic. He offered such a plan in detail, proposing certain concessions for the return of all captives.

He added his information on the buildup of troops in northern Mexico, ostensibly to control liberal insurrectionists, but possibly to invade Texas.

He concluded by revealing that he had decided to stand for

Congress, adding that if he were successful, he anticipated he and Lamar would work well together on many issues.

He signed and sealed the letters. Tomorrow he would send them on their way. He was not certain of their effect on the recipients. But at least he had not stood idly by and done nothing while his country, his family, his property, and his dreams were destroyed.

In the heat of August, Corrie's pregnancy became difficult to endure. She slept fitfully, and was often nauseated. Hattie spent hours bathing her with wet cloths. Consuelo prepared special delicacies to tempt her into eating. Through the long afternoons Prue read to her from the novels and dated newspapers that passed around the small community of Americans.

She saw little of Tad. His crops were approaching harvest and he spent much of his time in the fields. Often he was gone for days, clearing land titles.

So on a day in late August, when Tad came into the house in midafternoon, Corrie knew immediately something was wrong. He stood in the entryway, holding a bundle of mail. On top lay a letter edged in black. He held it out to her in silence.

Corrie felt a moment of giddiness. She took the letter and carried it to a chair. With the drapes drawn, the lighting was inadequate, but she could make out her father's neat hand:

Dear Cornelia and Pruella,
My heart breaks under the sad duty of conveying word to you that your mother passed from this world on Thursday evening last, a short while after sunset. She went easily, without complaint. Daughters, I truly believe she suffered no pain. We buried her yesterday afternoon, next to your grandmother and grandfather McNair. I cannot bring myself to write more. I only hope you may find solace in God's grace, as I must do.

Your loving father

Corrie searched for the date on the letter.

July 17, 1839.

Her mother had been in the ground four weeks, while this pitiful letter made its way across the country.

Strangely, Corrie felt nothing. She had wept scores of times through the months in anticipation of the letter. Now, with the letter in hand, tears seemed futile. Already she was thinking ahead to the ordeal of telling Prue.

Tad stood beside her, a hand on her shoulder. "Are you all right?"

She nodded and brushed away a lone tear, still surprised there were not more. "Father said she didn't suffer. I know she did. She just kept it from him. But now she's beyond pain."

A door opened at the back of the house. A moment later Prue burst into the long room, her face alive with excitement. "Consuelo said the mail rider came. Do I have any letters?"

She looked at Tad expectantly. Corrie reached for her hand. "I'm sure you have letters. But please sit down. Prepare yourself. We have terrible news."

Prue looked at her blankly and sank into a chair.

"We have a letter from Father." Corrie paused. She could not find a way to soften what she had to say. "Mother passed away a month ago."

Corrie held out the letter. Prue stared at the black edging. Her face drained of color. Her mouth worked ineffectively until she found voice. "How?" she asked. "Why?"

Corrie held on to her hand. "You knew she wasn't in good health. A year ago, she discovered a growth in her abdomen. The doctors told her then that there was no hope."

Prue unfolded the single page. Tad crossed to the window and opened the drapes to give her light.

Scanning through the letter, Prue showed no sign of comprehension. After a moment she looked up at Corrie. "You knew! All this time, you knew! Why didn't you tell me?"

"Mother didn't want you to know," Corrie explained. "She was afraid that if you knew, you wouldn't come with me to Texas."

Prue looked up at Tad, then back to Corrie. "Then this isn't a visit! You've brought me here to stay! It was all a charade!"

Corrie tightened her grip on Prue's hand.

Prue pulled away. "You tricked me! Your own sister!" Tears were streaming down her face.

Corrie felt that Prue was lashing out blindly. Still, the accusation hurt. "Prue, Mother swore me to secrecy. She thought that keeping it from you was the best course. I didn't have the heart to disagree. We were all trying to spare you."

Prue choked on her own words. "Well, thanks a lot! It would seem you could have at least given me a hint."

"If I had, then you would have suffered through every day with her, just as I did," Corrie snapped back.

"It was my right to do so!" Prue said. "It was cruel of you to keep it from me. I'm not sure I'll ever want to talk to you again." She looked up at Tad, rose and walked toward her bedroom, carrying the letter.

Corrie waited until the door closed behind her. "Maybe I should have told her," she said. "I thought it best not to."

"You and your mother were keeping it from a child," Tad said. "But that was no child who just left this room."

Tad's perception sometimes took Corrie by surprise. Prue was fast turning into a woman.

"Corrie, if you don't need me, I'd best be getting back to the office."

Corrie needed him. Badly. But she could not bring herself to beg him. "The only ordeal now is to tell Hattie," she said.

After Tad left, Corrie sat alone in the long room. Further tears would not come. It was as if she were depleted of emotion, and had no more grief to give.

She heard Hattie bringing in the laundry from the line. She raised her voice. "Hattie, come in here a moment."

Hattie hurried to her. "You need something, Miss Corrie?"

"Not now, thank you," Corrie said. "But I'm afraid I have bad news. I know you think a great deal of Mother. Miss Prue and I just received a letter from Father. Mother has passed away."

Hattie remained motionless, eyes widening. She could not absorb what Corrie was telling her. "Miss Sarah?"

Corrie nodded. "Yes, Hattie."

Hattie sank to the floor, weeping. "Hattie. There's nothing we can do for her now," Corrie said.

Hattie continued to sob. Despite her awkwardness, Corrie helped Hattie into a chair and hugged her.

"Oh, Miss Corrie, I love her so," Hattie said between sobs. "Miss Sarah took me in, *taught* me. She like my own mother."

"I know, Hattie. I know."

Hattie's uninhibited emotions triggered Corrie's own. After helping Hattie to her L-shaped room just off the patio, Corrie went to her own room, closed the door, and wept until she was exhausted. Afterward she slept.

Hours later she awakened to a gentle knock at her door. Prue came in and sat on the edge of the bed. Night had not yet fallen, but the heavy drapes cast the room into semidarkness.

Prue's voice was hoarse. "Corrie, I'm not taking back a single word. I won't apologize. I'm still furious with you."

Corrie lay without moving. "I don't expect an apology. Maybe I handled it badly. I don't know."

"What's going to happen to me, Corrie?"

Corrie did not understand. "Happen?"

"You had two years at Miss Lillian's. Do you see anything in Béxar resembling a finishing school? You made your bow in Savannah, had your pick of dozens of polished gentlemen. Where will I make my bow? At some fandango? Who'll be my suitors? Hays's Rangers, with their beards, buckskins, and spurs?"

"Béxar won't always be this way," Corrie said.

"Then when will it change? When I'm old and wrinkled? Look around you, Corrie. What prospects do I have?"

Corrie hardly knew what to say. She spoke the first thought that came to mind. "Outward appearances aren't everything. There are quite a number of educated, decent young men in Béxar."

"Name one. Just one! They're all adventurers, passing through. Here today, gone tomorrow. Full of big schemes that will never work out. I've seen them, heard them talking in the plaza. I haven't found a man in Béxar that even comes close to measuring up to Ramsey Cothburn."

Corrie remained silent. Was Prue saying she had made a mistake in jilting Ramsey for Tad? Corrie did not want to ask.

"What about Moultrie Hill?" Prue asked. "Will we inherit when Father's gone?"

"Prue, I'm not familiar with the specifics. But it's my impression that the indebtedness just about matches the value. We may inherit some. But not much."

"Then I'll have no dowry," Prue said. "There'll be no icing on this cake."

Corrie rolled over and faced her in the gloom. "Prue, you're turning into a beautiful woman. You're intelligent, a very likable person. Men will find you very desirable."

Prue laughed. "I'm skinny. My nose is too long. My ears stick out. I have freckles. I can't do anything with my hair. And I'm like that poor girl in the Song of Solomon, who 'hath no breasts.' Surely you remember the next line, 'What shall we do for our sister in the day when she shall be spoken for?' "

"You're too impatient," Corrie said. "I matured late. It seemed to take forever. Your day will come."

"You really think so?"

"I know so. One or two years will bring many changes."

"What if Béxar doesn't improve?" Prue asked after a moment. "What if I have no prospects for happiness out here? Will there be any way I can go back to South Carolina?"

Corrie thought the matter through. It was a reasonable request. She had no inkling whether her father would be able to help, or what Tad's attitude would be. But perhaps she could find a solution. She and Prue still had close and well-placed relatives in Savannah. Perhaps a promise was in order.

"Prue, if you want, when the time comes, we'll find a way for you to make your bow in greener pastures."

Two weeks later the summer heat abated. In the last week of September came the first hint of fall.

On a Sunday evening Corrie went into labor. Tad sent for Dr. Weideman. But he arrived too late.

With Consuelo and Hattie in attendance, the baby was born in the early hours of Monday morning, and was promptly named James Bowie McNair Logan, in honor of Tad's companion at the Battle of Concepción, who later died in the Alamo.

Hattie prepared Corrie and the baby for Tad's first viewing. He came into the room strangely unsure of himself. Hattie seated him in a cane-bottom chair and handed him his son.

Grinning his delight, he laughed as Jim Bowie's tiny infant fist tentatively grasped his huge forefinger. Corrie knew it was a picture she would always remember—Tad's proud first moments with his newborn son.

In the days that followed, Tad's visits became a ritual. Every evening he spent time holding and playing with Jim Bowie. Those hours brought Corrie intense pleasure. They were living proof that she truly had started her own family.

--- 9 ---

"I'm going," Prue insisted. "This may be my only chance to see a band of Comanches up close and live to tell the tale."

Corrie was fearful, but she conceded it might be a once in a lifetime opportunity. Moreover, if the newspapers were to be believed, her husband was largely responsible for the peace conference in progress on the Main Plaza. This was the third day and today the Indians were to bring in captives. Hopes were high the Rivas boy might be among them. "All right, I'll go with you," she said. "Hattie, why don't you take Jim Bowie out onto the patio for some air while we're gone? It's such a beautiful day."

"Miss Corrie, I don't want to be here by myself!"

"You won't be," Corrie told her. "Master Tad will be right in the next room. Miss Prue and I will be gone only a few minutes."

Corrie and Prue put on hats and shawls and walked to the Main Plaza. Soldiers from the newly mobilized army garrison were on guard. A large crowd had gathered, and most of the men were armed.

Corrie and Prue joined a group of women gathered in Mrs. Higginbotham's front yard, behind a white picket fence directly across the street from the building where the meetings were being conducted.

After a few minutes conversations around them abruptly ceased. Corrie stood on tiptoe and peered to the east. The Indians came toward the Main Plaza at a stately pace, the chiefs and warriors in front, the women behind. Every man held a long lance tipped with feathers. On one arm each carried an ornately decorated war shield. The eagle feathers of their headdresses rippled in the slight breeze.

168

Brilliant paint, gleaming bone breastplates, a loin cloth, and mocca-
sins were their only covering.

Prue whispered in Corrie's ear. "Did you ever see anything so
magnificent in your whole life?"

The Indians passed in complete silence, save for the soft drumming of unshod hooves.

Corrie was especially struck by the regal demeanor of a fierce old
chief who rode at the head of the procession. His skin was deeply
wrinkled, and he conveyed dignity and authority beyond measure.
He looked down at the Anglo women with the cold eyes of a bird of
prey. Corrie felt a chill as his gaze lingered for a moment on her.

"That's Muguara," Mary Maverick whispered.

The squaws, trailing behind the men, were almost devoid of
adornments. They wore their hair long and flowing. Only beads and
paint lent a dash of color to their deerskin dresses.

The chiefs halted in front of the Council House. Generals
McLeod and Cooke came out to receive them. On the plaza, Tom
Howard's company of troops stood at attention. The generals es-
corted the chiefs and a number of warriors into the Council House.
The Indian women, a few children, and the younger warriors seated
themselves on the Council House steps to wait. Mathew "Old
Paint" Caldwell, George Cayce, and several other Texians began to
talk with them in sign language and broken Spanish. Soon a game
started. Cayce wedged coins into cracks in the front of the Council
House. The young warriors backed off and shot arrows at them.

Corrie had dallied longer than she intended. "We should be
getting back home," she told Prue.

They walked toward home, and were only a few steps from the
front gate when the first scream came from the Council House. The
sound was followed instantly by a sustained roar of gunfire.

Corrie looked back. George Cayce stood in front of the Council
House, pierced through the chest by an arrow. He staggered and fell.
Old Paint Caldwell grappled with a young Indian. As Corrie
watched spellbound, Caldwell twisted the pistol from the Indian's
hands and shot him. The Indian fell at Caldwell's feet.

Indians came pouring out of the Council House. Tom Howard's
troops fired into them. Many fell. Others came on, running.

Belatedly Corrie saw that six Indians were running straight toward her.

She grabbed Prue by the arm. "Quick! Into the house!"

They hurried through the front gate. Corrie slammed and latched it, idiotically thinking it would stop the Indians. But the first one leapt the gate, landing on top of her, knocking her aside so violently she went sprawling into the rosebushes.

Then, to her absolute horror, he grabbed Prue by the wrist and dragged her toward the corner of the house. Prue resisted, digging in with her heels, striking at him with her free hand.

Corrie screamed and ran at the Indian, clawing for his eyes. But he was as tall as Tad, and tremendously strong. Looking at her with calm eyes, he held her off with a forearm. Without changing expression he tossed Prue away and hit Corrie in the left side of her face, knocking her flat.

At that moment Tad came out the front door, pistol in hand. In one smooth motion he brought the gun up and fired twice. The Indian fell backward and lay gushing blood from his throat.

"Get in the house!" Tad shouted. "Both of you!"

Corrie started to obey. But other Indians had jumped the fence and were running past.

"The baby!" she yelled to Tad. She ran along the east side of the house to the back, following the Indians onto the patio.

Hattie stood between an Indian and the bassinet. She held a big paving stone from the patio high over her head. "Git!" she shouted at the Indian. "You git!"

Hattie did not seem to understand that she was blocking the Indian's way. He danced cautiously around her, out of her throwing range, and ran on. Whit's bay saddle mare stood tied in front of the carriage house. The Indian raced toward it. Just as he leapt into the saddle Whit came out the back door and shot him. The Indian fell off the horse and tumbled against the side of the carriage house. There he lay still. The mare shied in fright, but the reins held.

Other Indians were running in the distance, heading toward the river. Whit raised his pistol and aimed at one Corrie thought too far away. But Whit fired and an instant later the Indian dropped.

Prue arrived at Corrie's side in time to see the Whit's feat of marksmanship. "Some shooting!" she said.

Corrie hurried to the baby. He lay awake, smiling up at her, oblivious to the danger.

Hattie still stood with the stone over her head. All strength had left her. She did not know how to set the stone down. Corrie went to help her. Together they lowered it.

Whit ran to his mare, swung into the saddle, and rode off just as Tad came out the back door.

"Whit!" Tad yelled. "Come back!"

Whit raced on, chasing the fleeing Indians.

Tad ran to the carriage house, opened the stable door, and hurriedly saddled Midnight. Corrie picked up the baby and waited until Tad led the horse out onto the patio.

"What happened?" he asked.

"I don't know," Corrie said. "There was a scream, then shooting, and suddenly there were Indians everywhere."

Tad cupped her face in his palm and examined where the Indian had hit her. In the excitement Corrie had forgotten about it. "Doesn't look bad," he said. "But you may have a shiner."

He stepped into the saddle and glanced toward the plaza. "Apparently it's all over. The shooting has stopped. Go into the house and bolt the doors. After a while, send Hattie or Prue to the plaza to tell Captain Fisher you need two or three soldiers here for protection. I've got to go and alert Jack and all our hands. They're in the upper field. They may not have heard the gunfire."

He put spurs to his horse and rode off. As he reached the corner of the horse pasture, Sam Maverick, his brother-in-law Andrew, and several other riders joined him.

Corrie started for the house with the baby. But Prue grabbed her by the arm. "That one's still alive!"

She pointed to the Indian beside the carriage house. Even from the patio Corrie saw the Indian's chest heaving. She put Jim Bowie back into his bassinet and walked closer to the Indian. He looked up at her, scurried backward a few feet like a crab, and pulled a knife. Hattie screamed.

Prue hurried to Corrie's side. "What'll we do?"

Frothy red bubbles flowed from a wound in the Indian's chest. He lay motionless, knife in hand, looking at her.

Hattie brought the double ax from the woodpile behind the kitchen. "I could hit him, Miss Corrie. I could kill him like a chicken."

"No, don't," Corrie said. "Let's leave him be. He's dying."

The Indian was young, no more than eighteen.

Prue touched Corrie's arm. "Let's get the soldiers."

"No," Corrie said. "They'd kill him." She felt only pity as the man struggled for life. "I wish we could help him."

She knelt close to the Indian. He raised the knife.

"I better hit him, Miss Corrie," Hattie said.

"No," Corrie said again. She was sure the Indian was too weak to be of any danger. His gaze moved from Corrie to the ax, and back. She leaned closer. "Water?" she asked. "¿Quiere agua?"

Comprehension came into his eyes. His free hand moved, rolling from palm-down to palm-up in a negative gesture. His mouth worked. Blood rolled down his chin. "Yo ya me muero," he said. Now I am dying.

Corrie placed her hand over his. He did not resist, or give any indication he noticed. "Tenemos confiar en Dios," she told him. We have to trust in God.

"I'm not at all sure they have one," Prue said.

"They do," Corrie said. "Maybe even the same one."

The Indian began a repetitious chant.

"I guess that's his death song," Prue said.

The Indian's voice was weak, but he continued until pain overrode his stoicism. He grimaced, and stopped. A shudder passed through his body. Corrie felt it. A moment later he ceased breathing. His eyes remained open.

"He's dead," Corrie said, rising. "Hattie, get that old blue blanket in the back of the carriage house, behind the landau. Throw it over him."

"Corrie, we shouldn't be here by ourselves," Prue said, looking at the dead man. "We don't know what's happened."

Corrie thought Prue's advice was sound. "We'll all walk over to the plaza. If you'll stay with Jim Bowie a moment, I'll go get a pistol."

She went into the house and retrieved the pepperbox revolver from her bureau drawer. Gathering several clean diapers, she put them in a bag, placed the pistol on top, and returned to the patio.

"Miss Corrie, I'm not staying here by myself!" Hattie said.

"Of course not," Corrie reassured her. "Bring the baby."

They walked down the drive. In the front yard Dr. Weideman was kneeling over the body of the Indian Tad had shot. At first Corrie thought the doctor was trying to revive the Indian. But then she saw that he was merely examining the body.

He looked up at Corrie with a smile. "The skeleton isn't damaged at all. Look at him! Must be fully two meters high. I hope you'll let me have him."

"I didn't know he was mine to give," Corrie said. "Be my guest. There's another in the backyard."

"I need perfect specimens. Most are damaged. But with this one, the ball passed through the jugular, leaving the bone intact. I'll send a cart for him."

Corrie did not know Dr. Weideman well. He was one of the eccentrics that seemed to abound on the frontier. He claimed to have been sent to Texas by the emperor of Russia to gather scientific information. In his cups he sometimes told of having buried a young wife and son in Russia, a tragedy he said had made him forever restless and set him to wandering about the world.

Leaving Dr. Weideman to his work, Corrie walked with Prue and Hattie to the Main Plaza, weaving through the bodies littering the street. In the plaza a group of Indian women was sitting on the ground, guarded by soldiers. Corrie walked to the Higginbotham house, where a crowd had gathered.

"Could you tell me what happened?" Corrie asked Mary Maverick. "What started the shooting?"

"I only know what I've heard," Mary said. "I'm told the Comanches claimed the two captives they brought in were all they had. But one of the captives, Matilda Lockhart, whispered to General McLeod that there were more. So he ordered the interpreter to tell the chiefs they would be held hostage till all captives were brought in. When Chief Muguara heard this, he gave his war cry, and the shooting started."

Everyone in the crowd had stories to tell. Corrie and Prue listened to various adventures. For a time Prue became the center of attention. She told her story and displayed the bruises on her arm. Corrie's left eye had swollen and darkened, and the bruise was duly inspected.

Corrie was astonished to see two severed Indian heads on one of Mrs. Higginbotham's windowsills. The heads—one male and one female—could have been mistaken for grisly sculpture, except that they were nestled into a pedestal of gore. "What on earth?" Corrie said.

"Dr. Weideman's trophies," Mrs. Higginbotham said. "Mary and I almost fainted when he came up and asked to leave them with us."

Across the street General McLeod emerged from the Council House. On sighting Corrie and the other women, he came straight toward them. His ingrained courtesy apparently was not affected in the least by all the excitement. He swept off his hat. "Ladies, I ask your indulgence. I have need of your good services. As you all may know, the Indians brought in two captives: a Mexican male, and Matilda Lockhart, taken two years ago from DeWitt's Colony."

Corrie remembered the name. Matilda had been taken at thirteen, along with the four Putnam children.

"We're questioning her now," McLeod went on. "The Indians have abused her terribly. We must clothe and feed her until her relatives can come for her. We need a place for her to stay."

"I'll be happy to look after her," Corrie said.

"Good. I'll have her brought over to you."

"Has she seen the little Rivas boy?"

"She has seen a Mexican boy, but doesn't know his name. She says the whites are held in different bands, and kept apart. She is a most observant young lady. All told, she has identified about fifteen captives, including the four Putnam children, who, thank God, are still alive."

Shouts erupted behind the Higginbotham house. Two Indians had taken refuge in Mrs. Higginbotham's kitchen. Corrie and Prue moved with the crowd to a better vantage point. Two soldiers were on the roof of the kitchen, lighting a candle-wax ball. When it blazed up, it was dropped through a vent hole, onto the heads of the Indians below.

The Indians burst out the kitchen door and were cut down with axes as the crowd roared approval.

Corrie was sickened. She knew that to her dying day she would remember the sound of axes striking flesh and bone.

Prue turned away, gagging. "Corrie, I can't take any more. For God's sake, let's go home."

"We must wait for the captive," Corrie reminded her.

"Then let's wait in the front yard. I've seen enough dead Indians to do me a lifetime."

They walked back through the crowd to the edge of Soledad Street, where Hattie stood with Jim Bowie in her arms. "He wet, Miss Corrie," Hattie said.

Corrie regretted she had committed herself to waiting for the captive. She still felt queasy. A half hour passed before three soldiers came, escorting the captive.

Although Corrie had been forewarned, nothing could have prepared her. Matilda Lockhart was wearing a grimy buckskin dress, plainly a castoff. Her hair was filthy, tangled, and matted. She came holding one hand to her face. Corrie could scarcely stifle her horror as Matilda lowered her hand.

Of her nose, no flesh remained. All had been burned away, leaving only two holes and encrusted scabs. Deep, vivid burn scars covered her face and arms.

Corrie fought to keep her composure. She put out her hand. "I'm Corrie Logan. We're so happy over your release. We hope you'll stay with us until your relatives come. This is my sister, Pruella McNair."

Corrie was pleased that Prue did not wince. Prue spoke by habit, but it served under the circumstances. "I'm pleased to make your acquaintance."

Matilda seemed in a daze. She did not speak.

"I'm sure you're tired," Corrie said. "My husband is out chasing the Indians. But apparently the immediate danger is over. We can go home and get you settled in."

Matilda's voice was hoarse. "I only want to sleep, ma'am. I'd like to sleep and never wake up."

They started home. Soldiers were now in the streets with big solid-wheeled Mexican carts, picking up the bodies. Matilda seemed not to notice. She trudged along as if sleepwalking.

The dead Indian Doctor Weideman had admired was gone from the front yard.

Hattie heated water. While Matilda bathed, Corrie hunted and found a dress Prue had outgrown.

The church bells rang for vespers. Corrie could hardly believe the terrible day was coming to an end. She said a silent prayer for Tad and Whit, who soon would be out in darkness.

Consuelo came in with a tray of food. Matilda ate, but sparingly, holding one hand to her face the whole time. Consuelo waited until it was plain Matilda would eat no more. "They say you saw a Mexican boy with the Indians," she said. "Would you please tell me about him?"

Matilda sat quietly for a moment, concentrating. With the setting sun, the room had grown dark, and she seemed more at ease. Corrie tried to envision her with a nose, and without the disfiguring scars. She concluded that Matilda once might have been called pretty.

"The boy I saw was little. About this high." She gestured. "He had big eyes. Lots of hair, real black. Straight, like an Indian. Not curly. Big front teeth."

"That's him!" Consuelo said. "I'm sure of it."

"They wouldn't tell me his name, and they wouldn't let me talk to him. I was told he was adopted by someone in the Quohada band. That may save his life."

Corrie did not understand. "How?"

Matilda looked at her. "When the Comanches hear what has happened here today, they'll kill all the captives—all except those already adopted into the tribe."

Consuelo began to cry.

"He has a good chance," Matilda told her. "Most of them don't. Not after today."

Hattie put Jim Bowie to bed and lit a lamp. Despite her stated desire for sleep, Matilda sat up and told of her two-year ordeal. She seemed to want to talk. She found rapt listeners in Corrie, Prue, Hattie, and Consuelo.

"They made me work day and night," she said. "I had to do all that the squaws didn't want to do. I scraped buffalo hides, chewed rawhide, jerked beef, carried water, chopped wood, packed and put up tepees every time we moved. Then at night I was told to tend the fires, not to let them go out. But after working all day I couldn't stay awake. Every time old Setimkia caught me asleep, he put a burning brand to my nose to wake me up."

"How perfectly awful!" Prue said.

"Sometimes we rode seventy-five miles a day, bareback, changing horses, never stopping. Once we camped in sight of Béxar. When they saw I recognized where we were, they burned the soles of my feet so I couldn't escape."

Matilda lowered her head. "All I want now is to go home and hide for the rest of my life. I don't intend to let myself be gawked at and made fun of. I'll die first!"

Corrie opened her mouth to say that this would not happen. But common sense told her Matilda was right. Matilda would be the object of unguarded curiosity until her dying day. Rather than mouth a meaningless platitude, Corrie remained silent.

After nightfall Tad and Whit returned, tired and hungry.

Corrie introduced Matilda. "She believes that after today, the Comanches will kill all the captives, except possibly those few who have been adopted," she told Tad.

He could not hide his fury. "It's worse than that. There'll be no end to it. By tricking the Indians—luring them into peace talks, then trying to take them captive—they've destroyed any hope of peace. I hope Lamar rots in hell."

"Some of the squaws captured today are the wives of chiefs," Matilda said. "Maybe the Indians will agree to an exchange. I've told this to General McLeod."

"Still, the Indians will get even," Tad said. "We can count on it. They'll hit somewhere. We can only pray it isn't Béxar."

Later in the evening he talked with Matilda, questioning her about the Comanches, where they traveled, where they camped, their day-to-day habits.

Matilda was intelligent enough to see what he was planning. "Mr. Logan, the minute the Comanches think you've come to take the boy, they'll kill him. That's their way."

"But if all else fails, it might be worth a try," Tad said. "He'd be . . ."

Tad stopped in midsentence. Matilda finished it for him.

"You're right, Mr. Logan. He'd be better off dead."

A week later Matilda's older brother came and took her home to DeWitt's colony on the Guadalupe.

Prue summed up Corrie's thoughts about Matilda. "You'll never hear one more word of complaint out of me about my big nose," she whispered.

But for Corrie, the worst aspect of the whole terrible experience was loss of the sense of peace and accomplishment the talks had brought to Béxar.

Now there seemed no end to the bloodshed.

Of the sixty-five Comanches who had ridden into San Antonio to talk peace, thirty-two had been killed, and the rest taken prisoner. Only seven Texians were dead, and ten injured. The army generals—Lamar's peace commissioners—immediately proclaimed the Council House Fight a great victory. Tad could hardly contain his fury. The question was not how the Indians would retaliate, but where and when.

His Negroes should be in the fields planting. But under the circumstances, he felt he must keep them close to home. He needed to keep appointments below the Rio Grande, buying *derechos* for himself, and for his associates in East Texas. But with an Indian attack a certainty, he could not leave his family, even for a day.

In their ignorance, the commissioners thought they had won peace. Tad knew they had incited a war.

He set out in search of a way to prevent it.

First he went to see Mathew "Old Paint" Caldwell. With the exception of Captain Jack Hays, Caldwell was the most experienced Indian fighter in Béxar. But as a Lamar appointee, Hays was in the chain of command. Caldwell tended to be independent minded, a free thinker.

Tad found him propped up in bed in his room at the Sam Maverick residence, his injured ankle resting on two pillows. Caldwell was called "Old Paint" not because of his age—no more than forty—but for the splotches of white in his thick black hair and beard. The random spots made him resemble an old paint horse.

Tad brought Caldwell a jug of Mexican whiskey. Caldwell thanked him profusely and waved him into a chair.

"Well, it's done," Tad told him. "They've turned the squaw loose. No one could talk any sense into them."

Old Paint made a sound that could have been a curse. The Indian woman was being freed to return to the Comanches with an ultimatum: If the rest of the white captives were not surrendered within fifteen days, the thirty-two remaining Indian prisoners—all women and children—would be killed.

"What do you think the Indians will do?" Tad asked.

Old Paint took another drink from the jug and rubbed his beard thoughtfully. "They'll kill all the captives. They'll drown their grief in blood."

"And afterward?" Tad asked. "Will they hit Béxar?"

Again Old Paint spent time in thought. "They know the army garrison is here. They've tested Hays and his Rangers. We whipped them good the other day from a standing start. I could be wrong, but I don't think they'll come to Béxar."

"Then where and when?" Tad asked.

"They'll send word for all the bands to come in," Old Paint said. "That'll take two or three weeks, maybe a month. My guess is that then they'll go down one of the rivers, pillaging and killing, taking captives. It'll probably be the biggest Indian raid this country has seen."

"Do you see any way of stopping it? Changing their minds?"

Old Paint shook his head. "Colonel, I know you've been on the peace route, and I've tended to agree with you. But I think it's time we both reconsidered. Let's look at it from their angle. Last fall the East Texians killed more than a hundred Cherokees—peaceable Indians—on the Angelina. Yesterday we killed thirty-two Comanches who came here to smoke the peace pipe. I'd say it'll be a cold day in hell before we'll get any of these Indians back into a peaceable frame of mind."

Tad remained silent. Houston had warned him this was coming.

"So the way I see it, there's nothing to do now but fight," Caldwell went on. "Destroy their means to make war, drive them back to the north. That's the only way we'll get shut of them."

Tad thought of the Indian woman he had killed. Her face came vividly to mind. "Maybe you're right, Paint," he said. "But I'm sick of killing Indians."

"So am I," Caldwell said. "Then I get to thinking. We chose to live in this country. Way I see it, we have no choice."

Tad considered Paint's argument. He envisioned for a moment his world with the Comanches driven back north once and for all. He could send his Negroes into the fields without worry. The wild cattle on his lands could be worked and branded. He could send the produce of his fields to Brazoria for shipment without the risk of losing it to Indians. He could take Corrie on carriage drives to beautiful sites she had not yet seen. His sons could grow up playing amid the woods and streams.

It would be the life he had envisioned when he first dreamed of coming to Béxar.

If Old Paint was right, there would be several weeks, maybe a month, to prepare.

"You think we could muster enough of a force to stop them when they head south?" he asked.

Old Paint shook his head. "Too much ground to cover. And they'll be moving right along. Time to hit them is when they come back north, worn out, loaded with plunder. If we start planning now, we could have quite an army in place."

"We'd need a network of spies, keeping watch," Tad said, thinking ahead. "We'll have to convince the army. Lamar."

"That's your department," Old Paint said. "You know the people who pull the strings. I don't. You know how to sell the idea. I don't. I only know this may be our one chance to remove the Indian threat from this part of the country."

Tad left Caldwell's room with mixed emotions. He was saddened by the likelihood that peace no longer could be achieved. But his frustration was eased.

At least now a goal was in view, and he could set to work on a plan of action.

Prue came into the house ashen faced after a trip to the Main Plaza. "Corrie, do you know what that crazy Russian doctor has done? After rendering out his Indians, separating meat from the bones, he dumped what was left into the acequia at daylight this morning."

Corrie felt her gorge rise. Every morning Consuelo went to the acequia for water. It was used for coffee, drinking, to wash vegetables, beans, Jim Bowie's bottles, everything.

Everyone in town knew that Dr. Weideman had been boiling his Indian specimens in a big soap pot to render his skulls and skeletons. The Mexicans called him a *brujo*, a male witch.

"Women are throwing up all over the plaza," Prue said. "They're yelling for the mayor to put him in jail."

Overriding Corrie's revulsion was her concern for her family's health. She had heard of bad water destroying entire communities. "Let's go see if there's any danger," she said.

Corrie took Jim Bowie inside, gave him to Hattie, and returned with Prue to the plaza. Prue had not exaggerated. More than two hundred people had gathered. The plaza reeked with vomit. Some of the women angrily told of finding body parts in the water they carried home for breakfast. Behind the women, some of the men of the town were laughing.

At last Dr. Weideman came out of the mayor's office and raised his hands for quiet. "My friends, there is absolutely no danger," he shouted in his heavy accent. "The meat was well cooked. There was no spoilage that could make anyone ill. I'm a scientist, a representative of the emperor. I'm dedicated to *saving* lives. I wouldn't cause you harm."

But Corrie thought Weideman's face gave him away; he could not hide his amusement.

Mayor Juan Seguín also spoke. "Dr. Weideman has assured us he meant no harm. But it is true he has violated a long-standing ordinance. Therefore, the maximum fine has been levied against him. Dr. Weideman has admitted his error, and he has agreed to pay the fine. He promises never to violate the ordinance again. I hope this puts an end to the matter."

Corrie turned away in disgust, furious with the men who stood laughing.

She returned home with Prue and tried to put her mind on things more pleasant, but the horrid incident started a chain of thoughts she could not control.

During the last few days she had seen conduct among the whites as atrocious as any ever attributed to the so-called savage Indians.

And now the army was threatening to put to death the thirty-two women and children taken captive at the Council House. The prisoners had been informed of their possible fate, and their death songs could be heard for blocks.

For the first time in months Corrie wondered if she had made a mistake in coming west. Despite its beauty, there was a harshness, a cruelty, to San Antonio she could not accept.

She felt she was a part of a slow deterioration. She remembered the savage fury that had driven her into attacking the Indian holding Prue, the primitive urge that sent her clawing for his eyes with her fingernails.

The battle in the front yard had introduced an aspect of herself she had never before encountered. The recognition left her frightened, and repelled.

Her glum mood lasted through the day. That evening she found those around her too quick to forgive and forget. Prue, as nauseated as anyone in the morning, was able to joke about it before supper. "I'm sending back to South Carolina a recipe for Texas Indian soup," she told Whit. "You take two Indians, boil in a big open pot until tender . . ."

"And add two heads to taste," Whit chimed in.

Corrie lost her composure. "Stop it! Both of you!"

She fled into her bedroom.

A few minutes later Tad came in and sat on the edge of the bed. "Corrie, I know this has been a rough experience for you. I should've insisted on your going to bed. Not only was it all disturbing, you also took quite a lick. Is it still painful?"

"Some," Corrie said. "But I'm just as upset over that crazy doctor as anything."

"Weideman may be odd, but he's as fine a physician as any in Texas," Tad said. "We're lucky to have him. We shouldn't antagonize him."

"But how could he do such a thing?"

"He's a medical doctor, involved in his work. He looks beyond what others might find disgusting."

"The other men laughed. Made jokes. They don't have such an excuse. And they cheered when the two Indians in Mrs. Higginbotham's kitchen were butchered."

Tad was silent a moment. "Corrie, when you're forced to shoot Indians in your own yard, you steel yourself against normal sentiments. Their joking was a brand of gallows humor."

"Does that explain Prue? And Whit?"

"Yes. They're still finding their way into adulthood. Whit's a boy one minute, a man the next. Prue hides behind her wit. There's a lot of woman there, waiting to emerge."

Corrie rolled over and looked up at him. "Tad, I've endured this Indian menace, the isolation of the life out here, thinking that eventually conditions would improve. Yet it has only grown worse. During the last few days I've seen precious little that raises the people of San Antonio above savages."

"Corrie, refinement follows in the wake of the frontier. As the frontier moves on, life will become better. It's always been so."

"But when?" Corrie demanded. "There's no reason we should be living like this."

"No, there isn't," Tad agreed. He leaned over her and gripped her shoulders. "Please, Corrie. Please endure a little longer. I'm confident change is almost here."

She nodded. He kissed her and returned to his supper. But Corrie had no appetite for food. She continued to lie in bed with her aching cheekbone, reflecting on the events of the last few days, and all that Tad had said.

He seemed so calm, so certain of the future.

She devoutly wished she could learn that art. Just as Prue was bordering on adulthood, Corrie felt that she herself was constantly poised short of the woman she should be. And just as Whit was a man one moment, and a boy the next, Corrie found she could not sustain her wavering bravery.

The wait to see what the Indians would do stretched into days, weeks. The men no longer went into the fields to work. Tad remained close to home. The suspense became wearing on everyone.

One afternoon a Comanche warrior rode boldly into the Main Plaza and announced in signs and broken Spanish that he and his warriors were holding captives at the edge of town, and that he was ready to make an exchange for some of the Indian women.

Tad and Jack Hays were sent to negotiate. The talks were difficult, but eventually terms were reached. In a swap for three Indian women and two children, Tad won the release of a Mexican male, one of the Putnam children, and two small boys.

One of the boys was Pablito Rivas.

The other was ten-year-old Booker Webster, a distant relative of the United States senator, Daniel Webster. A manly little fellow, Booker colorfully described the immense gathering of Comanches he had seen preparing for war.

"Do you know when they'll attack?" Tad asked.

Booker shook his head. "They looked about ready," he said.

Tension continued to build in San Antonio.

Then in late April the mail rider from Austin arrived with the report that he had seen several hundred Comanche warriors moving down the valley of the Guadalupe.

Captain Hays sent his scouts in that direction. They returned with tales of the horrors they encountered. The Comanches were moving south along the river, killing settlers, destroying and burning small settlements.

In the days that followed, the reports of devastation mounted.

Then came a confirmed report the Comanches had attacked Victoria, ninety miles southeast of San Antonio. After a battle, the Indians withdrew. When last seen, they were still moving southward.

"We have them now," Tad said that evening. "They can't come back north without being intercepted."

Whit and Jack begged to go. But Tad remained adamant. He rode off with a company of volunteers commanded by Old Paint Caldwell. Hays and his Rangers, Captain Fisher and his three army companies also left to join a force assembling near Austin.

Corrie became immersed in the floating sense of anxiety that had become a habit when Tad was away. She lived from moment to moment, trying to put her fears out of her mind.

Day by day the household doted on rumors. One afternoon Whit returned with the latest.

"A man and his wife just came up from Linnville. They said the Comanches burned and sacked the town. The man and his wife made it to a rowboat, crossed the bay, and escaped."

Corrie remembered Linnville from Tad's map. It was a port on Lavaca Bay.

"Now they have to go north for sure," Jack said. "I remember that town. They can't go farther south without swimming."

Again days passed without reliable news. Corrie and Whit fell back into the habit of staying up nights talking, seeking a measure of relief in companionship.

Whit remained dejected over Tad's refusal to take him along. He pointed out that several of the volunteers were younger, and smaller. "Corrie, will Tad ever treat me as a grown-up?" he asked one evening.

"Of course he will," Corrie assured him.

"I'm not so sure," Whit said after a thoughtful pause. "He doesn't seem to recognize that we're different. Already he's planning for us to become partners when Frank buys my part of Donegal. He said he has his eye on some land for me."

This was news to Corrie. But she liked the idea, for she had grown very fond of Whit. Without a brother of her own, the relationship was new to her. She relished the intimacy shorn of the usual entanglements. "I think that would be wonderful," she said.

Whit frowned. "I'm not sure I want to buy land with my money. I may want to do something else."

"Such as what?" Corrie asked.

Whit shrugged. "I don't know. I want to travel. I want to be free."

"Have you told Tad how you feel?"

"I've tried. He just starts preaching. Buy land and never sell. I've heard him say that a million times. He goes on about how Texas soon will be able to use what's here. Market its products. He says when that happens Texas will be one of the richest nations in the world."

"He could be right," Corrie pointed out. "You've seen the land, the wild cattle. Think of what you've done on a little bit of land upriver. Apply that to the whole Republic. It's almost frightening."

Whit nodded agreement, but remained silent. "Whatever I do, I want to do on my own," he said after a time. "Can you understand that?"

"Of course. But, Whit, after you've been on your own some, I wouldn't be surprised if you wouldn't be more receptive to a partnership with Tad. I think you'd make a good team."

"Maybe," he conceded. "But I'm not at all sure."

"I am," Corrie said. "Nothing could be more fitting."

A few days later came reports that Ranger scouts were tracking the Comanches and their captives north from Linnville, and that the main body of Texians was moving southward from Austin to join the Rangers and volunteers.

Then for days nothing more was heard. Corrie went around in a daze, unable to eat, think, or sleep. Whit and Jack haunted the Main Plaza, seeking any report, no matter how unimportant.

But the next news came from Tad himself.

He and the volunteers returned trail worn, battle weary, and jubilant. But Tad left the group before its arrival in the plaza and came straight home, ignoring the noisy celebration.

He seemed tired, but Corrie was more worried about his mood. He held her for an interminable time in a big bear hug, and ignored questions from Whit and Jack while he cradled Jim Bowie in his arms.

"What happened?" Whit asked repeatedly.

Tad's answer came reluctantly. "We met them on Plum Creek, and gave them a thorough drubbing. I was with Old Paint. We held the left flank. We captured about two thousand horses."

"How many did you kill?" Whit asked.

"I counted sixty-eight. Others claimed more."

Corrie observed that Jack also had noticed Tad's peculiar mood. "Why ain't you partying with the rest, Marsh Tad? Seems to me you deserve a drink or two."

Tad nodded. "I suppose so. It was a decisive victory. We put them afoot, drove them out of this country for good. San Antonio is safe. But I know we also lost. We've forever destroyed our chance for a lasting peace with the Indians."

PART THREE

A Quest for Empire

It is the rare and easy faculty of some people to make, as it were, postmortem examinations, and sit in judgment upon the best efforts of some of our best men, generally deeming an enterprise ill judged and wrong, if it be disastrous or unsuccessful. . . . Men who were true and disinterested and ready to die for Texas suffered much and occasionally suffered defeat and persecution in lawful enterprises. This Santa Fé Expedition is a case in point.

John Holland Jenkins
Recollections of Early Texas
1884

--- 10 ---

"I'll be civil to him, but that's all," Tad said. "Don't expect me to lead the cheering."

Corrie could not hide her irritation. Tad's animosity toward President Lamar threatened to cast a pall over the entire evening. "This isn't a political affair," she reminded him. "It's a social event. Social rules apply."

"That's the only reason I'm going," Tad said, carefully knotting his bow tie. "The man isn't a president. He's an embarrassment."

Corrie was not inclined to pursue the argument. After less than a year in office Lamar had relinquished the presidency, pleading his delicate health. Vice President David Burnet had assumed the reins. But now, only four months later, Lamar was saying he was sufficiently recovered to resume office. Now he was on an official visit to San Antonio. Corrie's feelings on Lamar were mixed. While she could not condone his trickery with the Indians, at least he had accomplished more than Sam Houston. There had been no Indian depredations around San Antonio since their defeat at Plum Creek.

Corrie hurried to Prue's room to see if she was still dawdling. She found Prue studying herself in the mirror. "Corrie, I'm not even sure I want to go," Prue said. "Not without a proper escort."

The remark elevated Corrie from mild irritation to anger. "What an ungrateful thing to say! Don't be so high and mighty! Whit Logan is as fine an escort as you'll find anywhere. Any young lady your age should be proud to go on his arm."

"Oh, Corrie, I didn't mean it the way it sounded," Prue said. "But Whit's family, and everybody knows it. They'll be looking at me and saying, 'There's that poor, skinny little McNair girl! Her sister had to recruit her brother-in-law as her escort. No one else was interested.' "

"You mean someone like John Morris." Corrie had seen Prue cutting her eyes at him in the plaza. Lieutenant Morris, with his small black mustache and sparkling black eyes, was currently setting all feminine hearts aflutter.

"Yes, now that you mention him," Prue agreed.

"I understand he's taking Miss Arceneiga. She's much more in his age bracket. You're still a bit young for him."

"I'm not! You had scads of gentlemen callers at fifteen."

Corrie could not offer a denial. "That was different. Conditions were not the same."

"How true! All the men out here can do is *look*."

Corrie also had noticed this social lack. She had pondered the reasons, and come to a conclusion. "Prue, listen to me. Many of these young men are from good backgrounds. They see you in the plaza and recognize you for what you are, a young lady of family and breeding. Then they look down at themselves and see buckskin. Most of them probably don't own a serviceable cloth suit. They feel inadequate around you. That's why they don't come calling. And that's the *only* reason."

"So what am I supposed to do? Buy them a suit?"

"Look beyond the clothes to the man. Lower your sights, where the social conventions are concerned. You tend to turn up your nose at rough appearances. You don't have to prove you've seen better. They know that. Encourage them. Show them you're aware material concerns don't matter."

Prue checked in the mirror again. She adjusted the stand-up collar. "This bodice seems to lack something."

Corrie silently agreed. On impulse, she reached behind her neck and unfastened her grandmother McNair's pearls. "Try these."

Prue seemed genuinely surprised. "Oh, Corrie! I couldn't. What'll you wear?"

"Don't worry. I have something that will do."

A soft knock came at the door. "It's time," Tad said.

Corrie hurried to her room for a simple gold filigreed necklace she had always treasured. By the time she returned to the front of the house, Tad and Whit were waiting.

With Prue and Whit leading the way, Corrie and Tad followed at a more leisurely pace on the short walk to the Yturri house. President Lamar's $2,300 carriage stood in the street. Although the Republic could not meet basic financial obligations, Lamar had ordered the coach from New Orleans. For many Texians the expenditure was symbolic of Lamar's wasteful extravagance.

Rangers and other single men lounged in the front yard, talking and smoking in the gentle light of lanterns in the trees. Corrie smelled liquor, but no jugs were in sight. The men swept off their sombreros as Corrie and Tad walked past them.

Inside, a reception line had formed.

As Corrie's turn came for introduction, Lamar gave her a warm smile. "Mrs. Logan! I regret I missed meeting you during your brief visit to Houston. I must say, the reports I heard of your beauty were not exaggerated."

The compliment was so unexpected that Corrie felt heat rush to her face. "Mr. President, it's clear not all of your poetry is confined to the pages of books," she managed to say.

He laughed and held her hand in both of his. "Well said! You *must* come visit our new capital in Austin. We're building quite a cultured society there. I believe you will find our diversions entertaining."

"I'm sure I would," Corrie said, passing on, not wishing to hold up the line. "I'll be looking forward to a visit."

In concentrating on amenities with Mrs. Seguin, Corrie almost missed Tad's exchange with the president.

"Colonel Logan," Lamar said. "I appreciated the long letter from you last year. Your suggestions were most valuable."

"I proposed peace talks," Tad said. "Not trickery."

He spoke too loudly. Nearby conversations stilled.

Lamar smiled. "As the Bard said, all's well that ends well. We won peace for San Antonio and this portion of the Republic."

"At the price of how many lives, sir?"

Lamar's smile did not wither. "Colonel, perhaps we'll find time to discuss our differences later this evening. I'll be looking forward to it. I'm pleased to see you, Colonel."

Corrie was furious. She fought for control until she and Tad were through the line. "Tad, how could you!" she whispered.

"He gave me no choice," Tad said. "He has plain as said many times that the Council House fight was my idea."

The reception line dissolved. All the guests crowded into the long room. Mayor Seguín made a brief speech welcoming President Lamar to San Antonio de Béxar.

Lamar's response was so low that Corrie had to strain to hear. He talked for a time of his affection for San Antonio, its place in the winning of independence.

"I now appeal to you to help the Republic bear yet another burden," he continued. "Since the birth of our Republic five years ago, we've woefully neglected our citizens on the upper Rio Grande. They deserve our protection. Moreover, considerable trade is being conducted between the United States and Mexico, through Santa Fé, and yet Texas receives no benefit."

Lamar paused. Corrie glanced at Tad. He was listening intently, frowning slightly.

"So I'm proposing an expedition to Santa Fé," Lamar went on. "Its purpose will be peaceful. It will map the unexplored country between here and there, perhaps establishing a route for trade between our seaports and Santa Fé. It will make possible the imposition of a tax on the commerce now being conducted between Mexico and Missouri. Its third purpose will be to welcome the people of Santa Fé and Méjico Nuevo into our Republic, and to free them from the despot's heel."

Corrie happened to be looking across the room at Whit. He was totally enrapt. Corrie could almost see the wheels turning in his head: Here at last was an opportunity for him to get out from under Tad's shadow.

"The expedition requires two kinds of volunteers," Lamar continued. "First, I'm seeking merchants willing to venture goods in an effort to establish trade with Santa Fé. Second, I call for men accomplished in arms, to protect the expedition from hostile Indians. As an added precaution, a garrison of light artillery will accompany the expedition. As commissioner I've selected General Hugh McLeod. He will be in charge of enlistment here. The expedition will depart Kenney's Fort on Brushy Creek about a month hence."

He closed his address with more flowery praise for San Antonio. The applause was long and sustained.

Mayor Seguín again spoke. "And now, President Lamar will open the baile."

The floor was cleared. A six-piece string orchestra launched into a tune. President Lamar led Mrs. Seguín onto the floor. Widely known as a romantic, Lamar definitely was not a dancer. His timing was off. His steps were awkward. His hand kept sliding up and down Mrs. Sequín's side, seeking her waist. But portly Mrs. Seguín had no waist.

The moment was volatile. A single spark could have set off an explosion of laughter. But good manners prevailed. President Lamar and Mrs. Seguín completed their turn. Other couples glided onto the floor.

Perhaps that moment of controlled humor set the mood for the evening. Spirits were high. Corrie was pleased to see that although Miss Arceneiga and Lieutenant Morris attracted considerable attention, Prue was emerging as the belle of the ball. The young men of Hays's Rangers vied for her attention. Soon it became apparent that Hays, Mike Chevallie, and John Howard had only one presentable coat among them, and were taking turns wearing it while the other two watched through the windows. Prue spent much of the evening dancing with the same coat, worn by a succession of admirers.

Corrie also was pleased to see that Whit never asserted himself in a proprietary way. Corrie felt he handled Prue's sudden popularity with admirable tact.

While dancing with Señor Ibarra, Corrie saw Whit and Tad in a secluded corner, embroiled in intense but subdued argument. She was certain she knew the subject. Her guess was confirmed later when Whit asked her to dance.

"Tad won't let me go on the expedition. He brought me west because I wouldn't have a life of my own at home. But now he's doing the same thing to me here," he said. "You've got to help me, Corrie."

Corrie was not sure she should meddle in this but she felt a wave of sympathy for Whit. Within months he would be eighteen. The time was coming for him to go out on his own. "Whit, I don't know what I can do," she said. "But I'll try."

President Lamar sank back into a deep leather chair, propped his boots on a low stool, and lit a long puro. Tad sat facing him across a small table. Brandy had been poured and the other gentlemen were unbuttoning their coats and arranging themselves comfortably. Lucifers flared as cigars were lit.

Lamar blew smoke and gazed at the glowing end of his cigar. "I'm told your election to Congress is a certainty, Colonel."

"That may be overstating the case, Mr. President," Tad said.

"Not at all," said Ibarra. "The Mexicans here give him credit, quite rightly, for saving the Rivas boy. And they know he has been dealing most honestly with Mexicans holding *derechos* to his land. His beautiful wife had been the only Anglo to comfort the Rivas family when the boy was taken. The Mexicans will elect him to Congress, sir. They also may canonize him."

The other gentlemen laughed. Embarrassed, Tad joined in.

"Then I'll no doubt be seeing you in Austin," Lamar said. "But, Colonel, I truly don't understand. From our previous talks, and from your letters, I thought our philosophies were similar. You oppose annexation to the United States. You champion expansion of the Republic, policies I've advocated. Yet I find us continually opposed. Tell me. What are your thoughts on my proposal for an expedition to Santa Fé?"

Lamar's tone was amiable. But his words had bite. The room quieted as the group awaited Tad's answer. For a moment the faint strains of the fiddles down the hall was the only sound.

Tad answered cautiously. "Sir, I think we differ more on method than on objectives. I fail to see where we gain by antagonizing Mexico."

"Then you're opposed to the expedition?"

Tad hesitated. His view would be unpopular. "If I were sending an expedition to Santa Fé, I wouldn't send less than a thousand men, all well armed."

General McLeod laughed. "Colonel, if we had a thousand men under arms, we could march on Mexico."

"Might be the same thing, General. An expedition to Santa Fé could provoke renewal of the war."

"But this is a *peace* mission," Lamar protested. "Where could there possibly be offense?"

"Let's look at it from Santa Anna's perspective," Tad said. "Here comes an armed body of my enemies, into territory I claim, where I govern. What am I supposed to do? Ignore the intrusion?"

Tad's words raised a murmur of dissent.

"Santa Anna has too many troubles of his own," General McLeod said. "With the revolt in Chihuahua, and unrest in the Yucatán, I doubt the matter will even come to his attention."

"The expedition won't be an intrusion," Lamar said. "General McLeod will be bearing sealed dispatches of friendship from myself to the governor of Méjico Nuevo. Our purpose can't possibly be mistaken."

"I hope not. I sincerely wish your plan well."

"The expedition needs experienced leaders. Can I prevail upon you to take part? It should require only two months or so."

Again Tad hesitated, uncertain how far to go in explaining himself. He decided the question deserved an honest answer. "Mr. President, during our long campaign against the Comanches, I greatly neglected my wife and family. I traveled a great deal in acquiring land. I may now be required to devote considerable time to Congress. With all due respect, I believe I should spend as many hours as possible at home."

"That's understandable," Lamar said. "Besides, we may need your talents more in Austin. I've let it be known that I'm supporting your candidacy."

Tad was genuinely taken aback. He wondered if Lamar had misread him entirely. "Surely you know, sir, that I've always supported General Houston."

"I'm aware of that. But I also know you're a level-headed man, not easily stampeded." He chuckled. "I'd even make a wager. I predict that if Houston is returned to the presidency next year, you'll find yourself among the opposition before six months have passed."

Tad held his temper. He did not take his loyalty to Sam Houston lightly. "How so?"

"You're a man of action. You'll soon weary of Houston's hot-and-cold position on annexation. You'll become exasperated as he takes repeated insults from Mexico without retaliation. You'll see splendid opportunities lost for alliances with dissident forces in Mexico. Colonel, you've become the largest landholder in this region. You have much at stake. Your patience with Houston will vanish. I'm so sure of this that I now proffer to you, in front of these witnesses, my solid support of your candidacy."

Tad felt further resistance would be ungracious. "I thank you, Mr. President. I accept. I hope you're not misreading me."

"I hardly think so. I doubt you realize the extent of your good reputation throughout the Republic. Thomas Rusk, Adolphus Sterne, Judge Love, Senator Gaines, dozens of our most influential citizens, have mentioned your name to me, and often, lamenting that we haven't utilized your abilities, especially in law. They all speak most highly of you."

"Perhaps that's because I've never run for office."

The room erupted in laughter.

Again Lamar chuckled. But as the room stilled, he turned serious. "The next few years will be most crucial to our beloved Republic. If Houston returns to the presidency, we'll need level-headed men in Austin. I hope you'll be there."

The puros had burned short. The political session ended. Tad followed the men back to the baile.

Corrie had sat down in the shade of the patio to nurse Jim Bowie when movement caught her eye. Tad emerged from the river on Midnight and came toward the barn at a gentle lope. Whit emerged from the barn. Tad dismounted and the two brothers stood talking.

Corrie felt a twinge of guilt. She had given her solemn promise to Whit, but as yet no occasion had seemed appropriate.

The argument at the barn apparently grew heated. After a time

Whit stalked off to the horse pasture, roped a gelding, and rode off bareback.

Tad came on toward the house. He stepped onto the patio looking back at Whit. "He just won't give up," he said.

He sank into a chair beside her and began to play with Jim Bowie, teasing him with a gourd rattle. Corrie felt she should speak now or never. "Tad, the expedition might be good experience for him."

Tad gave her a sharp glance. "You too?"

Corrie tried to speak naturally, even though she had been planning the words for days. "Tad, I don't think you realize how tight a leash you've held on Whit. You kept him from becoming a surveyor. You wouldn't allow him to go out with the Volunteer Rangers, even when boys younger were going. I can understand that. But everyone says the expedition should be safe. Whit only wants to get out on his own, learn to live among other men. I really think it might be good for him."

Tad studied her for a long moment. "Apparently you've done a lot of thinking about it."

Corrie nodded. "I have."

He sighed, looking off in the direction where Whit had disappeared from view. "Corrie, we don't know what kind of country lies between here and Santa Fé. We don't know what reception they'll receive when and if they get there."

"But think what a grand adventure it would be for him. An exploration into unknown country. It'd stay with him the rest of his life."

Tad shook his head. "I need him here."

"All the crops are planted. You have Jack and Newt. Harvest is months away. Whit will be back by then."

Tad frowned. "I'd have thought you'd want to keep him safe."

Corrie met his gaze. "Ordinarily I would. But, Tad, this isolation is beginning to wear on him. I see it. He's losing that wonderful self-confidence you gave him when you assigned him responsibilities coming west. Now he's beyond that. He's hungry for change, adventure, a chance to explore his capabilities. I believe this expedition might be the making of him. I can't explain it. It's just something I sense."

Tad sat silent for a time, playing with Jim Bowie. "I'll think about it," he said.

Corrie's appeal both surprised and disturbed Tad. Her arguments were logical, and her criticism stung.

Yet he was reluctant to grant his permission. On his forays to the north with the Rangers he had seen some of the rugged country the expedition would traverse. No one knew what lay beyond. More than twenty years ago a United States expedition had set out to find the source of the Red River. It failed, as had every attempt since. Most maps labeled the region "Comanchería."

His opposition was further undermined when he learned that Old Paint Caldwell had signed for the expedition as chief of scouts, and was taking his fourteen-year-old son. Tad knew he could depend on Old Paint to look after Whit.

He was wavering when a fresh bundle of mail arrived via San Felipe. Among the letters was a hurriedly scrawled note from Adolphus Sterne in Nacogdoches:

Dear Esteemed Friend Thaddeus,
The westbound mail is about to close. I'm rushing this to get it on its way to you.

This morning Wilbur Fowler was in town. I'm told he was making inquiries about you and your brother Whit, where you are located, etc. I do not know what he learned. But many people were aware of your destination. I'm sure he will get answers somewhere.

I know not why he has waited three years to seek you out. I can only surmise your shooting was more effective than you thought. I'm certain he is intent on making trouble for you and your brother. Please be on your guard. The Fowlers are a sly, mean bunch.

Your Friend
Adolphus Sterne

Tad took the letter seriously on first reading. Adolphus Sterne was a practical man, not an alarmist. His letter had crossed Texas. Wilbur Fowler might not be far behind.

He might already be in San Antonio.

Tad was not worried about himself. He would be cautious.

With Whit the situation was different. Whit tended to be too open, too trusting. And Whit was the one who had killed Cletus Fowler; logically he would be Wilbur Fowler's prime target.

Tad was still reluctant to send Whit off on the expedition. But it would take Whit out of town until this threat was ended.

He found Whit and Jack in the horse pasture doctoring a colt. When Whit saw Tad, he opened his mouth to start his latest plea. Tad stopped him with an upraised hand.

"I've changed my mind," he said. "You can go."

Whit seemed temporarily incapable of speech.

"Old Paint plans to leave day after tomorrow," Tad went on. "If you're bound to go, I want you to go with him. That doesn't allow you much time to get ready. We'll all help you."

Whit nodded, then ran toward the house, shouting the good news to Corrie.

Through the next twenty-four hours the household worked without rest to ready Whit for the expedition. His horses were selected and reshod, clothing carefully chosen, and guns and equipment prepared.

Then with the following dawn Whit was gone, riding away with Old Paint Caldwell, his son, and more than a dozen other men bound for Brushy Creek above Austin and the start of the expedition.

In the following weeks Tad felt as if he had lost his right arm. The empty place at the Logan table was a constant reminder. Tad caught Corrie and Prue glancing often at the empty chair. One evening Prue put Tad's thoughts into words. "I never thought I'd miss him so awfully much. But I do."

---11---

The end of the Indian threat brought glorious new freedom. Accompanied by Old Ben, Corrie and Prue explored the old missions in greater detail. Sometimes they spent the better part of a day among them, with Prue making sketches to send home, and Corrie walking through the ruins. On other days they rode into the hills west of town, basking on vistas of the missions glittering along the winding, tree-shaded river.

On most evenings Prue received gentlemen callers. Corrie became amused by Prue's growing coquettishness.

Around the Logan compound the Anglo community expanded. Corrie and Prue exchanged calls with the new residents, and Corrie began to see the fledgling start of a society like that she had known in South Carolina.

Each day she practiced her Spanish on Consuelo. With her growing command of the language she frequently called on the hidalgos. As she came to know them better, she found them exotic and charming, and regretted that the Anglo families chose to live apart. For her, the Anglos gave San Antonio its strength. But the Mexicans were its soul.

Gradually Consuelo became Corrie's friend, as well as her cook. A heavyset, jolly woman in her early thirties, Consuelo was intelligent, perceptive, and knowledgeable. It was from Consuelo that Corrie learned more of San Antonio's past, such as the fact that more than two decades before the Alamo, three hundred men of San Antonio were slain in an earlier revolt against tyranny. They were thrown into a granary, so tightly packed that eighteen suffocated. The remainder were taken out the next morning and shot. Their widows were forced to grind corn for the invading army.

202

"That's how Dolorosa Street got its name," Consuelo said. "There's where the men were imprisoned, and slain."

Corrie often had been struck by the beauty of the name, Dolorosa, meaning sorrowful. Now she was appalled that the Anglos who used the street every day remained ignorant that it was a memorial to three hundred heroes. Corrie told the story to some of her Anglo friends. But none was interested.

Yet Corrie could not shun her Anglo friends. In fact, she found herself becoming ever more involved in the tightly knit little community of Americans.

Early in the summer they prevailed on their husbands to build a bathhouse upriver, near Soledad Street. A large canvas structure was erected in the shade of huge cottonwoods. There each afternoon they gathered with their children and nurses. After a swim and bath they spread a delicious lunch. Recipes were exchanged. Novels and newspapers, now more plentiful, were read and discussed. Current gossip was aired, confidences shared. Tricks were played. Sometimes Corrie felt she had never had so much fun in her life.

One afternoon Corrie was in the river, dog-paddling in circles. Hattie played with Jim Bowie in shallow water. Prue was sprawled on the grassy bank, reading the latest issue of the *Telegraph and Texas Register* from Houston. Suddenly Prue squealed. "Corrie! Corrie! Come quick!"

Corrie panicked, assuming something had happened to Jim Bowie. But when she fought her way to shore, Prue held out a newspaper. "Look at this!"

Corrie knelt on the grass. The item was brief:

Mr. Ramsey Cothburn of this city, who returned this day from a trip to Austin, reports Congress devoid of hope that the much desired Franco-Texienne loan will come to pass. Mr. Cothburn quotes the knowledgeable as saying this solution to the Republic's soaring deficit was doomed by the recent Pig War, wherein Hostelier Richard Bullock's errant pigs broke into the private corn crib of the French chargé, Count Alphonse de Saligny. Faithful readers may recall that the count's servant remonstrated with the pigs and was soundly thrashed by Mr. Bullock for his trouble. Unable to obtain justice in our capital city of Austin for this insult, the count promptly decamped to France, where he currently is portraying the Republic, and most especially Austin, as a lawless outpost lacking the barest rudiments of civilization. This lamentable development would seem to recommend the return of the capital to Houston, where pigs are better behaved.

Mr. Cothburn also advises that he has purchased a league on the Brazos above Columbia, and has placed several hundred acres under cultivation there. He said recent rains have brightened prospects for his crop this year. Mr. Cothburn said he will continue his legal practice in Houston, as his plantation lies within a day's ride of this city.

"It's him!" Prue said. "It couldn't be anybody else!"

Corrie did not answer. She was unprepared for the emotional impact of seeing Ramsey's name in print—and of his being identified as a *Texian*!

She had never been able to envision him in Texas. "I really didn't think he would stay in Texas," she said.

"Why not?" Prue asked.

Corrie tried to explain. "He was so set in his ways. He didn't seem the type for adventure."

"He's as much of an adventurer at heart as Tad," Prue insisted. "I knew he was unhappy. I'm sure he felt boxed in by all the social conventions, what was expected of him by you, everyone. I'm not at all surprised he's starting a new life out here."

Corrie read the item through again.

Nothing was said of a Mrs. Cothburn. Corrie sat wondering about Ramsey, his new life, and if he had truly changed. Her marriage soon would enter its fourth year. Why was she so drawn to the past? Why did she still feel such a strong pull to Ramsey, as if their lives were entwined?

Columbia was not terribly far away. And if he was into Texas politics, as the newspaper implied, someday they probably would meet again. Texas might be big, but the population was small, and closely interlocked.

"There's an article about the Santa Fé Expedition on page one," Prue said. "At the bottom. Nothing really new in it."

Prue dived into the water, splashing Jim Bowie and Hattie. Jim Bowie laughed, thinking it great fun. But Hattie grumbled. Corrie searched and found the small item:

> Latest reports from Austin indicate that the Texas Santa Fé Expedition has vanished into the terra incognita of North and West Texas, after a late start from Brushy Creek. On last word the expedition, numbering 321 men and twenty-four ox-drawn wagons, was encamped along Cedral Creek on the upper Brazos, where additional beeves were awaited from Austin. While waiting, wagons were undergoing much-needed repair, as the journey thus far was said to be arduous in the extreme. This stop was some weeks hence. Thus far no further report has been received. By this writing, the expedition members should be well into the haunts of the wily Comanche, and filling in blank places on the map of the Republic, in regions hitherto unknown to the white man.

Corrie reread the article carefully, seeking any meaning she might have missed.

The expedition no longer seemed as safe as when proposed by President Lamar. She thought of Whit, traveling through unknown country, surrounded by thousands upon thousands of Indians.

A sudden chill swept through her. The sun was setting. Soon the bells of San Fernando would sound the call to vespers.

Her enchantment with the missions had made her much more conscious of the church, and the fact that San Antonio had no Protestant place of worship. On an impulse one evening she had donned a rebozo Consuelo had given her, and walked over to the cathedral. Not comprehending the ritual she witnessed, she never-theless had been moved by a deep sense of peace. In the plain, unadorned old cathedral, she indeed sensed that God was near, and that was enough. She prayed for her mother, her grandparents, her aunts and uncles who were gone.

The priest nodded to her, but did not speak. No one intruded on her privacy. She left the cathedral with a serenity that lingered into the following day.

Now vespers had become a habit.

Tonight she would say a special prayer for Whit.

Old Paint drew rein. "Boys, I'd bet my beard that's the Brazos. I think we've swung that far back south. What we've been following must be a *tributary* to the Red. The Wichita, maybe."

Whit studied the stream on the southern horizon. One river looked much like another. The expedition had been uncertain of its location for the last two weeks. With food running out, game non-existent, and water scarce, the question of their position on the map was fast becoming crucial.

"Let's rest the horses," Old Paint said. "We'll watch for a spell. If we come up empty handed, we'll head back."

Whit strained his eyes against the distance, alert for movement that might prove to be deer, elk, buffalo, or Indians.

The expedition had been far more difficult than he had expected. For two months he had been working harder than any slave.

From the time they left Brushy Creek near Austin they had had to make a road for the wagons. At each stream every wagon had to be unloaded, lowered with ropes, hauled back up the opposite bank, and reloaded. Only rarely did they find an adequate ford. Assigned to the fatigue company, Whit had helped wrestle every wagon at each crossing.

Farther up the Brazos they had encountered great herds of buffalo, deer, and elk. That had been a fun time, more like what he thought the expedition would be. When not involved with the wagons, he and the other men had been allowed to hunt. They had killed scores of buffalo. Old Paint had proposed laying over two or three days to jerk the meat. But General McLeod said he was concerned that they might not reach Méjico Nuevo before the first cold norther. The buffalo carcasses were left on the prairie to rot.

On northward they had passed Comanche Peak, a table mountain on the Brazos. Old Paint told Whit that Comanche Peak would be the last known landmark until they reached Santa Fé.

Within days they had entered a low forest of blackjack and post oak. The trees, stunted, gnarled, and twisted, were as solid as iron. Yet a road had to be cut through them for the wagons and cannons. Day after day Whit chopped wood until his hands bled, then chopped more. Thick underbrush had to be removed, rocks and boulders shoved aside. Progress of the expedition slowed to a crawl. Water became a memory. The bawling of thirsty oxen grated on everyone's nerves. Later, when water was found, it was muddy with buffalo manure, and bitter with minerals that sent the men scrambling into the brush with explosive diarrhea.

To lighten the wagons, General McLeod ordered tents and other luxury gear burned. The expedition's supply of meat was abandoned to the wolves.

In the two weeks they spent cutting their way through the Cross Timbers, Whit could not seem to get enough to eat. His clothing shrank, and his muscles grew.

The expedition emerged from the Cross Timbers onto a smooth, undulating prairie. Whit thought their troubles were over. To his joy, he was assigned to Old Paint's scouts. For a while the expedition made ten or fifteen miles a day. Spirits soared.

Then they came to a river, sluggish and dark red with silt. Belief was common that they had found the Red. Old Paint and a few others voiced doubt. But in one of the rifle companies was a man named Carlos, who claimed to have been reared in Santa Fé. He said that as a boy he had traveled with his father, trapping and fishing all along Red River. This, he said, was it.

So for weeks they had followed the river westward. Gradually the stream had led them southwest over increasingly rugged country. Doubts had been growing that this was the Red, but Carlos insisted that just a little way farther on, the river curved back to the northwest. General McLeod had believed him. Now the expedition's food supply was dwindling, and they had not yet seen a hint of the Rocky Mountains.

Old Paint rose to his feet and declared the rest period at end. "I don't see so much as a jackrabbit. We'd best get back."

"Couldn't we go look at that river first?" Whit asked. "See if it's the Brazos?"

"It won't have a sign on it," Old Paint said. "In this country, all rivers are red. They run through the same soil. But I think the time has come for me to lock horns with General McLeod over our situation."

Whit and the scouts rode back eastward. The sun was down by the time they reached camp. Two more of the expedition's oxen were roasting on spits.

Whit and Old Paint walked through the camp to the general's wagon. McLeod and his officers were seated on canvas stools around a campfire. As Old Paint approached they looked up. He spoke loudly and bluntly. "General, I've been giving it a great deal of thought. I believe the Red is fully seventy-five miles north of us. I'm convinced we've been following the wrong river."

McLeod frowned. "You have any more reason for this belief than you had yesterday?"

"Yes, sir. Today we sighted a good-sized river just to the south. I can only conclude it's the Brazos."

McLeod glanced across the campfire. "Lieutenant Hull, what do you say to that?"

Lieutenant Hull, late of Her Majesty's Royal Navy, often made sightings with sextant and transit. Whit had heard that his calculations had been inconclusive.

"I've come to believe us farther south than we expected," Hull conceded. "I now make Santa Fé as three hundred and fifty miles to the northwest."

Whit was aware of the theory behind Hull's figuring. Santa Fé's latitude and longitude were known. If the location of the expedition could be found, the way to Santa Fé could be charted.

McLeod turned to an aide. "Go fetch Carlos."

Whit and Caldwell were invited to be seated by the fire. They were given coffee. In a few minutes McLeod's aide returned with Carlos.

He was a short man of slight build, with a smiling, open face. He exuded sincerity. For a long while no one had doubted him.

"Carlos, Captain Caldwell and Lieutenant Hull are concerned that we've drifted so far to the south. I'm also concerned. Are you sure we're still following Red River?"

Carlos nodded eagerly. "Yes, My General. That is the way of the river. Soon now it curves north."

"Then you know exactly where we are?"

"Yes, My General. In two days we will see Los Cuervos. The Crows. They are three high mountains that the river passes through. Just beyond we will come to Las Angosturas. The Narrows. There the river makes its way through high mountains."

McLeod paused. "How far are we from the nearest ranchos?"

Carlos narrowed his eyes in thought. "Seventy-five miles, My General. I know this country like I know my mother's yard."

McLeod gave Old Paint a quizzical glance. "What do you say to that, Captain?"

"I suppose we have no choice but to give it a try, General."

But on the way back to their bedrolls, Old Paint confided his suspicions to Whit. "I'm beginning to think that Mexican is lying like a dog trotting."

They followed the river through the next two days, constantly searching the horizon for the first glimpse of the Rocky Mountains.

On the third morning, Carlos was gone. He and a friend by the name of Brignoli had fled camp, taking only their bedrolls and a supply of food.

General McLeod brought the news to Old Paint as the scouts prepared to go out on another day's patrol. Whit thought he saw a slight smile of satisfaction behind Old Paint's beard.

McLeod was apologetic. "You've been proved right, Captain. Apparently the man was lying. What would you propose we do?"

"I'd go north, General. Find the Red."

"That's my conclusion. All right. Today we'll leave this river and go northward."

For the next five days they climbed a long series of hills, each higher than the last. The country was rugged, filled with boulders and low brush. Each day Whit rode with the scouts, finding the easiest path for the wagons and cannon.

Water became the primary concern. Every stream was dry.

In the main body of the expedition, discipline vanished. Against orders small parties of men went out to hunt water on their own. Horses, mules, and oxen withered. The men shot and ate jackrabbits, prairie dogs, field mice.

One afternoon the expedition came to an abrupt drop-off of at least three hundred feet. A way was found to lower the wagons into the canyon with ropes.

"Go on and see if you can find water," McLeod told Old Paint. "Looks like we'll be tied up here quite a spell."

Two miles farther on Whit and the scouts found a few pools of brackish water at the bottom of a ravine. Whit dismounted and helped dig in the sand in an effort to find more.

From the direction of the wagons came a dull explosion. Whit assumed someone had fired a cannon. Dark smoke rose.

"Must be Indians," Old Paint shouted. "Come on, boys!"

They raced back to the wagons and found them burning. The entire canyon was on fire. Whit leapt from his gelding and helped pull trunks and goods from the blazing wagons.

Within minutes the crisis was over. The fire burned on up the canyon wall and into the distance.

The evening was spent in unloading the goods and assessing the damage. Two wagons were destroyed. All were damaged. The explosion had come from the expedition's main supply of gunpowder. It was gone, along with the coffee, flour, blankets, and a number of rifles.

The next morning, General McLeod summoned the expedition together. Standing on a charred wagon box, he made a speech.

"Men, we have no choice but to go on. According to Lieutenant Hull's calculations, we're only sixty miles from the ranchos of Méjico Nuevo. There we can buy food. I ask you to please do your best, and endure."

But in the following days the country rose in a series of steppes, with each hill higher than the last. Weakened by thirst, the teams of oxen had to be doubled to pull each wagon up the long slopes.

Rations were cut even further. The men butchered spare horses. In addition to the scouts, other groups were sent out in search of water. One evening Lieutenant Hull and four men failed to return.

The next morning, far out in advance, Whit and the scouts came to an escarpment almost a thousand feet high.

"Well, this puts the lid on it," Old Paint said. "Let's fan out, see if we can find a way for the wagons to go up."

They explored the bottom of the cliff. After several minutes one of the men called out. "Over here, Captain."

The bodies of Lieutenant Hull and his four men lay in the bottom of a gully, riddled with arrows. All had been mutilated in the way Whit first saw three years before, when Tad found the bodies of Bates, Shippen, and Sowers.

Whit looked up. On the lip of the cliff a half mile away a dozen Indians sat on their horses, boldly gazing down into the canyon. "Look yonder, Captain," Whit said quietly.

Old Paint studied the Indians. "Easy does it. No shooting unless they rush us. Let's back off the way we came."

"What about these bodies?" Whit asked.

"We'll leave them, for the time being. Nothing we can do to help them now."

They rode off at a trot, fully expecting pursuit. Whit kept looking back, but he saw none.

Old Paint led them straight to the wagons. There he went to General McLeod and dismounted. Whit held Old Paint's horse while he reported the discovery of Lieutenant Hull and his men, the impassable escarpment, and the sighting of Indians.

"General, way I see it, we've got ourselves in a hell of a fix," Old Paint concluded. "We're lost, pure and simple. The food's run out. In a week the men will be afoot, and starving. The only gunpowder we've got is what we're carrying on us. Hull and his men were killed by Kiowas, the worst there is. They'll be closing in on us, soon as they see the shape we're in. General, something's got to be done, and quick, if we're to get out of this alive."

∗   ∗   ∗

After Jack brought the mail over from Tad's office, Corrie carried it into the long room and examined the return addresses. All were familiar but one.

Curious, Corrie opened the letter from the stranger. It was written on legal parchment:

> My Dear Mrs. Logan,
> Please allow me to convey my most sincere condolences for the passing of your father. He was not only a favored client, but also a friend. His passing has impoverished the lives of all who knew him.

Corrie stopped reading, stunned and confused. Hurriedly she opened her other letters, scanning the first few lines of each. Not one mentioned the death of her father. She checked the postal markings. All the other letters were at least five weeks old. The letter from the stranger was more recent by two weeks.

Mail was often delayed by rain, especially in the bayou country of Louisiana and East Texas. Corrie assumed the letter from the stranger had come by ship to New Orleans or Galveston, often a faster route.

Holding the letter against her knee to still a sudden trembling, she resumed reading:

> Your father's last will and testament names me as the executor of his estate. I'm sure that in taking this action, your father took into consideration that I have served as his legal counsel six years, am familiar with the details of his holdings, and that you and your sister, sole heirs, are remote from the courts that have jurisdiction.
>
> I will forward to you, under separate cover, certified copies of the will, and the necessary legal papers. I'm writing you now to ascertain what route you and your sister wish me to take.
>
> As you may know, your father never fully recovered from

the Panic. His debts remain heavy. Unless relief is imminent in the form of considerable cash, I see no way the estate can escape falling to his creditors. But with care, and immediate dispersal, I believe a few thousand dollars can be salvaged after all obligations are met. I believe this to be the best course. But I am quite willing to attempt to save Moultrie Hill if you and your sister wish to do so.

Sincerely
M. Barnaby McQuaggue

Corrie gathered the letters and walked down the hall. Prue was on her bed, deep into Hawthorne's *Twice-Told Tales*. She looked up and saw the letters.

"Mail? Anything for me?"

"Four letters," Corrie said. "But there's terribly bad news, Prue."

She handed the letter to Prue and sat on the foot of the bed. Prue took the letter. A sad frown came over her face as she read it. "This is all?"

"The other letters were written earlier. Father must have passed away a few days before Mr. McQuaggue wrote."

Prue reread the letter. She looked up at Corrie. "I'm just numb. I guess it will hit me later."

"I know," Corrie said. "His life was so linked to Mother's. I somehow knew he wouldn't live long. . . . Still, I didn't think it would be so soon."

Prue gestured with the letter. "What will we do about this?"

"We don't have to decide right now. When we've had time to recover from the shock, we can discuss it."

"Would Tad help us save Moultrie Hill?" Prue asked.

Corrie hesitated. Tad seemed to have turned his back on the South. He was investing all of his capital in Texas. She did not know how much of his inheritance was left.

"He might, if I asked. But I hate to propose it. I know it's impractical."

Prue sighed. "I suppose so." She picked up her book, marked her place, and put it aside. When she spoke, her voice was husky with emotion. "Boy, howdy. All the bridges are burning behind me. I came out here on a visit. Now I'm an orphan, with no home to go back to. Corrie, I'm not ready for all this."

An idea had been forming in Corrie's mind for months. "I wouldn't mention this now, except you seem to want to talk. The money from Moultrie Hill, whatever it amounts to, is all yours, if you'll do one thing for me. Go back to Charleston or Savannah and a good school for at least a year. Make your debut. It isn't as if we're suddenly without family. We have aunts and uncles all over who would be proud to sponsor you."

Prue's eyes widened. "Alone?"

"You could take Hattie with you. Tad could escort you to Victoria or Galveston. We could have all arrangements made by the time the money is in hand."

Prue remained silent for a time, then shook her head. "It wouldn't work. Corrie, I can't be the glorious debutante you were. Don't you know that? The time is past. There are a million things to learn. A man holds his gloves this way, and it means something. A lady holds her fan another way and it means something else. On and on. That's a different world. I used to know some of it, but I've forgot what I did know."

"You could relearn it."

"What for? Corrie, your debut meant the world to me back then. I was thrilled to be a part of it. I thought I'd be in your place someday. But looking back, from this perspective, it all seems so *false*."

"Prue, there's nothing false about manners, proper conduct."

Prue made a sweeping gesture. "I'm talking about that whole way of life. I think Ramsey saw it for what it was. That's what I meant the other day, when I said I sensed he was unhappy with that life. The men so involved with their blooded horses and hounds. The women with their oh-so-correct little social tête-à-têtes. Corrie, I wouldn't want to go back to that. I once thought I did, but now I don't. I like what I see here. I've developed a preference for these men who talk grand schemes and smell of gunpowder."

"But how long will it be before their grand schemes come to pass?"

"I don't care. Most of the fun will be in the doing."

Corrie did not respond. Prue's lack of discrimination among her admirers had become a growing concern. Corrie often felt Prue encouraged only suitors she could manipulate.

She decided not to pursue the subject. "I won't press you," she said. "It's your life. But if you change your mind, the offer still stands."

Deeply troubled, Tad reread the long letter from Sam Houston. A worse litany of news he could not imagine:

> I have on the instant learned from dependable sources in Chihuahua that four thousand Mexican troops have marched through there, heading northward into Méjico Nuevo to intercept Lamar's Santa Fé Expedition. This I anticipated. From the Mexican perspective the expedition could only be regarded as hostile. I'm confident that before McLeod reaches Santa Fé he will find himself actively engaged with troops of the regular Mexican army.
>
> The question now is whether Santa Anna will follow with an invasion of this portion of Texas. I would appreciate any information you may have gathered from your sources, as to the disposition of Mexican troops below the Rio Grande, etc.
>
> Also, I would welcome, and hold confidential, any assessment you may forward concerning how my candidacy fares in Béxar. While I remain confident, nothing should be taken for granted. Of your own candidacy I have no doubt of success. The reports I hear from all quarters are good. As you probably know, I have spoken in your behalf frequently during the past few weeks. My motives are not altogether altruistic. We have a tough task ahead, my friend, in attempting to preserve our beloved Republic.

Tad was shaken. Nothing had been heard from the Santa Fé Expedition for three months.

Even at the moment, Whit might be fighting with the Mexican army, or dead.

And Tad's worries went even beyond his concern for Whit. If the Santa Fé Expedition was attacked, renewal of the war with Mexico seemed certain, and Texas was in no shape to fight.

After three years of Lamar's administration, the Republic was four and a half million dollars in debt. Lamar had failed in his attempt to obtain a seven-million-dollar loan from France. Diplomatic recognition had come from England, Belgium, and Holland, but France's turndown had made them also wary of lending Texas money.

To cover his lavish expenses, Lamar had issued two and a half million dollars in redback currency. The redbacks were rated as low as twelve cents to the U.S. dollar.

Now the election was weeks away. Sam Houston's return to the presidency was deemed likely. His opponent was David Burnet, a poor speaker further hampered by his ties to the Lamar administration.

Tad remained convinced that all hope for the Republic lay with Sam Houston. The Old Warrior had maneuvered Texas out of many scrapes. Maybe he could do so one more time.

Tad wrote a hurried reply to Houston's letter, pledging his continued support. He gave his candid opinion that Houston would carry Béxar by a significant majority.

He added a personal note:

> Your report from Chihuahua was also disturbing to me for private reasons. Against my better judgment, I allowed my younger brother Whit to accompany the Santa Fé Expedition. Any information you can forward concerning the expedition's fate will be most appreciated. He is young, and naturally I fear for his safety.

Tad finished the letter, sealed it, and put it into the box for Jack to include in the outgoing mail. He blew out the lamp and left the office.

The night was dark. An unseasonably cool norther had struck in midafternoon. As he walked along Commerce beside the plaza, canvas awnings fluttered and popped overhead.

He passed Black's Saloon. Voices and laughter came through the open door. Tad was tempted to go in for a drink. But the hour was late, he was tired, and he was in a hurry to reach home and bed. He was committed to leave at daylight with a team of surveyors to locate a plat of land down by the Nueces.

He reached the corner of the plaza and turned toward home. At that moment some sixth sense gave him warning. He heard nothing amiss, saw nothing unusual. But suddenly his every nerve was on edge. He stepped deeper into the shadows. The move may have saved his life.

Pain struck him an instant before he heard the gunshot. He felt himself falling. He rolled on the paving stones, drew his pistol, and searched for a target. Two more shots came in quick succession. Tad fired at the muzzle blasts, emptying his pistol.

He fell back, dismayed by his weakness. He reached for the other gun at his waist, but his arm would not cooperate. A wave of darkness came over him.

He fought his way back to consciousness. A crowd stood over him. He could see feet, but no faces. Someone was holding a lantern at knee level, blocking his view. He tried to sit up.

"He's coming around," someone said.

John Black, still wearing his bartender's apron, knelt beside him. "Colonel, just lie still. We've sent for the doctor. He'll be here in a minute."

Tad's back hurt. His left arm was numb. He had no feeling in his left hand. He struggled to speak. "Who was it?"

Black glanced across the street. "Nobody knows, Colonel. The man's been hanging around the plaza the last day or two. You put two or three balls into him. He's deader'n hell."

"Fowler," Tad said. "I think his name's Wilbur Fowler. He's a horse thief."

"Was," Black said. "He's nothing now."

Dr. Weideman pushed his way through the crowd. He knelt over Tad, lifted him with one powerful arm, and probed along his back with the other. "We must get this man home," he said. "We need a litter. A door. A blanket. Anything."

Again he raised Tad's body. Paralyzing pain shot through Tad's back. Blackness returned.

He awoke in his own bedroom, lying on his right side. Every lamp in the house was arranged around him. The flames were turned high, making the room as light as day. Corrie, Jack, and Prue stood near, holding lamps. Dr. Weideman was working on his back. Weideman was the first to notice that he had regained consciousness.

"Lie still, Tad," he said. "I'll be through in a minute."

Tad's back and side felt as if he were on fire. "What the hell are you doing?"

"Sewing you up like an old sack of potatoes. Your scapula—the shoulder blade—turned the ball. It ripped a gash up to your shoulder. If the man hadn't been so intent on shooting you in the back, he might have killed you."

"How bad am I hit?"

"You'll live. Part of the ball penetrated the chest cavity, but stopped short of the lungs. I fished it out. You haven't lost much blood. But you'll have to stay off your feet a few weeks."

Tad thought of his court commitments. "How soon will I be able to ride?"

"Oh, you could ride tomorrow, I guess. But if you did, it'd probably finish you off." Weideman laughed uproariously at his own joke. "Now, Tad, I'm going to wrap you up like an Egyptian mummy. After a couple of weeks, we'll unwrap you and see how much damage that fellow's done to your muscles. Then we'll talk about your travel plans."

"Just relax, Tad," Corrie said. "Try not to worry."

But he was besieged by worries. He had legal cases hanging fire in a dozen courts scattered over half of West Texas. His desk was loaded with papers demanding attention. Scores of clients were depending on him. Upriver, the crops were ripening. They must be harvested, taken to market. Thousands of cattle roamed his land downriver, as yet unbranded. His impending election to Congress would require his presence in Austin. And Whit was riding blindly toward an encounter with the Mexican army.

"I can't allow this to happen," he said. "I've got to get on my feet."

He tried to rise, and again sank into blackness.

Whit shoved his hunger aside and concentrated on keeping his face shielded from the icy north wind. Ahead the landscape was so flat that the horizon was a great distance away. He watched for movement, any sign of game. Aside from a few scraps of jerky, he had not eaten in twenty-four hours. But nothing stirred. The plains stretched away with monotonous lack of detail as far as the eye could see.

Eight days ago the expedition had been divided into two commands. The main body was to stay with the wagons and cannons in the big canyon. The best-mounted men were to travel on to the nearest settlements in Méjico Nuevo, hire guides and purchase supplies, and send them back for the rescue of the main body. Whit had been among the ninety-nine men chosen to go in the advance party.

Their first three days had been spent in crossing no more than ten miles of rough country. After they climbed the escarpment, onto what the men were now calling the Cap Rock, they found their way blocked by two more massive canyons. Each had required an exhausting day to cross.

For the last five days they had marched across immense, barren plains. It had been assumed they would find sufficient game en route. Thus far the pickings had been slim. A small bear and a lone, aged bull buffalo were all they had sighted and killed. The meat had not gone far among ninety-nine starving men. Yesterday a herd of wild horses passed well out of rifle range, but no other game had been seen.

For an hour Whit kept observing an odd cloud formation low on the western horizon. Strangely, the cloud did not seem to move. Whit's eyes were tearing from the cold wind. He wiped them dry and focused on the spot. Other clouds were moving. That one remained fixed. He spurred his gelding and moved to the head of the column.

"Captain Sutton, there's something on the horizon yonder," he reported. "I believe it's a mountain."

Sutton stood in his stirrups and squinted. His white hair fluttered in the wind. "Your eyes are better'n mine, Logan."

"I think I see something, Captain," said Lieutenant Lubbock.

"May be a rain cloud," Sutton said. "Storms tend to come from that direction."

"If it was a rain cloud, seems it'd be moving, sir," Whit said. "I've been watching it quite a spell. It hasn't moved. I truly believe we're seeing the mountains, sir."

"He's right," Lieutenant Lubbock said. "Other clouds are moving. That one isn't."

Word spread back down the column. A cheer went up. The plains had seemed endless. Now mountains were in sight.

"Logan, you were with Caldwell's scouts, weren't you?"

"Yes, sir," Whit said.

"You've good eyes. Ride up here with headquarters company. Lieutenant Lubbock may find use for you."

"That I will, sir," Whit said.

After another two hours the distant mountains grew more distinct. The plains gave way to undulating ground. Toward sundown they came to a valley with a small, free-flowing stream bordered by cottonwoods.

"Look, Colonel," Lubbock said. "Some of those trees have been felled by axes."

The cuttings were old, but there was no doubt. The marks had been made by axes.

"You can take heart, men," Sutton said. "We're drawing close to civilized habitation."

The men spread out, hunting game. By sundown they had found only terrapins, lizards, and skunks. In the twilight a few tried to cook and eat their harvest to the scornful taunts of others.

Whit did not participate in the byplay. He crawled into his bedroll painfully hungry, yet oddly content.

The Rocky Mountains were in sight. His long ordeal clearly was near an end. Soon he would be heading back home. For once Whit yielded to his homesickness and drifted off to sleep comforted by the thought that before long he would be back in San Antonio de Béxar with Corrie, Tad, Jack, and Prue.

In the depths of his fever, Tad reminded Corrie of a wounded animal. He seemed incapable of comprehending the extent of his injuries. He raged constantly against his helplessness, giving no one around him a single moment of peace. A dozen times a day he attempted to leave his bed only to fall back, weakened by the struggle against his harness. Corrie became frantic, for Dr. Weideman had made her responsibility plain.

"You've got to keep him quiet," Weideman had said. "The ball hit the edge of his left shoulder blade and split. A part went south, into his chest cavity. That apparently caused little harm, or he'd be dead by now. But the main part of the ball went up through his shoulder muscles, ripping them loose. They must have time to heal and reattach themselves. If they don't, he'll lose most of the use of that arm."

As his fever slowly subsided, Corrie thought his restlessness would fade. It only grew worse.

"I have things to do," he complained. "I can't waste time like this."

Jack shaved and bathed him daily. Corrie sought ways to pamper him, divert his attention. She conspired with Consuelo to cook his favorite dishes. Prue tracked down every recent newspaper and read to him by the hour.

In time the whole household came to revolve around Tad's sickbed. Yet he remained constantly fretful, tossing and turning.

In desperation Corrie turned to Jack, who knew him better than anyone else on earth.

"Only one thing puts Marsh Tad's mind at ease, Miss Corrie," Jack said. "That's work. Long as he's working, he's happy. When he ain't, he's miserable. He'll be miserable as long as he's in that bed."

Weideman had said Tad should remain in bed for weeks. Corrie was beginning to worry about his mental state as much as the physical. She knew something had to be done.

"Tad, you keep saying you should be up, working," she said one evening. "If you were able, what would you be doing? What is most important?"

Just thinking about it seemed to agitate him. He attempted a half-sitting position, but the harness held him back. "A million things," he said. "I have important letters that should be in the mail. The crops should be harvested. I've clients to write, cases to study, appeals to draft. Surveys to plat. Deeds to file." He spread his free hand to demonstrate the hopelessness.

"Jack could be supervising in the fields," she told him quietly. "He could go out and give orders in the morning, report back to you what's done, how the work is progressing."

"He doesn't have the eye for it. The hands would shirk on him."

"I think you're underestimating the loyalty of your men," Corrie said. "They know you're laid up, that Jack's out of his element. I doubt they'd take advantage of you."

Tad did not answer.

"It'd be better to try to work through Jack than allowing the crops to rot in the fields," Corrie said. "You might as well face it, Tad. You're not going to be yourself again for weeks, maybe months."

"Once I get these stitches out, and this harness off, I'll be able to get around," Tad said. "Weideman said three weeks."

"He also said you'll have to take it slow for a while, and that it'll be some time before you'll regain full use of that arm. He said any effort to rush it could be detrimental."

"Weideman doesn't know everything."

"Still, it will be a while. The work in the fields needs to be done now. Jack could be our salvation."

Tad clenched and unclenched his good hand. "I should never have let Whit go off on that expedition."

He remained silent, morose for a time. When he failed to argue further, Corrie knew she had won.

"I can't help you with the deeds and surveys," she resumed. "But I'm not exactly illiterate. I've been told I write a fair hand. You once said Sam Houston often reclines on a couch while dictating to his secretary. I assume you could do the same."

Again Tad did not answer. Corrie assumed he was reflecting that Sam Houston's secretary wrote with a properly bold male scrawl, not in a light feminine hand. But after a moment he surprised her.

"There's a letter that should have gone out weeks ago. You can inscribe it for me. Send Jack for my writing materials."

The promise of accomplishment improved his disposition noticeably. He waited impatiently for Jack to bring the stationery, and for Corrie to prepare for dictation.

"Address the first one to President Mirabeau Lamar, Texas Capitol, Austin. Dear Mr. President. I deem it incumbent on me to convey to you information I have received, on the very best authority—underline *very*—that troops from the regular Mexican army have been dispatched up the Rio Grande to intercept the Texas Santa Fé Expedition, presumably somewhere east of Santa Fé."

Corrie stopped writing. Tad had known about this for weeks! No wonder he had been so restless.

She thought of Whit, riding blindly toward battle. "What is that very best authority?" she asked Tad.

He hesitated before answering. "Sam Houston, but I don't want to put that in the letter."

"You think the report true?"

He nodded. "Sam has better sources of information than Lamar. It may explain why nothing has been heard from the expedition since its departure."

"Tad, why didn't you tell me? He's my brother too."

"I didn't want to worry you. There's nothing we can do."

Corrie thought of Whit, so young, so eager to please. "If there's a battle, what are their chances?"

Tad did not hesitate. Clearly he had been thinking about it. "They're well armed. They have cannon, quite a number of experienced men. General McLeod was a failure as a peace commissioner, but he's a graduate of West Point. Adolphus Sterne said he acquitted himself well against the Cherokees, and he was sufficiently in the action that he was wounded. All in all, I believe they'll give a good account of themselves." He pointed to the letter. "Let's get this written. I'd like for it to go out tomorrow."

Corrie resumed writing.

"Mr. President, I urge you, with all the strength at my command, to prevail upon the good offices of our friends among the nations of the world, to convey to Santa Anna that the expedition was conceived and executed with peaceful intent. The State Department in Washington may be inclined to act in our behalf, in light of the several United States citizens on the expedition. I also believe there was an English gentleman. London also might take note."

Tad offered other suggestions as to how Lamar might assure Mexico of the expedition's peaceful intentions. He read over the letter and apparently was satisfied.

The letter was the first of many. The Logan compound fell into a routine. Each morning before breakfast Tad gave Jack orders on what the men were to do through the day. Jack issued the orders at the slave quarters, then returned to shave and bathe Tad. By mid-morning Corrie was taking dictation. She and Tad worked until late afternoon, when Jack returned to report on progress made through the day. In the evening Prue read newspapers to him. Afterward Tad usually took Jim Bowie onto his sickbed and played with him.

Corrie was amazed by the breadth and depth of Tad's daily correspondence. He exchanged thoughts and opinions with foremost Texians, such as Sam Houston, Tom Rusk, Anson Jones, David Burnet, Adolphus Sterne, Senator Gaines, and Mirabeau Lamar. He not only kept them informed on events in San Antonio de Béxar, but also passed along reports he received from informants along the border. In addition, his correspondence with his legal associates in East Texas was extensive, and just as detailed.

Corrie remembered that Senator Gaines had once told her Tad was one of a network of close friends throughout Texas. With her glimpse into Tad's private world, she began to understand how the network operated in guiding the Republic.

For the first time since her marriage Corrie felt she and Tad were truly sharing. Often he stopped in dictation to explain the reasons behind an elliptical phrase, a vague reference, or some legal terminology. He told her of the complex system of *derechos*, ignored by many Anglos, who only wanted quick profits. He said he wanted unclouded titles so that none of their sons or grandsons would ever experience difficulty.

As they worked, Tad eagerly kept a running count on the days before Dr. Weideman's return to remove the wrappings and stitching. Corrie was less enthusiastic. Although she was glad to see Tad slowly regaining strength, she feared that once he was released from his harness he no longer would rest as he should.

But the day arrived. Tad ordered Jack to shave and bathe him early. He then waited restlessly until midmorning, when he lost patience.

"Jack, go up to Dr. Weideman's place and see what's keeping him," he said. "The fool must've forgot what day it is."

When Jack returned, he stood in the doorway for a moment with an odd expression. "Marsh Tad, they say Dr. Weideman's dead."

Tad jerked as if he'd been struck. "Who's 'they'?"

"Everybody at Dr. Weideman's place. They all crying. They say Colonel Hays came back from Gonzáles and say there was a cloudburst up there. Dr. Weideman drowned crossing a creek."

"You're sure about this?"

"They say it was Peach Creek. This side Gonzales. You know the place, Marsh Tad."

Tad hit the mattress with his fist. Tears welled in his eyes. "Damn fool. Never had a lick of caution about him. Shows how this country can get you the minute you're not looking."

Corrie knew Tad also was thinking of Whit, exposed to the same dangers.

Tad stacked the law books he had been consulting and put them on the table beside the bed. He wrestled his torso into a sitting position. "Jack, go get scissors, a pair of pliers, and a bottle of whiskey. I'm getting out of this rig."

"No, Tad, please," Corrie said. "Let's have another doctor do it."

"I don't want anyone else working on me. Weideman said it could come off today. That's good enough for me. Pulling stitches doesn't require a surgeon. Jack can do it."

Corrie knew he would not be dissuaded. When he settled on a course, there was no turning him.

Jack returned. Corrie lit a lamp. Jack held the scissors and stood awkwardly by the bed.

"Get the wrappings off first," Tad said. "Cut them straight down the back."

Tad rolled over, facedown on the bed. Corrie held the lamp so Jack would have ample light.

The heavy wrappings did not yield easily. Jack cut through layer after layer. The final bandage adhered solidly to the flesh.

Jack tugged at it experimentally. "It's stickin', Marsh Tad. This gonna hurt."

"Jack, you do have a talent for useless conversation," Tad said. "Get on with it."

Jack remained unperturbed. "I think maybe you better take a drink of that whiskey first."

"That's the best idea you've had all day."

Tad drank from the bottle. After a moment Jack retrieved it. "Maybe I better have some of that, too, Marsh Tad. It'll steady my hand."

"Don't drink it all. Way you're going, I'll need it."

Jack drank from the bottle, winked at Corrie, and resumed tugging the bandage free. As blood welled, Corrie could not bear to watch. She closed her eyes and concentrated on holding the lamp steady.

Jack pulled firmly until the wound was fully exposed. Bundling bandages and wrappings, he tossed them aside.

Tad rolled onto his right side. Holding his left hand with his right, he tried moving the injured muscles. "Stiff and sore," he reported. "I have no strength in it."

"You can't expect to use it right off," Corrie told him.

Tad again rolled onto his stomach. "Pull the stitches," he told Jack. "Just snip the thread, and pull each stitch through."

Corrie leaned over the bed for a close examination of the wound. It was dark and ugly, and more than six inches long. Weideman's sewing was neat, the thread taut across the wound. But festering pockets had formed around some of the stitches.

Carefully, Jack snipped the first three pieces of the heavy thread. He picked up the pliers and jerked the first stitch free.

Tad looked up in irritation. "Damn it, Jack! What'd you do, pull the knotted end through?"

Jack ignored him and continued to work.

After a time Jack paused. "That's twelve," he said. "Only twenty-two more to go."

"Pay less attention to counting and more to what you're doing," Tad said. "How does it look?"

"Not bad, Marsh Tad. Remember that old bull of Marsh Frank's that got gored? He was hurt worse. And he got well."

At last all the stitches were out. Jack covered the wound with fresh but loose bandages. Tad sat up and flexed his injured arm. He was not pleased. "Weideman said I'd probably regain use of it. Right now, I couldn't throw my hat with it."

"Doctor Weideman also said the healing would take time," Corrie reminded him.

Tad seemed not to have heard. He tried to raise the arm above shoulder level, but failed. "I suppose it doesn't matter," he said. "A man only needs one arm to get on a horse."

The next morning he ordered Jack to saddle a bay gelding. Jack helped him mount. Although still visibly weak, Tad went with Jack and the men into the upper fields. At midmorning he and Jack came by the house only briefly to pick up some papers before going to his office.

In the days that followed he seemed to be driving himself to exhaustion to keep his mind off Whit. He had only partial use of his arm, and took Jack with him everywhere he went. As he slowly recovered strength, he fell back into his habit of leaving the house early, and returning late.

Corrie was left desolate, feeling that somehow she had failed. Tad's narrow escape from death, his convalescence, should have renewed their marriage.

Instead, she now found herself more alone than ever.

* * *

The village lay in the curve of a clear stream, nestled into a grove of dark green cedars. Beyond, to the west and northwest, the spires of the Rocky Mountains rose deep blue, capped with white peaks. On his arrival the previous evening Whit had thought it the most beautiful sight in the world. Now he was not so sure.

"I'll be glad to be shut of this town," McAllister said behind him. "Something's not right here."

Whit nodded agreement. The Mexican captain with all the gold braid had come out from town an hour ago to announce that Governor Armijo would greet the Texians personally. But the morning sun was climbing higher and as yet nothing had happened.

The last few days had been a kaleidoscope of hardship and suffering. Forty-eight hours ago they had encountered a band of Mexicans returning from a trading expedition among the Indians. The Mexicans had shared their food with the starving Texians, and sent to nearby ranchos for more. Amazingly, they knew about the expedition and the wagons in the big canyon, which they called the Palo Duro. Colonel Cooke had hired the Mexicans to return to the canyon to rescue the main body.

Five men were sent on ahead under the command of Captain William Lewis to inform the Mexicans of the expedition's arrival. The advance party itself had come on to this village.

Now the expedition was strung out across two hundred and fifty miles of barren country. Whit knew this was not wise, but under the circumstances it seemed best, for the men were in bad shape. Cheeks were hollow, and eyes sunken. Some were so emaciated that they staggered about camp, feet dragging, arms hanging listlessly, their clothing in tatters. Whit himself felt an unfamiliar weakness to his muscles. He had been glad to see the Mexican traders, and the village, the first signs of civilization the expedition had seen in four months.

But as McAllister observed, something was not right. Last evening a four-man detail sent into town to buy supplies had been arrested. Later a Mexican officer rode out and apologized, saying it was a simple misunderstanding. The men were released.

And now the advance party was being kept waiting.

The morning was cold. The early sun struck full on the higher mountains to the northwest, placing them in bold contrast against the surrounding evergreens. Whit was moved by the haunting loveliness of the peaks, so different from any other in his experience. He thought of the hardships the members of the expedition had endured to see these mountains. He also thought of Lieutenant Hull and the other men who would never see them.

"They're coming out," McAllister said.

Whit turned his attention toward the town. A company of Mexican cavalry rode out at a trot, crossing the shallow stream.

"Form up, men," Lieutenant Lubbock called. "The ceremony's about to begin."

Whit helped McAllister to his feet. McAllister had injured a leg as a boy in Alabama, and walked with a permanent limp. Two days ago he had badly sprained the other ankle. Whit had been helping him in moving about.

The advance party fell into a semblance of military formation. Much of the previous evening had been spent in repairing clothing and equipment, in an effort to present as good an appearance as possible.

While they aligned ranks, another company of Mexican cavalry came out from town and moved to the left. Both Mexican companies halted about a hundred yards distant, sabers and pikes gleaming, guidons and plumes rippling in the wind.

"Good God, look!" McAllister said.

Whit followed his gaze. A third company of Mexican cavalry was emerging from the trees behind the Texians. A murmur of concern swept through the Texas camp. Whit felt cold chills up his back. Six hundred Mexican soldiers now faced the advance party on three sides, hemming it against the river.

Whit glanced toward Cooke, Sutton, and their aides. They were conferring in low voices. Lieutenant Lubbock strolled up close to where Whit was standing. "Don't be obvious about it," he said quietly. "But see to your weapons. Colonel Cooke has issued orders to prepare for action. Pass the word."

Whit found himself surprisingly calm. He carried his two Colt revolvers and a Colt revolving rifle. From what he could see, the Mexicans were armed with old flintlocks, muskets, and shotguns.

The advance party was outnumbered six to one. But Whit believed the superiority in arms would more than make up the difference.

"Sir, there's Captain Lewis!" someone called.

Whit turned to look. Lewis, one of the five sent on ahead two days ago, was riding leisurely across the stream from the village, accompanied by the Mexican army officer so amply bespangled with brass and decorations.

Lewis rode straight to Cooke and saluted. He spoke loudly. Whit had no difficulty hearing his words. "Sir, I regret to inform you that the country is up in arms over the expedition's arrival. In addition to the six hundred troops you see, there are four thousand more, better equipped, on the way here now. There are five thousand en route from Chihuahua, expected any day."

A buzz of anger swept through the Texian ranks. Cooke put his hands on his hips and took two steps toward Lewis. "That's not what I was led to believe last evening by Captain Salazar."

"I'm afraid Captain Salazar was talking a delaying action, Colonel. The army was preparing to fight. But I believe I've worked out a solution. Governor Armijo has agreed that if you'll give up your arms, the expedition will be allowed to go into Santa Fé and trade. At the end of eight days, your arms will be returned."

"Don't do it, sir!" someone shouted. A chorus of agreement rose from the Texians.

"Silence!" Cooke ordered. He turned back to Lewis. "Captain, I won't surrender our arms. You know me better than that."

"Colonel, this is the custom of the St. Louis traders who visit Santa Fé regularly. I pledge my honor that I've seen this policy in operation. Surely this is best, sir."

Cooke, Sutton, and the other officers moved away to confer. They talked in such low voices that Whit could not hear.

His initial alarm was turning to anger. He had not come six hundred miles to surrender. He spoke low to Lubbock. "Lieutenant, I'm not about to give up my guns without a fight."

A grumble of agreement came from the men around him.

"Let's not be foolish, Logan," Lubbock said. "If Lewis is telling the truth about those four thousand troops, we wouldn't have a prayer."

Whit felt emboldened by the support. "Please ask the colonel to consider our wishes, sir."

Lubbock nodded. He walked across the campground to where the expedition officers were now talking with Lewis. A heated argument seemed to be in progress. After listening for a time, Lubbock returned and raised his voice. "Prepare to stack arms, men. Captain Lewis has pledged on his Masonic oath that he speaks the truth, and that no harm will come to us."

Whit did not know much about Freemasonry, except that Tad was high on it. He wondered what Tad would do in this situation.

"I'm game to fight if anyone else is," McAllister said. "Logan, what about you?"

Whit studied the Mexican soldiers. They were a miserable looking, ragtag bunch. It was common knowledge that Mexico's army consisted mostly of convicts and conscripts. If the Texan Santa Fé Expedition was together, and in good order, it might be able to whip several times its number in Mexicans. But the advance party could not be considered a military unit. It now consisted of ninety-four men, some trained, most untrained. All had been half starved for the last three weeks. They were low on gunpowder.

Lubbock was right. With four thousand better-equipped troops entering the fray, there would be no contest.

"I guess I'll put my trust in Colonel Cooke and Captain Lewis," he said.

After another wait the order came: mark and stack arms. Whit scratched his initials on his rifle and pistols. Reluctantly he joined the long line and placed his guns on the growing pile. He returned to ranks feeling naked and defenseless.

A platoon of Mexican foot soldiers came out from town and faced the Texians. Captain Salazar, the one with all the braid, shouted orders to them in Spanish.

McAllister had lived in Mexico for a time and spoke Spanish well. "Good Lord," he said. "We're going to be searched! Does this sound like we've surrendered our guns for safekeeping?"

An argument erupted between the Texian officers and Captain Salazar. After an exchange, Cooke suddenly broke off and shouted at Captain Lewis. "You son of a bitch! You goddamned *traitor*! What is your honor worth? I hope you rot in hell!"

Salazar laughed and spoke to his aides. They laughed.

"I knew it," McAllister said. "We're prisoners. We should've fought while we had the chance."

Orders were issued for the Texians to form double lines. Helping McAllister, Whit failed to move fast enough to satisfy one of the guards. He punched Whit in the ribs with a rifle butt. Whit resisted the impulse to jerk the gun from the Mexican's hands and crack open his head with it.

They formed two lines and waited. Captain Salazar rode up and down their ranks, looking at them.

"Stand a little to your left, Logan," McAllister said behind Whit. "I'll try to hide my money, best I can."

Whit took a half step to the left to give McAllister cover. He resisted a strong impulse to touch the gold coins Hattie had stitched into a hidden pocket in his shirt. He felt he had a chance of diverting attention from them, but he could not think of a way to hide his watch, gold ring, and bowie knife.

They were marched forward to a search point. Whit's watch, watchfob, and ring were stripped from him and tossed onto a pile. A Mexican soldier pulled out Whit's shirttail and ran a hand over bare flesh. Whit looked him in the eye and raised his shirt, showing he had no money belt. He was waved on.

Again they were formed into ranks, and told each man could take one blanket from his personal baggage.

Still in double line, they were marched toward town. Whit put an arm around McAllister and helped him along, half carrying him at times. The stream was knee deep and icy cold. Whit's boots filled and his feet quickly numbed.

As they entered Antón Chico, Whit searched for any means of escape. But the plaza effectively served as a prison. On all four sides adobe houses formed a solid wall. Most had but a single door. None had windows. The roofs were flat. Only a small detachment of soldiers was needed to guard each of the four corners of the plaza.

They were ordered to sit in rows on the hard stones of the plaza, and to keep silent. But the guards withdrew some distance, and the Texians were able to talk in whispers.

Speculation on their fate ranged widely. Some thought they would be set free the moment Governor Armijo arrived, read the letters from President Lamar, and understood the purpose of the expedition. Others thought they would be shot. No one knew. As the hours passed, Whit grew weary of thinking about it.

All day they were given no food or water. Whit's hunger and thirst were bearable only because he had grown accustomed to such suffering. A few of the Texians were certain they would be given supper, but the day ended and no food came.

After sundown the temperature dropped rapidly. No fires were allowed. Whit and McAllister pooled their blankets and shared their body heat. Whit found sleep impossible. He could not stop shivering, nor could he keep his mind from what he might face at dawn. He remembered Tad's stories of the Texians who had surrendered at Goliad and Refugio. They had been taken out and shot. Whit saw no reason to hope the policy in Méjico Nuevo would be any different. He knew he must brace himself to meet whatever might come, for this might be his last night on earth.

Toward morning he slept from total exhaustion.

He awoke to a flare of trumpets. Governor Manuel Armijo rode into the square, accompanied by a personal bodyguard. All the Mexicans were in full dress regalia. Whit was stunned to see Captain Lewis among them, mounted, his boots and brass polished as if for parade.

A roar went up from the prisoners. Captain Lewis was called every name the Texians could think of or invent. Sentries cocked their rifles and moved forward menacingly. A Mexican officer shouted for the Texians to be silent.

Governor Armijo abruptly reined in his horse and began to shout. His Spanish was so fast and broken that Whit could make no sense of it.

"He's mad because we're not bound," McAllister whispered. "He says he wants us trussed up like hogs."

Lariats were brought. Whit was bound hand and foot and tied

into a string with McAllister and four other Texians. Again they were told to sit on the stones of the plaza.

There they remained through the long morning. At noon each prisoner was brought a wooden bowl of *miel*, a mixture of molasses and water. Then they continued to sit on the stones through the long afternoon.

After sundown Governor Armijo and his highest ranking officers met in the corner of the plaza, not far from where Whit and McAllister were seated. McAllister's hearing was unusually good. The other prisoners were asked to keep quiet so McAllister could monitor the discussion. He listened for a time in silence. At last he sighed. "Oh, Lord, boys, they're arguing over whether to shoot us. Armijo is for it. Some are against. At the moment, it sounds like this'll be another Goliad."

Whit felt mounting desperation. "We can untie each other, rush the guards," he whispered to the men around him. "Some of us might make it."

"What if we did?" McAllister asked. "You know how rough this country is. They'd ride us down. Hush now! I should be listening to this."

The argument continued. Deep silence fell over the Texians.

Whit was surprised to discover that he had no fear of death. His overriding emotion was regret. He wanted to see Corrie, Tad, Prue, Hattie, and Jack one last time. But mostly he was filled with a profound sadness for the life he never had.

Sitting in the icy wind of the Méjico Nuevo night, while his fate was debated, he yearned for the women he would never meet, never hold in his arms, never love.

Odd delights came randomly to mind: sunsets, watermelon, the sight of horses romping on cold, brisk mornings. He thought of the evenings shared with Corrie, the closeness he had enjoyed with Tad, his delightful running verbal competition with Prue. In thinking back on those moments, Whit felt he knew the true meaning of love.

The argument in the corner of the plaza grew more heated. Voices were raised.

"Some want to take us to Santa Anna in chains," McAllister

whispered. "Others say it would be less trouble to shoot us, and to send Santa Anna our ears. The odds are about even."

After a time the discussion died away. Soon there came only single words, in different voices: "*¡Sí!*" and "*¡Opuesto!*" time after time.

Whit tried to follow the voting, but lost count.

Governor Armijo made a short speech. McAllister gave a sigh of relief. "Immediate execution failed by one vote. Armijo said he would abide by the decision. We're to be marched to Mexico City and handed over to Santa Anna."

Again whispers carried the news down the rows of Texians.

"How far is it to Mexico City?" someone asked.

"About twelve hundred miles, as the crow flies," McAllister said. "But we ain't crows. The road'll be over some of the highest mountains and some of the worst deserts you'll ever see. And if we get there, Santa Anna still may order us shot. If he doesn't, we'll be thrown into prison. After our little two-thousand-mile stroll from Brushy Creek to Mexico City, I doubt many of us will survive a Mexican prison. I know I don't expect to see home again."

Whit wanted to say something encouraging to McAllister, but felt it a useless gesture. He could not imagine McAllister walking twelve hundred miles in his crippled condition.

"At least it beats being lined up and shot," someone said.

"I'm not so sure," McAllister answered. "I know Mexicans. Before it's all over, we may pray for a firing squad."

--- 12 ---

The first news of the Texian Santa Fé Expedition came only two days before Corrie and Tad were to leave for Austin and the inauguration of Sam Houston. For weeks there had been only rumors. But when Tad entered the house with the latest Houston and Galveston newspapers, she knew instantly from his gloomy expression that he judged the information both valid, and bad.

He sank into a chair by the fireplace, favoring his injured shoulder. "The expedition surrendered without firing a shot. They're being marched to Mexico City and prison."

Prue came out of her room in time to hear. "I can't imagine Whit surrendering," she said. "Is this another crazy rumor?"

Tad shook his head. "I believe it reliable. The newspapers quote eyewitnesses among traders just arrived in Independence from Santa Fé. They said they saw hundreds of Texians being marched south under guard."

"What does this mean?" Prue asked. "When will they be freed?"

Tad's eyes filled. "Prue, I don't know. There's some hope in that they weren't shot immediately. That's the usual Mexican practice. But any negotiations for their release will be long and difficult. Mexico doesn't recognize Texas independence. We have no diplomatic relations. We'll have to depend on other nations to represent us. That'll take time."

"Couldn't we buy Whit's way out?" Corrie asked. "Use bribery?"

"I doubt it," Tad said. "They'll be Santa Anna's prize prisoners. Any Mexican who helps them will be shot."

236

Prue was reading the newspapers. "This says two of the Texians were executed!"

"Howland and Baker, for attempting to escape," Tad said. "I knew Howland. I don't recall Baker."

"One witness says many of the Texians were barefoot," Prue said. "How can they march all the way to Mexico City barefoot?"

Corrie saw anguish on Tad's face. "I'm sure their suffering will be immense," he said. "But Whit's young. He's healthy. I keep telling myself he'll survive, if anyone will."

Corrie thought of Whit: he was of too gentle a nature for such circumstances. She also was concerned over the effect of the news on Tad. His election to Congress had placed further responsibilities on him. Two weeks ago he had returned from Austin exhausted. His shoulder was not healing properly.

She also thought of her own role in sending Whit off on the expedition. She wondered if Tad blamed her for changing his mind on allowing Whit to go.

"Tad, we must do something!" she said.

Again he nodded. "Most Texians won't take this lying down. It could mean a renewal of the war. That may be our best hope for freeing Whit and those men."

Corrie felt heavy foreboding. Resumption of the war had been a worrisome threat since the first day she crossed into Texas at Senator Gaines's ferry. "If the war is renewed, will Béxar become a battle-ground again?"

Tad looked up at her for a long moment. "Quite possibly."

Prue put down the newspapers and began to cry. "Well, I for one am ready to fight, if it'll free Whit," she said, sniffing. "One witness said the Texians are down to skin and bones."

Corrie picked up the newspaper, but was too upset to focus on the type.

"Apparently the trip was difficult, and the men were in bad shape before sighting the Mexicans," Tad explained. "That may account for their surrender."

"In the light of this, will the inaugural celebration be canceled?" Corrie asked.

"It may be more subdued, but it'll be held," Tad said.

Prue wiped her eyes. "I don't see how anyone can celebrate."

"Government must go on," Tad said. "In fact, it may be a boon, with prominent Texians coming in from all over the Republic. Sam Houston and the Congress may be treated to some firm popular opinion they might otherwise choose to ignore."

"How could they possibly ignore this?" Prue asked.

"There'll be a tendency to dismiss the expedition as another of Lamar's follies. Thank God I'm in Congress. I may be able to do something. I believe I know the minds of my constituents, but I'll spend the next two days making sure. From the moment we reach Austin, I'll start drumming up support for a firm stand against Mexico, even if it means resumption of the war."

"What will be President Houston's attitude?" Prue asked.

"Caution, delay, diplomacy," Tad said. "Ordinarily I might agree. But we have no emissaries in Mexico. And we can't depend on England, France, or the United States to present our case. They have too many concerns of their own. It's imperative that we deliver Mexico an ultimatum: Release those men, or we fight. I believe Santa Anna would back down. Much of his country is in revolt. I doubt he wants war."

Corrie knew Texas also was not in shape to fight a war. "Will Houston risk such a firm stand?" she asked.

"He's a politician," Tad said. "He's obstinate, but he may yield to pressure. I certainly intend to find out."

They left San Antonio at dawn on a cold December morning, accompanied by the Higginbothams, the Mavericks, the Bradleys, and the Johnstons. With drivers and servants, the caravan numbered more than sixty persons. In deference to his injury, Tad tied Midnight to the boot and rode in the carriage with Corrie, Prue, Hattie, and Jim Bowie.

Most of the way they talked little, each lost in his own thoughts. No one could forget for a minute that three hundred Texians were on their way to prison in Mexico.

They entered Austin in midafternoon of the third day. Corrie had heard many jokes on the primitive conditions of the capital, yet she was appalled. By comparison Houston was a polished city.

Austin consisted of two score log cabins perched in a bend of the Colorado River. Only three buildings were of any size. The Capitol, a two-story frame structure, perched on a hill a short distance from the village. The high stockade fence that had guarded it from Comanche attack was now gone. From its hillside, the Capitol dominated the village and landscape.

The second structure of any size was the Bullock Hotel, site of the infamous Pig War that had so angered the French chargé d'affaires that he had returned home. The big hotel obviously had been expanded several times, with patchwork extensions and cabins added in a random fashion. Tad said the hotel was a home away from home for most congressmen, and many political issues were hammered out in its rooms.

The carriage drew up in front of the third building of exceptional size. "This is the Eberly House," Tad said. "Here's where I retain a small room."

Corrie followed him into the hotel. He introduced her to the proprietress, Angelina Belle Eberly, a large, ruddy-faced, friendly woman talkative by nature. "We're crowded, but we'll make do," she told Corrie. "They say there are a thousand people in town for the inauguration! Can you believe it?"

Tad left to consult with other congressmen. Corrie lingered in the hall with Mrs. Eberly while Prue and Hattie went on to unpack. "The corner room is President Houston's," Mrs. Eberly announced. "I was hoping he'd bring his new bride to Austin. But she's not in the best of health, you know. So Sam rides back and forth to Houston on ol' Bruin. Can you imagine? Four days each way on a mule! Just to see his wife! He must truly be in love."

She said Sam Houston had burned her hotel in San Felipe during the Revolution to prevent it from falling into enemy hands. "I could have killed him cheerfully. Now he's my star boarder. You never know what turns life has in store."

She said she was now pro-Houston, anti-Lamar, and did not care who knew it. "President Lamar has all but wrecked the Republic. Maybe Sam can pull our chestnuts out again, but I doubt it. Congress has been in session since October and done nothing. Too many members are interested in matters other than legislation, if you get my meaning. There are women here not as proper as they could be. Oh, the stories I could tell you!"

Corrie was tempted to stay and hear some of the "stories," but too much remained to do in preparing for the inaugural events. She went on to her room.

Later Tad returned, deeply discouraged. "I don't understand it. There's anger. But most of Congress wants to wait and see if the United States will file a formal protest in our behalf."

Thinking of Whit, Corrie succumbed to a wave of despair. She did not feel she could endure the preinaugural parties. "Tad, I don't think we should go out this evening."

Prue agreed. "I don't see how anyone can have fun while those men are suffering."

"It's just as well," Tad said. "Most of the men are here without women. I expect the evening to be rowdy."

Tad went out to talk to more congressmen. Prue, Hattie, and Jim Bowie remained with Corrie in her room. Later they heard drunken shouting in the streets, and the firing of pistols.

Prue sniffed at the sounds of revelry. "Too bad they're so brave with their pistols here, hundreds of miles from where they're needed."

The next morning Corrie, Prue, and Tad walked up to the Capitol on a path cut through overhanging shade trees. A crowd gathered in front of a specially made canopy behind the Capitol. The day was sunny, unusually warm for mid-December. More than a thousand people milled before the platform as the band played martial airs and the cannons boomed.

Corrie had thought she would be among strangers, but it seemed every time she turned around she found someone she knew. While Tad lingered to talk with a group of men, Corrie and Prue chatted with Major Gaines, General Tom Rusk, and Adolphus Sterne. Gaines was now a senator. Rusk had served as chief justice of Texas and as attorney general. Sterne was now postmaster and land commissioner. Corrie had just inquired about Sterne's family, and brought him up to date on her own, when Prue grabbed her arm.

"Corrie! Look!"

Corrie looked. Ramsey Cothburn stood talking with three other men not thirty feet away. Corrie found she was not surprised to see him. The newspaper account Prue had found suggested he was involved in politics. She had half expected to encounter him sometime. The surprise was the emotional impact he still held for her after all these eventful months.

Corrie felt something stir inside of her. She had always loved him in a quieter, more basic way than the wild, impetuous emotions Tad aroused in her. And now, looking at Ramsey, feeling the absence of her parents, she found herself drawn to him as a tie to her past.

"He hasn't seen us. Should we stroll in that direction?" Prue asked.

"Absolutely not!" Corrie said. "The choice must be his whether to renew our friendship."

Even as she spoke he seemed to feel their eyes upon him. He glanced in their direction and recognition came. He smiled and nodded a greeting. He didn't seem surprised. Probably he had read of Tad's election in the newspapers, and anticipated that she would be here. He turned back to the men. For a moment Corrie thought he planned to ignore her, and disappointment came over her with a rush. But he shook hands with the men and came through the crowd toward her.

"Corrie! Prue! How delightful to see you. Where's the new congressman?"

"Over there," Corrie said, looking to where Tad stood.

Ramsey turned his attention to Prue. Corrie did not know whether he did so to hide his emotions, or to avoid an awkwardness he might feel with her.

"Prue, you were always such a charming child. I always knew you'd grow into a lovely woman. And you have."

"Thank you," Prue said with a smile.

Ramsey looked at Corrie. "And, Corrie, as beautiful as ever. I understand there's a little congressman. Where is he?"

Corrie supposed Prue's news of Jim Bowie's birth, conveyed in letters, had been disseminated back home. "He's with Hattie back at the Eberly House."

"I'd love to see him. I heard you were here. I hoped to see you and Thaddeus last night at one of the parties."

"We're not much in a celebrating mood," Corrie explained. "Tad's younger brother Whit is with the Santa Fé Expedition."

Ramsey winced. "A tragic affair. I can understand your concern. Everyone I've talked to is furious about it. Maybe there'll be enough pressure to win his release soon."

"Tad is gathering support for a firm stand. But we're worried so about Whit. Prue and I have grown quite fond of him."

Men were mounting the platform where the inauguration was to be held. Apparently the ceremony was about to begin.

Ramsey was studying her intently. "I hope to talk with you and Thaddeus more. Will you be at the ball tonight?"

"Our hearts won't be in it, but we'll be there."

She was saved from further conversation by Tad, who saw Ramsey, left his group, and came to her. He and Ramsey exchanged greetings and shook hands, each determined to do the proper, gentlemanly thing.

Ramsey congratulated Tad on his election. Tad asked Ramsey about his plantation on the Colorado. For a time they discussed mutual difficulties in getting their products to market.

Their conversation was interrupted as all the nearby cannons thundered in unison. Sam Houston mounted the platform to be inaugurated for his second term as president of the Republic of Texas.

A titter of amusement ran through the crowd. Houston wore a faded old red hunting shirt, a tattered pair of Mexican pantaloons, and a floppy wide-brimmed fur hat with a pelt a half-inch thick. The joke was plain: Houston's attire symbolized the poverty in which Lamar had left the Republic.

Corrie thought Lamar endured Houston's clowning with dignity. He sat quietly upon the platform, resplendent in a tasteful business suit. He declined an invitation to speak, a pointed contrast to his own inauguration, when Houston as outgoing president had hogged the speaker's podium for hours, bragging about the accomplishments of his administration. On that occasion Houston had appeared in powdered wig and knee breeches, portraying himself as the father of his country.

Corrie felt a moment of revulsion. She considered such pranks unworthy of the high office Houston held.

Yet she was enthralled by his speech. On their first meeting in Houston she had experienced the power of the man's personal magnetism. But on the podium his presence was infinitely multiplied. His timing, his diction, his dramatics, were flawless. She stood listening with Tad, Prue, and Ramsey, and somehow it seemed natural that they should be together.

Corrie and Prue did not feel equal to the mounds of food served at the conclusion of the speech. The crowd, the constant noise, were too wearing. They left Ramsey, promising to see him at the ball, and Tad escorted them back to the Eberly House.

When Corrie began dressing, she found that the yellow satin gown she and Hattie had labored over for a month was too snug. It had been a perfect fit before she left home.

She had suspected for weeks. Now she could not deny the evidence: She was again pregnant.

Hattie ripped out and resewed seams. By the time Corrie was ready, Tad and Prue were waiting impatiently.

They drove to the Capitol in the landau. The ball was held in the Senate Chamber, gaily decorated with buntings and flags, and with the seats and desks removed for dancing.

The women in attendance were outnumbered by men three to one. Corrie and Prue never lacked partners. Corrie was waltzed by the president, marched through a schottische by the vice president. She danced with senators and congressmen beyond counting, the secretary of state, the attorney general, and the diplomatic envoys to and from the United States. Under other circumstances it would have been a stellar evening. But Corrie could not put Whit, and how he loved to dance, out of her mind.

Again Prue was the belle of the ball. A superb dancer, she was much in demand. Corrie was pleased to see that she spent considerable time dancing with Adolphus Sterne, who had been so compassionate with her at the ball in Nacogdoches, when she was but a thin, gawky not-quite-fifteen-year-old.

Ramsey danced with Corrie but once, and she felt that was for the sake of propriety. He was attentive, but subdued. She could not fathom his emotions toward her. She had no doubts about her own: Ramsey still possessed a portion of her heart, and probably always would.

He devoted most of his evening to Prue. When Corrie began to tire in the early morning hours, Ramsey offered to stay with Prue, and to escort her home safely.

Corrie left the ball profoundly perturbed, convinced more than ever that her relationship with Ramsey was fated. She felt so frustrated. A part of her still yearned for him and her concern for him had not diminished in the least. She worried about her role in his decision to sell Osborne and to come west, and wondered how much of the guilt she felt was valid.

Too much had been left unsaid. She wanted so badly to confide her feelings with him, even though it would be improper.

President Houston turned his head, spat tobacco juice onto the bare floor, and fixed Tad with his eagle stare. "Diplomacy, not arms, is the best hope those men have."

"How can we negotiate with Mexico when she denies us recognition?" Tad asked.

"We'll prevail on the good offices of our friends," Houston said. "The United States. England. Perhaps France."

Tad fought back anger. "Mr. President, our diplomatic situation has been stalemated five long years. When will it change?"

Houston's eyes grew thoughtful. He seemed to be musing aloud. "Possibly—just possibly—the pot is coming to a boil. The trick will be to know when to take the morsels from the fire. As long as the United States fears the prospect of an English alliance with Texas, the issue of annexation will never be dead. As long as Mexico fears annexation, she'll never entirely close the door to peace."

Tad was determined to pin Houston down. "General, ever since

I've returned to Texas I've heard you're for annexation, and I've heard you're against it. How do you stand, sir?"

Houston looked at him a long moment. "I'm for whatever's best for Texas. On one day, annexation may be best for Texas, so I'm for it. On the next, annexation may be the worst course, so I'm opposed. If that's inconsistent, then I'm inconsistent. If it comes, I'll accept annexation *only* on the proper terms. I'll never endorse entering the Union as a supplicant."

Tad paused, searching for the right words to form his question. "General, if your brother were in the hands of the Mexicans, what steps would you take to get him out?"

Houston did not answer immediately. He worked his cud of tobacco into the opposite cheek. "First, I'd talk with Joseph Eve. He might be able to bring action through Daniel Webster."

Tad understood. Eve was the United States chargé d'affaires to Texas. Daniel Webster was U.S. secretary of state.

"I'd talk with James Reily before he leaves for Washington. He has considerable influence there. He may be able to help with the United States Department of State."

Again Tad nodded. Houston had just named Reily as Texas minister to the United States, replacing Barnard Bee.

"I'd write to Lachlan Rate, our consul general in London. He has wide acquaintance in Parliament, and with the Crown. Also, I'd write to William Kennedy. His interest in Texas is well known. I believe he'd be glad to help if he can."

Tad was not familiar with Rate. But Kennedy, an English journalist, had just published a two-volume work on *The Rise, Progress, and Prospects of Texas*. He had long advocated closer ties between England and Texas.

"Brantz Mayer is the U.S. secretary of legation in Mexico City," Houston continued. "I'd write to him. And to the United States minister there, Ellis. And to the British minister, Pakenham. If I were you, I'd leave no potential assistance uninformed of my brother's situation, and of his name. Santa Anna is only a man. He's subject to the pressures of diplomacy. If he receives it from all sides, he may yield."

Tad recognized the limitations. "All of this correspondence, especially overseas, will take forever, while my brother wastes away in a Mexican prison."

"He's young," Houston said. "As I remember him, he's robust. He should survive prison. War may kill him for sure."

Tad felt boxed in. Everyone in Austin thought only of politics, not the lives of three hundred men. "General, the Santa Fé Expedition was sent out by a duly elected president of the Republic. We can't turn our backs on those men, simply because of a change in administration."

Fire came into the Old Warrior's eyes. "Thaddeus, I'm *not* turning my back. But Lamar bears sole blame. He sought congressional approval for the expedition, and it was denied. He sent those men off on a mere presidential order. Now, thanks to him, those men constitute a serious diplomatic liability, as well as a constant burden on our conscience. I'll do the best I can for them. I cannot do more."

Tad felt himself losing control of his temper. "General, I believe we should do more than watch and wait. I'm giving you notice. I'm for renewing the war. Santa Anna's in financial difficulties, and busy putting down insurgents all over Mexico. I believe he'll yield to firm military pressure. As long as I'm in Congress, and Texians are in captivity, I'll work toward a military solution."

Again Houston fixed Tad with his eagle stare. "I'm sorry to hear that. I hope in time you'll see it my way. Thaddeus, as long as we talk with the enemy, there's hope. War should be the absolute last resort."

Tad stood. "General, I thank you for your counsel. You've given me good advice, and I'll follow it. But I see no future in attempting further appeasement with Mexico. I've already turned to the last resort."

Day after day they marched, often forty miles between sunup and sundown. Whit emptied his mind of everything but the determination to keep moving. Captain Damasio Salazar rode up and down the column like a man possessed, driving them on with the flat of his sword. Each night they fell to the ground and slept as dead men. The next morning they were awakened and staggered on.

Their boots long since had been traded for food. Their clothing hung in rags. To a man they were walking skeletons.

Nights in the high country of New Mexico were bone-chillingly cold. Whit and McAllister slept huddled together for warmth. There was little food. Governor Armijo had given Captain Salazar eighteen oxen with orders to kill or to trade them along the way to feed the prisoners. But the oxen plodded along behind the column, and none had been butchered. The Texians became convinced Salazar intended to sell the cattle and profit from the suffering of his prisoners.

On the sixth day they came to a village. Captain Salazar shouted orders for the column to move in double time. Whit helped McAllister, who could barely manage a normal pace.

The villagers came out of their adobe houses. The men stood watching without expression. But to Whit's amazement, the women swarmed into the streets and began handing out food.

The Texians slowed, double timing almost in place. Captain Salazar stormed up and down the column, striking with the flat of his sword. The Texians absorbed the blows. After days on thin molasses and water, a stinging back was a small price to pay for a bite of solid food.

Whit and McAllister were near the rear of the column. For an agonizing moment Whit feared they would be overlooked. But as he passed a row of houses a slim wisp of a girl came flying to him, clutching a rebozo filled with frijoles wrapped in tortillas. Jogging double time, Whit and McAllister wolfed the food. The girl ran beside them, serving her movable feast, and even in his preoccupation with the food Whit was struck by her beauty. Her long black hair coursed down her back like a waterfall. Her golden skin was perfection, her teeth white, and her mouth enticingly sensuous. She wore a simple chemise, and nothing else, her body as free as the wind. When the last of the food was gone she looked at him with chocolate-drop eyes and touched his cheek. "¡Pobrecito!" she whispered. Poor little one.

Whit was beyond speech. Salazar rode by, sword flailing.

"Mil gracias, señorita," McAllister said.

Again she touched Whit's cheek. *"Un momento,"* she said.

She ran. Whit tried to see where she went, but his view was blocked by the guards. The column moved on.

At the edge of the village she reappeared, holding two *melones*. Salazar moved to intercept her but she eluded him, taking refuge amid the Texians. She handed the *melones* to Whit. *"Vaya con Dios, Tejano,"* she said. Go with God, Texian.

"Mil gracias," Whit said.

A moment later she was gone and the column again marched in open country. Whit did not understand; never before had Salazar tolerated any act of kindness.

"Why did Salazar let them give us food?" he asked.

McAllister laughed. "As long as they feed us, he profits. He saves on expenses, and doesn't have to kill the oxen."

All through the long day Whit marched with the image of the Mexican girl's face before him. That night her voice, touch, and presence persisted.

Never before had he been around women unfettered by corsets and bindings. The memory of her lithe body engendered a different kind of hunger.

Pobrecito, Whit said to himself.

They passed through a succession of small villages with lovely, melodic names—Sandía, Alameda, Albuquerque, Los Placeres, Valencia. At each place it was the same. The populace lined the street. The men of the village remained stoic, but the women made no secret of their sympathy. They brought out food, and that was Whit's salvation. Frijoles in wooden bowls, or wrapped in tortillas. Chile con carne. Candies still warm from the kitchen. *Melones.*

"¡Pobrecitos!" the women would whisper. Poor little ones. The word followed Whit south like a sigh, lingering like a gentle caress. Faces, bodies, blended, melding into a pervasive homesickness.

In his newfound worldliness Whit thought often of his closeness with Prue. He fervently wished he had been mature enough to build on that closeness, and to convey to Prue how much she meant to him. At odd moments he took immense pleasure in remembering her wit, her fascinating turn of mind. Memories of Prue helped him through the long days and nights.

One morning in the high country Whit and McAllister awoke and found the man beside them dead, frozen during the night.

The prisoners were drinking their morning *miel*. They stood back from the dead man respectfully, anticipating some measure of compassion from the Mexicans. But Salazar came and sliced off the dead man's ears. He added them to the rawhide cord already holding those of Howland and Baker, executed for attempting to escape. The man's body was stripped, carried to the edge of the village, and dumped into a ditch.

A low rumble of anger swept through the Texians.

McAllister still lay in his blanket. He had not bothered to move. "Whit, this is probably as far as I'll go," he said.

Whit knelt beside him. The sprained ankle had blackened, and swollen to twice normal size.

"I can't stand on it, let alone march on it," McAllister said. "This looks like the end of the road for me."

Captain Salazar had promised to shoot anyone who dropped behind.

Whit thought of the gold coins sewn into his shirt. He had not yet resorted to them. This seemed a fitting occasion. "Don't give up, John," he said. "I'll try to arrange a ride for you."

The guards were saddling their mounts, prepared to resume the march. Whit searched for Old Paint, among the prisoners from the main body. Whit found him and explained the situation.

Caldwell looked toward the village plaza. "The alcalde of this place was here a while ago. He seemed sympathetic. Maybe he can help us. I'll go see what I can do."

Whit slipped Caldwell a gold piece. Caldwell hurried off. A few minutes later he returned. "Money talks. The alcalde arranged with Salazar for a cart to carry the lame and sick as far as Socorro."

The cart and burro arrived. Whit passed the word that transportation had been arranged for the lame. Room was made beside McAllister for the New Orleans newspaperman, George Kendall, who had a broken leg, and for Old Stump, so called because that was all he had for a right foot.

The column left the village and marched on southward. For a time they passed through vast expanses of cultivated fields and pastures. Whit was thirty yards ahead of the cart when a series of shouts made him look back. The right wheel of the cart had shattered. Repair was out of the question.

McAllister, Kendall, and Old Stump had spilled out onto the road. Whit moved toward the cart to help McAllister, but before he took two full steps he was struck and knocked aside by Salazar's horse. Salazar drew his sword over the three lame men. *"¡Adelante!"* he shouted. Forward!

McAllister looked up at Salazar and pointed to his black and swollen ankle. "I can't," he said. *"No puedo."*

Salazar dismounted and handed his reins to an aide. He pointed down the road and shouted a string of Spanish too fast for Whit's ear. Sheathing his sword, he pulled his pistol.

"John, you'd better move," someone shouted. "He's going to shoot you."

McAllister threw off his blanket and spread his shirt, baring his chest. He spoke in English. "Then shoot, you son of a bitch. The quicker the better."

The gun roared. McAllister fell backward.

Whit lunged, fully intending to tear the pistol from Salazar's hands and batter him to death with it. He was seized from behind in an iron grip. "Easy, Logan," said Old Paint. "John's dead. We can't help him. We can only help ourselves."

A guard knelt, cut off McAllister's ears, and handed them to Salazar. The captain added them to the rawhide cord at his waist. The guards methodically stripped McAllister's body and rolled it naked to the side of the road.

Salazar glanced at Whit, still held by Caldwell. Only now did he seem to realize he had almost been attacked.

"I'm fine, Paint," Whit whispered. Caldwell released him.

Salazar rode by, looking down at Whit. *"¡Adelante!"* he shouted, striking Whit on the back with the flat of his sword.

The blow stung, but Whit managed to keep his temper.

The column resumed the march southward, leaving McAllister's body to the buzzards and wolves.

That night, with a group seated around a roaring fire, Old Paint made a joke of the day's events. "Anybody happen to notice Ol' Stump this morning?" he asked in a loud voice. "When the cart broke down, Ol' Stump said he couldn't possibly go another step. But after John was shot, Ol' Stump marched to the head of the column and set us a lively pace all day."

The prisoners roared with laughter. For an instant Whit's anger flared. McAllister was hardly dead and already they were laughing about it. He opened his mouth to protest, but stopped when he saw the faces of Salazar and the guards.

They listened in open-mouthed amazement, and their thoughts were plain: These Texians laugh at death itself!

After that it became a game. At night, on the heels of a forced march of perhaps fifty miles, they sang like a bunch of schoolboys out on a lark.

They reveled in jokes of the road. One morning when a Texian was slow to move, Salazar whacked him a good lick with the side of his sword. In his shock, the Texian felt moved to say something to Salazar in his own language, and shouted the only words of Spanish he knew: "¡Muchas gracias!"

Infuriated that the man would mock him, Salazar gave him a harder blow. Again the victim shouted "¡Muchas gracias!" The situation was escalating fast, and would have ended fatally if the Texian's friends had not told him to shut his mouth.

Thereafter "muchas gracias" became a catch phrase. Every time they were served a flour-and-water gruel, or forced to march miles over rough ground in the dark, a voice would sing out "muchas gracias" and the column would ring with laughter.

Whit could tell from the reactions of Salazar and his men that they thought the Texians crazy. Often Whit himself suspected that they were.

They passed through Socorro, where again women came to them, whispered, "Pobrecitos," and gave them food. Then they were back in the desert, moving ever south, following the Río Grande, with barren mountains on the horizon and vegetation ever more sparse.

From his hazy acquaintance with maps, Whit knew that San Antonio lay somewhere to his left, across deserts and mountains. On many occasions he toyed with the thought of escape. But he recognized the futility. The land was too bare to support even jackrabbits. He had no food. Salazar's mounted men would track and overtake him in less than a day, and his ears would join McAllister's on the rawhide cord at Salazar's belt.

Whit trudged on, guarding his strength with care. While his body suffered, he continued to keep his mind free with memories of home. He thought of how it had been, walking with Prue in the shade of the cottonwoods, with the leaves of the weeping willows trailing in the pale-green water of the San Antonio River. He remembered her sparkling eyes and quick laugh. He thought of Jack and his love of jokes, his childlike enthusiasms. He dwelled on memories of Corrie and their late-night talks. He thought of Tad, his love and generosity, the way he could be stern and gentle at the same time.

Living with his memories, Whit transcended the struggles of his body as it worked its way southward.

They came to the tiny village of Fray Cristóbal, where the river curved away to the west, and the road to El Paso del Norte continued on south.

Salazar made a speech. He said they had come to what the Mexicans called the Jornada del Muerto, the journey of the dead man. For the next ninety miles there would be no water and no stopping. They would cross the region in one long march. Anyone who fell behind would be shot.

Whit studied his fellow Texians. None seemed capable of another mile, let alone ninety without water.

Salazar ordered an ox killed and cooked, and the prisoners were fed, a singular event in itself. The ox, also a survivor of the long trek from Brushy Creek, was gaunt, almost devoid of flesh. When Whit's small portion came, he devoured not only the meat, tough and grisly, but also sinew and bone, for whatever strength they might contain.

He was determined that his ears would not be added to the

rawhide cord. He fully intended to live through all Captain Damasio Salazar could devise.

He resolved that somehow, some way, he would live to return to the cool green glades of San Antonio de Béxar, and share them once again with Prue.

--- 13 ---

Corrie stopped in the hall, listening, doubting her own ears. The bells of San Fernando had not sounded an alarm since the last Indian scare, two years ago.

Consuelo ran in from the kitchen shouting. "Señora! The Mexican army is coming! You must leave!"

Corrie went numb. The specter of invasion had persisted so long that the threat had faded. Now all her fears were renewed in an instant. "How close?" she asked.

"South of the Nueces," Consuelo said. "A whole army. Captain Hays's men have seen them."

Corrie's fright soared. If the report came from Hays's Rangers, it was not a rumor. She and Prue were home alone. Tad and Jack had not yet returned from Austin. The second session of the Sixth Congress had ended, but Tad had lingered to confer with British and American ministers, seeking help for Whit's release. She was pregnant, and must think of her unborn child. She also had responsibility for the lives of Prue, Jim Bowie, and the Negroes.

She could not merely stand and wring her hands. "Prue, go find Ben," she said. "Tell him to go to the upper fields and tell the men to hurry home."

Prue hurried out. There came a knock at the front door. Corrie did not wait for Hattie to answer, but went herself. Sam Maverick stood at the door. "Mrs. Logan, you've heard the news?"

"I have, Mr. Maverick. How serious is it?"

"As serious as can be. We probably have only two or three hours to prepare. Everyone's packing. We're planning to travel in a body. Has Thaddeus returned?"

"Not yet. I expect him momentarily."

254

Maverick hesitated. "Mrs. Logan, I don't believe you should wait. Do you require assistance?"

"No, thank you. I've sent for the men. We can manage."

"Then I'll see to my own family," Maverick said. "But if you need help, don't hesitate to ask."

Corrie thanked him and turned back into the house. "Hattie, gather all Jim Bowie will need. Clothing, blankets, two or three of his favorite toys. Put them on the patio. We'll load from there. Prue, pack sensible clothing. None of your party dresses. Serviceable shoes. And coats."

Ben returned with Newt and the men. Corrie went to meet them. "Newt, I want you to prepare the carriage and two wagons for the road. We'll use double spans of horses instead of oxen. Do we have enough harness?"

Newt stood for a moment thinking. "Yes, ma'am. If the wagons are light enough."

"They will be. We'll take only essentials." She raised her voice, so the other men could hear. "We're all going to a safe place. You hear? We must work and get ready to leave quickly, as Master Logan would want us to do if he were here."

The next two hours were hectic. The men readied the wagons and carriage. Grain was loaded at the barn. Ben drove in the horses from the pasture to be harnessed.

Messages flew among the Anglo families. With such a perfect day, Mary Maverick and Annie Bradley sent word they chose to ride. Corrie and Prue agreed. Corrie ordered their horses saddled.

The time to leave arrived. The Anglo families assembled in the Main Plaza. The two Logan wagons and the carriage stood ready at the edge of the patio. Corrie could not bring herself to leave. She was afraid Tad and Jack would ride into town unaware, and be captured. "Prue, you go on with the others," she said. "I'll wait for Tad awhile longer. I'll catch up with you this side of the Salado."

Hattie, Jim Bowie, and Prue took their places in the carriage. The men climbed on top of the loaded wagons, and the three Logan vehicles joined the rest in the plaza.

Corrie watched the train of riders, wagons, carriages, and carts move out of town.

She returned to the house and quickly went through each room, seeking any small, precious item she might yet take with her. As she passed among the family heirlooms, the emotional toll was overwhelming. Not only was this her home, lovingly built through three years of hard work, it also contained treasures dating to times long before she was born.

Overcome for a moment, she wept. There Consuelo found her.

"Señora! You haven't gone?" Consuelo asked in Spanish. "You'll be taken! I cannot say what might happen to you!"

"I'll be leaving in a few minutes," Corrie promised. "My horse is saddled. I'm only waiting because I'm expecting Señor Logan any moment."

"Oh, señora, surely he'll learn of the invasion long before he gets home. Some people left when the bells first rang. I'm sure the word has traveled to the east." She stared at the furnishings. "Señora! I thought you were loading all your lovely things! Why are they still here?"

"There wasn't room, nor time," Corrie said. "That's why I'm crying. Much of this was given to me by great-grandparents."

Consuelo slapped a hand to her face. "*Aye, ¡qué lástima!* This cannot happen." She went to the sideboard. "All your lovely dishes. Your silver."

Corrie did not answer.

"Quick," Consuelo said. "Do you have boxes?"

"There are some in the barn."

"Then we must hurry. We can take your things into our own homes. The Mexican army won't search our houses. They're trying to bring us over to their side, make friends of us."

"Consuelo, I couldn't put you in such danger."

"*No hay de nada.*" Corrie·remembered that Señor Ibarra had told her she would hear that phrase often: It is of nothing.

"I thank you," Corrie said. "But I doubt we'd have time."

"Watch is being kept in the church tower," Consuelo said. "When the army comes in sight, the alarm will be sounded."

Corrie considered the risk. Her horse was fast, and she could be out of town in minutes. By staying a half hour, she might save some heirlooms, and Tad as well. "Let's hurry," she said.

"Get the boxes!" Consuelo said. "I'll send Pedrocito for Carlos and his cart. Your precious things will be scattered in many homes. The army will never notice."

Corrie rushed out to the barn and pulled down boxes. Most still contained the packing brought from South Carolina. Consuelo sent her oldest boy home for the cart.

By the time the first boxes were packed the cart was standing in the patio. Consuelo's husband, Carlos, loaded them. When the cart was full, he tossed hay over the boxes.

Carlos and Pedrocito made two trips while Corrie and Consuelo finished boxing the dishes and silver.

"Carlos and I can come back tonight and get the furniture," Consuelo said. "It'd be a shame for it to be lost."

They were loading the last of the boxes when Pedrocito came running from the plaza. He spoke to Consuelo too rapidly for Corrie to understand. Consuelo put a hand to her face. "The army is here!" she said. "On the Salado. You can't leave now. They'll see you."

Corrie understood. She was cut off from the wagon train. "I'll go north, and around," she said.

"No, please, señora. That way is too rough. Not even the Rangers will attempt it without a good horse. You'd be alone." She touched Corrie's waist. "Come home with me. We'll hide you."

"I couldn't. They'd know the instant they looked at me."

Consuelo grimaced enigmatically. "I have tricks. We'll change your appearance. Come along! There's no time to waste!"

Corrie could think of no other course. She went out, stripped the saddle from her horse, and turned him into the horse pasture, doubting she would ever see him again. Carlos helped her into his cart and covered her lightly with hay. Slowly she was trundled through the streets to Consuelo's jacal, a one-room structure of mesquite logs, straw, and mud. The roof was thatch and the floor was dirt. Chickens and children wandered in and out.

Corrie could not imagine spending a single night in it.

Mi casa es su casa, Consuelo said. My house is your house. A simple courtesy. But as Señor Ibarra had taught her by example, it was more than a mindless phrase. "Thank you," she said.

Consuelo shelled a handful of walnuts and pounded the meat in a stone pestle. Gently she rubbed the juicy pulp on Corrie's face with broad strokes. "We'll turn you into a *morena*," she said. "A dark brown one."

When Consuelo had finished, Corrie studied the results in a mirror by lamplight. Her face was streaked in places, but from a distance no one would notice. She was indeed a *morena*. "What about my hair?" she asked. "It's far too light."

"More tricks. You'll see."

Consuelo made a concoction of boot blacking and olive oil. She shampooed Corrie's hair thoroughly and swept it into a bun in the Mexican manner. On close inspection the result was hardly palatable, but again would be convincing from a distance.

After Corrie changed into one of Consuelo's dresses her confidence grew. The difference in her appearance was amazing.

"You speak Spanish well, but not perfectly," Consuelo said. "If you are questioned, answer yes and no and simple words."

With darkness visitors arrived. Carlos brought the boxes from behind the jacal. The dispersion of Corrie's heirlooms became a ritual. Each visiting woman was introduced to Corrie. Polite words were exchanged. Then the woman was given a handful of silverware or china. The items were slipped into the visitor's rebozo, and the visitor vanished as another appeared.

By midnight all Corrie's treasures were gone. Word came that the Mexican army was camped on the Salado, five miles from town.

"We have time to get the furniture out of your house," Consuelo said.

Again they took the cart through the streets to the Logan compound. Messages came, offering Corrie help. Señora Ibarra took the exquisite old armoire into her home. The Navarros took the huge black laquered chest. One by one, Carlos hauled the most valuable articles to safety.

Corrie returned with Consuelo and Carlos to the jacal, wondering where she would sleep, for their five children were bedded down about the house. Consuelo led her to a secluded alcove behind a low partition. The cot was comfortable. The chickens apparently roosted outside, for Corrie was not bothered.

Once during the night Corrie was awakened as Carlos and Consuelo made love less than ten feet away.

At dawn the Mexican army marched into town, band blaring and cannons booming. Corrie did not dare venture out, but she heard the shouted commands and bugle calls in the plaza.

All day she sat inside the jacal and worried, wondering if Prue, Jim Bowie, and Hattie had made it to safety, if Tad and Jack had learned of the invasion in time. Slowly the hours passed.

In the evening Carlos returned elated. His Spanish was more difficult for Corrie to understand than Consuelo's. She gathered that he had sold all his sheep to the army for a good price. A few minutes later Consuelo came with bad news. The Mexican army was burning and looting in the American section.

With darkness, Consuelo built a fire in the yard and started cooking. Corrie offered to help, but Consuelo said it was too dangerous. Some child, not knowing, might point her out. Corrie remained inside the doorway and enjoyed the spicy smells wafting in from all over the barrio. Carlos brought out his guitar and a bottle of mescal. Two of his male friends came to visit. Both carried guitars. After elaborate tuning, the three sang corridos and love songs.

They ate in the moonlight, leisurely, hardly interrupting the singing. In the spirit of the evening, Corrie drank some of the fiery mescal. The party continued long after she had retired to her private alcove. Later she again was awakened by Consuelo and Carlos making love.

Consuelo apparently considered it no secret. The next morning, after Carlos had gone, she rubbed her abdomen and sighed. "It is the way of a man," she said. "What can you do?"

In a rush it came to Corrie that Consuelo was supremely happy in her marriage. Consuelo and Carlos had no forty-thousand-acre ranch, no financial empire. But they had each other, and in this Corrie envied them. Through the day Corrie saw their love in every moment. Carlos could not pass Consuelo without a playful pinch or a caress of her ample buttocks, and Consuelo was not past a furtive squeeze of his penis each time they kissed good-bye. Corrie could imagine them growing old with their love, completely happy.

When she awoke the third morning, the Mexican army was gone, marching off to the south, the way it had come.

Before noon, Carlos came back to the jacal. With him, he brought Tad and Jack. Tad stared at Corrie in disbelief. "Good Lord! Look at you!" Then he laughed, profoundly relieved to see her alive.

Corrie ran into his arms and for a while she could not stop crying. "I was sure you'd been taken," she told him.

Holding her, kissing her, Tad explained that he and Jack had met the San Antonio refugees just east of town. There they joined with other volunteers and were awaiting reinforcements when the Mexicans pulled out. "Prue was sure *you'd* been taken," he said. "Are you sure you're all right?"

Corrie looked at Carlos gratefully. "Consuelo and Carlos saved my life."

After Tad thanked Carlos profusely in Spanish, he took Corrie back to the Logan compound.

"This is not much of a homecoming, I'm afraid," Tad said, surveying their home.

Corrie dismounted and walked through the house, heartsick. The furniture she had been unable to move was splintered beyond repair. The heavy doors had been battered from the hinges. An attempt had been made to burn the house, but the thick adobe walls were impervious to fire.

She stepped over the fallen back door, onto the patio. The carriage house and barn had been burned. Only the slave quarters were left unscathed. Her horse was gone.

Corrie looked at her violated house through the blur of tears. With all her being she wanted all back as it had been. "Tad, can we start over?" she asked. "Build again?"

He looked away. "Yes, but not right away. Corrie, it's too dangerous for you to stay here. There's unrest all along the border. We don't know when the Mexicans will come back. I know of a place down by Brazoria. You and Prue will be safe there. The Mexicans will probably make Austin their next target. I believe the coastal region will be safe."

Corrie searched his face. "Prue and I? Where will you be?"

He held her by the shoulders. "After this, surely there'll be some kind of retaliatory action against Mexico. I've been one of the most outspoken in agitating for it. Now I must be a part of it."

Tad talked Hays and his Rangers out of a spare horse for Corrie. But her sidesaddle was gone, burned with the barn. She could not ride astride in her present condition. Hearing of her plight, Señora Ibarra sent Corrie her own sidesaddle.

Tad took a last rueful look at the house. "There's nothing left for us here," he said. "We'd best make use of the daylight."

He summoned Jack, and they rode ten miles before darkness. Jack built a low fire in a ravine, and there they camped.

Jack expertly boiled coffee and warmed beans and tortillas. He kept looking at Corrie. "Miss Corrie, you blacker'n me," he said, laughing.

"Shut your mouth, Jack," Tad said.

"It's all right, Tad," Corrie said. "Jack's right. I am darker than he."

"I meant no harm, Miss Corrie."

"I know. It just strikes you funny that now I'm so dark, but still the same person. Backing off and looking at the situation, I suppose it *is* funny."

"Light's one way, and dark's another," Jack said. "You don't get into trouble until you're in the middle, like me."

"I've never noticed you suffering any," Tad said.

Jack was silent a moment. "I guess you right, Marsh Tad. I never have. Not really."

The next afternoon they caught up with the wagon train. Prue and Hattie came running and hugged Corrie, crying with relief. They said they had been certain she was captured, and carried off to Mexico.

The wagon train was disbanding, the various families making separate plans for exile. The Mavericks intended to go to a place on the Colorado, and sit out the Mexican troubles there. The Bradleys, the Riddleys, were scattering elsewhere.

Corrie hugged her friends in tearful farewells. They vowed to return to San Antonio as soon as the threat ended.

But Corrie now was well aware of the capriciousness of life. She doubted she ever again would know such an idyllic existence. She thought of her wrecked home and cried even harder.

Then Tad started the wagons, and they moved southward toward Brazoria and their new home.

Whit slipped in and out of a succession of dreams. In them he struggled across endless deserts and over mountain passes so high that breathing was pain. In vivid colors he saw scenes of startling beauty, of mountains stretching away into the distance, of charming villages clinging to the sides of awesome canyons. Often he dreamed of a dark-eyed señorita who looked at him, whispered, *"Pobrecito,"* touched his cheek, and gave him a *melon*. He dreamed of Prue. At other, worse times, he dreamed of Captain Salazar and a cord strung with rotting ears.

In dreaming this, Whit reached up frantically to make sure his own were still attached.

"Easy, Logan," someone said. "You're among friends."

Whit opened his eyes. He was lying in a huge dark hallway. Countless people were coming and going. An indistinct form leaned over him. "You've been sick," the form said. "Out of your head. A week or more. Feeling better?"

"Yes," Whit said, thinking back. It had been as McAllister had predicted. They had crossed great deserts, high mountains. He remembered the Jornada del Muerto, ninety miles without water. He remembered El Paso del Norte, and the wonderful people there who had taken them into their homes and saved their lives. He remembered Guanajuato, Querétaro, and at last the city of Mexico shimmering in the distance. He looked at the long, dark hallway. "What is this place?"

"A hospital. Go back to sleep. We'll talk tomorrow."

"I mean where?" Whit said. "What town?"

"Mexico City," the voice said. "A long two thousand miles from Brushy Creek. You've survived, Logan. You're entitled to a rest."

Whit's mouth was dry. He worked his tongue in an effort to speak. "What's wrong with me?"

"Smallpox. You're much better. Sleep now, while you can."

The figure turned away. Whit attempted to raise his head and was stopped by dizziness. He tried again. He was in a darkened room about three hundred feet long and perhaps thirty-five wide. He lay on a cot. Other cots were arranged all around him. On one side was solid wall, decorated with large paintings, indistinct in the dim light. On the other side were windows, open to air the full length of the room. Heavy grates covered each window. Whit lay back. Why would the windows of a hospital be grated, unless it also was a prison?

Again he slept. He awoke with the gray light of dawn seeping through the windows. Someone, or something, was staring at him from a few feet away. The man, if it was a man, had no nose, eyelids, or ears. Involuntarily Whit reached up to discover if his own were intact. They were. The ghostly apparition aped Whit's movement, reaching up to where his ears should be. The man had no fingers or thumbs. He grinned, a hideous sight. Much of the man's mouth was gone.

Convinced he was hallucinating, Whit closed his eyes. When he opened them, the figure was moving away, on crutches and the stumps of legs. The man had no feet.

Whit raised himself up on one elbow and looked around him. Other ghostly figures were moving past. Noses, ears, and fingers seemed to be in short supply. Most of the figures were on crutches, or limping, and Whit deduced that perhaps those with feet were lacking in toes.

Hurriedly he checked his own nose, fingers, toes and, by way of complete inventory, penis and testicles.

All were still in place.

"You're awake early," said the voice of the evening before.

Whit rolled over. Major Bennett, the quartermaster of the expedition, sat on the adjacent cot. He was six feet tall, slender, erect, and dignified in manner. Whit recalled hearing that he was from Massachusetts, a devout Puritan, and had fought at Velasco, Concepción, the Siege of Béxar, and San Jacinto.

"The physician will be making his rounds in a few minutes," Bennett whispered. "Don't try to get well too soon. When he thinks you're able, he'll release you to a work gang."

"What *is* this place?" Whit asked again, gesturing to the mutilated people passing by.

"San Lázaro. Saint Lazarus. A hospital for lepers. Santa Anna
apparently thinks it fitting for sick Texians."

Whit now saw that many of the lepers were covered with open
sores.

"Won't we catch it?"

"The physician claims it's only mildly contagious."

Whit could not take his eyes from the spectacle. "Poor bastards," he said.

"You'll be surprised how much they enjoy life in this place,"
Bennett said conversationally. "They play cards and games most of
the day. Wait till you see them shuffling a deck and dealing without
fingers. Sometimes at night the women are allowed to come over
and they have dances. The disease does something to their voices.
Yet they try to sing. On Sundays their relatives come and bring gifts.
Before, they were forced to beg on the streets. They became so
numerous, they were rounded up and put in here. Now they're
treated well. But their only way out is through the grave."

Whit shivered. "And us?"

"Speculation is that we're more valuable to Santa Anna alive
than dead. Otherwise we long since would have been shot."

"Is anyone trying to get us released?"

"The American ministers are working to free those who can
claim American citizenship. The British minister has won release for
Falconer. It seems we Texians must take our turn."

A few minutes later the physician came, took Whit's pulse, and
asked if his bowels were regular. Whit could not remember the last
time he had defecated. He lied, saying his bowels were fine. The
doctor prescribed salt. Breakfast came. Whit was able to eat some
bread and soup. He returned to sleep.

Hours later he awoke in dim light to discordant screeching. Sitting up on his cot, he found that the female lepers had been admitted to the hall, and were offering a performance. All wore gaudy
finery, as if in defiance of their condition. The faces of some were
covered with masks. Hardly had Whit steeled himself to the
unearthy, shrieking chorus, than began an elaborate ballet on

crutches. The light of a hundred candles sent grotesque shadows dancing on the wall in eerie counterpoint. The prima ballerina, pirouetting on stumps, used her crutches as macabre wings, flying from one part of the makeshift stage to the other.

The men responded with gyrations of their own, accompanied by musicians on harp and mandolin. Whit thought they played their instruments rather well, considering that they had only knuckles and limited digits.

Then the dancing became mixed, and even more spirited. Banshee laughter sent chills up Whit's spine. The familiar smell of mescal grew stronger. Whit clung to his cot as the strange rite rapidly turned into a drunken orgy. Couples left the dance floor for cots, and their choreography became even more fundamental, and ancient.

Major Bennett was asleep. Apparently he had seen the spectacle so often it no longer held his interest. Whit remained awake, watching the lepers copulate.

Later the church bells of the city struck midnight. Guards came through, ordering all the lepers back to their own beds. A few were so drunk they needed assistance. Soon the hall again was quiet, save for the eternal coughing that persisted throughout each night. Again Whit slept.

Day by day Whit grew stronger. Major Bennett urged him to pretend, but Whit did not try to hide the new, solid flesh on his ribs, or the muscles cording his arms and legs. He found the hospital routine wearing, the sights sickening, and he was desperate to get away.

He could not believe prison would be worse.

But Bennett tried to warn him. "You'll be sent to one of three places. My guess would be the old Convent of Santiago across town, where you'll be put to work repairing the streets. You could be sent to Puebla, where you'd be caged with the worst criminals in Mexico. Or you may be sent to Perote. That's an old fortress between here and Vera Cruz, turned into a prison. It's the worst of all. You could be thrown in there and forgotten."

Three nights later the guards came, awakened Major Bennett,

and marched him away. Whit was left with six other Texians, and hundreds of lepers.

Mirrors were rare in the hospital, but he borrowed one long enough to study the effects of his smallpox. Each side of his face, between jawbone and cheekbone, looked as if he had received a dose of birdshot. The pits were deep but not especially unsightly.

Not with lepers as a frame of reference.

That night he was prodded awake. A Mexican army officer stood over him. "¡Vayamos!" the officer said. Let's get going.

Whit was not especially dismayed. Anywhere away from the lepers would be an improvement. He gathered his blankets and gear. Thirty minutes later he was signed out of the hospital. Flanked by six soldiers on each side, he was marched toward the heart of the city.

"¿Dónde vamos?" he asked the soldiers. Where are we going?

"¿Quién sabe?" a soldier answered. Who knows?

They marched more than three hours through the main part of the city, and beyond, into the outlying country. They passed small houses where dogs came out to bark.

Well past midnight they arrived at a large and gloomy building. As they walked up to the front entrance, Whit heard the familiar cry, "¡Centinela alerta!" repeated ad infinitum, ever fainter and farther away.

He was going into a prison.

But which one?

His guards marched him through an entrance and down a long hall. Soldiers were asleep on the floor, rolled up in blankets. Whit and his escort were passed through guarded doors. They entered an inner courtyard, and marched up a flight of steps and down another long, dark hall. He passed a door with a single word hand-painted over it in crimson: CASTIGO. Punishment.

He was halted before another door. Sign and countersign were given. The door swung open, and he was admitted to a room that appeared to be part of the living quarters. He was ordered to stand at attention.

An elderly man entered the room adjusting his suspenders. He wore a morose scowl. Whit assumed he had been awakened from sleep. He demanded Whit's name, and wrote it into a book. Rising, he ordered the officer to place Whit in a cell.

Whit was marched back downstairs. He tried again. "What is this place?" he asked the officer.

He received no answer.

The officer halted in front of a large iron door and inserted a key. From within, Whit heard the rattle of chains.

The door swung open. Whit was thrust inside so hard he almost fell. The door slammed shut behind him. Again the key turned.

"Logan!"

It was not a single voice, but a roar of greeting. Colonel Cooke, Dr. Brenham, Captain Sutton, Major Bennett, more than fifty men from the main body of the expedition surrounded him and pounded him on the back.

Whit was disheartened by the constant rattle of chains. Some of the men were shackled in pairs. Minutes passed before Whit could ask questions.

"You're in the old Convent of Santiago," Colonel Cooke told him. "Tomorrow you'll be marched out to build a road to Santa Anna's castle. If you're lucky, you may see the Napoleon of the West himself, passing by in his grand carriage."

"We work hard at not doing any work," Captain Sutton said. "You become expert at throwing a shovelful of dirt out of a hole, while allowing three to fall back in."

"If we ever finish, we'll be sent to Perote," someone said. "We manage never to finish."

Whit was unnerved by the chains. Every man wore ankle irons. Some had slipped out the rivet, and were wandering around without their tether.

"No doubt you'll be fitted with one in the morning," Dr. Brenham said. "But you can bribe the blacksmith not to set the rivet solid. That way, you can slip the chain off at night, if you put it back on quickly when you hear the key in the lock."

With a fresh set of ears to listen, some of the men sat up and talked. Whit learned the fate of many friends. Old Paint Caldwell, left behind critically ill with smallpox at Guadajuato, had survived, as had his son Curtis. Lieutenant Lubbock had escaped, jumping from the second story of the convent. Others were at Puebla. Some were at Perote.

Various plans for escape were afoot. Each had drawbacks. No one had found how to reach the coast safely and to purchase passage home.

No one doubted that the penalty for such an attempt would be the firing squad.

Most of the men complained of being forced to do common labor in the streets. They said if they were prisoners of war, then international rules should apply. But in reality Whit did not shy away from the thought of hard work. He found himself wanting physical activity of any kind; better that than rotting with the lepers. His only revulsion lay with the chains.

Captain Sutton seemed to read Whit's mind. "The chain isn't too disagreeable," he said. "Once you get *used* to the idea."

Whit was opening his mouth for a reply when the whole room erupted in laughter. All had been awaiting his reaction. Whit knew that once again he had been made the butt of a joke.

It was a good one, the kind of crude subtlety these Texians loved:

In time a man might grow accustomed to being shackled.

But he would never get used to the idea of it.

--- 14 ---

Corrie quietly eased out the front door and walked down the path to the pond. Earlier the day had been insufferably hot, but the wind had shifted, and now a cool breeze came off the Gulf fifteen miles away.

Feeling awkward, gargantuan, she lowered her weight onto a log and idly watched the birds and the billowing clouds gliding across the deep blue sky.

She treasured these solitary moments. But today her self-indulgence was brief. Prue called from the house, caught sight of her, and came trotting down the path. "Corrie, you shouldn't be out here by yourself! Suppose something happened!"

"It's high time something *did*," Corrie said.

Prue arranged her skirt and sat on the log beside Corrie. "You shouldn't be going through this alone. Tad should be here."

It was a sore subject. Prue would not let it alone. "Prue, Tad has his work, his responsibilities. I understand that. I don't see why you can't."

"His first responsibilities are here. Besides, Congress hasn't done a thing all summer to help Whit and those men."

Corrie did not answer. She had reread the last letter from Whit until she knew it by heart. He sounded so discouraged. Many of his friends had been freed. But still he lingered in prison.

He said he had struck a guard under extreme provocation, been flogged, and now his outlook for release appeared doubtful.

She had written him, trying to sound cheerful. But under the circumstances, optimistic phrases were difficult. Prue was right. Nothing was being done.

Instead of uniting the Republic, General Rafael Vásquez's brief

269

invasion of San Antonio had thrown Texas into even greater confusion. With the prospect of further incursions, President Houston had declared Austin unsafe. He had moved the government back to his namesake city.

The uproar over the relocation of the capital filled every newspaper. That and the bloody land feud in northeast Texas. Editors and politicians appeared far more concerned over those issues than with freeing members of the Santa Fé Expedition.

Prue sighed, looking at the pond and the nearby pecan grove. "I hate it here. When will be able to go back home?"

"I don't know," Corrie said. "I'd leave today, if I could."

They had been living on Bailey's Prairie four months. It was a wild, gloomy place, well off any beaten path. She recognized that Prue was ill equipped to deal with the isolation, and was bored. Here she had one suitor, a former sea captain twice her age who came every Sunday. Prue did not seem to regard him seriously.

Prue remained silent for a time, watching the sea birds. When she spoke, it was as if her emotions suddenly bubbled over. "Well, you chose this, Corrie. You had your chance."

Several times lately Prue had made similar pointed references to Corrie's rejection of Ramsey. Corrie had ignored them. But they rankled. She wanted to put a stop to them. "Prue, it was *my* choice. It didn't concern you. Why keep bringing it up?"

"It *did* concern me," Prue shot back. "It *still* does. I didn't come out here to stay. Your whims affected the lives of a lot of people. Ramsey. Me. Tad. Whit. Jim Bowie." She jabbed a finger at Corrie's abdomen. "And whoever there."

Corrie's anger flared without warning. She raised her voice: "My marriage isn't a whim! I love Tad. Can't you understand that? I chose Tad because I love him."

"But where is he when you need him?" Prue snapped.

"Prue, you don't want to understand, do you? Don't you dare make judgments you know nothing about!"

"I know you haven't seen Tad more than two days at a time since we've been here. I know you feel neglected, miserable."

Corrie attempted a denial. But half-truths were difficult to refute. She could only manage a pitiful plea. "Prue!"

Abruptly Prue left the log and went to the edge of the pecan grove. She stood there, her shoulders heaving with sobs.

Corrie put her face into her hands and surrendered to tears. Prue was right. She was miserable, living in this awful place. Her long, troublesome pregnancy was only part of it. Even when Tad was home, his mind was elsewhere, planning his next speech, his next maneuver to free Whit. Corrie understood his total involvement. But understanding did not make enduring it easier.

She could not stop crying. Whit was constantly on her mind. She wept for him. She wept for her wrecked San Antonio home. She wept in dread of her uncertain future.

She heard Prue's footsteps returning. "Corrie, I'm sorry. I don't know what's wrong with me these days."

Corrie knew. They *both* were miserable. She raised her head and wiped her eyes. Prue sat on the log and embraced her. Corrie put her arms around Prue and held her.

After a time she pushed Prue away. There was yet something that needed to be said. "Prue, Ramsey was a dear, sweet man, and I loved him. But not in the way I love Tad. Ramsey could have made me happy in many ways, but not in other, essential ways. That's all I'm ever going to say about it."

Prue nodded, but did not respond.

The moment of anger was past. Corrie sought to lighten the mood. "You can't seem to forget Ramsey."

Prue laughed. "Well, he does have a flair."

"He isn't exactly ancient. You might still have a chance."

Prue sniffed. "It was you he was interested in."

Prue's eyes were red from crying. Corrie wondered about her own. Suddenly she was restless. She rose and started walking around the pond. Prue followed.

Wild turkeys flew, but the water birds refused to be disturbed. Corrie and Prue walked on, past the pond. In the trees they came to the lonely grave of James Bailey, the pioneer who had settled this place, built the house, and planted the grove in which he was buried.

"That thing gives me nightmares," Prue said.

The grave was round, and no larger than a wash tub. Bailey had asked to be buried standing up, facing west, with his favorite rifle cradled in his arms, bullet pouch and powder horn slung at ready. He said he had grown up on the eastern slopes of the Great Smoky Mountains, and spent his life in westering. On the Day of Resurrection, he wanted to be prepared to march, and pointed in the right direction. On his death his friends had accommodated him. They also placed his jug at his feet, with the thought that Bailey might need a stiff snort on Judgment Day. Now his house was believed to be haunted.

Bailey had been one of Austin's Old Three Hundred. Here the early colonists had met several times in their efforts to keep peace with Mexico.

Walking up the path toward the house, Corrie felt pain. She stopped. Prue looked back quizzically. The pain sharpened, then passed. There was a familiarity to it. "I think you'd best send Ben for Mrs. Giles," Corrie said.

Prue took her arm. "You *had* to walk around the pond!"

"If it'd speed matters, I'd run around the pond three times. Go on!"

Prue hurried toward the stables. Corrie walked into the house and to her room. Gently she lay down across her bed. She heard the drumming of hooves as Ben rode out the corral gate to fetch the midwife, four miles distant.

Corrie fought back a moment of panic.

What if the birth went wrong?

She was not acquainted with the midwife. She yearned for the reassurances of Dr. Weideman, the comfort of friends such as Annie Bradley, Mary Maverick, and Elizabeth Riddley.

Prue returned. "I hope Ben gets there in one piece. He was riding on his nose like a jockey. You feeling any easier?"

"For the moment. But it's started. I have no doubt."

"Shouldn't I send Newt into Houston to find Tad?"

Corrie wanted to say yes. But she thought of Tad's concern for Whit, the chance his efforts might yet be successful. "That'd serve no purpose whatsoever. By the time he could get here, surely it'll be over."

She endured three more contractions before Mrs. Giles arrived.

A tall, thin Scot, Mrs. Giles immediately took charge, ordering towels, sheets, and hot water readied. She glanced around the house. "None of your menfolk to home?"

"No," Corrie said. She did not feel like talking about it.

Mrs. Giles offered a curt nod. "It's a woman's place to abide and suffer. We're surely the better for it."

Corrie was still pursuing that logic when she was struck by another labor pain.

A half hour after midnight, Albert Martin Logan was born. His first gasps were weak, hesitant. He cried in pitiful wails. Mrs. Giles promptly labeled him "sickly."

Corrie studied the new baby intently. Where Jim Bowie tended to be wide of face, resembling the Logans, Albert Martin was oval faced and more delicately featured. Corrie felt he would more resemble the McNairs.

She drifted in and out of consciousness. Mrs. Giles sat up with her through the night.

Toward morning, Mrs. Giles put a hand to Corrie's forehead.

"I thought so. Mrs. Logan, you've got childbed fever. I've seen it before. I'm sending to Brazoria for a doctor."

Senator Gaines and Tad walked together toward the Capitol. Tad had just returned to Houston from Galveston, where he met with the British consul.

"You have any luck with the consul?" Senator Gaines asked.

Tad shook his head negatively. "He spent two hours explaining to me that Her Majesty's government is in a delicate situation. If they help the Texas prisoners too aggressively, they'll damage relations with Mexico and open the door to the French. He claims the British ambassador is working quietly on our behalf, but I don't know how much credence to put to it."

"If you've just arrived back, maybe you haven't heard the news," Gaines said.

Tad looked at him quizzically.

"Sam Houston let it out this afternoon that he has vetoed the War Bill."

Tad stopped in his tracks. For a moment he could hardly contain his anger. With a single stroke of his pen Sam Houston had wiped out Tad's many months of hard work. The bill had been the best Tad and his friends could obtain. In order to gather needed support, it stopped just short of a declaration of war on Mexico. Instead, it gave the president dictatorial powers to wage war, if necessary. By vetoing the bill, Houston was sending a clear signal to Mexico that he did not intend to retaliate for the San Antonio invasion, and the imprisonment of the men from the Santa Fé Expedition. With his veto, Houston was ignoring the will of Congress, and of the people. "This'll end Houston's political career," Tad said.

"Oh, I wouldn't be so rash as to say that," Gaines said as they resumed walking toward the Capitol. "Sam has gone against popular opinion before and survived. He will again. You've got to admire the old reprobate. He bided his time, saying nothing, until Congress stood adjourned. In a way, it's a victory for us. He obviously feared we might muster enough support to override his veto."

"We've lost a priceless opportunity," Tad said. "If he had acted against Mexico, I'm sure Britain would've come in on our side. At least they would have come through with a loan."

"Well, now we'll never know."

They were preoccupied for a time dodging horses and carriages. Houston had become even livelier in the last three years, and there was a growing sense of permanence about it. Many of the buildings now were of brick and stone.

"What happened today must be unprecedented in politics," Gaines said. "A legislative arm granting an administration total power, unsolicited, and then the measure is vetoed by that administration. I can't see where we faulted. We upheld our responsibilities."

Tad hardly listened. His thoughts were on the abuses heaped on Whit and the other prisoners, on his own destroyed home in San Antonio, and on his land lying unproductive and useless. "We must put pressure on Mexico," he said. "Sam Houston won't do it. Congress can't. If it's done, we citizens must do it."

"I think that's popularly called taking the law into your own

hands," Gaines said with a wry smile. "But you're right. That may
be what we'll eventually have to do."

They reached the old Capitol, now restored as the seat of government under Houston's administration. Tad left Gaines at the
door of the senator's office and continued on down the hall to his
own, shared with three other congressmen.

Darkness was descending. He lit a lamp. A half dozen letters lay
on his desk. Prominent on top was one edged in black. Tad sank into
his chair and opened it. Frank's tone was formal:

> Dear Brother,
> This is to inform you that our father passed away last eve-
> ning of apoplexy. Today we buried him in the family plot.
> My lawyers tell me that since you have signed a quitclaim to
> your portion of the inheritance, assigning all proceeds to
> me, no further action is required on your part. The situation
> with Whit is more complicated, but can be held in abeyance
> until he reaches his majority. Times have been hard here. I
> have been forced to sell some Negroes to meet taxes, and
> now I am hard put to work Donegal with the labor remain-
> ing. Times must improve soon.
>
> Your loving brother, etc.
Frank L. Logan

Tad reread the letter twice, analyzing each phrase. It was legally
correct. And as Tad had long anticipated, Frank promptly had trans-
lated the death of Larkin Logan into monetary terms.

The only surprise the letter held was his own emotional reaction. An hour ago, if required to do so under oath, he would have
said he retained not a shred of love for his father, that with verbal
and physical abuse, Larkin Logan had killed all filial affection years
ago.

But the letter brought a vastly different response than what he
had expected. He recalled that years ago a judge had remarked from
the bench that few events in a man's life were as profound as the
death of his father. At the time Tad had dismissed the remark as of

the judge's limited perspective, and certainly not applicable to himself. Now he saw wisdom in the observation.

Larkin Logan's death left too much unsaid, unresolved. With death, Larkin Logan had escaped his parental crimes too easily.

Tad would have predicted that with his father's death, his long-smoldering, deep-seated angers would have been eased.

Instead, he now found them intensified.

Seated with the baby by the fireplace, Corrie heard the rider stop in the front yard. But no knock came at the front door. Curious, she handed Albert Martin to Hattie and went to a window. The rider had not dismounted. Tad stood at the horse's neck, holding the bridle, talking intently with a stranger.

Tad stepped back from the horse and pointed, apparently giving directions. The man rode off at a gallop. Tad came on into the house, his face grim. "San Antonio has been invaded again," he said. "Judge Hutchinson was holding fall court. Judge, attorneys, bailiffs, plaintiffs, and defendants were captured in a body. Fifty-some-odd in all. Sam Maverick was among them."

Corrie's first thought was of Mary Maverick, in lonely exile on the Colorado River. "What will happen to them?"

"Imprisonment in Mexico, most likely, if we can't retake them." Tad struck a door facing. "Sam Houston can't ignore this! Two armed invasions! Interruption of a duly constituted Texas court! Fifty more Texians in chains! Surely he'll be forced to act!"

He stormed through the house to the back bedroom. Corrie followed, her sense of panic growing over what he might do. He had only been home two days. His town clothes, cleaned and pressed by Hattie, were hanging on wall pegs. Tad was moving back and forth across the room, assembling his homespuns and buckskins.

Corrie reached for his arm. "What are you doing? Where are you going?"

He stuffed clothes into a saddle wallet. "Colonel Hays has issued a call for volunteers. I've got to go."

Never before had Corrie interfered with what Tad saw as his

duty, whether it was chasing Indians, or devoting time to politics. But now she felt compelled. "Tad! You can't!"

He stopped packing and looked at her. "Corrie, a Mexican army is in San Antonio, looting and pillaging. Our home! They hold my brother in chains! Now they've seized fifty more of our friends. How can I not go?"

"Tad, look around you!" Corrie pleaded. "Can't you see? The baby's sick. I'm sick, still running a fever half the time. Winter's coming. We've had no harvest to speak of. The men need supervision. Tad, I can't run this place alone. I'm not able."

"I'll leave Jack. He can help."

"Jack, all the other Negroes have been told what to do every day of their lives. We can't expect them to assume responsibility! My knowledge is limited. I don't know what orders to give."

"I'll be back in time for spring planting."

"You don't know what may happen. What if this becomes another Runaway Scrape, and I have to flee? Where will I go? How will I manage?"

Tad took her by the shoulders. "Corrie, you'll be safe here. If the Mexicans move beyond Béxar, it'll be toward Austin."

"Why should they march on Austin, when the government has moved back to Houston? Wouldn't it make more sense for them to move along the coast? Maybe even land troops and supplies at Brazoria? Tad, this place could become a battleground."

Tad shook his head. "Not if we hurry, hound them out of Béxar, and back across the Río Grande. Corrie, I've got to go. Colonel Hays told the messenger to speak with me personally. Hays is depending on me."

"So are your sons," Corrie said. "Don't you care what happens to them?"

He took her by the shoulders and shook her gently. "Corrie if I didn't care about them, about you, I wouldn't go. Can't you see that? I want my family safe! This is the only way I know to achieve that."

Corrie looked up and met his gaze. "And what if you're killed?" she asked quietly. "What's to become of your sons?"

Tad sighed. He seated her in a chair and knelt beside her, still holding her. "Corrie, we can't sit paralyzed by what *might* happen. We have to go forward. I'll take every precaution. But I've *got* to go!"

Corrie thought of his long service to the Republic. Concepción. San Jacinto. Skirmishes with the Comanches. The Battle of Plum Creek. "You've done your share," she said.

Again Tad shook his head. "For months I've advocated action against Mexico. Now it's here. What am I to do? Turn tail? What excuse could I possibly give?"

"You can tell the truth. You have a new son who barely survived birth and is still clinging to life. The injury to your shoulder hasn't healed completely. Your wife has had childbed fever, and hasn't yet recovered sufficiently to run the household. You're needed at home. No man could find fault with you under those circumstances."

Tad rose and walked to the window. He stood a long time without moving. When he turned, his eyes were moist. "I simply *must* go. There's no other way. I'll try not to be gone long."

Corrie had no strength left. Since the birth of the baby she had been spending half her time in bed. "Then go," she said. "I can't promise you who or what will be here when you return."

Tad looked at her, questioning. Ignoring his gaze, Corrie got up and went to the front of the house to nurse the baby. When Tad had finished packing, he came to kiss her good-bye. Corrie did not return his kisses. She no longer felt capable of sending her man off to battle with a brave smile.

Then Tad was gone, riding away to the west on Midnight.

Hattie was changing Jim Bowie and Corrie was seated by the fire, nursing Albert Martin when a rider stopped in the front yard. Prue went to a window and looked out. "It's a stranger," she said. "He's coming to the front door."

Corrie felt a moment of panic, fearing it might be a messenger come to inform her that something had happened to Tad in the big battle on the Salado. Numbly she handed Albert Martin to Hattie and buttoned her dress. Prue went to the door.

"Ramsey!" Prue cried out, plunging into his embrace. He kissed her full on the mouth. Corrie felt an unaccustomed twinge of jealousy. She wondered belatedly what might have transpired when Ramsey escorted Prue home from the inaugural ball in Austin.

"I didn't even recognize you!" Prue said. "You look so different!"

Ramsey laughed. He was wearing a homespun shirt and buckskin trousers and coat. He was thinner, leaner, somehow more robust. "I went to help fight the Mexicans. I'm afraid I'm worse for wear."

He came across the room to Corrie, searching her face intently, and kissed her on the cheek. "Corrie, how are you? Thaddeus told me you've been ill."

"I'm better," she said. "You've seen Tad? Is he all right?"

"We only had a minute together, after the battle. He's fine. He left with Hays's Rangers to chase the Mexicans to the river. He said he was worried about you. I decided to come by to see you on my way home."

Corrie was immensely relieved to know that Tad was safe. But if Ramsey could come home, why not Tad? She felt there was something Ramsey was not yet telling. She assumed her duties as hostess. "Hattie, Master Ramsey has had a long, hard ride," she said. "Prue and I can look after the babies while you fix us toddies."

Ramsey strolled over to examine the babies. He laughed aloud at Jim Bowie. "He's a perfect miniature of Tad," he said. "Even to the color of his eyes." He moved to Albert Martin. "Maybe it's too early to tell, but this one seems more inclined to take after his mother."

"He's a McNair," Corrie said.

Corrie and Prue made Ramsey comfortable by the fire, where Hattie served the toddies.

"I can't get over how different you look," Prue said.

"I suppose I've lost weight," Ramsey said. "It was a hard campaign. Men with considerable experience said so."

"We only heard it was a decisive victory," Prue said.

Ramsey winced. "Perhaps so. We drove the enemy from the field. But a wonderful opportunity was lost. I suppose you've heard all the recriminations that followed."

"We've heard nothing," Corrie said.

"And we're dying to hear," Prue added.

"Not much to tell, really," Ramsey said. "I was with Caldwell. Tad was with Hays's Rangers. Hays made a feint, engaged the enemy, then fell back to draw him out. The ruse worked. All we three companies had to do was descend on the enemy's exposed flank and destroy him. Colonel Caldwell issued the orders. Before they could be executed, a dispute arose over command. By the time it was resolved, the opportunity was lost."

"That's Old Paint Caldwell?" Prue asked. "I thought he was still a prisoner in Mexico."

"As I understand it, he fell ill this side of Mexico City, was hospitalized, and released when he recovered. He arrived home just in time to take command at Salado. He was absolutely mortified over the dispute."

"Why?" Prue asked. "Was he wrong?"

"Apparently so. He was elected by the men. Colonel Moore held formal commission. That wasn't the worst of it. Thirty-five men under Nicholas Dawson tried to join us. The enemy cut them off, chewed them up with artillery, killed seventeen, and captured fifteen. Only three made it to our lines. So even our partial victory came at high price. Among those killed was Sam Maverick's body servant."

"Griffin?" Corrie asked. "What was he doing there?"

"Story was that Mrs. Maverick had given him gold to take to Béxar, to try to buy Sam Maverick's freedom. He fell in with Dawson's command in trying to reach Béxar. They say he fought valiantly, taking several Mexicans with him."

Griffin and Jack were good friends. Corrie dreaded breaking the news to Jack. She also thought of Mary Maverick, in exile on the Colorado, taking such a desperate gamble to try to win her husband's release.

"Did Tad say when he might be coming home?" she asked.

"No." Ramsey hesitated. "But perhaps I should tell you. There's high sentiment for a punitive expedition against Mexico. I've heard that Tad is among the leading advocates. I believe they'll go, with or without government sanction."

"But you're opposed?" asked Prue, forever perceptive.

Ramsey nodded. "I can understand their anger. But I tend to agree with President Houston on this one. Once we invade Mexico, we've lost our moral stance, and probably the sympathy of the United States and other nations who might help us."

"But with Whit and those other men still in chains, isn't a punitive expedition justified?" Prue asked.

Ramsey frowned. "Perhaps. Perhaps not. I don't know. Thaddeus and his friends may be right. Santa Anna may yield to pressure. My view is different. When I stand in my fields and imagine Mexican troops marching through, trampling my cotton, feeding their horses with my grain, I have no qualms about helping to force them back out of Texas. But to my mind, once we cross the Río Grande and wreak havoc on the populace, we've descended to the level of the enemy."

Warmth from the toddy spread through Corrie. But the liquor left her upset, not relaxed. "Then Tad isn't coming home? Is that what you're telling me?"

Ramsey studied her a moment before replying. "He didn't say. But from the tenor of the situation in Béxar, I wouldn't expect him home anytime soon."

Ramsey spent the night, then rode on in the morning.

During the next few days Corrie kept herself occupied preparing for winter. The pecan drop in the grove was heavy. She put the men to work gathering and storing the nuts.

A week after Ramsey's visit a letter arrived from Tad. His account of the battle was much the same. He called the dispute over command "disgraceful."

"We're now preparing to march on Mexico," he concluded. "We're only waiting for President Houston to act."

The next newspapers arriving from Houston and Galveston chastised President Houston for not approving military retaliation. Under intense pressure, Houston yielded. In early October, three weeks after the Battle of the Salado, he at last authorized a punitive expedition under the command of General Somervell.

Tad wrote once more. His letter was brief:

As you may have heard, Houston has acted. I've enlisted for the expedition. Since we'll be marching against a foreign country, I've resigned my seat in Congress.

Corrie, please send Jack to me with the rest of the bullets he and I cast two years ago. Also more gunpowder, that pair of heavy boots, and the fringed buckskins in the bottom of my trunk.

Corrie, we're not anticipating a long campaign. I'll be coming home to you and my dear family as soon as possible.

Corrie sent a long reply with Jack, begging Tad to come home, renewing all her arguments.

Tad did not answer.

In November the first hint of winter arrived with a cold norther and driving rain. Albert Martin remained sickly. Corrie feared he would not survive the winter.

Word came that Somervell's expedition of seven hundred men was finally organized, and marching south to attack Mexico.

"Seven hundred Texians," Prue said. "On their way to give a million Mexicans a good thrashing."

"Jack, I want you to stay here with the baggage," Tad said. "If anything should happen to me, you go straight home and take care of Miss Corrie. You understand?"

Jack moved his feet in a little dance of frustration. "Marsh Tad, please take me with you. I can shoot as good as any of these men. You know that."

They were standing on the east bank of the Río Grande, less than four miles from the village of Mier. A cold rain had been falling since early afternoon. "Jack, it's too risky," he said. "If you were taken, I'd never get you back. Don't disobey me! Stay right here!"

Tad left Jack, mustered his company, and waited beside the river, impatient to get moving. But there was delay. Cold rain continued to fall.

During the last few days the expedition had all but disintegrated. Of the seven hundred men who marched south from

San Antonio a month ago, only two hundred and sixty-five re-mained. The rest had decamped, some at Laredo, then more at Guerrero. General Somervell had been unable to establish disci-pline. The men ridiculed his extreme caution and called him "Old Granny," even to his face.

At Guerrero the general announced he was disbanding the expe-dition. Tad was among the officers who tried to convince him to continue. But Somervell had made his decision.

"Sam Houston authorized me to attack Mexico 'if success seems likely,' " he said. "I now see no chance for success. There are six thousand Mexican troops in this area. Our supplies are gone. The men have become nothing but an armed rabble."

So Somervell and two hundred of his command marched north toward home, and Christmas with their families. Tad and the re-maining two hundred and sixty-five Texians had marched on east.

Now they were attacking Mier.

At last the order came to cross the river. Tad led his men into the water. In the darkness he soon became disoriented. But muzzle blasts on the far bank showed him the way. "Hold your fire," he shouted to his men. "Don't give them a target."

On his right, Ewen Cameron's company reached the bank first and fired a volley. The Mexicans fell back.

Tad led his men up the bank. Again there was delay. One of Cameron's men had fallen into a ravine in the darkness. Hardly more than a boy, he had broken an arm and a leg and was in great pain. It was decided to leave the boy in a small hut with a doctor and two-man guard.

"We'll no doubt be needing the doctor," Tad said to Cameron. "My man Jack is good at treating wounded. I'll send for him."

A shuttered lantern had been lit for the doctor. Tad knelt in its light and wrote a note to Jack:

Jack, come tend a boy who is hurt. This messenger will show you where. Stay there until I come for you.

"Can he read?" Cameron asked doubtfully.

"I taught him. He'll recognize my handwriting. He'll come."

They moved on. Firing was sporadic as they advanced through the streets. But as they approached the center of town a sustained barrage came from the vicinity of the main plaza.

Within a hundred yards of the square Tad and his company found two vacant stone buildings. The expedition moved into them to await the dawn. The night was so inky black they could not see targets. Shooting was useless. The constant fire from the Mexicans was ineffective. Thus far, the expedition had lost only one man.

Yet the Mexicans continued to shoot, hour after hour, their bullets passing through the windows to strike harmlessly on the opposite wall. The buildings were ideal fortification. Slits in the walls offered protection for marksmen. The walls were thick, the windows heavily barred. The Texians felt so secure that some dropped off to sleep. Tad remained awake.

With the dawn their situation seemed good. In mounting an attack on them from any direction, the enemy would be exposed to heavy fire.

The Mexicans started a steady bombardment with six-pounder cannon. The shot either bounced off the stone walls or passed harmlessly through the windows and splattered on the back wall. Mexican sharpshooters fired from the rooftops, exposing their head and shoulders. The Texians easily picked them off. Soon the gutter spouts along the roofs were spilling blood into the streets. Hour after hour the battle continued. Targets were plentiful. Firing his Colt revolving rifle, Tad frequently had to stop because the gun was overheating.

After failing with cannon and sharpshooters, the Mexicans tried a massed assault. The Texians held their fire until point-blank range, then cut them down. The Mexicans charged repeatedly, taking deadly fire. The slaughter continued through the morning. At noon a Mexican delegation appeared with a white flag.

The Texians cheered. Tad thought the battle was over.

A quick count was taken. Only twelve Texians had been killed. Eighteen others were wounded.

Mexican dead littered the streets.

Tad hunted for Commander Will Fisher and found him seated in a corner, vomiting from pain. A musket ball had carried away his right thumb and the fleshy portion of his palm. Ewen Cameron was attempting to stanch the flow of blood.

Tad knelt to help. His eyes and nose burned from the acrid bite of gunpowder. He had not eaten since the previous evening. His mouth was dry, and his canteen empty.

A message was brought to the Texians by a Mexican captain under a flag of truce. Cameron opened the folded paper.

"This isn't what we expected," he said. "General Ampudia proposes a one-hour truce. After an hour, if we don't surrender, firing will be resumed. He claims we're surrounded by three thousand men. He says if we continue to fight, every one of us will be put to the sword."

Fisher glanced up at Cameron. "What do you think, Ewen?"

"I believe he's bluffing. We've turned back everything he's sent against us."

"Thaddeus?"

Tad thought of the many months he had worked to start a fight with the Mexicans. He thought of Whit. "Ewen, I'm for continuing. I think we've about got them licked. Otherwise they wouldn't have called a one-hour truce."

"I'm acquainted with Ampudia," Fisher said. "He's a humane man. We're out of food, water, ammunition. He may know that, and think we'll accept the best terms he offers."

"We could fight our way out to the river," Tad said.

"Ampudia would cut us down with his cavalry," Cameron said. "Few of us would make it. We'd have to leave the wounded behind. No one would want to do that."

"Let's put it to a vote," Fisher said. "I'll abide by whatever the men want to do."

The alternatives were hotly debated. Before the vote was taken, Fisher went under a white flag to confer with Ampudia. On his return, he called the command together.

"I've known General Ampudia for years," he said. "He's an honorable man. He promises us safety and good treatment. I believe him. If we accept his terms, you'll march into the square and stack arms. If you elect to fight, I'll stand with you. But I must tell you the outlook would be gloomy. I recommend we surrender. Does anyone else wish to speak?"

Tad was tempted to seek support to fight on. But Fisher's arguments were valid; food and ammunition were almost exhausted.

Tom Green, an old West Pointer, said he would lead an effort to reach the river if enough wanted to chance it. Fewer than twenty men volunteered. "That isn't enough," Green said. "It'd take at least a hundred."

"If no one else has a plan, we'll surrender," Fisher said.

Tad was worried about Jack, but hoped he had slipped away in the confusion, and would find his way home.

As they marched out, the Mexicans divided them into two groups, relieved them of their arms, and placed them in different houses under guard. They were fed, but the houses were so small there was hardly space on the floor to sleep.

Late the next afternoon they were marched into a large court-yard. Tad was apprehensive. A company of Mexicans with rifles lined up facing them.

Other prisoners were brought in. Tad's heart sank. Jack was among them.

Tad made his way to him. "What the hell are you doing here?"

"Not exactly my idea, Marsh Tad. I did like you said, stayed in that little house. They came after us. We held them off awhile. But they brought a big cannon and blew that house to pieces, with me in it. Killed that boy, the doctor, everyone but me and another fellow. And they got Midnight, Marsh Tad. I saw a Mexican captain riding him."

Tad went to Fisher. "They've captured my man Jack. He's not a soldier. They have no right to hold him."

"I'll mention it," Fisher said.

Soon the reason for the assembly in the courtyard became evident. As the men were marched out, one by one, they were searched. Knives and money were taken.

Later that evening Fisher came to Tad. "I mentioned Jack's situation to Ampudia. I think he was receptive. But General Canales was standing there. He said that light-skinned Negro killed six of his men. I'm sorry, Tad."

The next day Jack was called before a Mexican officer, who explained that Mexico did not condone slavery, and that in Mexico he was a free man, responsible for his actions. Therefore, he would be treated equally with the other Texians.

In the days that followed the Texians learned that General Canales had ordered them shot, saying six hundred of his men had been killed by them. But General Ampudia countermanded the order. Tad now wondered if General Ampudia might yet be overruled, once President Santa Anna heard of the battle.

Six days later they were ordered to prepare for the road. Flanked by infantry and cavalry, with cannon trundling along fore and aft, they started southeast toward Camargo and Matamoros.

Jack marched beside Tad. Jack glanced back at the Río Grande and laughed.

"Marsh Tad, on the other side of that river I was a slave. On this side, I'm a free man on my way to prison. You tell me this ain't a funny world?"

--- 15 ---

One morning in late January, Corrie came to a decision. "I've decided. We're going back to San Antonio," she told Prue over breakfast.

Prue stared at her. "How?"

"We'll just load the wagons and go. I'm sick of this place."

"Corrie, you're still too ill! You're not strong enough."

Corrie had anticipated this argument. When word of the Mier battle came she had gone to bed three days. Prue and Hattie had been certain she was suffering a relapse of the fever. But now Corrie was sure it was only emotional exhaustion. "I'm growing stronger every day," she said.

Prue continued to look at her as if she had lost her mind. "What about Tad?"

"I'm certain he was in the battle. He would've been the last to quit the expedition. If he escaped, he would be back by now. If he's dead, I shouldn't stay here. I should go back to where we have property. If he's a prisoner, he won't be coming home anytime soon. I must fend for myself. I can't do it here. In Béxar, perhaps I can."

Prue sank into a chair. "What about the Mexicans? What if they invade again?"

"I'll get Ben to teach me how to fire his shotgun. If a Mexican, or anyone, sets foot in my home again without my permission, I'll blow his head off."

"How'll we live? At least here we have pecans."

"If we hurry, we can plant and harvest vegetables through the spring and summer. We have cattle on our land downriver. We can send the men there to shoot and butcher. We may not prosper. But we won't starve."

288

"How far is it, from here to Béxar?"

"About two hundred miles. Farther, maybe, the way we'll have to go."

"What about Indians? A family was murdered no more than a week ago near Bastrop."

"Tad taught the men to shoot. We have those old rifles. I have my pepperbox pistol. We can all practice shooting before we leave. On the road, we'll keep a guard mounted, and pray."

"Isn't Albert Martin too young to travel?"

That was the only consideration that had made Corrie hesitate. She had thought it through carefully. "We'll take the carriage. It's warm enough. I really believe part of his trouble has been this low, damp air. Spring in San Antonio may save his life."

Her arguments exhausted, Prue grew excited with the prospect. "When do we leave?"

Corrie smiled. "As soon as we can get the wagons readied and loaded." Corrie thought a word of caution was necessary. "Prue, it'll be different now. All the Americans have gone."

"I don't care," Prue said. "Anyplace beats here."

Corrie went out to the stables, called the Negroes together, and told them they were moving back to San Antonio. They seemed happy at the prospect.

"Newt, I'm trusting you to see that the wagons and harness are in good order. Ben, you prepare the carriage. Miss Prue and I will ride sidesaddle most of the way, but Hattie and the babies will use the carriage. Before we go, we'll get out the guns and see who's the best shot among us."

The next few days were spent in preparation. Each evening they took turns shooting at marks, making a game of it.

Corrie went through the house, choosing what she would take, and what she would leave behind. Slowly the wagons were loaded.

In early February they set out. Corrie first planned to go westward hugging the Gulf, thus keeping her distance from hostile Indians. But she soon learned why most of the roads across Texas went far inland. Near their mouths, the rivers were wide and deep. So she turned the wagons northward, toward the well-used crossings.

Her fear mounted with every mile they traveled. The Negroes said nothing, but Corrie could see that they also were scared.

Corrie and Prue led the way, trying to avoid the rough places, steering clear of brush where Indians might be waiting. Newt, on a sturdy mule, kept the wagons and carriage moving.

At last they reached Columbus. No one was waiting to make up a convoy for the hazardous stretch to Gonzáles. Corrie decided to go on. She did not have provisions or money to wait.

Between the Colorado and the Guadalupe, in the vast spaces where Comanches still raided, they moved more cautiously. The days fell into a routine. In late afternoon they cooked over a smoke-less, dry-wood fire and extinguished it at sunset, even though the nights were cold.

Corrie and Prue took turns standing guard with the men, and lost much sleep. Yet in scouting ahead the next day they had to be vigilant every moment, carefully studying the land, every bush, every ravine and gully. Several times each day they were scared out of their wits by distant herds of wild mustangs, deer, or drifting droves of cattle.

Windy days were worst, when the whole countryside seemed in motion. Corrie often halted with her heart in her mouth, convinced a bobbing plumed bush on a far hillside was an Indian.

They reached the Navidad. Prue returned from her long day of scouting exhausted. She flopped on her bedroll and closed her eyes. "I saw twenty-six Indians today who vanished into thin air."

"I saw more than that," Corrie said.

Prue rolled over to face her. "Corrie, has it ever occurred to you how you've changed?"

Corrie did not understand. She waited.

"Before we came west you couldn't have done this. You'd have been helpless. You'd have written to Captain Hays for an escort. Appealed to the army. Someone. You'd never have taken it on your-self to come all this distance alone."

Corrie recognized the truth in Prue's observation, and sought the reasons. "Well, since Tad isn't here, I have to do what he would do, for the sake of our sons."

"And those hot letters you wrote to Sam Houston," Prue went on. "You would never have done that. Not to the president!"

Corrie did not respond. Her letters to Sam Houston had been written in fury. Total silence from Sam Houston after the Mier disaster would have been enough. But through the newspapers Houston had announced to the Republic, and to the world, that the Texians who invaded Mier had acted without authorization, in effect labeling them bandits, deserving of whatever punishment Mexico wished to mete out.

Houston had not yet answered. Apparently he was too busy with the continuing dispute over where to locate the capital. He had made an attempt to remove the archives from Austin. The residents of Austin had protected them with cannon fire. Corrie was disgusted with the whole affair. Texians fighting Texians, while five hundred of their fellow citizens languished in Mexican prisons.

"And you never would have been daring enough to move back to San Antonio so soon," Prue continued. "I doubt Tad would be moving us back yet. Certainly no one else is returning."

Prue's last observation planted a seed of doubt in Corrie.

Was she acting irrationally, driven by her desires, rather than by logic?

In this frame of mind she reached Gonzáles and heard speculation that General Canales, angered by the slaughter of his men at Mier, was preparing yet another invasion.

Only sixty miles short of her goal, she seriously considered turning back. But she was out of money, low on provisions, and the wagons were deteriorating rapidly. She went on, and two days later they reached San Antonio.

Corrie rode ahead of the wagons, hardly able to control her emotions. The Alamo and the river crossing looked exactly the same. The Main Plaza, San Fernando Church, appeared unchanged. Corrie turned toward home. Unable to curb her impatience, she spurred her horse into a lope.

The yard fence lay flat. The front of the house was defaced. The front door hung by one hinge. All the window glass was shattered. Corrie dismounted, stepped over the fallen front door, and entered.

It was as if she were walking in a nightmare. Her home was in *ruins.* Tad's letter had not begun to describe the extent of the further damage from the last invasion, when troops were quartered in the compound.

Every inch of the floor had been dug up in search of hidden valuables. The flooring stones were tossed about at random. Some were broken. The walls were chipped down to bare adobe. Sunlight came through large holes in the roof. Corrie wandered on through the house in a daze. Not a stick of furniture remained. The fireplace in the long room was now a gaping hole, unusable, filled with bat guano. The Mexicans had urinated on the walls, defecated in the dirt that once was the floor.

"We traveled two hundred miles for this?" Prue said behind her. "Corrie, what in the world will we do now?"

Corrie knew she had to retain her composure. The men were hungry. They must be fed. Life must go on.

"Prue, send Newt to tell Carlos and Consuelo we're back, and that we want to buy one of their sheep, if Consuelo will come cook it. Maybe all this won't look so bad on a full stomach. Tomorrow, we'll go to work."

"We can't sleep here!"

"We'll sleep in the wagons. The far back bedroom isn't so bad. Maybe we can fix it up in a day or two."

Consuelo came within minutes and hugged Corrie in tears. "My poor little *morena.* What have you heard of Señor Logan?"

"Nothing," Corrie said. "The Republic apparently doesn't know or care, and the Mexican government won't say, whether he's dead or alive."

Consuelo put a hand to her face. *"Aye, ¡qué lástima!* He came to see us while he was here. He is so *simpatico.* I have said many novenas for him."

"I believe he's alive," Corrie said. "I have to keep believing that."

The sheep was roasted on the patio. Carlos brought a jug, and the liquor was shared with the Negroes. Carlos played his guitar and sang. The evening became an impromptu party, making bearable a sad homecoming.

The next morning Corrie allowed Hattie and the children to

sleep late in the wagon. She went by herself to examine the house. Slowly she walked from room to room, estimating the amount of work that would be required. The further she explored, the more damage she found, and the more unlikely it seemed that her home ever could be made livable again.

Standing by the ruined fireplace, she was overcome with the enormity of her situation. The money Tad left her was all but gone. She could not buy provisions enough to go back to Bailey's Prairie. The chances of selling land or slaves seemed remote, considering the pitiful shape of the Texas economy.

After weeping quietly for a while, she went out to face the day. She put the men to repairing their own cabins and sent Consuelo and Prue to the market.

She was inspecting the kitchen when a familiar voice asked, "Do you need some help?"

Corrie could hardly contain herself. "Ramsey! What are you doing here?"

He took a step toward her, but hesitated. "I went to Bailey's Prairie, but you'd left. I've chased you halfway across Texas in the hope that I may have good news for you. Have you heard about Tad?"

"No. Nothing."

"He's alive. A prisoner."

"How do you know? I've written everybody! No one knows anything!"

"I was in Galveston when an English ship arrived from Tampico. A man aboard saw the Mier prisoners marched through Matamoros. He had a partial roster. Tad was on it. The man said the prisoners were under heavy guard, but not in chains."

For a moment Corrie felt faint. Ramsey rushed over and held her. Slowly her head cleared. Tad was alive, and a prisoner, like Whit. "I'm all right," she said. She looked up at him. "Ramsey, you'll never know how grateful I am you've come all this way to tell me." She pulled away and gestured to the shambles of her house. "I wish I could be a good hostess. But you see my situation."

They left the kitchen, walked back into the house, and Ramsey circled through the rooms, examining the damage. "The walls are still sound," he said. "The *vigas* are intact. It'll require a lot of work, but I believe it can be made as good as new."

"Yes, but I don't know much about the construction of houses," Corrie said. "I won't know what to tell the men to do."

Ramsey did not look at her. He was gazing up through a hole in the roof. "I can stay awhile, help you get started."

Corrie badly needed his help. But after the way she had treated him, she did not feel right in asking for it. "I couldn't put you to that much trouble."

"No trouble. I've been lonely on the Colorado. My only fee will be for you and Prue to offer me some much-needed company."

Corrie reasoned that Ramsey was indeed a lifelong friend. "It's a deal," she said. "And I'm sure Prue will agree."

"Repairing the floor will be the biggest job. If I can look around, I'll see what needs to be done."

"Go ahead," Corrie said. "*Mi casa es su casa.* Have you eaten? Prue and our cook have gone to the market. We should be able to serve you something."

"That would be fine," Ramsey said, walking into the hall, examining the rooms.

Corrie left him to his inspection and went out to waken Hattie and start the day.

She felt much better. Tad was alive. She had Sweet Ramsey back. She no longer was so alone.

The Mexicans again marched them into a stone corral to bed down amid manure and filth. At the gate Tad drifted close to Ewen Cameron. "We can't wait much longer," he whispered.

Cameron nodded agreement. "Morning will be best. Tomorrow we'll try. Spread the word."

Escape had been in the air since Matamoros, three hundred miles back. Many plans had been made, rejected, held in abeyance. Conditions had never seemed ripe. Now they were far below Saltillo, at a small place called Rancho Salado, and marching deeper into Mexico every day. They must make a break soon if they hoped to cross the vast, arid lands of northern Mexico to reach the Texas border.

They had settled on the desperate course of rushing the guards. Cameron had been named escape captain. He would give the signal at the appropriate moment.

Tad made a circuit of the corral, evaluating their chances. The cavalry was bedding down on the other side of the ten-foot stone wall. Already two sentinels were on the wall, keeping watch on the corral. A double guard—eight men—had been posted at the gate. The infantry companies were stacking arms just beyond. They would bed down in the courtyard for the night.

Tad completed the circuit and found Jack squatting beneath an overhanging shed, warming their beef-and-flour broth.

"Marsh Tad, I could pluck one of those fellows off that wall like a chicken," Jack said in a low voice.

Tad replied in the same tone. "Cameron says we'll go in the morning. The trick will be to get past the guards quick enough to reach the rifles before the troops get to them."

"I still think the best way would be to go out at night, take our chances."

"The cavalry would track us down," Tad said. "The only way is to put them into a rout. Then maybe we can break away."

Tad and Jack ate in silence. Around them, the other prisoners were subdued. During the day they had crossed thirty-five miles of desert, much of it without water. And now the water at Rancho Salado was brackish.

Tad thought of Corrie. He hoped that by now she knew he was alive, and that she would be making direct appeals to President Houston. In Matamoros he and the other Texians had been allowed to write letters, through the benevolence of a German merchant named Schatzell. Tad knew delivery would be slow. But three weeks had passed. Surely she knew by now.

Already he was making plans for his return to Bailey's Prairie. The Mexicans had robbed him of two years of cash crops. The house in San Antonio would have to be repaired before it could be occupied again, and most of his cash was gone. He would have to sell land or, failing that, some of his Negroes.

Jack spoke softly. "Marsh Tad, we ever going to get home?"

"Of course we will," Tad said. "Let's get some sleep now."

Hours later Tad dozed. He awoke in the interval between first light and dawn. Jack was already up, warming their breakfast of corn mush. Tad glanced around the corral, seeking Cameron. He was seated near the gate, calmly eating breakfast.

Tad and Jack hurriedly ate their own.

"Let's drift over by the gate," Tad whispered.

The atmosphere in the corral was so charged that Tad could not imagine how the guards could remain oblivious to it. Every eye was on Cameron, looking, glancing away, returning again. Tad and Jack ambled to the gate and stood, pretending to be readying their gear for the road.

Two guards came joking, laughing, and unlatched the gate. Cameron rose and casually studied the courtyard, the stacked arms beyond. His voice rang over the compound.

"Now, boys! Now we go it!"

The two guards who had opened the gates were seized. Tad ran past them. Another guard was raising his musket, hauling back the massive hammer. Tad grabbed the gun, whipped it free, and struck the guard in the head with the butt. He turned. Another soldier had reached his rifle. Tad shot him. A third raised his gun and took aim at Tad. But as he fired, Jack stepped between them, grasped the gun, and jerked it clear. Using the rifle as a club, he battered the guard to the ground.

Then Jack staggered and fell against the wall.

Other prisoners were streaming past, snatching up the stacked arms. Gunfire became general. With the Texians in possession of their weapons, the Mexicans were fleeing on foot into the surrounding sandhills. But several officers had taken refuge in the rancho's buildings. They were shooting at the prisoners with pistols.

Jack lay facedown against the wall. Tad hurried to him and rolled him over. He was conscious, but blood was welling up from the center of his chest. Tad sat on the ground and held him in his arms.

Jack grinned. "Who would have thought it would end this way, Marsh Tad?"

Tad found speech difficult. "Hush now. I'll send for Dr. Brenham."

Jack strained to look down at his chest. "Doctor won't do no good. Did we scatter them?"

Tad glanced at the compound. The Mexicans had fled. The Texians were in possession of Rancho Salado, at least for the moment. "We did it," he said.

Jack closed his eyes. Tad thought he was slipping away. But a moment later he again looked up. "Marsh Tad, you ever hear that story that maybe you and me are some kind of cousins?"

Tad had first heard the story many years ago. He was unaware Jack knew of it. Nothing had ever been said. "I've heard it."

"You think maybe it's true?"

"Hell, I don't know, Jack. Could be. Great-grandpaw Logan was a randy old bastard."

Jack laughed, blood catching in his throat and cutting it short. "What would that make us? If'n it's true?"

Tad could hardly speak around the knot in his own throat. "I don't know. With the same great-grandfather, we'd be some sort of kin, I guess. There's probably a name for it."

Again Jack smiled and closed his eyes. "That'd be good, Marsh Tad. Damn, but that'd be good."

He lay quiet so long that again Tad thought he was going. But without opening his eyes, he spoke. "Marsh Tad, you 'member when we was little, and Miss Jane used to put us to bed. Then we'd sneak out the window, climb down that weeping willow, and go walking along the river in the moonlight?"

Tad remembered. "Hush, Jack," he said. "You're talking too much."

"You 'member?"

Tad made two attempts before words came. "I remember."

"Marsh Tad, those were just about the best times in my whole life."

Tad squeezed Jack's shoulder. "Mine too," he managed to say.

Jack grinned, then fell back. He lay limp, unbreathing, a hint of the old familiar smile on his face.

How long Tad held Jack in his arms and wept he did not know.

After a long while Ewen Cameron came and put a hand on his shoulder. "Colonel, you'll have to get hold of yourself. We must leave here. Barragan is out with some of his cavalry. He may try to rush us."

Cameron knelt and helped Tad lay Jack on the ground. Tad felt he could not leave. But he knew he must.

Corrie and his sons were depending on him.

He turned away from the body. For the first time since the start of the fight he became aware of his surroundings. Dr. Brenham and a man named Lyons lay only a few feet away, apparently killed in the initial attack on the guards.

"How many did we lose?" he asked.

"Six dead, five wounded. Twenty have elected not to go with us. They'll take care of the wounded."

The other prisoners had been preparing for the road. They now had among them one hundred sixty muskets and carbines, many swords and pistols, and three mule-loads of ammunition. They had rounded up almost a hundred mules and horses, all the provisions they could comfortably carry, and fourteen hundred dollars in cash.

Tad armed himself with a musket and pistol, and stripped a canteen and sandals from a dead Mexican. With Cameron in command, they set out north. Some rode double. Others trotted along, taking turns riding.

The satisfaction of moving toward home gave them wings. All day they moved without stopping, and on through the night. By morning they had put seventy miles between themselves and Rancho Salado.

After a brief rest they went on. Twenty miles farther they turned off the main road. Behind them they saw scouts from the Mexican cavalry, following at a distance.

Twice they stopped at remote ranches for water, and once they were fired upon by a Mexican army garrison guarding a waterhole. Not wishing a fight, they circled the soldiers and went on. Around them the smoke of signal fires in the mountains kept track of their movements.

Unexpectedly they came to the Monclova road. A tall, lanky American rode out of a grove of trees and approached them.

"I've just heard of your escape," he said. "I wish you luck. You should know that Colonel Barragan has sent messages to every ranch and town within two hundred miles to be on the lookout for you. But there's no organized force ahead of you. Keep to this road until you're at least through the Pass of Benado. Whatever you do, don't turn north into the mountains."

"Who are you, friend?" Cameron asked.

"It doesn't matter. My man will go with you a way, serve as your guide."

The American retreated back into the trees, and was gone.

For a time they followed his advice. But some grew wary. Twice they passed ranches where red flags warned them away. Flintlocks were poked through loopholes of the houses.

The guide abruptly disappeared. Suspecting a trick, most of the men wanted to turn north into the mountains.

"I wouldn't do it, Ewen," Tad advised. "We're making good time on the road. Surely we'll come to a stream of good water."

"Why wouldn't that American give us his name?" Cameron asked. "Why did his guide cut out on us without as much as a good-bye? Maybe the Mexicans want us on the road so they can bring up artillery."

After considerable debate, they turned northward into the mountains.

Within a day of travel everyone was convinced of their mistake. The mountains of Coahuila appeared to be the most arid, desolate, rugged region on earth. Soon their water was gone, and no more was to be had. Every canyon and ravine was dry. Vegetation was so scant they had no protection from the sun. They saw no birds or wild animals, or any sign of them, proof enough that the mountains were uninhabitable.

Hoping for better terrain beyond the distant peaks, they moved on. The mules and horses, then the men began to fail. First by twos and threes, and then in small groups, the most exhausted of the prisoners turned back.

Tad, Cameron, and about seventy men made their way over the mountains. But they found that more mountains lay ahead, as barren as those they had just crossed.

Worn out, dying of thirst, they saw campfires late one evening. Hoping to find a rancho where they could buy water and food, they turned toward the glow in the night.

In this way they walked into the hands of a troop of Mexican cavalry sent to hunt them.

At the moment, Tad did not care.

He gladly would have traded his life for a drink of water.

--- 16 ---

Corrie reveled in again having a man in the house. Under Ramsey's direction the Negroes removed the filth from beneath the floors and hauled in clean earth. He showed them how to lay sand-and-gravel bedding for the flooring stones. With a new coat of plaster, the battered walls were reborn. The holes in the roof were repaired. Newt made new hinges of wrought iron and the doors were rehung. Gradually her home again became habitable.

Her china, silver, and furniture were returned. Not a single piece was missing. Only the big fireplace in the long room continued to serve as a reminder of the destruction. It was made serviceable, but the ornately carved mantel Corrie had loved could not be duplicated.

She consulted with Ramsey on almost every day-to-day decision. He advised concentration on the house, so as to get the work out of the way before planting the fields upriver. When she confided to him she was worried about money, he offered to go into Tad's office, examine the books, and determine her situation. Corrie's hesitation was brief. Tad certainly would not return for months, and possibly years. Meanwhile the men had to be clothed, and food purchased. She gave her permission.

As she suspected, Ramsey found that Tad's money had gone into land, and that none was left.

When she mentioned that the inheritance from Moultrie Hill was still tied up in litigation, after two years, Ramsey spent an evening with the legal papers and found shortcomings in the handling of the case. With Corrie's permission, he wrote the court, demanding quick closure. Corrie felt relief. The money would be enough to see her through.

Since the Anglos had not yet returned to San Antonio, Corrie, Prue, and Ramsey kept mostly to themselves. In the evenings they sat in front of the fire and talked, content with each other's company. When Hays's Rangers returned, and suitors came calling, Prue held them at arm's length, obviously preferring to spend her evenings with Ramsey. Occasionally when Corrie was preoccupied with the babies, Ramsey and Prue went for strolls together along the river. Neither gave Corrie a clue to what, if anything, was happening between them.

Then, after a month, Ramsey returned to his plantation on the Colorado, leaving as abruptly as he had arrived. "If I can find a proper overseer, I'll be back," he said. "Señor Ibarra says that with Thaddeus, Maverick, and the others gone, Béxar is badly in need of a lawyer. I told him I'll try to help."

Corrie missed him even more than she had expected. But while she was upset, Prue was devastated.

"I don't know what to think," Prue confessed one evening. "I'm sure Ramsey cares for me. He shows that he does, in so many ways. Yet he'll only go so far, and no farther. Nothing like a declaration, or even a hint of his intentions."

With her own feelings so heavily involved, Corrie recognized that she probably was the last person in whom Prue should confide. She could not imagine Ramsey and Prue as a married couple. Still, she listened.

"Sometimes I think my difficulty is that Ramsey is such a decent man," Prue said. "In his gentlemanly way, he has mentally put you off limits, and included me."

Corrie was silent a moment. "You may be right but, remember, Ramsey is ten years older than you. He probably still sees you as a child."

"Then what can I do?"

"Go out with other men. Let him see you through their eyes."

One afternoon a packet of mail arrived, forwarded from Bailey's Prairie. Among the letters was one from Tad, mailed from Matamoros more than two months ago.

It contained only a few lines:

Dearest Corrie, I have but a few minutes to write, to let you know that Jack and I are alive, and being marched under guard to prison somewhere in Mexico. I have attempted to explain Jack's situation, to no avail. Please write to President Houston, Senator Gaines, British consul William Kennedy in Galveston, the British chargé to Texas William Elliott, the American chargé Joseph Eve, and anyone else you can think of, telling them what has befallen us. I'm not hopeful of our release anytime soon. Sickness is prevalent, but Jack and I are in good health. I am praying for you and our sons, and for our quick return home. Your most loving husband, Tad.

Corrie cried over the letter for some time before looking at the others. One was from President Houston. She skipped to the pertinent paragraphs:

I was most disheartened to learn that Colonel Logan was taken at Mier. As you may know, the Colonel and I have disagreed on the Republic's course in world affairs. The plain fact is that authorization for punitive action was invested solely with General Somervell, and ended when he deemed it inadvisable to continue the expedition. Since the Mier engagement occurred without the sanction of the Republic, my official capacity is limited, regardless of my strong personal desire to assist in your husband's release.

As you may know, I am conducting a peace policy toward Mexico. I assure you that implicit within any treaty will be a measure calling for prompt release of your husband, your brother-in-law, and the other citizens held in Mexican prisons.

I remain,
Yr. Most Humble Servant
Sam Houston

The letter left Corrie furious. Couched in the flowery language was a plain message: the Republic had abandoned Tad and the other Mier prisoners to their fate.

She also received letters from Senator Gaines, Adolphus Sterne, and General Tom Rusk. They offered encouragement. But Corrie could read between the lines: Without the support of the administration, all efforts were doomed to failure.

The letters brought Corrie to a harsh reality: Odds were long she would not see her husband again for years, if ever.

Yet she knew she must not surrender to total despondency. The responsibilities Tad had left her must be met, for the sake of her sons, her sister, and the Negroes.

Fortunately, there was much to do. Following Tad's instructions, she wrote to those he had named, urging any and all help. Day after day she labored in a corner of the long room, gradually enlarging the scope of her attack.

After three long weeks Ramsey reappeared. He leased a nearby house for himself, his man Rufus, and the three horse handlers he had brought with him. He opened an office off the plaza and began a legal practice.

Corrie could hardly restrain her joy, and her confidence in him was soon justified. He inspected the fields upriver, laid out plans for irrigation, and put the men to planting.

Again he came almost every evening for supper and a quiet glass of wine with Corrie and Prue before the fire. They often talked well into the night.

But Prue was taking Corrie's advice. When Hays's Rangers were in town, Prue often received gentleman callers, and sometimes walked with them along the river.

On those evenings Corrie and Ramsey were alone and the talk between them slowly became more intimate.

One evening, relaxed from the after-supper wine, Corrie asked a question that had long been on her mind. "Ramsey, your life seemed so established back home. What led you to give it up and come west?"

Ramsey stared into the fire a long while before answering. "Corrie, after you called off our wedding, I took a good hard look at myself. I saw that everything in my life had been handed to me intact. I'd created nothing, built nothing. No one took me seriously. Including you."

Corrie was aghast. "Oh, Ramsey, that's not true!"

He smiled as if he did not quite believe her. "My life seemed inconsequential. I believed—knew—I had greater capabilities. So I suppose I came west to prove to myself, and to others, that I was worthy of greater challenges."

Corrie was appalled that Ramsey had ever doubted her belief in him. "Ramsey, I've always known your worth."

He was silent a moment, looking into the fire. "Still, your faith in me was just that—faith. Unproven. I felt I had to build a life for myself, away from the context of the past. Now, I think I'm doing so."

"I'm not at all surprised," Corrie said. "I only wonder that you haven't yet allowed some young lady to share it with you. Surely you've had many opportunities."

Ramsey's dark eyes were soft in the low lamplight. "My trouble is that with you I've known perfection. I've never encountered it again. I doubt I ever will."

Corrie sat still, her heart beating furiously. She was deeply moved. What had she done to this dear man, who meant so much to her? "Ramsey, I'm not perfect! Please don't place that burden on me. I can't bear it. I love you. I've always loved you, always will. In many ways our love is constant, satisfying. My love with Tad is wild, tempestuous. He needs me so. You are so complete within yourself. Somehow, I've never felt such depth of need in you."

Ramsey choked off a laugh. "Oh, God, Corrie! If I never conveyed how I need you, then I *have* failed. In everything!"

He came to her chair, knelt, and put his arms around her. "I thought that was plain for all to see!" he whispered. She held his head and stroked his hair, as she had done so often long ago. The closeness felt so familiar, so right.

Unexpectedly, desire welled up within her. She recognized it had always been there. She hugged him tightly, kissed him. She felt no longer alone. The glow of the wine convinced her she could endure the months, years, of loneliness she faced, if she but yielded to the present.

As if walking in a dream, she took him into her bedroom, and they made slow, gentle, delicious love. With Ramsey it was as Corrie had always anticipated: comfortable, quietly passionate, and deeply satisfying.

For the moment, all again seemed as it should be.

On the fourth day out from Saltillo, at three o'clock in the afternoon, the Texas prisoners again arrived at Rancho Salado and were marched into the same filthy corral from which they had made their escape. Thinking of Jack, Tad looked for any evidence of fresh graves. He saw none.

Tad and Major Robert Dunham had now been shackled together with handcuffs for seven days, and were growing accustomed to each other's movements. They walked across the corral together and sat down beside Ewen Cameron, who was shackled individually, hand and foot.

Cameron was once again thinking about the nine days he and his men had spent in the mountains. The Mexican cavalry had not caught up with them in seven days, which meant they were more than a week ahead of them when they turned off the road. In fact, they had averaged sixty and seventy miles a day on the road. By now they would have been across the Texas border.

"I knew we should have kept to the road," Cameron said. "I don't know why I let the men talk me out of it."

"Don't blame yourself, Ewen," Tad said.

"I always will. All this suffering could have been avoided. Now there'll be no more opportunities."

That was true. The Mexican soldiers, so careless before the escape, now held their muskets at the ready, even though most of the prisoners were now pitifully weak. "I just wonder what will happen to us now," Tad said.

"I think we'll know soon," Cameron said. "Look yonder. Something's afoot."

Tad followed Cameron's gaze. The Mexican officers were entering the courtyard in full regimentals. Bugles sounded. The troops assembled in formation.

The corral gate opened. With pointed rifles, soldiers drove Tad, Dunham, and the other prisoners to the far side of the corral. A

Mexican army colonel entered, holding a rolled parchment. An interpreter took up position at his side.

The colonel began to read in high, stentorian tones. The Spanish words were clear to Tad. But their meaning seemed preposterous, even after confirmation by the interpreter: Every tenth man among the Texians was to be shot. Selection would be made now, by lot. Execution would follow immediately.

Tad stood stunned. For brutal callousness, this was worse than Goliad, where prisoners had been shot without warning.

What could be more cruel than a lottery of death?

The colonel said that under the original order all of them were to have been shot, but that the humane government of Mexico had graciously commuted the sentence to this plan of decimation.

Tad remembered Jack's first words after he was shot: "Who would have thought it would end this way?"

A clatter of chains rose as some of the Texians attempted to free themselves for whatever last-ditch action they might be able to make. The Mexican officers shouted orders. Rifles were cocked, raised, and aimed. The Texians were ordered to move back. A deadly silence fell.

With the possibility of his death only minutes away, Tad found his reaction far different than he would have expected.

Instead of fear, he was filled with an overpowering hunger for life. Corrie's face came to him as clearly as if she were standing before him; he thought of his sons; he yearned to see them grow up, become men, have children of their own. He desperately wanted to live to see his grandchildren.

While the Texians waited in dazed silence, a low bench was brought into the corral. On it was placed a plain earthen crock covered with a large handkerchief.

"This is the way the selection will be made," the colonel said. "This bowl contains one hundred and seventy-four beans. One for each prisoner. Seventeen are black. The rest are white. You will each take a bean from the pot. Each man who draws a black bean will be shot."

The handkerchief was removed. An officer tipped the bowl to

show that it truly held white beans, and black. Then the bowl was shaken. A list of names was handed to the interpreter.

He called out the first. "Captain Ewen Cameron."

Cameron stepped forward, his stride limited by his ankle chain. The crock was held high, above his head. With his face devoid of expression, Cameron reached into the bowl, felt around for a moment, and pulled out a bean. He held it out between thumb and forefinger.

It was white.

Cameron handed it to an officer. The bean was recorded.

The bowl was shaken, and again raised.

"Colonel Tad Logan."

Tad did not have time to think. He stepped forward, pulling Major Dunham with him.

His mind reeled, seeking a way out. It seemed to him—just an impression—that the black beans had been slightly larger. He had only been accorded a glimpse. The difference in size might have been a trick of lighting. But it was his only hope.

He put his free hand into the bowl, plunged deep, and felt with thumb and forefinger for the smallest bean he could find. After rejecting two, he seized one that seemed smaller. Carefully he pulled it out. His heart skipped a beat as he looked down at it.

White.

He felt his heart thump. For a moment he thought he would faint from sheer relief. He handed the bean to the officer as calmly as he could manage.

The bowl rattled as it again was shaken.

"James Ogden."

With a faint smile, as if the outcome would be of no more importance than a dance with a pretty girl, Ogden reached in quickly and drew a bean. He held it up between thumb and forefinger for all to see.

Black.

Instead of feeling compassion, Tad wanted to exult. He felt like dancing for joy, shouting to the skies for his deliverance.

But the emotion quickly passed. Death was spreading around him. Seventeen men were to die in the next few minutes.

"Major Robert Dunham."

Because of the handcuffs, Tad was compelled to make another trip to the bowl. Dunham reached in with his unfettered hand and pulled out a bean.

It was black.

Only in that moment did the full horror hit Tad.

He was chained to a doomed man. They had shared the handcuffs for a week. Now Dunham would be shot. And there was nothing Tad could do to prevent it.

The drawing continued until the seventeenth black bean was drawn. The list was then reviewed. Each man who had drawn a black bean was moved aside. Since Tad was still attached to Dunham, he was marched out of the corral with the condemned men.

"Major, is there anything I can do?" he asked. "Write to your family?"

Dunham seemed to be walking in a mental fog. "My wife," he said. "There are letters in my blanket. Please write her. Tell her my last thoughts were with God, and with her."

A blacksmith punched out the rivet and knocked the handcuff from Dunham's wrist. Holding the cuff, Tad was driven aside.

The blacksmith continued to work, removing handcuffs. All who had drawn white beans were herded beside Tad.

Two priests were brought in to hear confessions. One whispered to Dunham, whose voice rose in reply. "I'm a Protestant, Father. I'll shrive myself, thank you."

He knelt in the dirt, folded his hands, and began to pray silently.

"Pray for us all, Major," said one of the condemned, his voice breaking.

Dunham threw back his head and raised his voice. "Our heavenly Father . . ."

"¡Silencio!" the colonel shouted. In Spanish he decreed that since Mexico was a Catholic nation, no Protestant prayers would be permitted.

Dunham was prodded to his feet.

Tad and the other white bean prisoners were escorted back into the corral.

Events had unfolded so rapidly the prisoners had not yet had time to respond emotionally. But as two files of soldiers marched across the courtyard, and the band struck up the death march, an angry murmur swept through the corral. The Texians surged forward. But the guards had been forewarned. Waving their rifles, they forced the prisoners back.

An officer ordered them to sit on the ground. Guards took up station on the opposite side of the corral, their rifles at full cock. The officer warned that anyone who spoke or moved would be shot.

The afternoon had flown. Already the redness of sunset was gathering in the west. Tad sat in helpless rage as the death march continued. Around him, men were crying openly. The procession of musicians and soldiers passed the gate and marched around the wall of the corral, disappearing from sight. The music stopped. A silence followed, broken by shouted orders.

A low murmur came from beyond the wall, puzzling Tad until he caught a few words and understood that he was hearing the final prayers of the doomed men.

Then came the signal taps of a drum and rattle of muskets.

The thunder of the salvo from the firing squad was followed by shrill cries of anguish and a few pitiful groans.

Then, at spaced intervals, pistol shots rang out as the dying were given the coup de grâce.

After a few minutes, again came the signal taps on the drum, the clatter of muskets, another volley. The pistol shots this time came at shorter intervals.

The seventeen men had been executed in two groups.

Cautiously, rifles still cocked, the guards withdrew from the corral.

The prisoners were now oddly subdued. As if sleepwalking they ate the food shoved through the gate. Conversations were few, and conducted in whispers, as if in respect for the dead. Tad found Dunham's bundle of letters, tucked them in his shirt, and stretched out to sleep. He placed the empty iron cuff on his chest, where it rested against the letters.

He thought of the men who had been alive only a few hours ago, blithely unsuspecting their impending deaths.

He had known all seventeen, marched with them, fought beside them, suffered with them.

He lay awake, thinking of the newly dead, reveling in his own restored life.

And there in the manure of the corral at Rancho Salado, he suddenly was filled with more love for Corrie than he felt he possibly could contain.

The revelation came to him that she *was* his life, that all else was insignificant by comparison. He yearned for paper, the opportunity to write and tell her what was in his heart.

Slowly the emotions of the day swept him into exhaustion. He slept.

The next morning he was awakened early and shackled to an Alabaman, Captain William Davis. Then he and the other Texians were marched out of the corral, past the crumpled bodies.

On their horses, the Mexican officers set a lively pace. They told the Texians that the next stop would be the Hacienda Saint John, forty-two miles down the road, and that much closer to prison.

In the harsh light of day Corrie could barely force herself to face what she had done. While she could blame the wine, the fire, the relaxed mood, and her enduring love for Ramsey, she felt overwhelmed by self-recrimination.

A court commitment in Austin took Ramsey out of town for four days. Corrie spent the hours trying to decide how to handle the situation. She was determined the mistake would not be repeated. Yet she owed Ramsey so much, and she did not want to lose him.

By the time Ramsey returned she had devised a number of polished speeches. None sounded adequate, and she knew the reason. What she had done could not be defended.

On his arrival home he came for supper, as was his custom. Corrie was careful to act naturally around Prue and Hattie. After supper, Ramsey lingered as usual. Prue left with a beau. When Hattie put the boys to bed, and retired to her room, Corrie spoke quickly, allowing Ramsey no room for false assumptions. Abandoning her speeches, she fell back on honesty.

"Ramsey, we must never allow that lapse the other night to happen again," she said.

They were seated before the fire, in the way they had spent so many other evenings. Ramsey did not respond immediately.

"Still, it happened," he said after a moment. "I wouldn't undo it for the world. And we're changed by it. I know I'll never be the same again. Nor, I think, will you."

"But it was *wrong*," Corrie said, more sharply than she had intended. "So very, very wrong."

"No. It was right," Ramsey insisted. "I think deep down you realize that. We owed it to ourselves. And we haven't harmed anyone."

Corrie fought back tears. "Yes, we have. Tad, for one. Even if he never knows, the harm has been done. And you. Maybe I've misled you into invalid expectations. And I've harmed myself. I'm ashamed. Nothing will ever change that. And I've harmed my sons in spirit. Certainly they have every reason to expect a mother beyond reproach."

Her voice caught in her throat. Ramsey started to move toward her. She held up a hand, warding him off.

"Corrie, you're much too hard on yourself. Times, situations change. There are what we lawyers like to call extenuating circumstances. We've been thrown together a lot lately. You have every reason to wonder when, if ever, you'll see your husband again. You have every right to be thinking of yourself."

Corrie shook her head. "No! I should be thinking of Tad."

Ramsey spoke quietly. "Was he thinking of you when he went off on that foolhardy filibuster to Mier? Leaving you, and your sons, without money?"

"Please! Don't talk against Tad. It doesn't become you. He saw his duty. If his politics were in error, that's one thing. But no one can question his dedication. His valor."

"And I don't!" Ramsey protested. "I only question his common sense. Surely consideration of his family should have come first."

Corrie could not argue the point. She allowed it to pass. She had something more important to say. "Aside from what I've done to Tad, what I regret most is the change in our relationship. I've forever valued you as a friend. Now, I'm afraid we've destroyed that. We can never go back."

Ramsey laughed gently. "Corrie, you have some very odd ideas about life. Don't you know that the best love has solid foundation in friendship? That's why you should have married me. We would've had a wonderful life together. I think the other night proved that."

Corrie again held up a hand, palm outward. "Ramsey! Please!"

"I'm only saying our friendship is still there, indestructible. That friendship could grow, expand into an even more rewarding relationship. We've enriched it. Corrie, you haven't lost me as a friend. You never will."

Corrie tried further to explain herself. "In a way, I know that. But I also know it can go on only if I can trust you, trust myself, to avoid repeating what happened the other night."

Ramsey shook his head. "I can't promise that. I'm no saint. But I do promise that, for your sake, I'll try."

One of Ramsey's most endearing traits was his total honesty. Corrie felt somewhat relieved. But there was yet something that needed to be said. She waited until she could control her voice. "Ramsey, you'll never know much I treasure you. I hope I'll *always* be your friend. But perhaps it'd be best if we don't spend so much time alone together, especially at night this way. I can't undo what's been done. But perhaps I should pay more attention to appearances."

Ramsey remained silent a long moment. "Well, I can take a hint. I'll see you in the morning."

He came to her chair. Corrie turned her cheek for a kiss, as was their habit. Instead, Ramsey kissed her full on the mouth. He then walked out of the house without looking back.

Disturbed, Corrie picked up her needlepoint, intending to work until she became sleepy. She was awake when Prue returned.

Prue looked at the vacant chair. "Where's Ramsey?"

Corrie tried to speak casually. "He left early."

Prue hesitated. "You two quarrel?"

Corrie laughed. "Of course not."

Prue glanced at the front door, as if suspecting Ramsey might still be lurking there. "That's like a bee leaving honey. Something's happened you're not telling me."

Corrie took care not to miss a stitch. "What makes you think so?"

"Well, it's obvious."

"You're imagining things," Corrie told her.

Ramsey continued to come to the house almost every day for supper. He often sat late with Corrie and Prue before the fire. But Corrie took steps to make certain she and Ramsey were never alone. If Prue went out, Corrie invented reasons for Hattie to delay her departure for bed until after Ramsey left.

"I can't figure you two people out," Prue said one evening after Ramsey had gone. "There's something different about you."

"In what way?" Corrie asked.

"I don't know. I thought at first you'd quarreled. But now you seem thicker than ever."

Corrie could not deny that. Ramsey's prediction had proved apt. Their night of love, never repeated, had deepened their relationship immeasurably.

"Well, keep your little secret," Prue said. "I'll bet I find out what it is, someday."

Once more the Texian prisoners were counted. Six Mexican army officers fussed over papers, their work hampered by illiteracy. While waiting, Tad carefully eyed the Castle of Perote, the most infamous prison in the Western Hemisphere. The moat was dry, but sixty feet across, and ten deep. The size of the castle itself was staggering. The walls were thirty feet high, and ten to fifteen feet thick. Twenty-five acres were contained within them. Cannons protruded from the star-shaped buttresses.

Tad judged that an army would be required to break into—or out of—the place.

Seldom in his life had he been so tired. He and the other prisoners had marched all the way from Puebla, ninety-six miles, with only a few brief stops. Now darkness was minutes away, and they had not been fed.

"¡*Adelante!*" an officer ordered.

Tad marched with the other prisoners across the moat, and under the thick deadfall gate. They clattered down steps and entered a long, dungeonlike corridor. The guards counted and divided prisoners, and locked them up for the night.

Tad and two dozen others were marched into a gloomy hole six steps one way, and ten the other. The big, solid door slammed behind them. A key grated in the lock.

Tad examined his surroundings. The only light came from a barred window at the top of the wall, thirty feet over their heads. Soon the sun would set, and they would be in complete darkness. No blanket or sleeping mat had been provided. The stench from a bucket in the corner was staggering.

Moving to a wall, Tad lay down on the hard stones. A few of the men stood at the door for a while and shouted for food. None was brought. Eventually they quieted.

With his head pillowed in the crook of his arm, Tad drifted off to sleep.

He was awakened as the key again turned in the lock. Daylight was showing in the window overhead. The guards wheeled in carts loaded with buckets of coffee and stacks of bread. They left the door open. A guard informed them in Spanish that since today was Sunday, they had the run of the prison until the evening lockup.

The bread was plentiful. Tad ate his fill. After rearranging his clothing and making himself as presentable as possible, he walked out into the immense corridor. A few prisoners were stirring, going from cell to cell, visiting. Most were in chains.

Tad stopped two men shackled together. "I'm looking for Whit Logan. You know where I might find him?"

The taller one pointed. "That way. Southeast corner."

Tad thanked him and moved on. The stench grew stronger the deeper he moved into the prison. He passed cells where men lay sick and delirious, groaning with pain. Tad recognized the symptoms of *el vómito*, an especially vicious form of yellow fever. He had seen it before. The disease was invariably fatal.

Twice more he asked directions and, in the gloom, found the

corner cell. He entered. A half dozen vague forms lay along one wall in semidarkness. "Whit?" Tad asked. "Whit Logan?"

One of forms rose from his reed mattress. The deep yet familiar voice was heavy with sleep. "Tad?"

Shock made Tad momentarily speechless. The man before him bore but slight resemblance to the seventeen-year-old youth who had left San Antonio just over two years ago. The pockmarks in the hollows of his cheeks enhanced his age. But mostly the change was in the eyes. Whit now had a wary, knowing look that made him seem two decades older.

"Whit? Is it really you?"

Whit laughed. "Nobody else."

They staggered into an abrazo. It was awkward, for they had been reared never to show affection. Never before had they embraced.

Stepping apart, they looked at each other for a long moment.

"What kept you?" Whit asked. "Corrie wrote months ago you were taken at Mier. I was growing worried."

"They kept most of us about three months at the Santiago Convent," Tad explained. "A chain gang, working on the streets."

Whit nodded. "I had a shot at that. You'll find it better here in some ways, worse in others. The food's better. But the dankness is bad. Lots of sickness."

He gestured to the mat. They sat down. Tad noticed for the first time that Whit was shackled to another man, who still lay asleep. Somehow the chain on Whit's ankle seemed more galling to Tad than the one he himself had worn in the Santiago Convent.

"What's the talk in Mexico City?" Whit asked. "Any chance of release?"

"Everybody figures it won't be soon. American, British embassy people are working on it. But Sam Houston has turned his back on the Mier prisoners, same as with the Santa Fé Expedition. I don't look for wholesale release until he's voted out. What exactly was that trouble you were in? I've heard different reports."

Whit smiled ruefully. "A guard at the convent kept hitting me every morning with his rifle butt. Right in the kidney. It stayed sore.

I knew I had to put a stop to it. So I did. I laid him out. I was flogged."

Whit turned, raised his shirt. Tad winced. He had seen few Negroes beaten worse. Angry red scars covered Whit's back.

"When the first release came last June, my name wasn't on it," Whit went on. "When I asked why, I was told charges are still pending."

"Even though you've already been punished?"

Whit laughed. "That's Mexico for you. When did you last hear from Corrie? You know she's moved back to San Antonio?"

Tad nodded. "I received two letters at Santiago. Apparently two or three others went astray." He paused. "Whit, I have bad news, of sorts. Father died about a year ago. I didn't write, thinking there'd be a better time to tell you."

Whit remained silent a moment. "Well, what the hell. He was an old man. It was to be expected, I guess. Now Frank's got clear sailing."

"I'm told he's in bad health. I don't really know. We deal mostly through his lawyer. He still owes me money. It isn't long until he owes you a bundle."

Again Whit laughed. "If it's enough to buy my way out of Perote, I'm interested."

"What kind of work will we do here?"

"The work of asses." Whit grinned at Tad's puzzlement. "We're yoked to carts like burros, go out and load them with rocks, and pull them back into the prison. Either that, or we bring sand from a mile away with wheelbarrows. The material is used to repair this old place. We're well guarded. Two companies of infantry and one of artillery. Little chance of escape."

Talk of escape reminded Tad. "Jack's dead. Corrie write you?"

Whit nodded. "But not the details."

"You know Jack. . . . When we jumped the guard at Salado, there was no holding him back. He took a ball that was meant for me. Died in my arms."

Whit was silent for a time. "Corrie also wrote that Old Paint Caldwell is dead."

"I heard," Tad said. "He blamed himself for that mixup in command on the Salado. Someone said he died of pure mortification. That's probably true."

Whit shook his head sadly. "Seems like every day I hear that someone else from the expedition is dead. We must be down to about half."

"We're losing men from Mier right along. Seventeen in one bunch at Rancho Salado. Even then the Mexicans weren't satisfied. Later they took Ewen Cameron out and shot him. On Santa Anna's personal order, they said, because he was our escape leader."

Whit nodded. "My best friend was shot down in cold blood, right before my eyes. I've seen men beaten to death with rifle butts because they were so sick and helpless they couldn't walk. I never dreamed anything like this country existed."

"They can make a believer out of you," Tad agreed. "When I drew that white bean at Salado, and those seventeen men were taken out and shot, I made up my mind right then and there I was going to survive."

Again Whit chuckled. "Hell, brother, I made *that* decision a long time ago, on the Jornada del Muerto. And we will, Tad. We'll survive. No matter what."

Tad reached for him, and again they clung to each other in a warm abrazo.

Corrie kept up her letter writing campaign throughout the summer, fall, and winter with meager results. When spring came again, it seemed Tad and Whit would remain prisoners forever.

Then came a glimmer of hope. Texas envoys in Washington succeeded in hammering out a treaty for the annexation of Texas to the United States. Drafted and approved by the U.S. State Department, the treaty was sent to the U.S. Senate for approval.

Annexation had always been popular in Texas. But now it became a fever. Attention shifted almost overnight from Washington-on-the-Brazos, now seat of Texas government, to Washington-on-the-Potomac, where the all-important treaty was under consideration.

The treaty boldly proclaimed that, during negotiations, Texas must be "free from molestation." To enforce the provision, United States troops assembled along the Louisiana border.

With the new support, Texas was no longer a tottering republic. Corrie saw evidence of renewed excitement around her every day. Land speculators returned to San Antonio in droves. Béxar became headquarters for a steady stream of immigrants arriving direct from middle Europe. An impresario named Henri de Castro acquired a large tract fifty miles to the west and settled French families around a new town called Castroville. The German Association of Noblemen—the Adelsverein—acquired land to the east of San Antonio and brought in settlers. The plazas of San Antonio took on an international air. Corrie now heard not only English and Spanish in the streets, but also French, German, Polish, and languages she could not identify.

All the exotic activity brought a different, invigorating flavor to San Antonio. Corrie's hopes soared. Upon ratification of the annexation treaty, Tad and Whit would become de facto United States citizens, virtually guaranteeing their release.

Corrie went from day to day expecting good news any moment.

Then came a stunning reversal. Ramsey returned from Houston with a newspaper revealing that the annexation treaty had been rejected by the United States Senate.

Corrie was devastated. "What will this mean?"

"Mexico already has taken it as a clear signal," Ramsey said. "General Woll has informed President Houston that Mexico will resume hostilities."

Corrie thought of the impact the news would have on Tad and Whit's situation. No doubt General Woll's threat doomed any hope for their release. It was Woll who had last invaded San Antonio, and most of the Mier prisoners had helped drive him back across the river.

Prue was reading the newspaper Ramsey had brought home. "This says Houston has sent a letter to the U.S. Senate, proclaiming that Texas has the alternative of becoming a greater Republic, peopled with industrious European immigrants, joined with Oregon and northern Mexico in a natural union. He sounds more like Lamar than Lamar."

"Then he's closing the door to annexation," Corrie said.

Ramsey disagreed. "No, he's handling it well. I believe he thinks, as I do, that there'll be a backlash in the States to the Senate vote. Certainly Texas annexation will be a principal issue in the United States presidential election this fall."

"We're right back where we started," Corrie said. It was her lowest period since Tad's capture.

The U.S. presidential campaign that summer was followed as avidly in Texas as in any part of the United States. Corrie read every newspaper that came her way, doting on the chances of the proannexation candidate, James Polk.

Her hopes again soared with his election in November.

But newspaper writers were quick to point out that Polk still lacked the necessary two-thirds majority in the U.S. Senate.

Ramsey was privy to the maneuverings in the Texas capital. "Polk's forces plan to try a new tactic," he told Corrie. "Instead of annexation by treaty, requiring two-thirds majority in the Senate, they'll seek a joint resolution from Congress. That requires only a simple majority in both houses."

The ploy worked. On the last day of February in the new year of 1845, Texas annexation cleared the U.S. Congress.

But it still had to be ratified in the Texas Congress, and as yet the new president, Anson Jones, had not declared himself on the question. As secretary of state he had worked with Houston in the negotiations. But no one knew his views. He had made no speeches during the election campaign and, curiously, had not mentioned the subject in his inaugural address.

After some delay, Jones promised the chargés of England and France that he would delay action on annexation for ninety days.

"What's in his crazy mind?" Prue complained. "Plainly the people want it. Why is he waiting?"

"He wants to effect the best deal possible," Ramsey explained. "It's a brilliant maneuver, worthy of Sam Houston himself. I'm sure it'll work in Tad's favor."

The public was not so perceptive. It was widely assumed that Jones was scheming to defeat annexation. He was attacked by the newspapers, and burned in effigy.

But the maneuvering bore fruit, as Ramsey had predicted. Britain and France put pressure on Mexico. Soon there came from Mexico City an offer: If Texas would reject annexation, Mexico would recognize Texas Independence.

For Texians, it was a difficult choice. On all sides, Corrie heard the pros and cons debated heatedly.

"Whatever the outcome, this is a boon for Tad and Whit," Ramsey insisted. "Mexico is making every concession. Maybe release of all Texas prisoners will be among them."

President Jones called for the Texas Congress to meet in mid-June to vote on the choices: statehood, or independence.

Sentiment in Texas appeared to favor annexation. Perhaps this was Santa Anna's assessment, for in the first week of May Corrie received a letter from Waddy Thompson, United States ambassador to Mexico:

Dear Mrs. Logan,
In haste I write you wonderful news. On Thursday last President Santa Anna issued an executive order for the release of your husband and his brother. I had the pleasure of delivering the order personally to the commandant of the prison at Perote. While there I visited briefly with the Texian prisoners. I'm pleased to report that Thaddeus and Whit are in moderately good health, considering the hardships they have endured. They will be released immediately, and should be able to secure passage from Vera Cruz on the next ship.

> Yr. Obedient Servant
> Waddy Thompson

Corrie went to bed and wept for sheer joy, so emotionally depleted she could hardly stir.

Whit had now been a prisoner three and a half years, and Tad two. She felt as if she had endured all of their ordeals.

It was Prue who saw the irony.

"Tad always opposed annexation. Now it has won his freedom after all else failed."

--- 17 ---

Alert for the sound, Corrie heard Tad and Whit in the drive the moment they arrived. She called to Prue and ran out the front door. Ben was holding the reins of both their horses while trying to take off his hat and exchange handshakes. Tad and Whit were in high spirits, laughing with Ben as they pounded him on the back.

Tad saw her coming and stepped through the gate to meet her. He swept her into his arms beside the rosebushes. Lost in his embrace, Corrie found she retained not the slightest trace of anger over his having left her two years before. All resentment had vanished during the long months of worry.

He held her at arm's length and looked at her. "You haven't changed a bit. You're as beautiful as ever."

"Irish blarney," she said, although she had hardly heard. She was studying the changes in him. He seemed older, and more weathered. He had lost weight. But she sensed a new calmness in him, a more deliberate manner. She remembered how the tone of his letters had altered abruptly after the black bean episode, growing ever more thoughtful and introspective.

She glanced at Whit, still standing by the horses. For a dizzying moment she thought Tad had brought home a stranger. Only the grin was the same. Whit walked toward her, holding out his arms. She hurried to him, keeping tight rein on her dismay.

Gone was the open-faced boy she had known. Once so unguarded, his eyes now were impenetrable and knowing. When he spoke her name, his voice came as the deep rumbling of a bear of a man.

He held her for a long moment, while Corrie searched for a

322

tactful way to comment on the differences in him. But she was spared. Whit looked past her toward the house. Corrie turned.

Prue had taken time to put on her best dress, the blue brocade that contrasted so well with her coloring. She had brushed her long hair out onto her shoulders. She was posed beautifully, using the doorway behind her as a frame.

"My! Look at that!" Tad said, holding out his arms. Prue came to him, hugged him, and kissed his cheek. She stood back, looked at Whit, and moved hesitantly toward him.

Corrie stepped aside. Whit and Prue came together slowly, each searching for changes, and finding them in abundance. When Prue spoke, Corrie heard her anguish for what the years had done to him. "Oh, Whit!"

They moved into an embrace and exchanged ardent kisses.

Corrie was mildly surprised. Their relationship must have deepened more than she knew through their letters. She glanced at Tad. He also seemed to recognize that more was happening between them than was evident on the surface.

"Where are the boys?" Tad asked.

"They're playing on the patio," Corrie answered.

Tad walked down the drive beside the house. Corrie, Whit, and Prue followed.

Jim Bowie and Albert Martin were playing with a toy wagon. Albert was seated in it, legs outstretched, and Jim Bowie was pulling him across the patio.

Tad knelt on one knee. "Hey, Jim Bowie! Remember me?"

Jim Bowie dropped the wagon tongue and stood looking at his father, uncertain what to do. Tad scooped him up. The boy squirmed. At six he considered himself too old to be carried. Albert Martin scrambled out of the wagon, looked for a place to hide, and found none. He stoically endured Tad's manhandling.

"I know you don't remember me," Tad told him. "But we'll get acquainted, and make up for lost time."

Hattie came out of the house and welcomed Tad and Whit home. The Negroes stood gathered by the barn, grinning and laughing their pleasure over Tad and Whit's return.

"Let's go say hello to the men," Tad said to Whit.

As Tad and Whit walked out to the barn, Prue stopped at the edge of the patio. "What have they done to him?" she whispered, watching Whit. "He looks older than Tad."

"I'm sure they put him through more than we'll ever know," Corrie said. "But they've turned him into a man."

"And then some. Did you see his eyes? And that voice! Oh, my God!"

Tad and Whit finished their brief ceremony with the men and came back toward the house. They paused to admire the decorations on the patio.

Corrie felt she should explain. "I knew everyone in town would want to come welcome you home. I thought if we turned it into a single celebration, we could save you the ordeal of its lasting for days. If you've no objection, I'll send Ben out now to confirm that we're giving a welcome-home party tonight."

Tad put an arm around her and laughed. "We're past ready to celebrate. But Whit and I best go dunk ourselves in the river before we greet company. We rode all the way from Columbus without stopping."

"Shall we go in?" Corrie suggested. "Ben can bring your baggage."

Tad walked through the house, examining the walls, floors, ceilings. He gave a low whistle of exclamation. "When you wrote you were fixing up the house, I thought you were just patching and making do. I had no idea you had restored it."

"Ramsey showed the men how to reseat the floor tiles, plaster the walls, fix the ceilings. They worked hard at it."

Tad inspected the ceiling in the long room. Corrie knew he was remembering the large hole there. "Where is Ramsey?" he asked without looking at her.

Corrie found herself tense. She admonished herself, and spoke as casually as she could manage. "He'll be over later. I asked him to come early, so we could have a few minutes together with him before the other guests arrive."

Tad nodded without comment. Corrie did not know if it was her imagination, but she thought he had acted differently from the first mention of Ramsey's name.

Taking along fresh clothing, Tad and Whit left for a bath in the river. Corrie helped Hattie with final preparations for the party. She then hurried to her room to change dresses.

She returned to the patio just as Ramsey arrived. He greeted Tad and Whit so effusively Corrie could see he was ill at ease. Tad did not help him, but stood listening politely, his deep reserve as solid as a stone wall.

"Everywhere I go your friends ask about you," Ramsey said. "Only last week Sam Houston mentioned hearing of your release. He said he was looking forward to seeing you again."

"I'm not sure I'll have anything to say to him," Tad said.

Ramsey saw his error. "I know the Texas prisoners have blamed Houston for his stance. But I truly believe he handled the situation best, playing other nations against each other, using the specter of annexation to win concessions from Mexico."

"You could be right," Tad said, refusing to discuss it.

An awkward silence fell. Tad seemed to see he had spoken too abruptly.

"Ramsey, I want to thank you for helping Corrie while I was gone," he said. "I saw the shape the house was in after Woll's troops got through with it. You've done wonders restoring it."

Ramsey was relieved to be on firmer ground. "The basic structure was undamaged," he said. "Your men became quite adept with plaster and stone. We did a rather hasty job on some of the lintels. You may wish to replace them before long."

"They look fine," Tad said.

Again an awkward silence fell. Whit stood with a slight smile, as if amused by the exchange.

Corrie felt moved to intervene. "Our guests will be arriving soon," she said. "Would you gentlemen help us light the *luminarias?*"

Both Tad and Ramsey seemed to welcome the opportunity to end the conversation. They produced lucifers and helped Hattie light the shrouded candles. The patio assumed a soft glow. By the time they finished, guests were arriving. The band started to play, and the party began. Soon the patio was filled with dancing couples.

As hostess Corrie was preoccupied with her guests. But she noticed that the two men in her life carefully avoided each other as the evening progressed. Their obvious coolness toward each other left her upset, for she wished with all her heart that Tad and Ramsey could be friends, and she blamed herself that the situation was not as innocent as it should be.

Prue understood the growing animosity between Tad and Ramsey but she did not know what to do about it. She could sympathize with Tad, returning home after two difficult years to find another man solidly entrenched in his house, and in his wife's affections.

Yet Prue's heart went out to Ramsey, who had been granted the unexpected opportunity of serving the love of his life for two long years. And now with Tad's return he once again was out in the cold. Prue saw evidence of his anguish on his face, in his manner. She had known him all her life, and tonight was the first time she had ever seen him unsure of himself.

Prue understood the situation because she had seen it coming. For the last year the question had been on her mind: Would Ramsey settle for second best?

Earlier she thought that tonight she might learn the answer. Several times during the last few months, on their walks together, Ramsey had seemed on the verge of speaking his heart. Prue was certain he had seen this situation coming, while hoping it would not. Now, faced with the reality, he was shattered.

Prue had prepared herself to pick up the pieces. Since her childhood Ramsey Cothburn had been considered a prize beyond measure. Prue was confident she could have him, if she played her skills right.

But she was also confused. Tad had brought home a most exciting stranger. She had loved Whit for his gentle humor, his essential good nature. His letters from prison had continued to convey those qualities. She was totally unprepared for the changes in him. Plainly he now was as much a man as Tad or Ramsey. She felt she should get reacquainted with him before making any hasty commitment. If the Whit she knew was contained somewhere in that imposing man, she might be his for the taking.

She danced with Ramsey. He was in a glum mood. "I shouldn't have come," he whispered into her ear. "I'm out of place here."

"Ramsey! What a terrible thing to say, after the friend you've been to us."

"I'm Corrie's friend, and yours, but not Tad's," Ramsey said. "This is his night. He sees me as Corrie's former fiancé, and that rankles. I've seen it in him every time we've met."

"That could pass in time," Prue insisted. "Tad, if nothing else, is generous. I'm living proof of that. I'm sure you'll always be welcome here. I can't conceive of it otherwise."

Ramsey seemed to find that reassuring. "I'd like to have a good relationship with Tad. I like life here. I'm thinking of selling my plantation on the Colorado. I've received a good offer from the Adelsverein. I've decided I'm more suited to law and politics."

"I think that's wonderful," Prue said. She had always considered the plantation as one of Ramsey's drawbacks as a potential suitor. She did not intend to be stuck away on one.

She wanted to ask what kind of home he planned in San Antonio, to replace his rented quarters, but she felt the question would be too forward. For a moment she sensed Ramsey was thinking on the same subject. Again he seemed on the verge of revealing himself. But once more he stopped short of speech. The waltz ended and Whit came to claim her. Prue danced away with Whit, wondering what Ramsey had almost said.

"I can't get used to the changes in you," Whit whispered.

"Look who's talking," Prue said.

Whit chuckled. "All those years I thought of you as I remembered you. I've always thought Corrie the most beautiful woman in the world. Once a long time ago Tad said that when you became a woman you'd be just as beautiful. He was right."

"Mexican prisons must be detrimental to the eyesight," Prue said. "But please rave on."

Whit laughed. It came like the rumble of a drum. "I kept thinking of you as fifteen. Seeing you as a woman was a shock."

"I've tended to do the same with you," Prue admitted. "If you remember, you were skinny as a rail when you went away. Now look at you. And that's not fat. I can tell."

"Hard labor," Whit said. "For three years I loaded big stones on a cart, then pulled the cart three miles into Perote. They fed us well. Some of us thrived on it physically. Of course mentally it was a different story."

Prue looked up at him. "Whit, I haven't had a chance to tell you. I'm so very, very glad you're home."

He held her close. "You don't know how good it is to be home."

They danced for a time in silence. When Whit spoke, his tone was jocular. "Hattie let it slip you've been receiving plenty of callers. You have a steady beau?"

"Nothing serious," Prue said.

"I hope we have the chance to do some catching up with each other."

"Then stick around," Prue said. "I'm not going anywhere."

The party was a complete success. Of that Corrie had no doubt. Tad and Whit danced with all the women, and were besieged by old friends. Both drank too much, but Corrie felt that was their due.

Perhaps sensing that the honorees were tired, the guests did not stay late. By midnight all were gone.

Corrie helped Tad into the bedroom. Fully clothed, he tumbled into bed on his back.

She went out to make sure all the lights were extinguished. When she returned, Tad was asleep. She eased into bed beside him. He scarcely stirred.

For a time she lay awake, examining his face in the low lamplight. He indeed had aged beyond the two years he had been gone. There were new, deeper wrinkles and creases. His hands were thick and callused from the harsh prison labor.

Corrie cringed with guilt. In the last few months she had regretted her one night with Ramsey thousands of times.

Yet there was nothing she could do to erase it. And there was a danger. If she sent Ramsey away now, she would only be adding fuel to any speculation Tad might have. It was best to go on treating Ramsey as the dear friend he had always been.

Corrie wept for her guilt. After a time, she slept.

She awoke as Tad struggled to sit up. "I'm thirsty from all that liquor," he said. "I'm going to get a drink of water."

"I'll get it," Corrie said. Gently she pushed him back into bed. She glanced at the clock. After two-thirty in the morning. She hurried through the house to the water bucket, filled a glass from the dipper, and returned with it to the bedroom.

Tad had removed his clothing and was under the sheets. He was smiling with amusement. "This isn't exactly the way I've pictured my homecoming. Drunk and passed out in bed with my wife."

"I should have delayed the party," Corrie said. "But I was certain everyone would come over anyway."

"Corrie, I'm glad you didn't put it off. We got all that over with, and it was a great homecoming. I'm just laughing at myself, the way I'd imagined it."

Corrie moved to get out of bed, intending to change into a nightgown. Tad took her by the wrist.

"There's something I want to say." He paused. "I've done a lot of thinking during the last two years. I don't know if I've found answers. I'm still of two minds. One minute I think I shouldn't have gone off on the Mier adventure. On the other hand, what's a man to do if his home's invaded? How can he sit still? So maybe it was proper that I went. I still don't know."

Corrie waited.

"But I want to devote more time to you and the boys from now on," he continued. "It won't be easy. I've lost two years. When Whit and I went through Houston, Anson Jones sent word he's appointing me to the Constitutional Convention in July. If annexation passes the Texas Congress, we'll have the chance to write a solid foundation of laws for statehood. It'll probably take several months. But it must be done, and there are ideas I want to work into it, especially in the area of jurisprudence. So I'll probably accept."

Again he paused. "I want to resume my law practice. The land downriver must be put into production. Somehow, I must juggle all this, without neglecting you and the boys. Albert Martin didn't know me. A boy going on four, not recognizing his own father. Scared of me. That's a crime."

"He's a bit shy," Corrie said.

Intent on making his point, Tad hardly listened. "So I'll enlist Whit as a full partner, to take some of the load. But I want you to know that even when I'm overburdened, I won't deprive myself of enjoying ample time with you and the boys. Seventeen black beans taught me what's truly important in life."

Corrie yielded to his kisses. Several minutes later she pushed away and rolled from the bed. She began changing into her nightgown, troubled by a nagging worry.

Would he find a difference in her, in some subtle way, that might lead him to suspect?

For years she had been awaiting the words she had heard tonight. But now she herself had cast the biggest flaw of all on her marriage.

Tad pointed. "The Peralta Grant begins at that knoll over there. The south line parallels that creek, and runs six miles to the east. I'll show you the map at the office."

Whit seemed distracted. He acknowledged the information with a nod and followed the creek with his gaze. But his expression remained distant.

Tad touched his horse lightly with a spur and started on eastward. Whit's sorrel fell into step alongside. "Whit, if this is what you think you want to do, I'll draw up the papers, cutting you in for half. Fee simple. One dollar and other considerations."

"Hell, I couldn't do that," Whit said. "It's yours. Frank going broke is just my bad luck."

"Donegal money bought all this," Tad said, gesturing to the horizon. "We can look on it as your share."

"There may be Donegal money in it. But you also plowed in all the money you made from your lawyering. Besides, it isn't my share of Donegal. Frank lost that."

"There's money from my law practice in it," Tad conceded. "But you also were contributing, running the place upriver. Consider this your share, plus pay for your work. All I ask is that if anything should happen to me, you'll look after Corrie and the boys."

"Hell, I'd do that anyway. You know that. It's just I'm not sure yet what I want to do."

Tad remained silent for a time, thinking. Whit had been taken out of the natural flow of his life at a crucial point, when he should have been developing a goal in life. Now, he seemed to have lost all ambition.

"During the next year I intend to concentrate on putting this land into production," Tad told him. "Horses. Cattle. Maybe sheep down toward the Nueces. There's not enough irrigated land upriver to merit expansion. It'll never equal what Jared Groce has built on the Brazos. I may have made a mistake on the work we've put into it. But down here there's no limit. We may be troubled for a few years by Indians and Mexican renegades. And we must find a market for the cattle. But the makings are here."

"Sounds like too much work for me," Whit said.

Tad knew he was being put off. Whit had always been a willing worker.

Tad drew rein. Whit also stopped his horse, and they sat in their saddles, facing each other. "Whit, I'm not pushing you," Tad said. "After what you've been through, you deserve a rest. But you ought to be thinking ahead, to what you want to do with the rest of your life."

Whit looked off toward the south, his eyes narrowing in the glare of the sun. "I've been talking with Colonel Hays. I may enlist in the Rangers."

Tad winced inwardly. "Not much money in that."

"I'm not interested in the money," Whit said. "Hays says he's been kept busy lately by Mexican renegades along the border. I figure I have a few old scores to settle."

So that was it. Tad stood in his stirrups for a moment, readjusting his weight in the saddle. "I can understand that. But I wouldn't consider it a life's work."

"I do," Whit said. "I doubt I'll ever get my fill of it."

Tad took off his hat and wiped the sweatband. "You're of age. I can't tell you what to do. But Whit, Rangering is a dead end. A year or two of it wouldn't hurt a young man. You've lost three and a half years. With Hays, you'll just be throwing away more."

"Maybe not. Hays says war's coming, over the drawing of the boundary, if nothing else. You've said so yourself."

He glanced at Tad for confirmation. Tad nodded agreement. Mexico had always placed the border at the Nueces, eighty miles and more above the Río Grande.

"I'd have to be in it anyway," Whit said. "Hays thinks if war comes the Rangers may be taken into the United States army."

"That could happen," Tad conceded.

"Anyway, that's what I want to do."

Tad touched his horse with a spur. Again Whit's sorrel fell into step alongside and they moved on eastward.

In a way Tad understood. He remembered his own restlessness at Whit's age, a dissatisfaction that first brought him to Texas. He spoke cautiously. "I hope you won't be in any hurry about it. Corrie and Prue are enjoying having you home. I'd appreciate it if you'd indulge them awhile."

"They've got Ramsey to entertain. I'd say he's a handful."

Tad did not respond. It was the first time Whit had showed any indication of irritation over Ramsey.

Whit refused to let the subject die. "Why's he always hanging around? Why does Corrie put up with him?"

Again Tad was inclined not to answer. But Whit was living amid the situation. Perhaps he deserved an explanation. "Corrie and Ramsey have known each other since childhood. He was a great deal of help to her, when I couldn't be. He's a big part of her life. Also, I think he's a tie to home for her."

Whit rode for a distance in silence. "I think there's more in his head than Christian charity," he said after a time. "If it was left up to me, I'd run him off."

Tad had considered doing exactly that. He offered Whit the only reason he had not. "It'd only make matters worse. She'd be hurt, and it'd be my doing. If he's left alone, I believe he'll eventually move on of his own accord."

"I'm not so sure," Whit said. "I predict that someday you'll tangle with that son of a bitch."

Tad glanced at Whit, seeking a judgment on whether he spoke from jealousy, or if he had seen something that made him suspicious. From the moment he returned home Tad had been wary of Ramsey's motives.

"I tolerate him for Corrie's sake," Tad said. "But you're right. My patience may wear thin." He gestured. "Look yonder."

In a flat less than three quarters of a mile away a herd of several hundred wild cattle grazed.

"Every one of those cattle would be worth good money in Cairo or St. Louis," Tad said. "They're grazing on our grass. But not one wears a brand. I don't know how many are here. Several thousand, for sure. Right now anyone could come and take them. They're not marked."

Whit sat looking at the cattle in silence.

"We'll build log corrals to trap them," Tad continued. "Put the iron to them. Castrate all the bulls, except the best. It'll take a year or two. Maybe longer. But when a market develops, we'll have a fortune on the hoof, with our name on it."

Still Whit remained silent. Tad felt moved to try once more. "I need you, Whit. Putting this land in operation, keeping it going, will be too much for me alone, especially if I keep my law practice and dabble in politics, which I'll probably do."

He paused. "Half of it, Whit. I'm hoping you see what I see here."

Whit leaned forward and stroked the neck of his horse. "I'll think about it," he said, picking up his reins.

Whit held aside branches of the weeping willow. Prue slipped through and they sat beside the river in the shade of the tree. Whit trailed a hand in the water, then allowed the excess to run down his fingers onto his tongue. "This river kept me alive all the way across the Jornada del Muerto," he said.

He saw, from her expression, that she did not understand. He explained. "We'd march all day on a cup of water. The thirst would drive us crazy. I kept thinking of this river, how you and I used to walk along beside it, the way it looked, all the cool water flowing along. It helped put thirst out of my mind."

Prue positioned the picnic basket and took out a tablecloth. "We talked about you every day," she said. "Even before Tad was taken, you were never out of our thoughts."

She spread the tablecloth on the grass. Once again Whit was struck by how much alike Prue and Corrie were in many ways, yet so different in others. Prue's long auburn hair was tied back with a narrow leather thong. Corrie would never have worn anything so plain. She would have used a colorful barrette, a Mexican-style comb, or at least a bright ribbon. There was a simplicity, a neatness, a starchy crispness, about Prue. Corrie tended to wear soft fabrics, more comfortable styles. Whit did not necessarily prefer one mode over the other. He just noticed, and appreciated, the difference.

Since his return, he and Prue had not been able to spend much time together. A steady procession of old friends came to welcome him home. Several members of the Santa Fé Expedition, released earlier, traveled long distances to shake his hand, to reminisce about those who had not returned.

Thus far, his homecoming had been wearing.

He had suggested to Prue that they slip away, stroll along the river, as they used to do. She had proposed a private picnic, and prepared a basket, saying that would give them an excuse to be away the whole afternoon.

Prue looked up at him. "What do you plan to do, now that you're free?"

Aside from Tad, Whit had not yet discussed his plans with anyone. "I'll probably enlist in the Rangers," he said.

Prue closed her eyes and shook her head. "Oh, Whit! I'd think you'd have had enough of that harsh life."

Each time she turned her head a bow of hair gathered over one ear. He wanted to run his hand along it, stroke it, kiss it. He contented himself for the moment with the fantasy.

He pulled his mind back to what she had said. "There's war coming with Mexico. I want to get into it from the beginning. I figure I have a few debts to pay."

Prue put a hand on his arm. Her fingers were long and slim,

perfection in motion. "Whit, why don't you give yourself some time? You're angry now. That's understandable. But you've been away from all this too long." She gestured to the river, the trees. "You should become reacquainted with the better side of life. It might help you forget your anger."

Whit watched a stem of willow leaves at play in the current. Since coming home, he had not wanted to talk about his experiences. Now, suddenly, he did.

"Prue, on the walk through Méjico Nuevo, the man I shared blankets with every night was shot down right before my eyes. I saw other prisoners beaten to death with rifle butts simply because they were too weak to stand. I had to watch helpless. Their ears were sliced off and strung on a string. That was the way the Mexicans kept count. Their bodies were stripped and left at the side of the road like the carcass of a dog. I was thrown into prison with lepers whose fingers, noses, feet, had rotted away. The stench . . ."

He stopped. Prue's face had paled. She sat rigid, eyes wide.

"I'm sorry," he said. "I shouldn't have told you all that."

Prue swallowed. "Don't apologize. I want to know those things. It helps me to understand." She looked away for a long moment. "But the memories are still fresh in your mind. In time perhaps they'll fade, become like a bad dream. Why subject yourself to more horror?"

Whit found he badly wanted to explain. He glanced around them. They were well screened by the drooping willow branches, the surrounding trees. This was a secluded spot. "The memories are a part of me," he said. "I'll never be allowed to forget. I'll carry the evidence to my grave."

He unbuttoned his shirt, peeled it off, and turned his back, looking past his shoulder for her reaction.

She cringed at the sight, reached out a hand to touch him, hesitated, and put her fingertips to her lips instead.

Whit longed to feel those hands on his bare flesh. "It's healed," he said. "Even though I know it doesn't seem so."

She reached, touched his back. Chills raced through him as she traced the curve of his shoulder, along his ribs. He basked in the pleasure, then moved to put on his shirt.

But as he turned she came into his arms. Tears were running down her cheeks. Those marvelous hands went along his face, past his neck. Her mouth sought his. They rolled onto the grass, straining, taking and giving pleasure with their kisses.

For Whit the next few minutes brought to life all the fantasies he had entertained through countless long nights in reeking cells. All of that pent-up desire mushroomed within him.

Then incredibly Prue was helping, tugging aside clothing, uncovering new flesh for him to caress, to kiss. Whit's senses built into a roar in his ears.

Suddenly it was over. Whit lay breathless, feeling disheveled, awkward.

Prue held him close. "Don't move," she whispered. "I want to stay like this forever."

She ran those hands along his jaw, into the hollows of his eyes, through his hair. He kissed her delicate cheekbones, the arc of hair over her ears, the soft recesses of her throat.

The world dropped away. Time hung suspended. After an interval, Whit's desire began to rebuild. But he was hesitant.

"Anytime," Prue whispered.

They made love leisurely, reluctant for the ecstasy to end. Whit was aware that Prue derived greater pleasure from his slower pace. She clung to him, quietly saying his name. Eventually necessity drove him to depletion.

They lay in each other's arms, content. The hours passed. Twilight came. Across the river, a full moon rose.

"Today you've deflowered a nineteen-year-old virgin," Prue confided with a smile.

With that Whit was struck by the enormity of what he had done. If it came to light, Tad might give him a worse flogging than he had received from the Mexicans.

Certainly Corrie would.

"Prue, I love you," he began.

"I know," she interrupted. "And I love you. That's what makes it so perfect."

Whit persisted. "But my life isn't my own to give. That's what

I've been trying to explain. I have an obligation to all my friends who died."

Prue sat up and looked at him in the moonlight. "Are you talking about revenge? Whit, what you've told me was horrible. But it happened. Nothing will undo it."

Again Whit tried to make her understand. "I couldn't help them then. But I can do something now. What happened to them shouldn't go unpunished."

"You can't hunt up all those men who did those things."

"I don't intend to. I just want to kill Mexicans."

"Excuse me, but I don't see where shooting Pedro will punish Pablo."

He could not argue against her logic. But logic had nothing to do with it. "It's something I must do," he persisted.

"If you must, then go do it," Prue said. "I'll wait for you."

"But I can't pledge my heart to you, Prue. Don't you see? My life is already taken."

She began to dress. "Well, that was one short, sweet romance."

Stung, Whit pulled her back into his arms. "Prue, I'll manage, somehow, for us to be together. I just want you to know how it is with me."

He kissed her. She responded. But after a time she pushed him away. "Whit, I think maybe I do understand. Lord knows I've been mad enough at times to want to go off and kick the tar out of somebody. Anybody. Is that the way it is?"

"Something like that," Whit said. "But a million times worse."

"We'll work it out," Prue said. She stood and arranged her clothing. "You hungry? A good roll in the grass always leaves me famished."

Whit laughed. Memories of Prue's humor also had sustained him in many trying circumstances.

"We've got to eat this stuff. If we go back home with a full basket, they'll think we've been doing something else."

They sat in the moonlight and ate the picnic lunch. When they had finished, Prue refolded the tablecloth and picked up the basket.

As they left the glade, she paused for a lingering look back. "I don't know whether you know it or not, Whit Logan. But you've made this one of the most important days of my life."

"Glad to be of service," he said.

Prue laughed, then reached for his hand. "Whit, this is important. I don't want you to feel any sense of obligation over what happened today. I've been waiting for you three and a half years. I suppose it was plain I wasn't exactly reluctant. But I want you to want me for me, not for what happened."

Whit hugged her. "Prue, I love you. I want you for you."

Later, as they walked back toward home, Whit felt in his heart that he was being sincere, uncompromising.

But he was beginning to wonder how he would manage to do what he felt obligated to do, as well as what he wanted to do.

P A R T   F O U R

Statehood, and War

Hays's Rangers have come, their appearance never to be forgotten.
. . . The Mexicans are terribly afraid of them.

Brig. Gen. E. A. Hitchcock
Diary entry, Dec. 6, 1847

--- 18 ---

Albert Martin and Jim Bowie watched in awe as U.S. army soldiers carried skeletons out of the Alamo and placed them on the ground. Soldiers were everywhere, repairing the old Alamo to use as a storehouse. In clearing out the rubble they had found the skeletons. "Who you suppose they are?" Albert asked.

"How the hell would I know?" Jim Bowie said. "Probably some damn Meskins."

Ever since Albert could remember, the Alamo had lain in ruins. He knew vaguely that battles had been fought there a long time ago, back before he, or even Jim, was born. The skeletons had been found beneath a ramp where he and Jim had played many times.

Soldiers and a sprinkling of officers gathered around the bones. Among them Albert recognized Colonel Hays, who was Uncle Whit's commanding officer. Albert and Jim crowded close. Five skeletons were lined up in a row. Two were missing jawbones.

"Colonel Hays, you have any idea as to their identities?" asked one of the army officers.

Hays knelt for a closer look. "Offhand, I'd say they're probably Mexicans killed in the Siege of Béxar in thirty-five. That was before my time here. But it's my understanding that General Cós knocked down a wall and built that ramp to get his cannons up on the roof. Travis later reinforced it, before the Siege of the Alamo. I'd say they were some of Cós's men."

"What happened to the bodies of those in the Alamo?"

Hays removed his hat and wiped his forehead. "According to all accounts, they were stacked and burned. Then the ashes were taken out and buried. No one knows exactly where."

"Well, whoever these fellows were, we'll give them a decent

burial," the officer said. "Sergeant, put them in plain pine boxes for the present, until we decide what to do with them."

Across the river the bells of San Fernando sounded. Albert and Jim glanced at each other, then hurried toward the Commerce Street bridge. They were expected home for supper.

"Let's go tell Uncle Whit," Jim Bowie said.

Albert glanced uneasily at the setting sun. "If we don't get home pretty quick, Aunt Hattie's gonna tan our hides."

"Scairty-cat. It'll only take a minute."

They ran across the bridge, and all the way home. As they had expected, Whit was down at the stables, working with Newt to get his horses ready to go off to war with Hays and the Rangers. Albert's mother and Aunt Prue had been crying all week.

He was standing with hands in hip pockets, his lanky frame bowed forward, watching Newt size a shoe to the big red roan. As Albert and Jim came running up, he punched Jim on the shoulder and mussed Albert's hair. "What you two been up to?" he asked. "Somebody chasing you?"

Jim, the better talker, told the story. Whit listened, unlike most adults, who tended to give Albert and Jim only half an ear. All of Albert and Jim's friends agreed that their uncle Whit was the toughest man in San Antonio. He had fought in all the renegade scrapes along the border. "Colonel Hays is probably right," he said after Jim had concluded. "I'd imagine they're Mexicans killed in the Siege of Thirty-five."

"Were you in that one, Uncle Whit?" Jim asked. He and Albert could never get all the battles straight.

"No, but your daddy was. He helped chase ol' General Cós out of Béxar and back to Mexico. I was just a boy then, not much older'n you two. I didn't come out here till four years later."

He stopped and asked Newt if the shoe should not be placed higher on the hoof. They debated how the hoof should be filed.

Albert wished they could get Uncle Whit to talking. He loved the stories about Indians, like the one of how his mother and his aunt Prue fought the Comanche in the front yard with their bare hands until his father came out the front door and shot him. Or how Aunt Hattie held a big rock over her head to keep an Indian away from Jim's bassinet—a rock so big she afterward needed help to set it down.

Albert wished with all his heart that he had lived in such exciting times.

Uncle Whit glanced at them. "You two better get on in to supper. Tell them I'll be there in a minute."

Albert and Jim ran into the house. Aunt Hattie made them wash their hands and change their shirts. By the time they got to the table their father was home, and Aunt Prue had come out of her room. Uncle Whit entered the house just in time to hold Aunt Prue's chair. Sometimes Uncle Ramsey also ate supper with them, but not often. Jim's theory was that with their father and Uncle Ramsey both being lawyers, and often on opposite sides, they did not like each other. Albert was pleased to see that no plate was set for Uncle Ramsey today. When he was at the table no one talked much.

After saying grace, Albert's mother asked Whit when he was leaving.

Uncle Whit gave her his slow smile. "First thing Wednesday."

"Oh, Whit! So soon!"

He nodded. "Word came this afternoon. Wheels began to turn after we were taken into federal service. Now they want us somewhere down there quick. We don't know where yet."

Albert's father thumped the table. "For two cents I'd go with you."

"I've got two cents," Whit said.

Aunt Prue began to cry so abruptly that all turned toward her. Uncle Whit looked at her as if he did not know what to do.

Albert's father filled in the silence. "I never dreamed it'd be so soon. Washington must be pressing the war."

All but Jim Bowie had forgotten about eating. Prue was quietly weeping.

"Whit, you don't have to go," Albert's mother said, her voice breaking as if she also were about to cry. "We waited and prayed for you three long years. Surely you've done enough."

Uncle Whit answered Albert's mother, but he looked at Aunt Prue. "If I didn't go, I couldn't face myself in the mirror."

Albert's mother persisted. "Whit, we couldn't stand it if something like that happened to you again."

He hesitated. "It won't. I've got the whole U.S. army behind me. I intend to do my duty, and come back."

Aunt Prue quit making so much noise.

Albert's father carefully put his napkin on the table. "Whit, I intended to tell you this in private. But now there's little time, and perhaps this table is the most fitting place. I closed a deal today to supply beef to the army, range delivery at Corpus. This is only the beginning. The offer I made you before still stands. When you come back, we can work together, put that land into full production, on the halves."

Whit shook his head. "I couldn't do that. You have heirs coming along. I'm not about to do to them what was done to me."

"They're still very young. Besides there's enough here for all and I can't do it alone."

Whit looked at Albert and Jim. "Tad, you'll soon have plenty of help."

Albert's father seemed angry. "I'll say no more for now. But the offer's still on the table. It'll be here when you get back."

Whit hesitated. "All right. We'll talk about it then."

Suddenly Aunt Prue burst out crying again. She covered her face with her hands, rose, and fled toward her room.

A long silence followed. Albert looked from one adult to the other, hoping for some explanation.

Whit rose, excused himself, and left the table. He walked in the direction of Aunt Prue's room.

Albert's father also left the table, but without saying a word. He went toward his library, next to the long room.

Jim Bowie had finished eating. Albert had hardly started. But now he did not feel hungry.

Their mother seemed to become aware they were still at the table. "Can you boys go play in your room? Please keep quiet. We're all upset over your uncle Whit's leaving."

Albert followed Jim to their room. "What's going on?" he asked.

Jim began whittling on a leather scabbard he was making.

"Haven't you figured it out yet? Momma wants Uncle Whit to marry Aunt Prue."

Albert was confused. It was his understanding that people related to each other could not marry. "Can they do that?"

"I don't know," Jim admitted. "But I don't think Uncle Whit's going to marry her anyway."

From the back door Corrie glimpsed the red glow of Whit's cigar at the far edge of the patio. Sometimes he went there in the evenings to smoke, to be alone. On impulse she spread a rebozo over her shoulders and walked out into the crisp fall night. Crossing the patio, she allowed her heels to strike the stones so he would not be startled.

"I'm sorry to interrupt your solitude," she said. "But I thought this might be my only chance to see you alone before you go."

Whit's voice rumbled in the darkness. "No interruption, Corrie. Not at all."

"I suppose there's no hope of talking you out of going."

"No."

Corrie had not found a suitable way to phrase what she wanted to say. But she felt she must try. "Whit, I've been careful never to interfere in your relationship with Prue. But now I'm at a loss. I really don't understand your attitude. Maybe I'm mistaken in the way you feel about her."

Whit's cigar flared briefly in the darkness before he answered. "I love her. I love both of you, and Tad, with all my heart. The three of you are my whole life."

Corrie was more puzzled than ever. "Is it that you don't love her in that way?"

Whit chuckled. "I don't know what you mean by 'that way.' But if you mean what I think, yes, I love her in that way."

"Then why in God's name are you going off and leaving her as bereft as she is tonight? You know how she feels about you. She's hardly been coy about it."

"I'm doing her a favor. I'll not leave her a widow, out of my own selfishness."

"Better a widow than a broken heart grieving for what's never been."

"Corrie, if she doesn't take my name, there'd be healing with the passage of time. But as a widow she's marked forever."

"You talk as if it's a certainty. Do you have some sense of premonition? Is that it?"

Whit laughed. "No. Not exactly. But Hays will always make certain we're in the forefront of action. We've lost ten men in the last three months in skirmishes with renegades. What'll it be like when we go up against cannon? I can only guess."

Corrie shuddered in the darkness. "Lord knows I've tried, but I still fail to understand why you think you must go."

"Prue said she understands. At least a little."

Corrie was glad to learn that they had talked about it. Yet there seemed to be a failure of rapport somewhere. "I come closer to understanding Tad leaving me with two small children to go off and fight. His brother was in prison. They had driven us out of our home, left it in ruins. But you'll be fighting so far away. And nothing you hold dear is threatened."

Again the cigar flared briefly. "It's the same people who wrecked your home. The same government. The same Santa Anna who sent soldiers to shoot my friends in cold blood. To beat them to death as they lay helpless. To make Tad draw a bean in that lottery. If we don't act now, they'll be back. We've got to put a stop to them once and for all."

Corrie felt that was the responsibility of the U.S. army. Texas had given up independence on the promise of protection. She believed it was time for the United States to make good on that promise. Yet from all accounts the Mexican War was unpopular in the eastern states. Antiwar, anti-Texas sentiment was running high. As a new state Texas had sent Sam Houston and Tom Rusk to the U.S. Senate. In fiery speeches Houston kept reminding the United States of its bargain. He told them they were now getting a taste of what Texas had endured for ten long years in their behalf.

"I pray our troubles will indeed be ended," Corrie said. "I just wish you weren't going." She paused. "Whit, I've never told you, but I want to now. I've always loved you. And I care deeply about you and what happens to you."

Whit tossed the cigar onto the ground. "There's something I never told you, Corrie. That's how much I treasure those nights we used to sit up and talk. In prison I thought back on them a lot. I reconstructed whole conversations in my mind, the way you looked, the way you always put your tongue to your lips when you're thinking. Remembering those nights helped keep me sane."

"I often think fondly of those nights," Corrie said. She reached for his hand in the darkness. "Whit, please take care of yourself," she said. "Come back."

"I assure you I have every intention."

Corrie felt she knew him well enough to ask. "And what then, Whit? About Prue, I mean."

He did not hesitate. "Corrie, I've told her. If the war is truly over for me, and all the bad feelings are gone, I hope to marry her, if she's still single and willing."

"I'd love to see that happen, Whit. I truly would. That'd make all of us very happy."

"**P**rue, we're all probably worrying needlessly," Corrie said. "I wish you'd get up, get dressed, and come on to supper. You haven't eaten a decent meal in days."

Prue did not intend to endure another lecture. Maybe time had arrived for the truth. Certainly it would not stay hidden much longer. She rolled over in bed and looked up at Corrie. "I've reason to worry. I'm carrying Whit's baby."

After a moment of stunned silence Corrie sank to the edge of the bed. "Prue! How could you!"

Even under the circumstances the remark somehow struck Prue as funny. She laughed. "With Whit around, the question was not how *could* I, but how could I *not*."

"How far along are you?"

"Three months, I think. On the way to four."

Whit now had been gone more than two. In that time General Taylor had defeated the Mexicans at Buena Vista, and General Scott had taken Vera Cruz and was moving on Mexico City. Thus far no one knew where Whit was serving.

After a brief letter from Monterrey, they had heard nothing.

"Have you written Whit?"

"More than six weeks ago," Prue told her. "Twice. Since then there's been nothing but silence."

Corrie put a hand on her arm. "That doesn't necessarily mean anything. Tad believes he may be fighting in some remote area, and is unable to write. Prue, I have every confidence he'll be pleased, and come home as soon as possible. I know he'll do the right thing."

Prue had been thinking that almost two months. "And if he doesn't?" she asked.

Corrie hesitated. "Let's face that possibility only if we must. I do know there are ways. I've heard the Negro women chew cotton root."

Again Prue burst out laughing. Sometimes Corrie could be so naive. "Corrie, that's what they do to keep from landing in this fix. Once they do, they take turpentine and calomel. No thank you. Turpentine! I'd rather have the baby."

Corrie sat for a time in silence, absorbing the situation. "I thought you had more sense."

"Unfortunately, sense has nothing to do with it."

"I feel I've failed you. I promised Mother I'd look after you. I thought you knew how important it is to wait."

Prue could not contain her irritation. "Please don't give me any holier-than-thou claptrap. As far as I'm concerned, Whit and I are all but married. This war just got in the way."

"Still, it was a stupid thing to do. As far as I know nothing like this has ever happened in our family. At least not for generations."

Prue did not answer. No doubt she would be hearing more on the subject.

"I'll have to tell Tad," Corrie said.

"Please! Not yet," Prue said. "He'd go through Washington, have Whit ordered home, make a federal case out of it! It'd make Whit mad, and rightfully so. If he doesn't want to come home and be a father, I'm not going to force him."

"I'm certain Whit isn't at fault. I know him!"

"That's what I keep telling myself," Prue said. "But the weeks are passing. Susan Hays received two letters last week from the colonel. Others have heard."

Corrie lowered her face into her hands. "This will take a while to get used to."

"I've been working on it two months," Prue said. "I haven't become the slightest bit accustomed to it."

After a long silence Corrie rose from the bed. "Well, under the circumstances you must eat. I'll have Hattie bring a tray." She paused at the door. "Try not to worry. Whatever happens, Tad and I will stand by you."

After Corrie left, Prue rolled facedown and tried to make her mind blank. But that trick never seemed to work.

She thought back over Whit's promises: Once the war was over they would be married. He would take Tad up on his offer. They would build a house to the west of Tad's compound and live apart, yet beside Corrie and Tad.

Hattie brought a tray. Prue ate a few bites, but left the rest. The food seemed tasteless.

The bugle at the Alamo encampment sounded taps. The brassy notes came across the river and through her open window lonely and sad. She was not at all happy with the changes statehood and war had brought to San Antonio. Hundreds of United States soldiers were in training in Béxar, and others were passing through on their way to the war. The town was mushrooming. In the once-empty spaces beyond the Alamo a village, Irish Flat, had sprung up to house the Irish teamsters in army service. Freight wagons and the shouts of the drivers ruled the streets, day and night. There was no escaping the war.

Prue's thoughts kept coming back to the same questions: Could she have been wrong about Whit? Was there a possibility that she did not know him at all?

The mountains were painfully familiar. Whit remembered coming this way to Puebla and Perote, handcuffed to another man. Now he rode with one hundred and thirty-five Rangers and a small force of

Dragoons, on their way to destroy nests of guerrillas holding the mountains east of Mexico City.

During the last six weeks Whit had killed one hundred and twenty-six Mexicans. He had found it satisfying work.

At times he daydreamed of going back to San Antonio, marrying Prue, and going into partnership with Tad. But that life now seemed so tame, so confining.

Colonel Hays believed that after the war the Oregon country and California would be free, and wide open for exploitation.

In a way, he had been putting off making a decision on what to do after the war. He loved Prue, but he could not imagine her in the life of exploration and adventure he now envisioned.

The night seemed interminable. But eventually daylight struck the distant peaks. After the exertion of the high passes, the horses were faltering as the column made a sharp descent. Ahead appeared the outskirts of the town of Sequalteplan.

Hays and General Lane rode forward to reconnoiter.

"Make ready," Captain Daggett said. "This may be lively."

Whit checked the loads on his rifle, his brace of Colts. He looked back. The Dragoons were coming down the steep slope, closing up the column.

Hays gave hand signals to advance. They moved forward, passing a row of houses. The streets were deserted. A Mexican army officer stepped out of a door, fumbling with his fly in preparation to urinate. He almost collided with Colonel Hays's horse. The man was seized, trussed, and gagged.

Hays moved on at a trot. They reached the center of town. A sentinel stood sleepily on a wall surrounding a row of barracks. On hearing the Texians, he yelled a warning and ran to close the gate into the compound. But Hays spurred his horse into the gate and knocked it wide open. Whit and the Rangers dashed through.

Guerrillas poured out of the barracks half dressed, shooting. Whit jumped from his horse and abandoned the reins. Firing steadily, he advanced with a small group of Rangers.

On Whit's right, Hays was taking a detachment to meet an attack coming from the town's main plaza. For a time the gunfire was as fierce as Whit had ever experienced.

But within minutes the firefight was over. Two Rangers were down. More than sixty Mexicans lay dead.

Acrid fumes filled the air. Inside the corral the Mexican horses were milling, screaming, some injured in the shooting.

Another intense firefight had erupted farther up the street.

Whit's guns were empty, his heart pounding. He was certain he had killed six. Kneeling beside an adobe wall, he reloaded.

"Men, this way!" Captain Daggett yelled.

Whit ran to Daggett, who was assembling his men. "The colonel sent word General Lane is in a fix," he said. "We're to go to his assistance."

They ran toward the fresh gunfire. Lane and his company of Dragoons were pinned down, heavily outnumbered by regular Mexican troops. Some of the Mexicans were shooting from a long barracks. Lane also was taking concentrated fire from a large detachment in the streets to his left. Caught in the crossfire, he could not move.

Whit gathered with the rest of Daggett's men behind an adobe wall. "We'll rush the barracks," Daggett said. "Logan, you and Hicklin get the door open. We'll give you cover."

Whit hunched by the wall and awaited the signal. The instant the company opened fire, he raced around the wall and ran toward the barracks door, firing with every step.

Several paces short of the door he felt a sledgehammer blow on his right side. At first he thought he had collided with Hicklin, or that Hicklin had accidentally struck him with his rifle barrel. But when Whit glanced in that direction, he was surprised to see that Hicklin was a good ten feet to his right.

Still on his feet, Whit reached the door and gave it a hard kick. The door did not yield. Bullets came through the thick wood. Whit and Hicklin took turns kicking until the door swung open. Captain Daggett and his men went past, shooting.

Strangely, Whit's knees would no longer support him. He sank to the porch and leaned against the front of the building. Sustained gunfire came from inside the barracks. Now freed from the crossfire, General Lane was advancing against the Mexicans in the street. Whit looked down. His lap was bathed in blood.

As yet, he felt no pain. Only a numbness. He put his revolvers on the porch and probed the wound. Entry was on the right side, just below the ribs. The exit wound was on the left.

Whit did not delude himself. He had seen enough wounded men to know he probably was bleeding to death, internally.

Captain Daggett came out of the barracks yelling. "There's some kind of passageway at the rear. Get four or five men around to the back. Where's Logan?"

"Here," Whit said.

Daggett knelt beside him. "How bad is it?"

"Not good," Whit said. "Not good at all."

"We've got to stop that bleeding."

"Then you better send for a horse blanket."

Daggett did not argue. "Rest easy. We'll get you taken care of in a minute."

But in the street the battle flared anew. From the porch, Whit had a ringside seat. Several companies of Mexican lancers had arrived, and were driving the Americans back.

Even in his helpless condition, Whit could see the humor of the situation. Hays and Lane had expected to destroy a hidden guerrilla stronghold. Instead, they had stumbled upon a large concentration of the Mexican army.

For a time he watched the battle. The Americans were pushed farther down the street. In a few minutes they were out of sight. The sounds of battle faded.

Whit drifted into a twilight sleep. As he had on so many other difficult occasions, he lay remembering more pleasant times: joshing with Prue, talking with Corrie, riding along beside Tad. He recalled the glorious mornings on the Santa Fé Expedition when he awakened wondering what discoveries the day would bring. He savored the memory of making love with Prue.

He felt unexpectedly content. He had known the love of a good and beautiful woman. Surely that was enough.

He sensed a deeper sleep approaching. Slowly he drifted toward it. He had closed out all accounts. He did not resist.

*   *   *

Tad waited patiently while the men tied their horses and prepared to work on foot. Inside the corral, Chancy Denton eased his horse through the longhorns, culling out those to be sent into the branding chute.

"Start 'em through, Chance," Tad called.

Sensing a way out of the pen, the first longhorn came down the chute. At the proper moment, Dorman Simpson closed a heavy gate that blocked the narrow passageway. Bud Childers closed another gate behind the longhorn, boxing him in. It was a dangerous moment. Always the wild cattle fought, battering the wood, leaping, trying to clear the six-foot fence. Chancy Denton stepped forward with a hot iron and stuck it to the longhorn's left hip. The gate was opened, and the animal was allowed to run on into the holding pasture.

The chute was not an ideal arrangement. The brands went on haphazardly. Sometimes they burned too deep, or else hardly marked the hair. But the results would serve for road brands.

Tad put a knot in his quirt for every ten longhorns processed. He needed five hundred more to close his most recent army contract.

These cattle were scrub longhorns. When Whit came back, Tad planned to begin ranching in earnest. Calves would be castrated, marked, and branded. He would experiment with stockier breeds from the east, to see if more beef could be added to the longhorn's bony frame.

It had long been axiomatic that a cow could be raised cheaper than a chicken in Texas. But as yet no one had found a consistent market. Tad intended to find a solution to that problem. Perhaps the answer lay in cattle boats, operating out of Texas harbors. Maybe the longhorns could be driven up through Missouri, right into the populated east. Or butchering and preservation might be perfected to the point that smoked or salted meat could be shipped to the growing market in the east.

Tad was confident a way would be found.

He shifted his weight in the saddle, easing his cramped legs. Counting the cattle without effort, he allowed his thoughts to wander back to the evening before, when he had located the site for his future house. It stood on a rise a half mile from the river, commanding a view in every direction. Along a small creek grew pecan and cottonwood trees. Riding back and forth over the site, Tad envisioned his future house. It would be of three stories, with galleries encircling the lower two floors. The front, facing the rising sun, would be graced with fluted pillars like those of the grand plantation houses in Georgia and the Carolinas. Behind the house, in the trees, would lie the stables and horse barns. Farther back he would erect cabins or long houses for the ranch hands.

The brunt of Indian raids were now falling on the German communities to the west and north of San Antonio. Years had passed since hostiles had penetrated this far south. The ranch house would be just over forty miles from San Antonio, a comfortable day's drive on a good road. His main difficulty would be with Corrie, so preoccupied with her life in San Antonio. He doubted she willingly would leave her circle of friends. But the time was soon coming when he should be training his sons for their future. He had great hopes for Jim Bowie, who was aggressive, ever aware of his surroundings, unfazed by obstacles. In contrast, Albert Martin showed a tendency toward being too dreamy headed.

Tad also would like to get Corrie away from Ramsey. He was reaching the point where he could hardly endure the man's presence. A ranch house might be the most tactful solution.

Without taking his eyes from the branding chute, Tad thumbed the rawhide cord, confirming his count, then tied a double knot, signifying another hundred. He and his men worked steadily. Within two hours of sundown, the last of the five hundred were branded.

"It's getting late," he said to Chancy. "But we'd best move them off their bed ground, keep them from mixing with the rest. Tell the men."

With Chancy Denton and six men Tad started the cattle toward Corpus Christi. Many of the longhorns were smarting from the fresh brands. They moved along at a good pace.

At twilight Tad called a halt, established a dry camp, and set up watches through the night to hold the cattle. He was spreading his bedroll by the fire when Ben caught up with them.

"Mastah Tad, Miss Corrie want you home right away," Ben said.

Tad was swept by a heavy premonition. "Ben, what is it?"

Ben shook his head. "Please, Mastah Tad. I don't want to be the one to tell you."

Tad's first fear was of an accident to one of the boys. He reached out and seized Ben's arm. "You know you don't have to fear me. What is it?"

"It's Mastah Whit," Ben said, choking on the words. "They say he dead."

--- 19 ---

Corrie moved silently through the deathly still house by the first light of early morning. Almost a full month had passed since the report of Whit's death and nothing had changed. Prue remained in her room prostrate with grief. Repeatedly she had said she no longer wanted to live. Corrie had hidden the laudanum, calomel, arsenic, all spare pistols and rifles. She had thought of taking Consuelo into her confidence and hiding the knives in the kitchen.

Now Prue might have her way in the face of all precautions. She had stopped eating.

Corrie found Hattie in the sewing room, mending the boys' shirts. She spoke from the doorway. "Hattie, when Consuelo brings in Miss Prue's tray this morning, I'll take it to her."

Hattie's eyes were red from crying. "Miss Corrie, I've tried all I can with her."

"I know, Hattie."

"She can't go on this way!"

"I'll try talking to her."

Corrie returned to her room. As usual, Tad had left the house well before daylight. Officially Whit was listed as missing, for his body had not been recovered. But early hopes had been dashed. Whit's captain wrote Tad that Whit was all but gone when the Rangers were pushed back. He said from the nature of the wounds, and the amount of blood lost, he had no doubt.

Corrie had not told Tad about Prue and the baby, for he could not yet talk about Whit.

But the days were passing. A decision had to be made soon.

Corrie lay across the bed and dozed until there came a soft rap at the door. Hattie pushed it open. "Miss Corrie? Here's Miss Prue's breakfast."

Corrie rose and carried the tray to Prue's room.

To all appearances, Prue had not moved in days. She had lost more weight, and her skin was sickeningly sallow. Corrie placed the tray on the bedside table and opened the curtains, flooding the room with sunlight. "Enough of this, Prue," she said firmly. "You must eat."

Prue's reply was muffled by the pillow, but Corrie could make out the words. "I'm not hungry."

"Then eat for the baby. He deserves better from you."

"Like what? A life of shame?"

Corrie sank into a chair. "Listen, Prue. I have a plan. What if I claim the baby as mine? We could both stay in the house through the spring and summer, and put it out that you're ill, mourning for Whit. I could have a difficult confinement."

Prue laughed in her humorless way. "You think the whole town wouldn't guess? You think servants wouldn't talk? We'd be the laughingstock."

"No one would know for sure. It'd only be idle gossip. Pure speculation. In time, people would forget."

Prue rolled over on her back and looked up at the ceiling. She raised an arm to shield her eyes. "Even if it'd work, I couldn't do that to you, Corrie. Leave you with someone else's child to raise."

"It wouldn't be 'someone else's' child," Corrie said. "It'd be yours, and Whit's. That'd make all the difference in the world. Don't you know that?"

Prue frowned, thinking. "Does Tad know?"

"Not yet. I'll have to tell him soon."

"I doubt he will agree to do that. He's too proud. He couldn't abide scandal in his own house."

Corrie suspected Prue might be right. She offered her only hope. "But since it's Whit's baby, it'll be different. He'd endure a great deal before he'd turn his back on family."

"I've been thinking about it for days," Prue said. "I see two courses open to me. One, I can go away somewhere, have the baby, and accept the shame. Or I can kill myself *and* the baby."

"Oh, my God, Prue! No!"

"On the whole, the last course makes the most sense," Prue said dispassionately. "If done decently soon, no one ever need know I died in disgrace. I died of love. Quite romantic."

Corrie forced herself to speak calmly. "Prue, listen to me. There's a way out of this. We only must find it. Neither of us is thinking properly at the moment. But we'll weather this. Promise me you won't do anything rash."

Prue did not answer.

"Promise!"

Prue looked at the ceiling and sighed. "Corrie, I don't know from one minute to the next what I'll do. At times I think I'll have Whit's baby and spit in the eye of anyone who says a word. At other times all I want to do is crawl into a hole and never come out."

"Promise!"

Prue looked up at her. "I'll try. That's all I can do."

Corrie left Prue's room in a quiet panic. She badly needed help, and there was no one. She went back to the sewing room and tried to speak in an offhand way. "Hattie, I must go out awhile. I'm worried about Miss Prue. She's not herself. She's so weak, I'm afraid that if she gets up she may hurt herself accidentally. So I want you to watch her closely. I don't expect you to do anything else today but that. You understand?"

Hattie nodded. "She eat?"

Corrie had forgotten the food. "I left the tray. She may."

She returned to her room and dressed. She left the house quietly by the front door, walked to the Main Plaza, and climbed the stairs to Ramsey's law offices.

As she entered, Ramsey's secretary looked up, then rose from his desk. The old gentleman appeared quite discomfited to be receiving an unescorted female in the all-male preserve.

Corrie attempted to put him at ease. "Mr. Whittier, I wonder if I may see Mr. Cothburn on a rather urgent matter. He handled my inheritance, you know."

Whittier recognized his cue. "Yes, I remember, Mrs. Logan. If you'll please be seated, I'll inform him you're here."

He scurried down the hall. Corrie remained standing. As she

had anticipated, Ramsey came to her immediately. "Corrie! What a pleasant surprise. What can I do for you?"

Corrie allowed her eyes to flick significantly in Whittier's direction. "A matter has come up. We need to talk."

"Of course. Come right on back."

She followed him down the hall and into his private office. She had never seen Ramsey in his working environment. One wall contained law books, perhaps two hundred volumes. The furniture was walnut, cushioned in black leather.

Ramsey closed the door and held a chair for her. Then, instead of going behind his desk, he sat in a chair facing her. "Well, now. What's this all about?"

Corrie found words difficult. "It's about Prue. I'm frantic about her. I don't know what to do."

Ramsey waited.

Corrie saw she could not avoid plain English. "She's carrying Whit's baby. She's threatening suicide."

Ramsey's eyes narrowed in an expression that could have meant anything. He rubbed his mustache thoughtfully. "Oh, my," he said. "That *is* a pickle." He paused. "Have you told Tad?"

"Not yet. He's in such a melancholy state over Whit. I haven't wanted to burden him further. As Prue pointed out, he's such a proud man. Scandal would trouble him greatly."

Slowly, Ramsey nodded agreement.

"I've thought of a possible solution," Corrie continued. "But it involves Tad. I don't know if it would work."

She described her idea for an elaborate charade, leading to her claiming Prue's baby as her own, and of Prue's reaction.

Ramsey shook his head. "Prue's right. Secrets like that don't keep." He paused, thinking. "Her plan for a trip out of town might serve better. I could arrange it, distancing you and Tad from it. I know of an ideal place in Houston. There she would have privacy, and servants to tend her."

Corrie felt a wave of relief. "Ramsey, could you do that?"

Tad nodded. "Perhaps later we could concoct a suitable story to explain the baby—a cousin in New Orleans who died of yellow fever. It happens."

"I think Tad might agree to that."

Ramsey hesitated. "You might wait a few days before telling him. You understand, I'm talking to you as a friend, and not as your lawyer. Given time, I might think of a better solution. May I talk with Prue?"

"Ramsey, she has always thought most highly of you. But I'm not sure she would receive anyone right now."

"Then don't tell her I'm coming. Let it be a surprise. I'm sure that if I can only talk to her a few minutes, alone, I can convince her this would be best."

Corrie rose from the chair and put out her hand. "Thank you, Ramsey. I don't know what I'd do without you."

He kissed her cheek and opened the door. "I'll be over in the morning. Just don't tell her I'm coming, and give me a few minutes alone with her."

Prue pulled the blanket over her head, furious that Corrie would dare bring Ramsey right into her bedroom unannounced. She had not washed her face or combed her hair since yesterday, or maybe the day before that. "Ramsey, I mean it!" she shouted from beneath the covers. "Please leave! I'm not receiving!"

"I'll just be a minute," Ramsey said. "We must talk."

Prue heard the door close, Ramsey's footsteps, and the creak of a chair. The air grew stifling under the blanket. Prue thought Corrie had left the room, but she was not sure.

"Prue, Corrie told me your condition. It isn't the end of the world."

Prue could not contain her rage. "She had no right to tell you!" she shouted. "Please leave me alone!"

"Prue, I know that with Whit gone, the future looks bleak to you right now," Ramsey went on. "But it isn't. You're a wonderful person. You have your whole life ahead of you."

Prue was smothering. She shifted position to make a tent for air. "I don't want to talk about it. Least of all now."

"I just want to leave you some ideas to think about. Corrie said you've thought of going away for a while. If so, I could drive you to

Houston. You could take Hattie, and stay with a friend of mine. She runs a rooming house. We could depend on her for discretion. I think it a very good plan."

Prue choked back a sharp retort. Soon she must do something. This sounded like a feasible possibility. "And the baby?"

"We'll have more time to decide about that. Perhaps you would want to arrange an adoption."

"No! Never!"

"Then we could make up a story to explain it."

"No one would be fooled for a minute."

"Perhaps not. But no one could prove anything."

Prue remained silent. The future still looked bleak enough.

"I have another alternative for you to consider," Ramsey went on. "It's much more to my choice. Will you marry me?"

Not long ago, Prue would have given half her life to hear those words. Now the circumstances cheapened them. "I won't accept charity," she said.

Ramsey spoke quietly, intently. "Prue, you know me better than that. You know I've always loved you. I think you suspected, correctly, that I was on the verge of proposing to you before Whit came back. Then you two became involved, and the opportunity was lost. If conditions were otherwise, I'd wait a decent interval to propose now. But I think we should bow to facts."

Prue badly wanted to see Ramsey's face. But she did not want him to see hers. "I'm damaged goods," she said.

A tone of anger crept into his voice. "Don't you ever say that! Believe me, I know how it was between you and Whit. No one can blame you."

"Still, an illegitimate baby is hardly a good foundation for a marriage."

Prue heard his weight shift in the chair. "Prue, listen to me. I'm going to say this once, and I never want it brought up again. I'll accept the baby as my own. Believe me, I wouldn't have proposed if I entertained the slightest reservation in this regard."

Prue enlarged her airhole. "Ramsey, I can't talk now."

"I understand. I apologize for forcing my way in like this. But I knew you wouldn't see me otherwise, and I didn't want to propose through Corrie."

"She doesn't know?"

"Of course not. It was for your ears alone. I told Corrie I'd tell you of the Houston plan. The rest is between us. I do hope you'll consider all I've said. Prue, I love you. I know I'll make you a good husband."

Prue felt trapped, pressured. "Ramsey, I'm so confused. Please give me time to think."

His chair creaked as he rose. "I apologize. I promised Corrie I'd only be a minute. I'll visit in a day or two. I hope we can discuss it then."

Prue heard him move across the room. The door opened and closed. A moment later she heard him talking with Corrie and Hattie in the long room. Then there was silence.

The absurdity of the situation struck her, and she began to giggle. Had any maiden ever known such an hilarious setting for a proposal of marriage? She envisioned Ramsey, so neat and proper, sitting upright in his chair, making his ardent appeal to a pregnant lump under a brightly colored Mexican blanket. It was so unlike Ramsey, so far removed from his innate dignity. Certainly no one would ever catch Ramsey Cothburn disheveled. She would lay bets he awoke each morning with mustache neatly trimmed, every hair in place, and not a wrinkle in his nightshirt. For a time, reliving the scene, she was convulsed.

She surrendered to the emotional release. It was her first good laugh since hearing about Whit.

In the wake of laughter came sober reflection. Long confinement in a Houston boarding house could only be horrible. Under no circumstances would she give up the baby. It was hers, and Whit's. She would never consider giving a horse or dog to a stranger, and certainly not her own flesh and blood. Yet, if she kept it, the baby would require *some* explanation, however flimsy.

Even if Ramsey Cothburn had been an unwashed, illiterate ruffian, his proposal merited consideration, given her circumstances. And he was no ruffian. Prue knew she could search half the world without finding a better man. He was honest. If he said he was prepared to rear Whit's child as his own, that was the last word on it. Marrying Ramsey would be no sacrifice. She loved him, and had always loved him. Not in the way she loved Whit. Surely such passions came but once in a lifetime. Still, Ramsey was a prize beyond measure. When her girlhood friends learned she had married Ramsey Cothburn, she was sure they would turn lovely shades of green.

She crawled out from beneath the blanket, went to a mirror, and assessed the extent of repair needed.

If Ramsey Cothburn was willing to settle for second best, perhaps she should harbor no qualms about doing the same.

On the morning after Ramsey's visit Corrie came to a stunning revelation that changed everything. Two previous pregnancies had sharpened her perception.

She waited until that evening after Tad came to bed. "I've just learned," she told him. "We're soon to have another child."

He smiled. It was the first time his dark mood had lifted since the news about Whit. He hugged and kissed her, and Corrie could see that he was immensely pleased.

She was emboldened. "You also might as well know. Prue's carrying Whit's baby."

Tad sat up in bed. "How far along is she?"

"Over four months."

He seemed stunned. "Why didn't you tell me?"

"She kept it to herself for a long time. Then you were grieving so. I didn't have the heart. I kept thinking there must be a way out for her."

"What do you mean, 'a way out'? Like what?"

Corrie told him of her plan to take Prue's baby and raise it as her own. She told of going to Ramsey, and his solution.

Tad's eyes flashed. "Why did you go to Ramsey? That baby is a Logan. Surely we can look after our own."

"I went to him as a friend," Corrie explained. "I was too upset to think straight. You were so miserable, I didn't want to burden you further. I wanted some level-headed advice, I thought Ramsey could help."

"That's no solution, hiding Prue away, making up some cock-and-bull tale. She'd still reappear with the baby. Everyone would put two and two together."

"What would you do?"

Tad seldom smoked in bed, but now he lit a Mexican cigar. "Why don't we go back to your original plan? You and Prue aren't far apart. When your time comes, we could let it out you've had twins."

Corrie could see how that might work. Her close friends could witness her pregnancy. Prue could remain indisposed with grief. When the babies came—double cousins—their close resemblance no doubt would be convincing even to skeptics.

"Prue might agree to it," she said.

She lay awake most of the night, thinking the plan through. She foresaw no difficulties. The household would be sworn to secrecy. They could use a midwife from the barrio. Consuelo would know someone to trust.

The next morning she hurried to Prue's room. But halfway through her explanation Prue interrupted. "Thank you, but all that won't be necessary. I've decided to marry Ramsey."

For an instant Corrie thought Prue's macabre humor was at work. But in the next breath she saw that Prue was deadly serious.

She felt faint. "You what?"

"Ramsey has offered to make a respectable woman of me. I believe I'll allow him to do just that. Frankly, Ramsey Cothburn beats the scarlet letter. Or suicide. Long before the baby is born, I'll be Mrs. Cothburn."

Corrie suddenly felt as if the world did not contain enough air. She sat down in the chair by the window and fought for breath. "He deceived me!"

"It would seem so. But his impetuosity suits me fine. I'm really not in the mood for a long courtship. I'd prefer a wedding sooner, rather than later. My wedding dress will have to be rather full fashioned as it is."

Corrie was so confused that she said no more, fearing she might say words she later would regret.

But during the next few hours an ugly suspicion began to fester:

she wondered if Ramsey's offer stemmed not from his attraction to Prue, but from his desire for a permanent tie to Corrie McNair Logan.

While the wedding would solve the immediate crisis, she could see that the foundation possibly was being laid for worse difficulties in the future.

Yet, she could say nothing. To make such accusations smacked of unbridled conceit. But Tad, in his offhand way, let her know he had reached the same conclusion.

"Ramsey has been seeking a chair at the Logan family table the last five years," he said. "He now seems to have found one."

Albert Martin lingered in the shadows and listened as his father told the story for the third time during the evening. Most of the wedding guests were dancing out on the patio, but here in the long room the men had gathered to drink, talk politics, and tell stories.

"So when the yearling ran into a little motte of mesquite, Jim Bowie sailed in after him at a dead run. A limb raked him off his horse, right into a patch of prickly pear. Took us two hours to get all the stickers out of his backside."

The men had been drinking all evening. They laughed louder than usual. Albert personally thought the prickly pear story stupid. He had been riding right behind Jim and had the good sense to stop his horse. He had circled the mesquite and turned the yearling calf on the other side, while Jim Bowie had injured both himself and his horse with his dumb derring-do.

Jim Bowie stood ramrod straight beside his father, basking in the attention, the cuts on his face abundant proof of his mindless bravery. Albert could not understand why everything Jim Bowie did won praise from their father, while whatever he himself did was ignored. No mention had been made that he was the one who had outsmarted the yearling, and returned it to the herd.

In the wake of the laughter, Albert's father spoke to Hays. "I just can't believe you're leaving the Rangers."

The room fell silent. "It's time for me to move on," Hays said quietly. "Our work is done. With the U.S. army building forts all across Texas, the future appears tame. California sounds lively. I believe I'll push on west."

"California and the Oregon country should have been made a part of the Republic," Albert's father said. "That was our golden opportunity. We failed. Now the United States will reap the profits from blood we spilled."

"Your thinking's dated, Thaddeus," Sam Maverick said. "We must remember that *we* are the United States now. *We* will profit from the new territories."

"It was probably inevitable we'd wind up one nation," Colonel Hays said. "I'm told that in early spring a thousand people a day leave St. Louis for Oregon. It'll be the same with California. And statehood may double the Texas population."

Albert listened with dismay. By the time he was grown, all the country would be filled up.

Talk turned to how the new territories would affect politics in Washington. Jim Bowie still stood by his father's side, as if he understood it all. Albert grew bored. No one seemed inclined to tell more stories of Indian fights.

He left the long room and went back to the patio. The fiddlers were stomping as they ground out a tune. Uncle Ramsey and Aunt Prue were leading a cotillion, and there was much laughter. Aunt Prue was still wearing the flowing, lace-covered dress in which she had been married beneath a bower on the patio in late afternoon.

Albert was still confused and disturbed by the wedding. Aunt Prue had been sick in her room for weeks, weeping over the death of Uncle Whit. Now Uncle Whit seemed forgotten. Aunt Prue had married Uncle Ramsey, who had not been Albert's real uncle before, but was after today. Now Aunt Prue would be going to live with Uncle Ramsey in his house over in the next block.

How could Uncle Whit be forgotten so quickly? Even Albert's father, who had been so sad through the last few weeks, no longer seemed to be thinking of Whit. Throughout the day and evening he had been in high spirits, teasing and joking with Albert's mother. But she seemed sad, although she smiled a lot and tried to act cheerful. And so did Aunt Prue.

After a while he grew tired of watching the dancers and went to his room.

He was looking through his kaleidoscope in the lamplight when his mother knocked. "Are you sick?" she asked.

Albert shook his head.

"Then why'd you leave the party? Get bored with all the adults acting silly?"

He did not know how to explain. But she would understand if anyone could.

"Just days ago Aunt Prue was still crying over Uncle Whit. We all were. Now, everyone has forgotten him."

In the glow of the lamp, tears glistened in his mother's eyes. "Albert, it isn't that way at all! No one has forgotten your uncle Whit. Not for a minute. But he's dead, and life must go on. Your aunt Prue grieved for a while, but she had to pick up the pieces, make a future for herself."

"But she still looks sad," Albert insisted.

For a moment his mother did not seem to know what to say. She wiped away tears. "Albert, you are a very perceptive little boy. I hope you never lose the ability to understand people's feelings. But this is more complicated than you realize. A woman's wedding day is a joyous occasion, one of the most important days in her life. But for the same reason, you're right, it's a little sad. Can you understand that?"

In a way, he could. He nodded.

"That's why people cry at weddings. When you're older, you'll understand better." She kissed him on the forehead and walked to the door. "I should be getting back to our guests. I just came to see if you were sick. I was worried about you."

Albert wished she would stay. He wanted to ask her why his father always favored Jim Bowie. But there was never a right time to ask the really big questions.

--- 20 ---

At first Tad thought it a cruel fluke of the mail. He opened the envelope with trembling hands.

Dear Tad,

I understand my friends left me for dead. I sincerely hope this false report was not told to you at home. As you can see, I lived, though it was touch and go for a while. I owe my life to the village women who tended me. I was held by the guerrillas, and got to know them well. Last week I escaped and made my way into Mexico City. I have quite a tale to tell, and I hope to tell it to you soon. The doctor here at the station wants to probe for a bullet, and I may oblige him. That will keep me here awhile.

Tad, I've had plenty of time to think of that future you talked about. If your offer still stands, I'll take you up on it. My roaming is done. I've seen the Grim Reaper face to face. He convinced me you were right.

So I'm coming home to that, and to Prue. I've written her a letter, saying so. I'm sending both with a man bound for Texas. You should receive both about the same time. Tad, if Prue has changed her mind, and not waited, please hold her letter.

I will write again as soon as I have a permanent location.

Your loving brother
Whit

Tad shuffled through the rest of the mail. He found a fat envelope addressed in Whit's handwriting to Miss Pruella McNair.

Seldom did Tad feel the need of a drink. But he went to a bookcase and poured himself a glass of brandy. He then sat down at his desk and tried to determine what to do.

Prue and Ramsey had now been married seven weeks. She was in her fifth or sixth month of pregnancy. Tad thought through the courses of action he might take, the results of each.

In the end he felt he could not withhold the letter from Prue. The fact that she was carrying Whit's baby changed everything. Only Prue could decide what she wished to do.

He blew out the lamp and rode on home. The hour was late. Corrie was in bed, reading a book. Tad took off his coat and sat down facing her. "I've great news, Corrie. Whit's alive."

She dropped the book in her lap and stared at him. "How do you know?"

He handed her the letter. She read it open mouthed. Abruptly she put both hands over her face and moved her head from side to side as if to clear it. She looked at him, her eyes glistening. "Oh, Tad! This is absolutely marvelous! I'm so happy. For Whit. For you."

"Did you read the last part? I'm at a loss on what to do."

She again picked up the letter and finished it. He handed her the letter addressed to Prue. Corrie looked at it a long moment. "We'll have to give her the letter. There's no way around that."

"That's my thinking," Tad agreed. "But we're faced with an impossible situation."

"The fact that Whit's alive is what's important," Corrie said. "We're adults. All of this can be worked out some way."

"But will it be the right way?" Tad asked. "That's my concern. If Whit hears she's married, he'll back off. He's too decent a man to interfere in a marriage. Before he learns, we must undo what's been done."

"How?"

"If Prue wishes, I'll file an action in her behalf for an annulment. It'd be as if the marriage never existed."

Corrie sat still, thinking. "That might be what she'll want to do."

"There's a danger. If Ramsey contests the action, we'd have to show cause. It'd come out she's carrying Whit's child."

Corrie moved to the edge of the bed. "I'll go over, tell her, and give her the letter."

Tad put a hand on her shoulder. "Corrie, it's late."

"We can't keep this marvelous news from her overnight! That'd be cruel!"

"We don't want to tell her in front of Ramsey. Wait until tomorrow. You can go over, give her the letter, and explain our thinking that if Whit hears about her marriage, he'll light a shuck for California. He may be a terror on the battlefield, but he'd go to great lengths to keep from bringing pain to those he loves. She knows him. She'll understand."

"Maybe you should talk to her too," Corrie said. "I don't know enough about the legal aspects to explain it."

Tad hesitated. He did not want to put himself in the position of entering another man's house with the plain intention of interfering in his marriage. "It'd be best if you talk to her first. Then, if she wants, I'll serve as her attorney."

"What about a divorce? Wouldn't that be better?"

"It'd take longer. Cause would have to be shown. This way, with Ramsey's cooperation, it could be easily done."

"Ramsey moved heaven and earth to bring this marriage about," Corrie said. "I don't know that he'll cooperate."

"He must," Tad said. "He's the key to this situation."

Prue was resting on a couch in a back bedroom. Corrie sat beside her and took her by the hand. "Prue, I want you to get ahold of yourself. I have shockingly good news. Whit's alive."

Prue's mouth flew open. Her hand closed on Corrie in an iron grip. She tried to rise. "Alive? Where?"

"We don't know the details. He was badly wounded, and held for a while by guerrillas. Now he's in Mexico City."

Prue was so dazed that Corrie doubted her words were registering. She handed Prue the sealed letter.

Prue looked at it as if in a trance. "Whit? Alive?" She put a hand to her abdomen, over Whit's baby, and looked up at Corrie. "Oh, my God! What have I done?"

"Prue, try not to get upset," Corrie said. "Read Whit's letter, and then we can talk. Want me to leave you alone a few minutes?"

Prue shook her head negatively. She opened the envelope, took out the pages, and began reading. Tears came, but she read on. When she finished the first page, she handed it to Corrie.

The first paragraphs were almost identical to those in the letter to Tad. But then came an eloquent appeal. Whit said that with sufficient time to think, he now understood he had done her an injustice, that they should have married before he left home. He said he wanted to make amends as soon as possible.

Prue passed the pages to Corrie as she finished reading each. In the remainder of the letter Whit unburdened himself of his feelings. He told Prue of his love for her, that she was the world to him, and that if she would have him, he would devote the rest of his life to her.

Corrie treasured a similar letter she had received from Tad after the drawing of the beans.

Prue put both hands to her face. "Oh, God, what have I done?" she said again.

Corrie reached for Prue's wrists and pulled her hands down. "Prue, listen to me. You have two men. You only have to decide which one you want."

"But I'm married!"

"If you wish, that can be fixed. Tad can file for an annulment, wipe out your marriage."

Prue's eyes were wide. "I couldn't do that to Ramsey!"

"That's your decision to make. But, Prue, you must be certain. You don't want later bitterness over what you now see as an obligation. Ramsey is a generous man. I believe he'd release you, if that's what you want him to do."

"I couldn't ask him to do that! He saved my life!"

"I know. He's a wonderful man."

Prue was biting her fingers, as she sometimes did when upset. "But Whit will know this is his baby!"

"Most likely," Corrie agreed.

"Corrie, I can't lose Whit again. Not when I'm carrying his baby."

"Then you should ask Ramsey for the annulment. Tad says if you want to do it, you must act quickly. He thinks if Whit hears you're married, he'll bow out."

Prue nodded. "He'd do that."

"So you must think about it," Corrie said. "You've two good men. You can't go wrong with either. No one else can make your decision. It must come from your heart."

Prue was still in a daze, her face pale. "I don't know what I'll do."

"Wait until you're over the shock," Corrie said. "Then talk with Ramsey. He's level headed. I'm sure he'll help in whatever you decide to do."

Corrie returned home, hoping she had not influenced Prue one way or the other. She felt in her heart that Prue and Whit belonged together, that Prue and Ramsey's marriage was basically wrong. But once more she found herself cast in the role of being cruel to her Sweet Ramsey, just like hard-hearted Barbara Allen, even though her sympathies lay with Ramsey. She hoped that, through continued friendship, she might be able eventually to make amends for the terrible sacrifices to be required of Ramsey during the next few days.

Prue had decided that she would not tell Ramsey of the letter until after supper, but the minute he arrived he knew something was wrong. "Are you ill?" he asked.

Prue saw she could not postpone the news. "Not exactly," she said. "Corrie was over today. She brought this letter. Whit's alive."

Ramsey sat in a chair facing her, leaning forward with elbows on his knees. His expression did not change. She handed him the letter. He read it dispassionately, as if it were a bloodless legal document. Only once did he glance up at her. When he had finished, he leafed back through the pages, as if to reaffirm certain points.

He refolded the letter. "Well, this complicates matters immensely," he said. "How do you feel about it?"

Prue hesitated. "At this point, I'm not sure," she admitted. "You know I love you. And I've never made it a secret that I love Whit. But I feel I shouldn't be guided by personal considerations."

Prue took a deep breath. "I'm trying to make the proper decision. Beyond what I feel, I keep coming back to two basic facts. This is Whit's baby, and I promised him I would wait for him. I feel I've let him down. In retrospect, the evidence of his death was insufficient for me to make assumptions."

Ramsey tossed the letter onto an end table and leaned back in his chair. "Prue, no one could condemn you for not waiting. Captain Daggett is an experienced man. He judged Whit's wounds mortal. You have no cause to be guided in this by misapprehensions of guilt. As for the child"—he paused—"I'm confident it will be better off in its present situation. Surely you recognize that Whit would not be an ideal father."

Prue looked at the letter. "He says he's changed."

"A deathbed conversion. The worth is yet to be proved. Prue, I've never spoken against Whit, because it's unseemly to criticize the dead. But he lacks Tad's ambition, drive, purpose. He has accomplished nothing on his own. His stated goal for the last few years has been to kill Mexicans, hardly a prime requisite for fatherhood. He isn't above saloon brawls."

Prue badly wanted Ramsey to understand. "Whit had a lot of anger in him, from the flogging, from prison, from the atrocities he witnessed. All that anger seems to be gone now."

Ramsey again leaned forward. "Prue, we've started a good marriage, under difficult circumstances. Your happiness is most important to me. I honestly believe you'll have a better life with me than with Whit."

Prue thought that might be true. But would she be more content? Ramsey's arguments, even though filled with logic, were turning her more and more toward Whit.

"I've considered all that," she told him. "I keep returning to the fact that I love Whit, this is his child, and I promised him I'd wait. Ramsey, I regret with all my heart saying this. But I believe Tad's suggestion may be the best course, that I should simply erase this marriage, and wait for Whit."

Ramsey sat for a long interval in silence. Then he rose from his chair and stood over her. "Prue, I want you to think this through very carefully. I believe that if you do, you'll reconsider. I can't emphasize strongly enough I feel you're making a mistake. But if you want an annulment, I won't stand in your way." He paused for a moment. "I'd ask, however, that we do nothing for two weeks. That way you'll have time to think this through carefully."

Prue knew she would not change her mind. She started to disagree, but at the moment she felt miserable over asking for the annulment. She could not bring herself to argue further.

But the next morning Corrie immediately became upset when she learned of Ramsey's request. "Prue, Whit's deliverance will be stunning news to his friends. They'll all be writing to him. Anyone may let slip you've married. We must dissolve your marriage before Whit learns of it."

Corrie's reaction sent Prue's fears soaring. She was sure she would die if she lost Whit again.

When Corrie insisted on sending for Tad at once, she did not protest.

Tad arrived and gravely listened to the situation. "Corrie's right," he said. "We can't wait. Ramsey has already agreed to the annulment. Why wait? Prue, with your permission, I'll go ahead and draw up the papers and talk to him. I'm sure I can convince him to sign them."

Prue felt she had stated her case to Ramsey as well as she ever could. No more was left to be said between them. And it was true he had agreed to the annulment. Only the matter of delay was at issue.

"Go ahead," she told Tad. "You have my permission."

"Tad, Ramsey will resent your interference," Corrie warned.

"That can't be helped," he said. "Ramsey's playing for time, hoping Whit will hear about the marriage and back off. We can't allow that to happen."

Tad moved between Ramsey and the door. The atmosphere was tense. He was prepared for trouble. "I've brought the papers," he said. "A simple petition of annulment, and attendant clauses. All that's required is your signature."

Ramsey was behind his desk. Since Tad had declined a chair, he also remained on his feet. He smiled. "That's hardly necessary, Thaddeus. I've told Prue I'll release her. I'll file the required papers."

"I'm here as Prue's attorney," Tad informed him. "Since she's the petitioner, I'm initiating the action. In consideration of the circumstances, I want this filed as soon as possible."

They were alone. Tad had timed his visit to coincide with Old Man Whittier's departure, so there would be no witnesses to what was said.

Ramsey spoke with considerable heat. "I could have you disbarred. You've gone behind my back, entered my home without my permission, and sold my wife on this petition to destroy my marriage. I can prove undue influence. I told Prue I'll cooperate with her. But I won't cooperate with *you*. When the time comes, I'll file the papers."

Tad ignored Ramsey's anger. "There are two special provisions in this petition. One, affirming that you surrender all rights to the child. Two, that you'll keep your distance from Prue."

Ramsey shook his head. "I'd never agree to that. She has always relied on me. She can continue to do so."

"I don't want you hanging around her," Tad said. "Whit will feel the same way. I want it in legal terms."

"No court would impose such a ban without cause. And I'm sure any court would be sympathetic upon learning the situation of my marriage, and my long acquaintance with Prue."

"We're not trying this in a court of law," Tad said. "You'd better sign those goddamn papers."

Ramsey's eyebrows rose. "Is that a threat?"

"It'll serve as one."

Ramsey's face reddened. "Thaddeus, you really are an uncivilized man. I've always known it. This visit is ridiculous. I'll not participate in any legal transaction under these circumstances. If you don't leave my office immediately, I'll summon a law officer to put you out."

"I don't see one handy," Tad said. "And since you've brought up the subject, I'll give you another warning. Stay away from my wife."

Ramsey looked at him a long moment. "Is this from Corrie? I rather doubt she'll appreciate your severing our friendship."

Tad knew that was true. But the words had been on his mind for years. "I'll put it plainer," he added. "Stop hanging around my house like a lovesick puppy."

Ramsey's face turned a deeper red. "You're an oaf, Thaddeus. You never understood Corrie. You're incapable of it. You're an unfeeling, insensitive man. If you had one iota of decency, you'd have never gone off and left her broke, sick, and with two babies to feed. You never concerned yourself with what she went through during those years. I was there. I saw it. I know. I helped her as a friend, and I don't apologize for it."

"I'll tell you just once," Tad said. "Utter one more word on my marriage and I'll blow your fucking head off."

Ramsey's face paled. His hand made a tentative movement toward the small pistol at his waist. "You can't talk to me that way."

"I just did. Sign those papers."

Ramsey shifted his stance and raised his voice. "Someday Corrie will see you for exactly what you are, Thaddeus. A common clod. A lout. You've never been the man for her. You've never brought her the happiness she deserves. I've given her more pleasure in one night than you've managed in all your years of marriage."

Tad's hand went of its own volition to the revolver on his hip. The movement was so practiced that the gun was coming up, cocked, before he even realized he held it in his hand. Yet, to his amazement, Ramsey also was pulling his pistol with a bold, decisive expertise. Tad brought his gun to bear and dropped the hammer, aware even before the explosion that Ramsey also was getting off a shot.

The two pistols roared almost simultaneously. But even as he felt Ramsey's bullet strike him high on his leg, Tad thumbed another round into Ramsey's chest. The second shot was pure reflex, born of his years of fighting Mexicans and Comanches.

Ramsey went down hard under the impact of the two large-bore bullets.

Shouts came from the street below. Tad holstered his pistol, lowered himself into a chair, and examined his wound.

The ball had entered at the front, where his leg and torso joined. He could not find an exit wound.

Ramsey had not moved. Tad saw no signs of life.

Ignoring the pain, he scrambled crabwise to the desk and retrieved the annulment petition. He rolled the papers and stuck the edge in the chimney of a lamp. When they ignited, he held them while they burned, then dropped the residue into a metal spittoon. The room was so full of gunsmoke he doubted the additional fumes would be noticed.

Even unsigned, the annulment petition might have caused complications. Now Prue was a widow, pure and simple, and stood to inherit Ramsey's considerable estate. Her child was relegitimized, and she was free to remarry.

Tad spoke to Ramsey's corpse. "A lawyer has to think on his feet. Let's forget about that petition. Two lead balls just changed the whole picture."

Feeling faint, he dropped into a chair and waited for someone to come upstairs and investigate the source of the explosions.

The evening had turned into a nightmare. After Tad was carried into the back bedroom, and the doctor had commandeered all spare lamps for his work, Corrie went into the semidarkness of the long room for an agonizing wait. Through the undraped front windows came the amber glow of lanterns among the crowd in the yard. She was too deeply in shock to feel any emotion but horror. Her mind was paralyzed. Her child-swollen body seemed ready to fly into a thousand pieces at any minute. She battled to hold it together while she struggled to absorb what little she had been told.

Ramsey was dead.

And by Tad's pistol.

As she waited, her fear grew. Surely the gunfight had not been over the annulment. Ramsey had told Prue that he would sign.

She could think of but one other possibility, and it was a secret, known but to herself, and to Ramsey.

Thus far Tad had said nothing. Corrie was still awaiting an explanation.

Sam Maverick and Colonel Hays emerged from the bedroom, where they had been helping the doctor. As their eyes adjusted to the gloom they saw Corrie and came toward her.

She rose from her chair. "How is Thaddeus?" she asked.

"The doctor will be out in a minute," Hays said. "But the colonel doesn't seem to be in any immediate danger."

Corrie was apprehensive about the answer, but she asked the question anyway. "Did he say what happened?"

"Only that they quarreled, Mrs. Logan, and that Cothburn went for his gun. The colonel's in considerable pain. He's hardly up to questions."

"Mrs. Logan, would you like for me to send for Mary?" Sam Maverick asked. "You really shouldn't be here alone like this, in your condition."

Corrie considered the offer only briefly. It would be nice to have a friend to lean on. But who knew what revelations the evening might yet bring? No doubt the matter should be kept within the family as much as possible. "No, thank you, Mr. Maverick," she managed to say. "I'm quite all right. I have my girl, Hattie, with the children. As soon as I can leave Tad, I must go to my sister."

The doctor emerged from the bedroom carrying two lamps. He brought them into the long room and placed them on the mantel.

He spoke in subdued tones, as if for Corrie's ears alone. "The colonel's in no danger, Mrs. Logan. But I intend to stay the night with him. I probed for the ball, and couldn't find it. The hip is shattered. I could feel the raw edges. He'll recover. But the injury will probably prove permanent."

"Will he be able to walk?"

The doctor hesitated. "Time will tell. But my guess is that he'll have to depend on crutches."

Corrie felt driven to learn more, from any source. "As you may know, Mr. Cothburn was a longtime friend. Did you also tend his wounds before he died?"

The doctor gave her an odd glance. "No, m'am. Mr. Cothburn died instantly. He took two large-caliber balls through the heart."

The thought made Corrie weak. She searched for a chair. The doctor and Maverick helped her to the sofa.

Why would Tad shoot Ramsey once? Let alone twice?

"Doctor, may I see my husband? Is he awake?"

"He's resting. I gave him some laudanum for pain. He'll be groggy. He can talk, but I wouldn't tax him. Nor should you be exhausting yourself, Mrs. Logan."

Corrie gathered her strength. "I only want a few minutes with him."

The doctor escorted her down the hall. Corrie went into the bedroom and closed the door behind her. Tad lay full length, his head propped up on pillows. At first Corrie thought him asleep, but as she settled into a chair at bedside he opened his eyes and looked at her.

"Corrie, he tried to kill me," he said, keeping his voice low. "I want you to know that. He accused me of interfering in his marriage, and lost his temper. But I won't doctor the truth. I don't know which of us started the shooting. It seemed to be a mutual decision."

Never in her life had Corrie seen Ramsey lose his temper. "Did it have to come to this?" she asked. "Surely you could have backed off."

"We had an extended conversation," Tad said. "We read off each other's pedigree. Eventually I lost my temper too. I warned him to stay away from Prue and Whit, and from you. He bragged he had known you in the biblical sense." He paused. "Is that true?"

Corrie put her hands to her face. It was her worst fear realized. Why had Ramsey betrayed her?

"Were you intimate with him?" Tad asked again.

The secret had rankled too long. Corrie could not lie. "Only once," she said.

Tad looked away for a moment. "When?" he asked.

Corrie was surprised she could speak about it so calmly. "After you were taken at Mier. After I came back here."

Tad winced. He shifted his weight in bed. "I knew he was courting you while I was off fighting. But I trusted you, Corrie. Don't expect me to be sorry. I didn't set out to do it. But I'm glad I killed the son of a bitch."

Anger overrode Corrie's shock and grief. "Tad, you left me with two children, a household to care for, and no money. I didn't know whether you were dead or alive. I came back here and found this house unfit for pigs. Ramsey helped me, stood by me, when it looked as if you'd never come home again."

"Thank God I didn't know in that Mexican prison."

"I'm not condoning what I did. It was a mistake. I've regretted it more than you'll ever know. But you contributed. If you hadn't left me, it would never have happened."

Tad met her gaze, his eyes smoldering. "All the time he was hanging around here, he knew, you knew, and I didn't. I feel like a perfect fool."

"It was my fault. That was no reason to kill him."

"You never saw him for what he was. Even Whit had his number. He was nothing but a whorehouse dandy. If he'd been carrying a man's weapon instead of a woman's purse pistol, you could have buried us both on the same day."

Corrie felt it was time to leave. She had overstayed the doctor's orders. "I must go to Prue. She's alone. No telling what she's thinking. Or what she's heard."

"Tell her not to mention the annulment. I destroyed the papers. Thanks to me, she's now a moderately rich widow."

Again Corrie's anger flared. "Don't you ever think of anything but money?"

"I once did, quite often. But this late in life, I'm learning that money is about the only thing you can depend on."

Stung, Corrie left the room without another word. She summoned Old Ben to carry a lantern, and started walking toward Prue's house.

She knew in her heart she would never be able to forgive Ramsey for his betrayal.

Nor would she ever be able to forgive Tad for killing him.

And Tad was a proud man.

He would never, ever, forgive her one moment of weakness.

✳   ✳   ✳

Ramsey's body lay in state in the long room. Entering by a side door unannounced, as was her habit, Corrie came upon it unexpectedly and stood in stunned horror. Ramsey's professional associates had washed him, dressed him in fresh clothing, and arranged him on a bed of planks stretched across sawhorses. With the hint of his familiar smile, he looked quite lifelike, except for a bloodless pallor. Instinctively Corrie reached to touch him. The instant she grasped his cold, stiff hand every last trace of the delicate control she had maintained through the evening suddenly vanished. She screamed.

Men came running. Their voices reverberated as if arising from a deep well. She knew them. They were Ramsey's friends, Tad's friends. But she could not relate to them. It was as if they spoke from the other side of a glass wall. Still screaming, she fought them off. Cloistered in her grief, she wept for Ramsey, for her wrecked marriage, for her father and mother, and for her lost girlhood. She wept for her moment of weakness with Ramsey that now had cost him his life, and had cost her her marriage.

Prue came and joined the men, grasping at Corrie's arms. Corrie shoved her away.

Then Prue slapped her. And with the stinging blow the spell was broken. Corrie instantly regained her sanity. She struggled for breath, embarrassed, appalled.

Never in her life had she made such a public spectacle. Prue seized her by the shoulders. "Corrie, you've got to get hold of yourself!"

She found herself incapable of speech. She nodded.

Prue was haggard, and almost as pale as Ramsey. "Come to the back bedroom and lie down," she said. "Should I send for the doctor?"

Corrie shook her head. Prue and two of the men helped her down the hall to the bedroom. One of the men lit a lamp. The men withdrew, leaving Corrie and Prue alone.

Corrie lay back on the bed. "I'm sorry," she said. "Seeing Ramsey, it came over me all at once."

Prue touched Corrie's face. "I didn't intend to hit you so hard. I left my handprint. But I had to do something."

Corrie remained shaken. The slap still stung. But she dismissed it with a gesture.

Prue leaned close and lowered her voice so the men keeping watch over Ramsey would not hear. "Why, Corrie? Why did Tad do it? What really happened? No one will tell me anything!"

Corrie hesitated. The real reason behind the shooting must forever remain a secret. Carefully she repeated Tad's account of the events, down to the burning of the annulment papers. She left out only Ramsey's revelation of her infidelity.

"Corrie, even if Ramsey had been obstinate, and refused to co-operate, it shouldn't have come to this. Why did Tad warn Ramsey to stay away from me? I didn't want that! It was never even discussed!"

Corrie offered the only excuse that came to mind. "They irritated each other. I think the quarrel just got out of hand."

"And do you believe that about Ramsey losing his temper? Corrie, in all the years you've known him, did you ever see Ramsey lose control?"

A vague memory tugged for attention. "Only once when we were children," Corrie said. "At a picnic he fought an older boy over a fishing pole. I remember it was said then he was slow to anger, but when he lost his temper, people should look out."

"That's childhood stuff," Prue said. "You ever see him truly angry as an adult?"

"No," Corrie conceded.

"Nor have I. Corrie, if Ramsey reached for his gun, Tad goaded him into it. I'll never believe otherwise. I know Tad will claim self-defense and probably make it stick. But not with me. Ramsey was as nice to me as any man could possibly be. He was a good husband. And when we learned Whit was alive, he was wonderful about it. I'll forever be grateful to him. I'll never forgive Tad for what he's done."

Corrie remained silent.

Prue studied her for a moment and then went on. "I've been going crazy all evening, trying to imagine what happened. I went over to your house and it was full of people. I didn't want to talk to you with so many people around. I've been waiting for you to come over, knowing you would, hoping you'd have an explanation. But you have none. Corrie, what are you going to do?"

"Do?" Corrie asked, not understanding.

"I don't see how you can live with what Tad has done."

Corrie was coming to a conclusion in her thinking. "Prue, I have two sons. And now another child to think about. What *can* I do? I blame Tad for what happened. But I can't end my marriage."

Prue remained silent for a time. In the lamplight her color was sallow and her eyes red rimmed. Worry lines had deepened around her mouth and eyes. She looked years older. "Corrie, as long as you're married to that man I'll never set foot in your house again."

Corrie thought it best not to argue at the moment. She voiced a fundamental concern. "I hope you won't allow your anger at Tad to affect your relationship with Whit."

"Never. Whit can be violent, but I know that deep down he's gentle. He fights only after he's hurt. I understand and respect that side of him."

Corrie did not answer. Prue's eyes widened. She gave Corrie a knowing look. "It was about you, wasn't it? Of course! Not about me at all! And here I've died a thousand deaths tonight, blaming myself! When all the time it was you! I should have known!"

Corrie retreated to a partial truth. "Ramsey's attentions to me were a part of it. Tad resented Ramsey helping me while he was a prisoner. When he warned Ramsey to stay away from me—from us —Ramsey criticized him for leaving me when he went off on the Mier expedition."

"And there's more, isn't there?" Prue demanded. "If not, you would have mentioned all this when you first told me. What is it I don't yet know?"

Unable to answer, Corrie shook her head. "Prue, the quarrel was over the both of us. Tad was overly protective of you, because of Whit. The two men couldn't abide each other. I blame myself. I should have seen it coming."

"Yet knowing all this, you brought Tad into it, talked me into letting him handle the legal papers. Oh! I've done Ramsey an awful injustice! I truly wish he had been a better marksman."

Unbidden Corrie's anger flared. "That's a terrible thing to say! Tad has always been good to you. The doctor says he may be crippled for life."

"I wish I could say I'm sorry, but I'm not. I can't forget we'll be burying Ramsey at ten in the morning. I hope you're not planning to go."

Corrie had not yet thought ahead to the funeral. Even with her husband as the one who had killed him, she could not deny Ramsey one last gesture. "Of course I'm going," she said.

"Under the circumstances, I don't think you should," Prue said. "Not if you want to save your marriage. It'll anger Tad."

"I'm sure it will," Corrie said. "But I'm going."

"And you'll be adding fuel to the fire. Apparently Tad hasn't told anyone what set off the quarrel. I won't. And you won't. So this town is free to invent. I'm sure that little scene in the front room sent speculation soaring. A very pregnant lady slapping her very pregnant sister over the body of one husband shot by the other. I wonder what they'll make of that! We don't need you showing up at the funeral of the man your husband killed."

"It's no one's affair but our own," Corrie said.

"Ramsey may have been your fiancé, but he was my husband. And I'm telling you that you won't be welcome."

"I'll be there," Corrie said. She struggled to her feet. "Since I'm not welcome at Ramsey's funeral, I assume I'm no longer welcome in his home."

"My home," Prue corrected. "I don't know how I'll feel when this is over. Right now I'm just going from moment to moment."

Corrie paused in the door for one last shot. "Prue, Tad took you in without question. You owe him some loyalty."

"I know," she said. "That's one thing that's making this so difficult."

Corrie left without another word. She made her way down the hall and past Ramsey's body to the front yard, where Ben waited.

Heart pounding in anticipation, Whit turned at the Main Plaza and rode the final block toward home. In a way, his absence for the brief war seemed longer than his three years as a prisoner. Yet the house was exactly as he remembered, bone-white in the glare of the sun, with red-tiled roof, low picket fence, and Corrie's roses in bloom along the walk to the front door. Old Ben came hurrying down the drive to take his reins. Ben seemed to have something weighty on his mind.

"Mastah Whit, Miss Corrie said for you to wait right here till she come. I done sent Hattie to fetch her."

Whit laughed. How like Corrie to organize a celebration for his arrival. He was in the mood. He might party a week, nonstop.

Corrie came out the front door. On first glance Whit burst into delighted laughter. "Corrie! How wonderful! When's it due?"

She put a forefinger to her lips and came close before speaking. "Whit, I have a lot to tell you before you see anyone. That's why I had Ben waylay you." She stood on tiptoe and kissed him. "It's great to have you home."

Taking him by the hand, she led him down the drive. "Let's go sit on the patio where we can talk," she whispered.

Corrie was acting so strangely that Whit's concern soared. "What's wrong?" he asked. "Is it Prue? Is she all right?"

"She's fine, and waiting for you," Corrie whispered back. "Now be quiet."

But he was driven to ask one more question. "Is it Tad?"

They reached the edge of the patio. "I'll take you to Tad in a minute," Corrie said. "Please, Whit. Let me tell you. I've had spies out watching for you the last week. I didn't want you to walk into this situation unaware." They took seats on the far side of the patio. Corrie continued to hold his hand. "First, I want you to tell me something. Did you receive Prue's letters, telling you about the baby?"

Whit was bewildered. "Baby?"

Corrie squeezed his hand. "Prue is due to have your baby any day now."

Never in his life had Whit felt such unexpected joy. He slapped a leg with his free hand and laughed. He looked toward the house and started to rise. "Where is she? Can I see her?"

Corrie clung to his hand, pulling him back into his chair. "Wait, Whit. There's more. Much more. She's now a widow."

Whit's bewilderment was complete.

"Whit, you must understand her situation. She was unmarried, carrying your child. She wrote you, twice. She never received an answer."

All that now seemed so long ago. Whit experienced difficulty remembering. "We had no mail after we left Mexico City for the mountains. After I was wounded, my mail was held, probably returned to the States. I don't know what happened to it."

Corrie nodded, as if he had confirmed something for her. "Then shortly afterward we received the terrible news that you'd been killed. Captain Daggett wrote Tad, telling him the circumstances, saying there was no hope you were alive. Still Prue insisted on having your baby."

Whit was consumed for a moment with the shame of leaving Prue in that situation. "I should have married her. I thought I was protecting her by not tying her down."

Again Corrie nodded before continuing. "Then Ramsey, knowing the circumstances, surprised us all by proposing to her. With no hope of your ever coming back, she accepted."

Whit throttled a curse. Why Ramsey Cothburn, of all people?

Corrie seemed to read his thoughts. "Now, Whit, don't blame Prue. Look at her situation. She has always loved Ramsey. Not in the way she loved you. But she knew he was a good man. He promised to raise your child as his own. And, Whit, I really think it would have been a good marriage. But out of the blue, your letters came, and you were alive."

Corrie paused. "Think of the effect of that news on Prue. She was thrilled beyond measure. But at the same time she was burdened by guilt that she hadn't waited for you, as she'd promised. Her marriage, rushed for the obvious reasons, now seemed far too hasty."

Whit listened quietly, amazed to find that once again the world had not stood still while he was gone. During his three years in prison Prue had grown up. This time, in only a few months, her life had gone awry without him.

"Through me, Tad suggested she ask Ramsey for an annulment. Reluctantly, Ramsey agreed. Tad went to Ramsey's office to get him to sign the papers."

Step by step, Corrie described a sequence of events that was no surprise, for he had predicted them long ago. But he had not anticipated that Ramsey would manage to shoot Tad.

"Tad's in constant pain," Corrie said. The doctor thinks he'll never again walk normally."

Whit winced. He could not imagine Tad as a cripple.

"Whit, you've always been so sympathetic to the feelings of others. Now Prue needs your understanding. No one else can help her. She's angry at Tad, for she thinks he could have avoided killing Ramsey. She still feels a strong loyalty to Ramsey. He befriended her at a difficult time, then loved her enough to give her up so she could find happiness with you. She's very bitter at Tad, and with me."

Whit raised his eyebrows. He could not envision Corrie and Prue estranged.

"I brought Tad into it," Corrie explained. "And she's right. I shouldn't have meddled. I knew Tad resented Ramsey, and Ramsey resented Tad. I should have foreseen what might happen."

"It would have happened anyway," Whit said. "Ramsey couldn't seem to let go of you. I saw that."

Corrie was silent a moment, as if considering what he had said. "So Prue has no one but you," she continued after a time. "She's worried over what you may think of all this. Whit, you mustn't blame her for marrying Ramsey."

He did not answer. That was a tall order. He knew he would see Prue and Ramsey in bed together at odd moments for the rest of his life.

Still, she was about to give birth to his child, and she was free to marry. "Where is she?" he asked.

"Over at Ramsey's house. It's her house now. He had made a new will, leaving her everything he owned."

Whit was not pleased to hear that. His entire fortune consisted of six months of army pay, less what he had spent on the trip home.

"Corrie, I'll do my best by her," he promised. "I thank you for telling me. You're right. It would've been difficult to walk into this situation, not knowing. Word may be getting around town that I'm back. Maybe I'd better go on over to see her."

"Take a minute first to drop in on Tad. He's been waiting anxiously for days."

She led him into the familiar dim coolness of the house, and to Tad's sickroom. After opening the door, she closed it behind him, leaving him alone with Tad.

Tad lay trussed in a metal frame from waist to ankle, surrounded by books and legal parchment. He looked up at Whit and whooped. "I thought I heard that laugh a while ago. But I decided I was hallucinating on laudanum. Damn, but you look good! ¡Déme un abrazo, hijo!"

Whit leaned over the bed and embraced his brother.

"Fat as a butterball," Tad said. "With a gut wound, I was afraid you'd be down to skin and bones."

"I was for a while," Whit told him. "But once I could keep food down, I came back fast. The Mexicans in that place were mostly Indians. They chewed plants and made poultices. Every hour they gave me a soup spoon full of homemade pulque. My theory is that it cauterized my wound from the inside."

Tad laughed. "That may be. I've never heard of anyone surviving a wound like that, the way Daggett described it."

"Nor I. It went in here, and came out here. I later found I had two bullets in my leg and one in this arm. But after this one I didn't even notice the others. How bad you hurt?"

"Bad enough. I'm stuck in this contraption to let the bones knit. The ranch has gone to hell since it happened. In fact, a lot has happened since you left."

Whit nodded. "Corrie brought me up to date. If you remember, I once predicted you'd have to do something about Ramsey."

"I remember. But I didn't look ahead to what it would cost. Whit, I killed Corrie's pet. She's cold to me. I don't expect my marriage ever to be the same again."

Whit was surprised. Corrie had not even hinted at a breach with Tad.

"But I cleared the way for you," Tad went on. "Whit, you've got a lot of woman there. I liked the way she handled herself through this whole mess. I hope her marriage won't bother you."

"I haven't yet had time to think about it."

"Don't. You haven't the right. You treated her damn shabby."

"I didn't mean to."

"All the same, you did. From where I sit, it looks to me like you should make amends, rather than take offense over what she did. If I've learned anything, it's that you have to accept things for what they are, and work from there. Life is never as simple as you want it to be."

Whit rose from his chair. "One thing for sure. Life isn't going to be simple around here for quite a while. I should get over to see Prue."

They lay on the bed in a back room, Prue on her side, Whit on his back looking at the ceiling. With Prue's condition, his homecoming had been regrettably chaste. Yet he felt strangely satisfied. The nearness of his first child offered a certain contentment.

For hours they talked. He told her of his wound, his sense of abandonment as the Americans retreated, leaving him in the village. He described the Indian women who came and carried him to a hut, and cared for him.

He told her of his return to Mexico City, and his discovery that he had been presumed dead, and that everyone he knew had departed for home.

"There was a lot of confusion," he explained. "I was moved from one place to another. I don't know what happened to my mail. I didn't know anything of what was happening here until Corrie filled me in after I got home."

"I followed every step of the war," Prue said. "I still wonder if it was necessary."

"It was," Whit said. The results of the war were still being sorted out, but already he had reached some conclusions: "Mexico will never again be a threat to us. We've gained California, the Oregon country, and the land in between. Not for Texas, as Tad wanted, but for the States. And there's talk in Mexico City that

Texas may pay off its debts by selling its claim to land from the Rio Grande eastward to about the hundred and third meridian. Whatever we get for it will be a steal. I've walked every foot. I wouldn't pay a dime for it."

Prue told him of the discovery of her pregnancy, the agony of writing to him and receiving no reply. She described her devastation over the news of his death.

"Ramsey's proposal saved my life," she said quietly. "He made me see I owed it to your child to carry on, to attempt to salvage some kind of future."

Whit remained silent through her account. Never had he dreamed that his mindless pleasures would bring such suffering.

She told of her unlimited joy when word came that he was alive, and the pain of her loyalty to Ramsey.

"He believed the baby and I would have a better life with him. Yet he was willing to go through with the annulment."

She described the terrible night when Tad killed Ramsey, of her search for information, of her immense burden of guilt, and of Corrie's late-night visit.

"Whit, there are still some things I don't know. I've come to suspect that Corrie had more to do with the shooting than she'll ever admit."

Whit did not respond. He already had reached that conclusion. Just as Ramsey could never turn loose of Corrie, she in turn could never seem to turn loose of Ramsey.

"I'll never forgive Tad," Prue went on. "That may make matters difficult for you, working with him every day. But I can't help the way I feel."

"Don't worry about it," Whit said. "I can edge around it."

"I'm still very upset about Ramsey," Prue warned. "I still grieve for him. You'll have to understand that has nothing to do with our relationship."

Whit knew there would be days he would barely be able to contain his resentment. But he also recognized the situation was inevitable. "I think it would be best if we don't live in this house," he said. "You can sell it. I'll build another."

Prue did not answer. Whit took her silence as an acceptance.

"I want to marry you as soon as possible," he said. "But I don't know what would be proper under these circumstances. Do you?"

Prue smiled. "Hang what's proper. In a way I feel I've been married to you all along. We can call in a priest and say the words, with a minimal number of witnesses."

Whit hesitated. "I'm assuming you won't want to invite Tad and Corrie."

She looked at him, and they both knew the question was a test, one of many to come. "Absolutely not," she said. "I think it's high time we started living our lives for ourselves."

Corrie's confinement became increasingly wearisome in the latter stages. Mostly she kept to her room, contending with the heat of August. On a weekend in early September she went into labor. The delivery itself, of a baby girl, was not especially difficult. Since Tad could not come to see the baby, Hattie carried it to his room for viewing. Through Hattie, Tad agreed to Corrie's selection of the name Priscilla Louise, after Corrie's maternal great-grandmother.

From the first the baby conveyed a curiously haughty air, and it was Hattie who gave her the name she was destined to carry—Prissy.

Four days later Corrie learned through the Mexican servants that Prue had gone into protracted labor. "She's alone over there among comparative strangers," Corrie told Hattie, "I believe you should go over and tend her."

"But you need help here, Miss Corrie," Hattie protested. "And Mistah Tad needs me."

"I'll be back on my feet soon," Corrie said. "We've Consuelo and the hired girl. We'll manage."

Hattie spent a week with Prue. She reported that Prue's delivery of a baby girl was long and exhausting. Prue named the baby Cambria Elizabeth, after Grandmother Pendleton. Hattie said Whit quickly abbreviated the name to Bree.

"The little thing's a McNair, Miss Corrie," Hattie said. "Oval face, turned-up nose. Seems to me Prissy more favors the Logans."

Hattie was disturbed by the coolness between Corrie and Prue.

"Miss Corrie, I want you two to stop fussing. Your momma won't be resting easy in her grave, way you two acting."

Corrie thought of Prue, how close they had been all of their lives. "Hattie, in time Prue and I will probably put this behind us. But it'll take a while."

Hattie never commented on Corrie's estrangement from Tad, now evident to the whole household.

Clearly Hattie recognized that Corrie's rift with Tad would never be healed.

P A R T F I V E

Secession, the Confederacy, War

*Some of you laugh to scorn the idea of blood-
shed as the result of secession. But let me tell
you what is coming. . . . Your fathers and husbands, your sons and brothers, will be herded at
the point of a bayonet. . . . You may, after the
sacrifice of countless millions of treasure and
hundreds of thousands of lives, as a bare possibility, win Southern independence . . . but I
doubt it.*

> Sam Houston
> Speech Opposing Secession
> February 1861

--- 21 ---

"Late again," Jim Bowie said. "Damn it, where are they?"

"They'll be along," Albert said.

"They better be. If we're not there when Pa gets home, hellfire and brimstone will be cool by comparison."

That was true. Their father was coming down from Austin with old General Sam Houston, now governor of Texas, and other politicians. Tonight there would be a torchlight parade and political rally in the Main Plaza. Houston promised to give his views on the fall elections and the growing threat of secession. Before the rally Houston would attend a reception at the Logans'. If all the family were not present and on time, there would be hell to pay. Already the sun was low on the horizon. A German marching band was practicing before a crowd in the plaza, warming up for the night's activities.

Albert was stirred by the excitement in the air. As students at St. Mary's College, he and Jim had been studying the Lincoln Douglas debates through the last two years. Now those national issues were becoming far less abstract. Albert was now eighteen, Jim Bowie twenty-one. If Lincoln was elected, the South seceded, and war came, they both might become what their history professor scathingly called "cannon fodder."

That possibility was beginning to worry Albert.

"Here they come," Jim said. "Bree probably forgot."

Albert caught sight of their sister and cousin weaving their way through the crowd. Priscilla and Cambria came out of the Ursuline Academy laden with books. At almost fourteen, they were becoming young women. It was a standing rule that Albert and Jim were to meet them at the school each day and escort them home.

"We're late and it's your fault," Jim told Prissy. "We've been waiting fifteen minutes."

It had been closer to five, but Albert did not intervene. Jim and Prissy stormed at each other constantly. He and Bree were the quiet ones.

"We had an examination form," Prissy said. "I told the Sister we had to hurry home, but she wouldn't listen."

Prissy was the lively one. She used her extraordinary good looks to her own advantage. Quick witted, she stayed a half step ahead of everyone around her, plotting and scheming. Her long hair was light, almost blond, and she had laughing, flirty Irish eyes. She invariably could get her way.

Bree's beauty was of a quieter nature. She was darker, more thoughtful, considerate, and hesitant. Albert felt Aunt Prue bossed her too much, not allowing her personality to emerge.

They hurried toward home, Jim and Prissy leading, Albert and Bree behind them. Albert reached and took Bree's load of books. "Was it a tough one?" he asked, meaning the examination.

"*Niaiserie*," she said. "*Ouvrage de longue haleine.*"

Trifling, but a tedious task. Bree's French was improving. The monsieurs at St. Mary's called English a barbarous language. Classes were supposed to be conducted in Spanish and English, but the monsieurs made certain their students also were adept in French and German. So prevalent was French that St. Mary's was called "the French school." Now most of the Ursuline sisters also were from France. They, too, stressed French in classwork.

San Antonio had changed drastically since Albert's boyhood. The old Adelsverein, the Association of Noblemen, had gone bankrupt, but the flood of German immigration had continued. The titled aristocrats and their coterie of artists and intellectuals had made San Antonio their home. Their grand houses now surrounded the Irish Flat. They had taken over La Villita, pushing the Mexicans westward. Now Germans outnumbered the Anglos and Mexicans combined, and the San Antonio River was called "the Little Rhein." La Villita was filled with *biergartens*, each with a resident band. German marches, polkas, and lieder mingled with the softer Spanish music Albert remembered from his boyhood. At Casino Hall, an association dedicated to the "mother tongue" staged concerts of Beethoven, Bach, Mozart, and the new rage, Wagner.

They reached the corner of the plaza and turned toward home. "I told you," Jim said. "We're late."

Carriages and coaches were drawn up in front of the Logan compound. Jim and Prissy broke into a run, heading for the patio and the back door. Albert and Bree followed.

Aunt Hattie waited at the back entry. "Shame on you!" she said to them collectively. "Mastah Tad's been asking for you! Hurry and get ready, now!"

Albert and Jim went to their room and changed out of their school clothes. By the time they emerged, Hattie was motioning them toward the long room.

Governor Sam Houston was talking with Albert's mother. Albert's father stood apart, leaning on his crutches. Albert understood that his father and General Houston once had been close friends, then bitter enemies. Now they were halfway friends again. Albert followed Jim to their father's side.

"General, allow me to present my sons," Albert's father said. "This is Jim Bowie."

Houston shook Jim's hand.

"And Albert Martin."

Albert was generally considered more handsome. It also was widely acknowledged that he was by far the better student. Why did his father always relegate him to such a secondary role?

"I'm deeply honored, sir," he said, gripping Houston's hand.

Albert was well aware of the legends that had grown up around Sam Houston. He knew the man's awesome attainments. Brother Francis, director of St. Mary's, said that if Houston had not made the mistake of flirting with the Know-Nothing party, he now might be the Democratic candidate for the U.S. presidency, instead of Stephen Douglas. New York and Baltimore had gone heavily for Houston in the conventions. But Houston had received little support in his home state. His presidential bid had failed to gain momentum.

"What fine-looking young men," Houston said. "You two bear illustrious names. I'm sure you'll do them justice."

"And may I present my daughter, and niece," Tad said. "Priscilla and Cambria."

Albert moved aside so Prissy and Bree would have room for their curtsies.

"I'm gratified to see you young ladies have inherited the great beauty of your mothers," the governor said. "I've known and admired both many years, since they were not much older than you. I'm glad you're such a credit to them."

Bree colored slightly at the compliment. Prissy seemed to take it as her due.

Others were waiting to be introduced. Albert, his brother, sister, and cousin withdrew.

They lingered on the fringes of the crowd in the long room. A few minutes later a clamor arose in front of the house as the torchlight parade arrived to escort Houston to the plaza. Houston, Albert's father, and the other politicians went out to join the parade.

Albert and Jim followed at a distance. The crowd circled the plaza twice to martial music. Then the governor was escorted to a raised platform. Albert and Jim crowded in close to hear.

Houston opened by stating that if Abraham Lincoln proved victorious in the coming election, calamity would not necessarily follow, as many seemed to believe. "I'm here to tell you that if disaster comes, it'll come from the people, not from Lincoln. There's talk in the air of secession if Lincoln is elected. And I tell you now: secession is *treason.*"

A chorus of boos rose, and grew louder. Houston waited for the interruption to subside.

"But, if secession does come—and it may—I prefer we devote our energies to a separate Republic of the Lone Star."

This time the cheering drowned out the voices of dissent. Albert found himself clapping and yelling his approval.

"Don't make a fool of yourself," Jim shouted in his ear. "This is the same old swill."

"Look at Father!" Albert shouted back.

On the platform as state senator and host, Tad was on his feet, leaning on his crutches, applauding. He also had been saying that Texas should avoid all Southern ties and, if necessary, go it alone.

Houston's speech closed in that vein. Reaction in the plaza was loud but mixed. The pro-South element was noisy.

"Let's get out of here," Jim said. "This could get ugly."

Albert walked with Jim south into La Villita and its familiar aroma of beer, sausages, cheeses, and sauerkraut. Already their friend and classmate Karl Voigt had secured a table at their favorite *biergarten* on King William Street. He motioned for them to join him.

For a time, while Albert drank beer and listened to the music, Jim and Karl argued over a "solution" to the slavery issue. Albert did not take part. His views were considered too radical for serious discussion. He tended to agree with Lincoln. Yet he could not abide the self-righteousness of the Northern abolitionists, who thought they had all the answers. Jim was hot for secession. Karl argued that the United States needed to establish social classes, as prevailed in Europe. He said a good war might accomplish this.

Albert grew weary of the talk of war. "Father says there's nothing so bad about slavery that it couldn't be fixed without wiping out a generation of white boys," he said.

"Meaning us," Jim Bowie said. "You and me. That's what has shaped his thinking so far. But watch him change when the Northerners start shooting. He'll be pounding us on the back, telling us to get in there and fight, reminding us how many times he had to whip the Mexicans and Comanches."

Albert did not answer. That was probably true.

"If war comes, what'll you do?" Karl asked Jim.

"I'll join the best-trained outfit I can find," Jim said. "There'll be no reason to wait."

"Not me," Karl said. "Already my father is talking of sending me back to Europe. To put a polish on my education. Albert, you're the thinker. What will you do?"

Albert had lain awake many nights wondering. He believed slavery was wrong. Goethe, Schiller, Pope, Stendhal, Hugo, others, had convinced him of this before he ever heard of Lincoln. And if an idea was wrong, he could not bring himself to fight for it.

He had thought of flight to Mexico, to Europe. But deep down he knew he could not endure the shame of quitting his country in time of war. "I don't know," he said. "I don't know what I'll do."

Through the years Corrie and Tad's marriage had settled into a dreary stalemate. To the world they presented a picture of normalcy. But Ramsey and his death ruled their marriage. Tad's crutches were an omnipresent reminder of her infidelity, and its cost.

She had devoted her energies to her children, and was pleased to think they showed the results. She had achieved a cool truce with Prue. Yet they remained somewhat estranged, for Prue still would not enter Tad's house.

Around them San Antonio had grown into the paradise it had always promised to become. The roughness of the Mexican War years had gradually faded. Through the fifties a segment of European aristocracy moved in, bringing their culture intact. Concerts by professional orchestras and full-dress operas were standard fare. Corrie remembered her difficulty in acquiring Spanish; now her children routinely spoke four languages in the course of their daily lives. Their education was as good as any in the country. Corrie loved San Antonio more than ever.

Tad, however, was unhappy. Corrie saw it in his face. He had plunged back into politics, leaving operation of the ranch to Whit. Now, with talk of war, he spent even more time in Austin.

Events had moved rapidly after Lincoln's election in November. A Secession Convention submitted the question to a statewide vote. Secession carried in Texas three to one.

Now Texas—and the nation—were waiting to see what steps Governor Sam Houston would take. Would he bow to the will of the people, swallow his pride, and guide Texas into the Confederacy? Or would he resist, and fight one last political battle for his convictions?

Today Tad would be returning from Austin with the answer.

Corrie had not been so worried since the Mexican invasions and Tad's captivity.

In a way, this was worse, for the outcome threatened the lives of her sons.

She anxiously awaited Tad's return. When his carriage finally drew up in front of the house in midafternoon, she called to the boys, waiting in their room, and sent a servant for Whit.

Tad came laboring up the walk on his crutches. He entered, breathing hard, and made his way to his big chair by the fireplace. His face was creased with fatigue. Jim, Albert, and Whit arrived and took chairs facing him. Corrie remained standing.

"We're in for it," Tad said. "Houston declined to act. He has been deposed. Thrown out. The Legislature declared the office of governor vacant. There was no use of my speaking against it. Austin's in the grip of war fever."

"Then it's final?" Whit asked. "Texas has quit the Union?"

"All but the formalities. There's no question. War's here."

Corrie sank into a chair. Albert and Jim remained deathly quiet. Tad looked solemnly at his sons. "What I'm about to tell you is not to go beyond this room. General Houston has received communication from President Lincoln, offering him a commission as major general in the United States army, command of all Federal forces in Texas, and authorization to recruit a hundred thousand men for an effort to hold Texas in the Union."

Corrie glanced at her sons. Albert had paled. Jim was unusually solemn.

"I'm telling you this to show you what's at stake, and what's to come," Tad went on. "Lincoln's offer clearly signals his intention to block Southern secession by force of arms." He paused. "What's that infernal racket?"

"Prissy and Bree are having a party for their classmates," Corrie explained. "I'll go quiet them."

Tad put up a hand. "No. Leave them be. There'll be little enough cause for parties in the days ahead. Houston confided in me, and a few other trusted friends. That in itself is unusual. It's his habit to act on his own. He wanted to know if we saw a way to avert bloodshed. We felt—to a man—that the maneuver Lincoln proposes would throw Texas into an internal civil war, and make the state the focus of the coming conflict. We advised against it. Houston agreed. So as it stands the Federal forces will be withdrawn from Texas, and events allowed to take their course unimpeded."

"Will San Antonio be safe?" Corrie asked.

"I believe so. The bulk of the war will be fought elsewhere. Texas is too remote from armament and supplies. The Union won't wish to provoke Mexico into it with operations close to her border."

"I've never been a Houston admirer," Whit said. "But I was hoping the old reprobate could hold back the tide."

Tad shook his head. "No one can. Not now. War's coming. And it'll be far worse than the Mexican War or any we've fought with England. It'll be brother against brother. We Logans have a decision to make. We must stand united. The way I see it, there are not enough of us who favor Texas independence, who want to quit both the Union and the Confederacy and go it alone. That's a doomed hope. I can see no course but to cast our lot with the South. I haven't yet taken the oath of allegiance to the Confederacy. But it'll be required if I'm to hold my seat in the Senate. Before I commit myself, one way or the other, I'd like to receive assurances we stand together on this."

"I'll side with the South," Whit said. "I don't like being told what to do. I wouldn't mind freeing my slaves, if they'd let me continue to take care of them. But I don't like being told it's what I have to do. If it comes to fighting, I'll probably go with an outfit like the Rangers."

Tad looked at Whit under lowered brows. "Whit, you're what? Thirty-seven? You're too old."

"Tad, if I'm young enough to wrestle longhorns every day, I'm fit enough to fight Yankees."

"Jim, how do you feel?" Tad asked.

Jim Bowie spoke without hesitation. "If war comes, I'll enlist immediately, sir, and fight where I'm needed."

"Well spoken. Albert?"

Albert glanced at Corrie. She could not help him.

"I prefer to wait, sir."

"Wait? For what, in God's name?"

"To see what transpires, sir. You yourself said last week you hope there are men in Washington who'll listen to reason. So do I. I'm hoping to give them time in which to act."

"And if the fighting comes, what will you do?"

Again Albert glanced at Corrie. He hesitated. "Sir, I believe the institution of slavery is morally wrong. I'm reluctant to take up arms in its defense."

The veins stood out on Tad's temples. "Don't you preach to me about slavery! I've had to put up with it all of my life! Of course slavery's wrong! But two wrongs don't make a right. What if armed men came in here to carry off Aunt Hattie? Wouldn't you fight for her?"

"Yes," Albert said.

"This is the same thing. I fought Mexicans, Comanches, for years, taking comfort in the thought that if I prevailed, my sons would be spared finishing the job. But now I see the necessity will always be there. This is *your* fight. It's *your* responsibility."

Albert was pale, but he met Tad's gaze. "I prefer to wait before I make my decision, sir."

Tad looked at him for a long moment. "I know you're not a coward. If I thought so, I'd disown you. But you should know this. Already in Austin there's talk of enacting a law calling for every adult male to swear allegiance to the Confederacy or quit Texas. If that becomes the case, what will you do?"

Albert hesitated. "I'm trying to come to a decision. I'm thinking night and day. I'll keep doing so, sir."

Tad put a hand to his face and rubbed his eyes. "You do that. Let me know when you come to your senses."

Tad rose from his chair, picked up his crutches, and made his way down the hall toward the bedroom. Corrie followed.

She felt moved to speak up for Albert. "He could be right," she said as the door closed. "Perhaps if he waits, doesn't rush off to enlist, all this will blow over."

Tad lay on the bed fully clothed, rolled over, and prepared for sleep. "Waiting doesn't absolve him of his responsibilities. He's just weak natured." He was silent so long Corrie thought he had drifted off. But once more he spoke. "Why couldn't he be more like Jim?"

Albert attempted to lose himself in schoolwork. But the growing tempest loomed like a Shakespearean tragedy. The Southern states continued to secede. Federal arsenals were seized. Riots broke out in

Baltimore and St. Louis. Then, in mid-April, with stunning swiftness, Fort Sumter surrendered to the Confederates, and Lincoln
declared a state of insurrection and ordered a blockade of all Southern states, including Texas.

It was the blockade that finally kindled Albert's anger. Lincoln
had made it increasingly difficult for him to remain neutral. Around
him, the war became impossible to ignore. Former Rangers and
Indian fighters declared themselves captains, called for volunteers,
and organized a company for Confederate service. They obtained
uniforms and spent the afternoons drilling in the plazas. Albert
passed them daily on his way to and from school. Then one by one
the companies received their orders and marched off to war, flags
flying, friends and families cheering and weeping.

Still Albert hung back.

So did Jim Bowie. "I don't want to go with some ragtag outfit,"
he said. "I'm waiting for a good cavalry regiment."

In July came reports of the Battle of Manassas. Albert was stirred
by the descriptions of the vast armies maneuvering and clashing.
The numbers were staggering: twenty-nine hundred Union casual-
ties. Almost two thousand Confederate.

In August came the call Jim and Whit had been awaiting. Ben-
jamin F. Terry, a hero of Manassas, was authorized to return to
Texas and raise a regiment of volunteers. Houston newspapers were
billing them as Terry's Texas Rangers.

Jim and Whit enlisted.

Still Albert hung back.

On the evening before Whit and Jim's departure the family gave
them a farewell dinner.

For Albert it was a miserable evening. He was saddened to see
Whit and Jim going off to war, and was made even more desolate by
the fact that he was not going, that he could not yet bring himself
to do what was expected of him.

Although neither was yet in uniform, Albert's father seemed
unable to take his eyes from them.

"Whit, Jim, you've done us proud," he said. "If it wasn't for this
bum leg, I'd be going with you."

Albert's mother and Aunt Prue kept wiping away tears. Whit laughed and told jokes, most of a military flavor.

Jim teased Albert. "There's still time to go with us."

"I think it'd be wonderful, the three Logans, side by side in the Rangers," Prissy said.

Albert's father looked at him. "Prissy has a point. If you three were together, you could look out for each other."

Albert felt all eyes on him. He resented the pressure being placed on him. His father wanted to be able to brag in the Texas Legislature that he had two sons and a brother in Terry's Texas Rangers. Prissy wanted romantic uniforms. Jim wanted acclaim and glory.

Albert only wanted peace.

"I've not yet made up my mind," he said.

Prissy groaned. No one else commented.

He went with the family the next morning to see Whit and Jim ride off to the tune of a brass band. His mother and Aunt Prue put their arms around each other and cried. His father also shed tears, yet looked proud. Prissy shouted and waved a flag as long as Terry's Rangers were in sight. Bree wept silently. Albert felt an immense sadness, more for himself than for Whit and Jim.

He was unprepared for the emotional vacuum in the wake of Jim's departure. Suddenly he had their room to himself. All of his friends had gone. Shorn of students, St. Mary's closed

Albert spent his days in walking along the river and thinking. He read every newspaper he could find. Gradually, a set of convictions began to form. They were not derived from the major news items, but from the smaller, often tucked away on inside pages. In Maryland the Federal government arrested members of the State Legislature who disagreed with Union policy. In St. Louis, Major General John Charles Frémont ordered the arrest of a newspaper editor who had criticized his actions. President Lincoln ordered the suspension of the writ of habeas corpus from Maine to Washington.

Albert wondered. Was this a sample of what the Union might someday impose on Texas?

One morning he passed a company drilling in the plaza. He stopped to watch. The men went about their work seriously, and without ostentation. Albert crossed the street and talked with the officers. They said the company was preparing to join the Fourth Texas Regiment, currently being formed in Virginia.

After a day of careful consideration, he returned and signed enlistment papers. The officers told him he could take until the next morning to put his affairs in order.

It was his intention to leave without saying good-bye, except through brief notes. But at the last moment he relented and awakened his mother. "I've made up my mind," he told her. "The company is forming in the plaza now. You can write me in care of the Fourth Texas Regiment, Richmond, Virginia."

She left her bed in the dark and clung to him. She seemed dazed. "Albert, you can't go like this!"

"I don't want any fuss," he told her. "I'm only telling you because you'll understand it's better this way."

"Can't you wait until your father comes down from Austin?"

"We're on a tight travel schedule. We leave this morning."

He held her for a time while she cried. "Your father will have questions. What is this regiment? What made you choose it?"

"It was the one being formed when I made up my mind. Tell him I'll write all about it. I really must go now."

Slowly she released him. "Will you see Jim?"

"I don't know."

He kissed her again and backed toward the door. She held him for one last question.

"Who's the commander? Will your father know him?"

"I doubt it. All I know is, he's a West Pointer. A colonel."

He backed out the door.

"What's his name?" she called after him.

"Hood," he said over his shoulder. "Colonel John Bell Hood."

--- 22 ---

Tad put the team into a mile-eating trot, confident Newt would have fresh horses waiting at the camp on the Colorado. The buckboard hack was an irritation, but necessary. He had not ridden horseback in years. The pain was too great. But he had learned that with cushions, and his stiff leg propped against the dashboard, he could travel in relative comfort in a light hack, and go almost anyplace a horse could go.

He had been convinced from the start a way existed around the Union blockade. He had found it, and was now buying cotton for his third trip.

The smuggling was dangerous. The barren reaches of the Wild Horse Desert west of Corpus Christi were plagued by Mexican bandits. Twice Union troops had landed in efforts to stop the blockade-running. But the distances were great, and with prudence those hazards could be avoided. Tad worried most about the insurgent military forces gaining power across the border. After crossing the Río Grande at Brownsville by ferry to Matamoros, he was in their hands. Thus far he had been able to bribe them into allowing him to use the old smugglers' trail the fifty miles from Matamoros to Bagdad and the coast. There his cotton was ferried out to the island port of Brazos Santiago to be loaded aboard English ships.

He regarded his blockade-running as his contribution to the war. He longed to be in the thick of it with Whit and Jim, but he recognized such ambitions were impractical. He could not sit on a horse without agonizing pain.

Whit and Jim were covering themselves with glory. Terry's Texas Rangers had been mentioned in all accounts of the Five Days' Battle, Shiloh, Bardstown, Perryville, and Murfreesboro. Whit was now a colonel. His letters were usually brief and noncommittal. But Jim, knowing Tad's interests, always sent long descriptions of the fighting and strategy. At nights along the border Tad read and reread Jim's letters by the campfire and penned long replies.

Again he had been forced to abandon the ranch. All the young men were gone, and he could not muster enough competent people to keep it in operation. Thus far the ranch had been a disappointment. The market he long envisioned had not materialized. Once Whit drove a thousand head all the way to St. Louis, up through the eastern portion of the Indian Nations into Missouri. But when grazing expenses through the nations were totaled, the profits proved marginal. One spring Whit attempted a drive to New Orleans, and termed it one of the worst experiences of his life. He lost cattle to the tangled woods, the swamps, and the powerful currents of the Mississippi. In another experiment, Tad had loaded five hundred head of longhorns onto a steamboat, intending to take them across the Gulf and up the Mississippi to Cairo, Illinois. The longhorns proved to be poor sailors. They virtually kicked the steamboat apart. After Tad paid the damages, his losses were heavy, for few survived the trip.

Yet he continued to believe that the future of Texas rested in cattle, and that the realization of his dreams lay with Jim. Time after time Jim had proved himself a doer, a leader. Already he had won two promotions. Whit said Jim was idolized by his men. Tad wrote Jim long letters, laying out plans for what they would do together after the war.

In contrast, Tad hardly ever knew what to write Albert. He could not fathom the boy. With all his education and intelligence, why was he content to remain a common, foot-slogging soldier? One of the young men from San Antonio had written home that Albert twice was elected captain, and had turned down the honor each time. Albert had seen more than his share of the fighting, from Eltham's Landing, Gaines's Mill, Second Manassas, and Sharpsburg on Antietam Creek through to Gettysburg. Yet his letters were distant, formal. Not knowing what else to do, Tad always replied in the same tone.

Without Whit and Jim, Tad's life had become lonely. He and

Corrie seldom communicated beyond routine household matters. During his long convalescence years ago he had remained in the back bedroom until it became a habit. As a consequence, from the night he killed Ramsey, he and Corrie had slept apart.

As he had told Whit long ago, he never expected his marriage to be the same ever again.

At last he arrived at the camp on the Colorado. As he had expected, Newt had a fresh team waiting. After getting all the wagons together, Tad and the Negroes began their three-hundred-mile trip south to Brownsville, Matamoros, and the smugglers' trail to Bagdad.

After dark Corrie lit a lamp and returned to work at the loom. She was too upset for anything else. The monotony of sending the shuttle back and forth provided soothing diversion.

The war was entering its third year and life was becoming more grim each day. The long-established social order of San Antonio had crumbled, with some of the best families virtually destroyed. A few of the uneducated lower classes had become wealthy through speculation and black-market trading.

The value of Confederate money dropped every week, and the price of gold soared. The stores were empty. Manufactured goods, such as clothing and shoes, were impossible to obtain.

To meet the needs of the Logan family, Tad and Newt had built a loom and spinning wheel. Both now reposed in the long room. There Corrie, Prissy, and Hattie spent long days carding and combing cotton and wool, spinning it into thread, and weaving cloth for homespun shirts and dresses. Periodically Tad went out to the ranch, shot several of the older cattle, tanned the hides, and made moccasinlike shoes. He also brought home meat, and continued to plant patches of vegetables upriver. Unlike many, they did not want for food.

Corrie was thankful that thus far the war had not touched them in ways it had others in San Antonio. The wounded were streaming home. A small hospital had been set up, and almost every day Corrie, Prue, Prissy, and Bree went over to help tend the sick and wounded.

Karl Voigt was there. Twice he had tried to tell Corrie about the battle at Sharpsburg, where he last saw Albert, but each time he lost his composure and could not go on. From talking with Karl and the other young men, Corrie had gained an inkling of what her sons were enduring.

Nothing had been heard from Albert since the large engagement at Gettysburg. Usually he wrote as soon as possible after a big battle. This time, they had heard nothing.

Corrie was so worried she could hardly think of anything else. A pall seemed to lie over San Antonio as families awaited the lists from Gettysburg.

Corrie had been at work more than an hour when Bree came into the room. "You're almost out of wool, Aunt Corrie," she observed. "If you want to rest at that awhile, I'll spin, if you'll hold."

They moved to the spinning wheel. "We could use more hands," Corrie said. "What's Prissy doing?"

Bree's face did not alter expression. "She went to the Schneider party, after all."

Corrie stopped, her hands full of wool. "But she's the one who first suggested it wouldn't be appropriate to go."

"I know. I swallowed the bait. Hook, line, and sinker."

Corrie's anger flared. Prissy had talked Bree out of going, saying that since they had not yet heard from Albert after Gettysburg, they should not appear at a funfest. "She wanted Major Gruenther all to herself!" Corrie said.

The major recently had returned from the fighting in Arkansas. At first he had devoted his charms to Prissy. Now he was paying as much attention to Bree as to Prissy.

"She tricked me fair and square," Bree said. "Aunt Corrie, sometimes I feel like Prissy's pet monkey. I'm so mad! If it had been anyone but Major Gruenther I wouldn't have minded so much. I think he likes me. But every time he looks in my direction, Prissy steps in. She's only doing it out of pure devilment. She doesn't care for him."

Corrie did not argue. She had seen a coldness in Prissy that troubled her. She had wondered if the long, subdued estrangement between herself and Tad—and the lack of human warmth in the house—could be to blame.

Corrie had never been able to talk easily with Prissy. In many ways she felt closer to Prue's daughter than to her own.

After helping for a while at the loom, Bree went on home. Corrie continued to work until Prissy returned.

She came through the hall into the long room on tiptoe and obviously was surprised to find Corrie still up.

Corrie spoke calmly. "Young lady, where have you been?"

Prissy shrugged and waved a hand. "Out."

"Out where?"

"Mama, I'm sixteen. Surely I can come and go without an act of the Legislature."

"That depends. Certainly you raise suspicion by sneaking around. Who brought you home?"

"Major Gruenther. Surely he's beyond reproach. After all, he's descended from nobility."

Corrie was still seated at the loom. Prissy was standing in the center of the floor, her face in shadow. Corrie turned up the wick on the lamp. "If you've read history seriously, you've no doubt learned that nobility isn't necessarily a stamp of virtue. Not that I'm concerned about Major Gruenther. I'm confident he's a fine man. I'm concerned about you. I take it you went to the Schneider party after saying you wouldn't."

Again Prissy shrugged. "Can't a person change her mind? You do it all the time."

"Not in matters such as this. You told Bree you didn't think the two of you should go. She agreed. I heard you. Then you went so you could have Major Gruenther to yourself. Prissy, that's despicable."

"I changed my mind!" Prissy said again.

"And slipped out without telling anyone. Suppose your father had arrived home with terrible news, and you were out at a party. What could I tell him?"

"Mama, almost everyone there has someone in the war. They don't stop living because of it. Why should we be different?"

"Because that's the way we show our love, our concern. But you don't seem to care."

"Oh, Mama, I do!"

"Then show it. I've never seen you distraught for a moment when any of your young friends are in battles."

"Mama! I am! I care about them!"

"Are you seriously interested in Major Gruenther?"

Prissy cocked her head in the flirty way she had acquired. "What woman wouldn't be?"

Corrie tried to put what she had to say into the proper words. Early in the war a gaiety had prevailed. Prissy and Bree wore Jeb Stuart hats to show their loyalty and gave balls and cotillions for the troops. Prissy continued to correspond with many of the young men she had met. She wrote long, flirty letters that kept them dangling.

"Prissy, I've been disturbed over your attitude toward these young men for some time," Corrie said. "You're only trifling with them. You don't take their attentions seriously. Not in the way you should. That's cruel. Not only are you distracting them from other young ladies, who might treat them better, you're also suggesting to them that a more serious relationship may follow, when you know it won't. Do you understand me?"

Again Prissy shrugged. "I can't help it if men find me attractive."

"No, you can't. But you could be honest in your dealings, let them know you're prepared for friendship, but that you're thinking of nothing beyond. I want you to stop taking their attentions so lightly."

Prissy did not respond. Corrie went on.

"I'm telling you this for your own good. In time, men will come to see that you take no one seriously, and consider you nothing but a flirt. Then they won't take *you* seriously."

They stood facing each other. Prissy started sniffling. "I'm sick of this war!" she burst out. "I'm sick of people talking about the South losing. If it's worth fighting, it's worth winning. Why aren't we winning?"

After the recent Federal victories the newspapers were speculating that perhaps the tide of battle had shifted, that the Confederacy was losing the war.

"I can only quote your father," Corrie said. "He says if the South loses the war, the worst is yet to come."

By eight o'clock in the evening the battle had ended. Albert had not slept for two days and nights. He was staggering from exhaustion. The colonel told him to go get some sleep. He rolled into his blanket and dropped off immediately.

Two hours later he was awakened. A cavalry captain knelt over him, shaking him gently. "Albert Martin Logan?"

"Yes, sir," Albert said, still half asleep.

"I come from your brother, Jim Bowie. He's been wounded. You're to come with me."

Albert sat up, instantly awake. He struggled into his boots. "Jim? Here?" He had not heard from Jim since Murfreesboro.

"He's over on Dry Valley Road, toward McFarland's Gap," the captain said. "He took a bullet in the chest. It's bad."

Albert went to the colonel and obtained permission to go to his brother. He then followed the captain at a gallop north, through the battlefield taken by General Hindman's division only hours before. Under the three-quarter moon bodies were scattered along the road and through the fields on each side.

After an hour they came to a low hill. The captain slowed his horse to a walk and gave a peculiar whistle. It was answered. A man emerged from the trees.

"This is Albert Logan," the captain said.

"Sorry, Logan," the man said. "Jim Bowie died an hour ago."

Albert felt as if he might fall from his horse. He waited until the moment passed. "Can I see him?"

"He's over yonder a ways," the man said. "We got him off the road. We didn't know if the Yankees would come back."

Albert followed the officers through the trees. Troopers were cooking over a low fire in a ravine. Jim's body lay nearby. Someone had pulled a blanket over him. Albert was handed a shuttered lantern. He knelt and turned back the blanket.

Jim's face looked older, sadder. He had grown a small mustache. His eyes were closed. Albert raised the blanket higher and examined the wound. The bullet had gone into the center of Jim's chest. Albert found it remarkable Jim had lived more than minutes. He extinguished the lantern.

"Would you like some coffee, Logan?" one of the men asked. "Real coffee, not chickory. We lifted it off some Yankees."

"Thank you, I would," Albert said.

He reached for Jim's hand. Already it was cold. He did not know what else to do, so he sat on the ground beside the body. He felt depleted of all emotion. During the last two years he had seen so many deaths that one more hardly seemed significant.

Another officer came out of the woods. In the light of the fire Albert saw the insignia of a major. "I'm sorry about your brother," he said. "We were good friends. Anderson's my name. I'm from Bastrop."

Albert shook hands with him. "Jim and I hadn't seen each other since the war began."

"I know. He talked a lot about you. He was proud of you."

Albert did not answer. He could not imagine why Jim would be proud of him.

"He said you made the highest grades ever recorded at St. Mary's, and were so stubborn you wouldn't accept a commission."

Albert could think of nothing to say to that. The matter was too complicated.

Major Anderson rose. "We thought we would wait until morning to bury him. I'll leave you alone with him. When you're ready, come on over to the fire. We have some food, and a blanket. If you want, you can take Jim's personal effects."

Albert lay down by the fire and slept. Hours later he was awakened by hooves drumming on the road. For a moment he feared the Yankees had returned. But he heard Whit's voice answering the sentinel's challenge.

Still sleep-logged, Albert left his blankets and staggered to his feet. Whit enveloped him in a bear hug. Whit seemed older, his face more craggy. They stood for a long moment embraced by the fire. "I came as soon as I heard," Whit said. "Where's Jim now?"

"Over here, Colonel," someone said. "We have a lantern."

Albert and Whit walked over and sat down on each side of Jim. Whit took the lantern, looked at Jim's face, and examined the wound. He shook his head. "This will just about kill Tad," he said. "Corrie too. They put so much stock in both you boys."

Albert acknowledged the statement in silence.

"The captain said he found you with Headquarters Company. What do they have you doing?"

"I go to the forward areas, make an assessment of how the fighting's going, and report back to the colonel."

"They usually have a captain or major doing that."

"The colonel said all his field officers are illiterate. He wants reports he can send up to division."

Whit seemed amused. "Reports from a private? Sent up to division?"

"The colonel offered me a captaincy."

Whit shook his head. "You've turned down another one?"

"I don't want the responsibility for other people's lives."

"Jim would have laughed over that story," Whit said. "He got quite a kick out of the way you were holding out."

Albert felt he could not bear to talk much longer about Jim. "Have you heard from home lately?"

"Two letters from Prue, two from Bree last week. They said Tad and Corrie were worried about you. They'd read Hood took heavy losses at Gettysburg."

Gettysburg seemed so distant, it was like another lifetime. Since then Albert's division had spent nine days on a train, rushing from the Rapidan in Virginia to this battlefield. "Gettysburg was bad," Albert said. "But for us, yesterday and today were worse."

"You heard from home?" Whit asked.

Albert shook his head. "Not in quite a while. We've been on the move since Gettysburg."

Whit pulled back the blanket and straightened Jim's coat, forcefully tugging the wrinkles smooth, squaring the shoulders.

"Tad ever tell you what his body servant said when he was killed in Mexico? He said, 'Who would have thought it'd end like this?'

That's the way I feel now. Who'd have thought we Logans ever would be burying one of our own along a shitty little creek in Georgia?"

Albert did not trust his voice to speak.

Whit put a hand on his shoulder. "Albert, take care of yourself. Now you're all Tad and Corrie have left in the way of a son."

Again Albert did not answer. But he nodded to show that he had heard. Light was showing over the knobby hills to the east. Several troopers got up from the fire, went into the woods, and dug a shallow grave.

Whit folded the blanket over Jim's face. Another blanket was brought and the body carefully wrapped.

Albert and Whit helped carry Jim to his grave. They lowered him with bridle reins. The troopers covered him.

Major Anderson said a brief prayer, and it was over. The sun was just beginning to show on the rim of the hills.

"I must get back to my men," Whit said. "Albert, will you write the letter about Jim, or shall I?"

Albert felt it was his place. "I'll write it," he said.

"Then I'll leave it to you. And, Albert, you take care now. We're destined to have some good times together, you and me."

Again he seized Albert in a strong abrazo. Albert could not find the right words to say.

Then Whit was gone, riding off to the west at a gallop.

Albert piled rocks on the grave and drew a map showing its relation to the crossroads, the hills, and various trees.

"After the war, either I or my father likely will come back for him," he explained.

He rode with the major to where the Rangers were bivouacked. There he gathered Jim's personal belongings. Aside from Jim's pistols, sword, bowie knife, and a small amount of money, there was only a packet of letters.

"We travel light," the major said. "Don't accumulate much."

Albert rode back as far as the Widow Glenn's house with the Rangers, then sought out his headquarters.

The command post was quiet. A few final skirmishes had broken out earlier in the day, but by noon all guns fell silent. The Federals had pulled back, leaving the field to the Confederates.

The Battle of Chickamauga was over.

Albert sat down to the terrible letter that must be written. In preparation he spread Jim's meager possessions, hunting anything—even a trinket—to send with the letter. He opened the packet of mail. A few of the letters were from women. Some Albert knew, others he did not. There were letters from Corrie, Prissy, and Bree. The only surprise was the number from their father—bulky letters, unlike the brief notes Albert received. Curious, Albert scanned through them.

They were filled with plans for the ranch, to be put into practice after the war. Apparently Jim was to be in charge.

On some pages were drawings for a house—three stories fronted by fluted pillars. Other pages were filled with projections of the expected increase in the herds, year by year, and the additional land that would be required.

Slowly Albert came to realize that into Jim their father had poured all his hopes and dreams for the future.

He thought of his own paltry, preachy letters.

Where was his own place in all of this?

He had always known that Jim and his father were close. But this new discovery almost seemed a form of betrayal.

The revelation made his task easier. He wrote a dispassionate letter, bluntly informing his father that Jim was dead. He described being awakened, his nighttime ride, and his belated arrival in the cove. He told of Whit's visit, their talk, the coming of dawn, and the burial of Jim. He sealed the letter and sent it out with the evening dispatches.

That night he was summoned to the colonel's tent. A quick assessment of losses needed to be made, so the generals could determine whether to pursue the retreating Union forces, or to pull back to regroup.

Through the night the reports came in. Albert and the colonel tediously assembled the figures.

The toll was appalling. Of the sixty thousand men General

Bragg had taken into the battle, eighteen thousand were dead, wounded, or missing.

For Albert, the total held personal meaning.

One of those eighteen thousand was his brother.

--- 23 ---

Tad stood in the doorway, and from the first glimpse of his face Corrie knew that once again he was bringing home tragedy.

Without speaking he came across the room and handed her a letter edged in black. Corrie recognized Albert's handwriting. She felt such overwhelming relief she almost fainted. She unfolded the letter and began reading.

Albert's opening words were blunt, not at all like him. She scanned ahead seeking reassurance, even as the words registered.

Prissy came into the room and stood waiting. Tad had turned his back. The room was deathly still. As Corrie struggled to speak, she understood Albert's bluntness. This news could not be softened. "It's Jim Bowie," she said to Prissy. "He's dead. Killed in the fighting. Whit and Albert helped bury him."

Prissy wailed, a high, keening sound. Tad made his way to the hall door. There he stood leaning against the frame, head down, his back to the room. Corrie felt only a gnawing numbness. She knew the full onslaught of grief would come later, as it always did, lying in wait for her unguarded, weaker moments. This was a grief that would hang over her family from now on. It was a grief that must be faced. She forced herself to go back to the beginning and reread the letter carefully.

There was a stark poetry to Albert's grim description. "We had been fighting for two days with no rest," he wrote. Corrie's imagination supplied details the letter left unstated. What had Albert endured that he could write of his brother's death in such dispassionate terms? He told of being awakened in the night, his ride through darkness, and his belated arrival. He told of Whit's coming, and how they sat beside Jim's body. He described the dawn burial in a

419

wooded cove not far from Chickamauga Creek. "I mourn for Jim," he wrote. "But during the last two days thousands of men died at this place. They were all my brothers. Jim was important only because we knew him."

Corrie's concern shifted from Jim to Albert. Jim was at peace. Nothing could touch him now. But Albert was still alive amid the horror he had described.

She heard movement and looked up. Tad was gone from the doorway. She heard his crutches in the hall, moving toward the front door. She knew Tad all too well; he would be going off to grieve somewhere alone.

Corrie was determined he would not abandon her once again at a crucial time in her life. She hurried into the hall. "Tad! Don't you dare go off and leave us alone with this!"

He turned, leaning against the wall, using his crutches to hold himself in place. His eyes conveyed his anguish. "Corrie, I can't stay here and talk to people, say the proper words, just as if nothing has happened."

"Someone must!" Corrie told him. "Our friends will want to express their sympathy. We can't ignore them."

Tad waved a hand in a helpless gesture. His voice broke. "Jim was everything."

Corrie was having trouble with her own voice. But there was much that needed to be said. "Tad, Jim was my son too! Part of me is dying with him. But he wasn't everything. We still have Albert and Prissy. That thought should see us through this."

"Albert isn't Jim," Tad said. "He never will be."

Corrie found some relief from her grief in anger. Tad's favoritism had always rankled. "Jim was a wonderful son. But so's Albert. He's probably the most intelligent among us. He's loving and caring. You've never appreciated his best qualities."

"He's weak. I never expect him to amount to anything."

Corrie was shocked. This was not the time to argue, but she could not allow that statement to pass. "How can you possibly say that? Albert's not weak!"

Tad's head was lowered. He stared at the floor. "He always vacillates, seeks the easy way. He couldn't make up his mind to go off to war. Refused a commission. Didn't want responsibility. Jim marched right off to do his duty, served with distinction, won promotions and the admiration of his men. He was tough, strong minded, decisive. He would have gone a long way."

"So will Albert," Corrie shot back. "He delayed going and refused promotion because he's a man of principle. You've never understood that. Jim marched off because you told him it was his duty. He did all you expected of him, and probably more, just to please you. Well, now he's dead. I hope you're satisfied."

Tad opened his mouth to speak, but no sound came. With an abrupt shake of his head he turned back toward the door.

"Don't you dare leave us with this!" Corrie said again.

He struggled out the door without answering. Corrie stood in an emotional paralysis until she heard his hack pulling away in the gravel drive.

She turned back into the house. Renewed wailing came from the long room. Prissy had just told Hattie, and they stood embraced, crying.

Corrie felt she could endure no more. She went to her room and lay facedown across her bed.

She entered a twilight state, alternately reminiscing about Jim and praying for him. She also prayed for Albert and Whit, asking God to keep them safe. She was too angry at Tad to pray honestly for his solace, although she knew eventually she would.

After a time she heard movement in the room and felt a hand on her shoulder. She looked up, expecting Prissy or Hattie. But it was Prue. They embraced and clung to each other silently.

It was Prue's first visit to Corrie's house since Ramsey's death, years ago.

"The news has spread on the pantry grapevine," Prue said. "By now the whole town knows. Corrie, everyone loved him. Soon they'll be coming to call. Where's Tad?"

"Out," Corrie said.

Prue raised her eyebrows but made no comment. "Hattie is in no condition to tend to guests. I'll bring over some help."

Corrie and Prissy sat in the long room through the long afternoon, receiving guests, who expressed their shock, dismay, and sympathy. Corrie went through the formalities in a daze. Prue and Bree assisted, greeting callers at the door, and taking care of the large dishes of food brought to the bereaved family in keeping with Southern custom.

Toward evening the steady stream of visitors ceased. The house fell quiet for the first time since the letter came.

Prue glanced toward the windows, the setting sun. "When do you expect Tad back?" she asked.

"I have no idea," Corrie said. And she could not help adding, "Right now, I don't even care."

Tad made a cold camp on the creek below the site of the ranch house that now might never be built. He unharnessed his team and spread his bedroll under the cottonwood trees, not bothering with a fire, for he was not hungry. Night came moonless and with a sky so clear the stars seemed alive. Tad lay on his bedroll, looked up at the stars, and allowed himself the luxury of remembering Jim as he had been.

He thought of the time when Jim, pursuing an errant yearling, plunged heedlessly into a clump of mesquite, so intent on his task that he ignored all danger. Bleeding, full of cactus spines, he had remained stoic, not shedding a single tear. Tad recognized on that day that the boy was of rare value, and began to put his hopes into him. Jim had never disappointed.

Tad fondly recalled teaching Jim to shoot. He had been a most avid student. Albert never showed much interest in guns. Jim spent hours every day for weeks practicing with his weapons to perfect the skills Tad taught him. It was the same when he showed the boys how to track and read hoofprints. Jim soaked up every bit of information and put it to use. Albert had listened passively. Corrie was incapable of understanding that it would have been the same in the future, with Jim absorbing Tad's knowledge of cattle, and building on it.

He felt worn out, useless. Cotton crops had dwindled. He no

longer could find cargo to run the blockade. All the money he had received was in Confederate currency, now worthless.

Thinking of this lost dream, grief hit Tad full force. He could not envision a life without Jim.

Giving way to the agony, he wept, bellowing his rage into the darkness, even quieting the coyotes, who recognized howls more elemental than their own.

Tad continued to weep through the night.

Albert rode along the tree-lined trail at a trot. Overhead, squirrels chattered, warning of his approach. The country was remote, hardly more than a wilderness. For two hours he had not seen another human—an extraordinary experience in war.

The brigade had moved northeast of Chattanooga to assist General Longstreet in the Siege of Knoxville. Foraging parties were out in every direction.

Ahead, the trail curved. Albert slowed his horse to a walk. The colonel had sent him to assess the fighting strength of a brigade company. The report was not urgent. Caution took precedence.

From the curve the trail went down a slope and into a small stream. Watching the woods on either side, Albert walked his horse to the water and lowered the reins to allow him to drink.

A sudden apprehension came over him. At first he did not know why. Then he realized that the woods were silent.

Slowly he gathered the reins and lifted his horse's head. Easing out of the creek, he turned back in the direction from which he had come. The moment he reached firm footing, he put spurs to the horse and raced for the distant curve.

A volley of rifle shots from behind literally swept the horse from under him. Even as Albert fell, he felt pain in his right knee. He and the horse went down together. He hit the ground hard and sank into blackness.

He awoke to the agony of pain from his right leg. The horse was dead. His right leg was trapped under it. A group of Union soldiers stood over him. "Looks like we winged us a Reb," a lieutenant said. "What you doing out here all by yourself?"

Albert did not answer. The lieutenant searched him and found Albert's half-written assessment of the brigade company.

"I expect command will want to talk to you," he said. He motioned to his men. "Let's get this horse off him."

They lifted the horse with a fence rail and pulled Albert free. The lieutenant knelt to look at his leg. "You've lost blood. But not much. Let's see what the damage is."

He slit the trousers. Albert raised up to look. He saw bone.

"It's bad," the lieutenant said. "Looks like you took a bullet through the kneecap. The leg was busted in the fall. You'll probably lose that leg."

The soldiers gathered around Albert to carry him to a nearby wagon. When they lifted him the pain was immense, and he again sank into blackness.

The following days were torture. He rode north in a flatbed wagon. In Louisville he was taken to an old warehouse that had been converted into a hospital. There he was questioned. The Union officers refused to believe he was only a private. They said no private made assessments of company strengths.

His leg was treated. A Union doctor said he was doing him no favor by not amputating, for he would have a corkscrew for a leg the rest of his life. After a month in the hospital, Albert was shipped northward with a dozen Confederate officers, despite his protests that he was a private. He and the officers were unloaded on the edge of Lake Erie and taken by boat to Johnson's Island, a Union prison camp for Confederate officers.

Albert had never seen such a melancholy place. Swept by the frigid, damp winds off Lake Erie, the camp was surrounded by a stockade fence thirty feet high, patrolled by soldiers with rifles. Inside the compound were rows of two-story barracklike buildings. Paths led out to the privies, and to a water well.

Albert was given a bunk beneath an older man with white hair, a long white beard, and a big Bible. He said he was David Price Thomas from the Duck River country in west Tennessee, and had fought at Murfreesboro, and at Chickamauga.

"How is it in this place?" Albert asked.

"Here we have but one enemy," Thomas said. "Disease. Half of the first men brought here a year ago are dead. More die every day. The way I figure it, Johnson's Island will be our hardest battle of the war. Worse than Chickamauga."

--- 24 ---

The third winter of the war was the most severe anyone could remember. A succession of northers struck, accompanied by snow and ice. The repeated snowstorms drove thousands of cattle southward from the upper Colorado, down toward the Nueces, where they mingled with the wild herds. The Logan ranch was overrun with branded and unbranded livestock.

Nothing had been heard from Albert since Chickamauga. His brigade was mentioned in accounts of the fighting at Lookout Mountain and Missionary Ridge. Invariably Albert wrote after major engagements. But the months passed with no letter.

Tad wrote Albert's commanding officer, a Colonel Gordon, inquiring as to Albert's safety. Two months later the reply came: Albert was listed as a deserter. The colonel said Albert disappeared while on reconnaissance to a distant company. The colonel added that Albert was a brave and conscientious soldier, and that in his personal opinion the designation of deserter was in error. He said he was bound by the rules concerning men missing under such circumstances.

"That's ridiculous," Tad said. "Albert wouldn't desert. It's just a paperwork idiocy."

"Whom would one write to get it fixed?" Prissy asked.

Corrie was more troubled by the fact that Albert was missing than from the label placed upon it. "But what could have happened to him?" she asked.

"Let's pray he was taken prisoner," Tad said. "If he was free, and alive, we'd surely have heard from him by now."

Prissy wrote Confederacy President Jefferson Davis in Richmond, attesting to her brother's long service and faithfulness. She

426

cited the praise from his commanding officer, demanded an investigation be made, and the mistake corrected.

She never received a reply from President Davis, which further lowered him, and the Confederacy, in her eyes.

Corrie fell back on her overused talent for waiting. She continued to read newspaper accounts of the fighting. Albert's brigade took part in the Siege of Knoxville and the Battle of the Wilderness. Whit also was in the Siege of Knoxville, and the Battle of Five Forks.

The following winter was milder, as if in promise of better times. Corrie endured, and prayed.

In the spring the war receded like a great conflagration that had burned itself out. Flickering flames lingered here and there, but the heat was gone, the fuel consumed. By early April, after General Lee's surrender at Appomattox, and President Lincoln's assassination, the end was in sight. There were holdouts. Some segments of the Confederacy vowed to fight on, and skirmishes erupted, but the surrenders continued.

On a warm day in late May, Bree burst through the back door crying. "He's home! Aunt Corrie! Prissy! He's home safe!"

She flew back out the door. Prissy ran after her. Corrie paused only long enough to send Newt to the office for Tad, then hurried over to Prue's house.

Whit stood on the porch, dancing a little jig, his arms around Prue, Bree, and Prissy. When he caught sight of Corrie, he released them, came to her, and swept her up in his arms, lifting her feet clear of the ground. He rained kisses on her lips, cheeks, forehead. He smelled of tobacco, horse lather, the dust of the road. His deep voice boomed. "Corrie, Corrie. Lovelier than ever! God, it's great to see you again!"

Corrie could not take her eyes from him.

Tad arrived. The two brothers embraced and pounded each other on the back. "Thank God you're home," Tad said. "We'll have a celebration that'll set them to dancing in heaven."

The welcome-home party for Whit grew of its own volition. By evening beeves were cooking over low fires. Much of the town assembled. Whit sat on his patio, drink in hand, greeting friends and answering their questions on where last he had seen their sons, husbands, and brothers. Corrie lingered near and listened, marveling over Whit's easy manner with people, his basic goodness. She thought of all the troubles he had seen.

He was forty-one years old but appeared sixty. Yet his aging was different from Tad's. Tad was wearing away, disintegrating under the weight of his many injuries. Whit had weathered in the way of an old stone, growing smoother, harder.

Slowly the party waned as guests departed. Eventually Tad and Whit were left seated on a bench together, their arms around each other. Both were half drunk. Corrie, Prue, Bree, and Prissy sat around them, listening to their talk.

"You ever get by Donegal?" Tad asked.

Whit shook his head. "I doubt anything's left. Tad, you should see that country. Everything's burned, scorched, looted, destroyed. The South will never be the same. Texas has come out of the war comparatively well off."

"Except for our sons," Tad said.

"Tad, I believe Albert's alive. It's just a feeling. All's in confusion. It'll take months to get it sorted out. There's a chance we'll hear something before long."

Tad nodded.

"You should have seen him at Chickamauga, the way he handled himself with Jim, and Jim's friends. You would've been proud."

Again Tad nodded.

"I went over and tried to see him two days later. Albert was away on a mission. I sat and talked with his commanding officers. They were full of praise. They said at Sharpsburg, Gettysburg, and Chickamauga he went repeatedly into the worst of it and returned with fresh estimates of how the battles were going. Tad, I'm telling you. That boy's got a lot of bottom. That's one reason I think he may have survived."

Tad did not respond. But Corrie thought she saw evidence on his face that he might be reappraising Albert.

Within a month after Whit's return, he and Tad were spending most of their time at the ranch. Chancy Denton and other former ranch hands returned from the war and resumed work.

Except for the absence of Jim and Albert, life in the Logan compounds gradually returned to the routine they had known before the war.

Prisoners were still being released from both Confederate and Union stockades. Corrie followed the accounts, and read every list carefully, searching not only for Albert, but for the name of anyone who might have news of him.

But the first word of Albert came from an unexpected source. On an afternoon in early June, Tad came home from the office with a letter. He held it in his hand, not offering it to Corrie. She could not read his expression. "It's from a medical doctor in Ohio. He says Albert is alive, but very ill. He was wounded, captured, and held on Johnson's Island in Lake Erie. He has consumption, and a wound that won't heal."

Corrie's joy over Albert's deliverance was tempered by renewed fear and concern. "Tad, what can we do?"

"I'll go to New Orleans and upriver to get him. I don't know what the rules of Reconstruction will be. But surely the sons of bitches won't keep a father from his ill son."

With the aid of his cane Albert crabbed his way across the new river bridge into Alamo Plaza. Winded, he sat on a bench and waited for the heat of the afternoon to ease. His days had acquired a mind-numbing sameness. In the mornings after Hattie brought his breakfast he lost himself for a while in the classics he remembered from college. Plato. Homer. Seneca. Virgil. Caesar. Epictetus. Toward noon he lay quiet as Hattie changed his bandages. During the afternoons he came over to Alamo Plaza to watch the town sleep through siesta.

He was feeding pigeons when Whit rode up on the dun gelding he favored. He dismounted and came to sit on the bench beside Albert. "I'm heading back out to the ranch," he said. "I thought you might like to go along."

"No, thank you," Albert said. "I've got pigeons to feed."

Whit scratched his boot heel in the dirt. "You can't sit here on this goddamn bench the rest of your life. I think I know what's in your mind. The war. Albert, it's time to turn loose of it. Come on out to the ranch. Hard work will make you forget all that, and clear out your head."

Albert did not answer. What Whit had said was true. He often spent his afternoons thinking of the friends he had lost in the corn-field at Sharpsburg, the woods of Chickamauga, in the Devil's Den at Gettysburg. Around him, in Reconstruction, there was only mis-ery, no jobs, no means of livelihood. As a paroled Confederate, he could not vote, hold office, or practice law, the profession for which he had been trained. Nor did the ranch seem the answer. Before the war Tad and Whit had tried every way to get the cattle to market. Now Texas cattle were being turned back along the Missouri and Kansas borders because of "Texas fever," a disease fatal to northern breeds.

"Whit, the ranch isn't for me," he said. "The ranch was for Jim. Father had it all planned."

Whit had gathered himself to leave. He sat back down. "Albert, I'm going to tell you something. Your aunt Prue and I always wanted a son. But as it turned out, Bree was it. I was disappointed. So to some degree I always borrowed you and Jim for the sons I never had. And I'm telling you now. If I'd had a son, I'd want him to be just like you."

Albert did not respond.

"I know something of what you're going through," Whit went on. "Anger you don't think you can contain. Regret for things you weren't able to do. A sadness that just plain eats you up. Feelings nobody ever invented words to fit."

"That's a fair description," Albert said.

"You don't have a corner on anger. I came back from Mexico filled with it, from the things I'd seen on the expedition. I almost let it ruin my life." He paused. "Tad ever tell you about your grandfa-ther?"

"No," Albert said. Corrie often talked of his maternal grandpar-ents. He knew nothing about his paternal forebears.

"Larkin Logan, your grandfather, was a tyrant. He whipped Tad unmercifully as a boy. Me too. Underneath these Mexican scars, I've got marks my father put on me. I only wanted to get away from it.

But Tad wanted his father's love, something he never received. He's still angry about it, thirty-odd years later. That's part of what makes him what he is. I'm telling you to help you understand him better."

Albert remained silent. He needed time to think about it.

"So I'm talking to the son I never had," Whit said. "Stop sitting here stewing in your anger. It can ruin your life. I don't give a shit what you do, but do something. The way I see it, our only way out is cattle. Every cow we have would be worth money in the east, if we could figure a way to get it there."

Abruptly Whit got up and walked away. He swung onto his horse and rode off without looking back.

Later in the afternoon Albert was still thinking over Whit's words when a shadow fell across him. He looked up. The old Negro known as Oliver stood before him hesitantly. Albert remembered him. Oliver had belonged to the Elkins family.

"Mastah Albert, they tell me you're a lawyer. Mastah Elkins say he'd hire me, pay me a little, let me live in his house, if there was a way to do it. But he says there ain't."

"That's true," Albert said. One of the provisos of Reconstruction decreed that former owners of slaves no longer could keep them on the premises. As a result, many Negroes were walking the streets without shelter or work, and in most instances no one cared *except* the former owners. At home Aunt Hattie had been weeping day and night, fearing that after her fifty-six years in the McNair and Logan families she might be forced to leave. Thus far the Logans had ignored the order. Tad vowed the war would start all over again if they tried to move Hattie against her wishes.

"It seems there ought to be some way," Oliver said.

Facing Oliver, it occurred to Albert that he himself had never read the law. Maybe no one had. "Oliver, I'm not promising anything," he said. "But I'll look into it."

On his way home that afternoon he went by the old Council House, where the statutes were posted. In reading them, he found a loophole.

The next day he explained it to Oliver. "You and Mr. Elkins can sign a simple contract and file it with the Freedmen's Bureau."

"Where we get this contract?" Oliver asked.

"I can draw it up for you. All I need are the terms."

Albert wrote out the contract. Elkins came by Albert's bench and signed it. Albert also wrote out a contract for Hattie and three other Negroes who wished to remain with the Logans. Tad signed the papers. Albert filed them with the Freedmen's Bureau.

Three of Oliver's friends came to Albert and asked for contracts. One afternoon Albert was surrounded by Negroes, drawing up a new set of papers, when three pistol-packing white men approached. "Albert Logan?" one asked.

Albert nodded.

"You'll have to come with us. You're under arrest."

The man took out handcuffs. Albert resisted. "Wait a minute! What's the charge?"

"Practicing law without a license," said the third man.

After handcuffing him, they started Albert moving in the direction of the jail.

They had to halfway carry him, for Albert could not keep pace without his cane.

Tad slowed at the front door and allowed Albert to go on into the house ahead of him. He was still furious. He limped through the front door, passing Corrie and Prissy in the hall. Albert went on through the house, toward his bedroom.

"They gave me all kinds of trouble in bailing him out," Tad told Corrie. "I asked for personal recognizance. They refused. I said I'd vouch for his court appearance, and they refused that! I was serving in the Texas Congress before most of them were born."

"What did you do?" Corrie asked.

Tad moved on into the long room. "I put up this house as surety. It was either that or leave him in jail."

Albert's cane thumped as he came back toward them from his bedroom. Tad first noticed the fury on Albert's face. Then he saw the pistol on Albert's hip. He moved to block Albert from the front door.

"Don't try to stop me," Albert warned.

For an answer Tad swung his crutch, not at Albert, but at his cane. It went skittering across the floor. Albert was thrown off balance. Tad stepped forward on his good leg and hit Albert solidly in the jaw. Albert went down.

Prissy screamed. Corrie moved to help Albert. Tad pushed her back. He lashed out with his good leg and kicked the pistol free. It slid across the floor and lodged under a table.

Tad moved until he was standing over Albert. He could not hide his fear, his fury. "I lost one son to this war," he said. "I'll not lose another."

Albert was making no attempt to get up. Corrie picked up his cane and handed it to him. He took it, but continued to sit on the floor with his legs out straight. All anger seemed to have left him.

He shook his head as if to clear it. "I can't abide this life any longer. I have to do something."

"Is shooting them the only solution you can think of?" Prissy asked. "Surely there are more intelligent ways to fight."

"Like what?" Albert asked. "I can't practice law. I'm crippled. I can't work. They have me boxed in."

Prissy took a step toward him. "If I were a man, I'd show up these carpetbaggers if I had to walk on stumps."

"Prissy!" Corrie said.

Albert shook his head. "She's right, Mama. I should be smarter than that. Whit more or less said the same thing to me. He said the cattle are our best hope."

"I've said the same thing for years," Tad pointed out.

Albert looked up at him. "Whit wants me to go out and work with him. I think I'll do that."

Tad thought of Albert's leg, his own pain from the saddle. "Are you well enough?"

"I'll never know till I try," Albert said.

Tad doubted Albert would be able to do much work. But at least it would get him out of town, away from further trouble with the Reconstruction people.

It was Chancy Denton who first saw the handbill. It was printed in Kansas and sent to Texas to be distributed among cattlemen. The man who signed it, Joseph G. McCoy, said he had arranged a corridor for Texas cattle through the quarantine, all the way from the Kansas line to the railhead at Abilene.

"What do you think?" Whit asked, edging his horse alongside Tad's hack. "This could be the market we've always hunted."

Tad wanted to believe it, but he found himself skeptical. "Could be nothing but a harebrained scheme. Abilene's quite a way into Kansas. I doubt anyone could get permission from all the farmers involved. This man could be nothing but a blowhard."

Twenty yards away, Chancy and the men were still working cattle through the branding chute. Albert was on the far side of the catch corral, cutting back the heifers, pushing steers and bulls through. Tad winced inwardly at the constant pounding Albert was taking as his cutting horse came to repeated stiff-legged, bone-jarring stops in turning cattle. Tad knew the work must be painful for him. Why was he doing it?

Whit pushed his hat to the back of his head, wiped his brow, and spat into the dust. "Tad, it could be true. Logic's on his side. The east needs beef. The railroads need freight. And all we've got to do is get it there. I think this might be worth a gamble."

Tad thought of the route north. With spring rains, Whit and the men would encounter swollen streams, storms, hail, deadly lightning. A good portion of the drive would be through Indian land. No doubt the tribes would expect some kind of payment. "If you're turned back at the Kansas border, what then?" Tad asked. "There's no money to lease grass."

Whit shrugged. "We could pay in beef. Maybe we'd lose most of the herd. But what the hell? They sure as shit ain't making us rich just standing here eating grass."

Tad knew Whit had a point. Those longhorns would be worth ten to fifteen dollars a head in Chicago. And the ranch was overrun with them.

"How many would you figure on taking?" he asked.

"We could have fifteen hundred head ready in a week or two," Whit said. "Maybe two thousand. I'd say that'd be about the right size herd."

"How many men?"

"Twelve or fourteen in all, counting me and Albert."

"No," Tad said. "Albert won't be going."

Whit was silent for a moment. "Tad, his heart's set on it."

"He's in no better shape than me. Worse, maybe. I've seen that open place on his leg. It's a wonder he can walk, let alone ride."

Whit watched Albert working the cattle for a time, then looked down at his saddle horn. He seemed to come to a decision. "Tad, I've never interfered in your affairs. But I'm going to now. No one has worked harder through the last six weeks than Albert."

"He's not up to going," Tad insisted.

"How do you know what he can do? We got him off that damned bench. He has proved he can make a full hand. He's getting stronger every day. Tad, he's trying to prove something to you, and you're too goddamned blind to see it. I haven't seen anyone so hardheaded since Larkin Logan."

Tad did not understand.

"Tad, you were so wrapped up in Jim, you could never see what a treasure you have in Albert. Sure, he's different. He can quote you some Greek philosopher on any subject at the drop of a hat. I loved Jim. But, Tad, I'm here to tell you that Albert's probably tougher. Jim was your Frank. Albert's you all over again. He's in that saddle now, pounding himself to pieces, to show you he's worthy of your respect."

Tad was too disturbed to respond. He remembered that Corrie had said much the same thing. He could not believe he had been so wrong about Albert. Yet he could not marshal an adequate defense. "I'm no Larkin Logan," he said.

"And thank God for that," Whit said. "But it stands to reason we've both inherited some of his ways. I'm just telling you that if I had to choose between Jim and Albert, it'd be a damned hard choice. Tad, I love Albert. I need him. I want to work him into this operation. It's only right!"

"What if his leg breaks down on him up there somewhere in Indian country? What if he's hurt? How would he get home?"

"Same way I'll get home if a horse falls on me, or if some Comanche puts an arrow into me. The best way I can. Albert's been through worse."

Tad thought of the possibility of Albert assuming a place in his dreams for this land.

It was a new concept. Tad did not know if it would hold water.

"I suppose we can risk a couple thousand head on this Kansas scheme," he said. "If you'll get the herd ready, I'll see what I can do toward supplies."

"And Albert?" Whit persisted.

Tad found he wanted Whit's opinion of Albert to be valid. The Kansas drive could be a test for them both. He gathered up his reins. "If Albert wants to go, I'll not stop him."

At dawn Corrie rode out with Tad in his buckboard to meet the herd on its way north. Prue, Prissy, and Bree were mounted. They rode on ahead, amusing themselves with impromptu races. On the east side of the Salado, Tad stopped the buckboard on a site that gave them a good view to the south. They sat and watched the herd approach.

"I'm still not easy in my mind over Albert going," Tad said. "But Whit made an eloquent case. Maybe I'm wrong."

"I couldn't argue against it," Corrie said. "He has been so restless ever since he came home. If he can endure the work, I truly believe the drive may do him good."

Tad remained silent for a time, watching the rising dust heralding the approach of the herd.

"He doesn't talk to me," Tad said. "Do you have any idea what he wants to do in life?"

Corrie felt encouraged. It was Tad's first hint of interest in Albert's future. She answered carefully. "I really think he hasn't had much time to think about it. The war thwarted him so. Really, he hasn't had experience in the normal world since he was a student at St. Mary's, six years ago."

Tad appeared to consider that at length. When he spoke, it was almost as if he were speaking to himself. "Whit thinks Albert might want to become a part of the ranch operation."

"I don't know," Corrie said. "I think he's searching. He may need our help and encouragement in finding himself."

Again Tad seemed to be reflecting on her words. "Whit sets a lot of store by him," he said after a time. "Maybe it'll all work out."

Corrie sensed that Tad was speaking beyond Albert, to his marriage, their happiness. "I pray it will," she said.

Tad placed a hand on hers, confirming her impression that he was speaking of the future in general, and their place in it. She thought ahead. Bree had just announced her engagement to Major Gruenther. Prissy's romance with Colonel Morgan of Austin had just taken a serious turn. If Albert joined Whit and Tad in the ranch operation, the Logan family might remain close.

Corrie found herself wanting this with all her heart.

She sat with Tad in companionable silence as the herd came on, filling the valley. The longhorns were reluctant to leave their customary sources of water for the unknown. They kept attempting to turn back. Whit, Albert, and the riders had their hands full. Prue, Prissy, and Bree went out to help, waving their hats, helping to push the herd along.

Whit and Albert came hurriedly to hug Corrie, kiss her goodbye, and to shake hands with Tad. They dashed back to their work with the herd.

Slowly, the cattle moved on northward.

"They'll settle down, once they get away from bedground," Tad said. "The first two days are always the worst."

Gradually the herd disappeared to the north, leaving only a thin pall of dust in the air. Prue, Prissy, and Bree came trotting back, excited over their adventure, their horses well lathered. They rode on ahead.

Tad turned the buckboard toward home. Soon San Antonio de Béxar once again rose out of spring greenness like an enchanted mirage.

Finis